T0285395

MURDER AT
LORD'S STATION

By Jim Eldridge

LONDON UNDERGROUND STATION MYSTERIES SERIES

Murder at Aldwych Station
Murder at Down Street Station
Murder at Lord's Station
Murder at Whitechapel Road Station

MUSEUM MYSTERIES SERIES

Murder at the Fitzwilliam
Murder at the British Museum
Murder at the Ashmolean
Murder at the Manchester Museum
Murder at the Natural History Museum
Murder at Madame Tussauds
Murder at the National Gallery
Murder at the Victoria and Albert Museum
Murder at the Tower of London
Murder at the Louvre

HOTEL MYSTERIES SERIES

Murder at the Ritz
Murder at the Savoy
Murder at Claridge's

MURDER AT
LORD'S STATION

JIM ELDRIDGE

Allison & Busby Limited
11 Wardour Mews
London W1F 8AN
allisonandbusby.com

First published in Great Britain by Allison & Busby in 2024.

Copyright © 2024 by JIM ELDRIDGE

First Edition

ISBN 978-0-7490-3078-0

Typeset in 11.5/16.5 Adobe Garamond Pro by
Allison & Busby Ltd.

By choosing this product, you help take care of the world's forests.
Learn more: www.fsc.org.

Printed and bound by
CPI Group (UK) Ltd, Croydon, CR0 4YY

As always, for Lynne.

CHAPTER ONE

London, Saturday 8th March 1941

Outside in the streets in and around Leicester Square, the bombs fell, bringing their nightly destruction to London. Inside the Café de Paris, deep beneath a cinema in Leicester Square, Rosa Coburg did her best to ignore the noise and vibrations as she played the closing number of her set at the club's piano. She was glad she'd chosen a loud, raucous song, 'When the Saints Go Marching In', because one of her favoured gentler, slower numbers, such as Hoagy Carmichael's 'Georgia on My Mind' or 'Stardust', would have been all but drowned by the bombing. With 'Saints', the sound of the bombing almost gave a deep bass musical counterpoint to the rhythm.

Rosa ended with a rousing change of chords, and then stood and responded with smiles and bows to the thunderous applause from the packed audience.

Martin Paulson, the genial compere, stepped forward into the spotlight, gesturing towards Rosa. 'Ladies and gentlemen, let's hear it once again for the fabulous Rosa Weeks!'

At this, the audience rose to their feet, applauding. Rosa bowed again, then moved out of the light to join her husband, DCI Edgar Coburg, at his table.

'Wonderful.' Coburg beamed. 'You slayed them.'

In the spotlight, Paulson was addressing the audience. 'Ladies and gentlemen, there will be a short break while we reassemble the band on stage for their next set. Mainly because we've got to find them.'

There was genial laughter at this, then Paulson continued, 'But do, please, order your drinks now, and shortly you'll be listening once again to the magic sound of the brilliant Ken Snakehips Johnson and his West Indian Dance Orchestra.'

With that, Paulson moved out of the spotlight and joined Rosa and Coburg at their table.

'That was superb,' he enthused. 'Rosa, you are a star! Are you sure you can't stay and do another number with Ken and the boys?'

'I'd love to,' said Rosa apologetically, 'but I've got to be up early tomorrow morning. I'm on the early shift for St John Ambulance.' She stopped as another bomb struck somewhere not far away, then said, 'After tonight's raid I've got an idea we're going to be busy. But I promise that tomorrow night we'll come back, as punters, and I'd love it if I could do something with the boys.'

'Me and the boys would love it, too,' said the smooth voice of Snakehips as he appeared at their table. 'Gal, you are smokin'!'

Rosa gave the tall, slim man a hug. 'You, too, Ken. We'd love to stay on tonight, but seriously . . .'

'I know,' said Snakehips ruefully. 'It's your wartime duty.' He turned to Coburg and held out his hand. 'Edgar, my man, you are one lucky dude, and I thank you both for tonight.'

Edgar shook the young man's hand. 'We'll see you tomorrow, Ken. Have a good night tonight.'

'I hope so,' said Snakehips. He looked at the bandstand and saw that most of his musicians had returned. 'Hey, look at that, they're here!' he chuckled. 'And that's because they were hanging around listening to your set, Rosa, instead of heading to the john for a poker game like they usually do.'

As Snakehips joined his band on the stage, Paulson asked Coburg and Rosa, 'How are you getting home? It's not that safe out there.'

'The same way we came, on foot,' said Rosa. 'We'll be safe enough. It's not far to our flat in Piccadilly, and we can always dodge in and out of doorways. After all this time, we're getting used to it.'

'I don't think I can ever get used to it,' said Paulson with a shudder. 'Take care, and God willing I'll see you tomorrow night.'

He shook their hands and they made their way to the cloakroom, collected their coats, then climbed the stairs to the exit to the street.

'I think it might have died down a little,' said Rosa.

There was the sound of an explosion followed by what sounded like a building collapsing.

'It doesn't sound like it to me,' observed Coburg.

'That was some distance away,' said Rosa.

'Yes, you could be right.' Coburg nodded. 'Alright, let's go.'

They stepped out of the shelter of the club entrance, then moved along Coventry Street.

'Maybe we should have brought the car,' said Rosa.

'This way's safer,' said Coburg. 'We can keep moving and dodging.'

They were at the end of Coventry Street when there was a colossal explosion behind them, the force of it sending them

9

stumbling, and then falling to the pavement. They got up and looked in the direction of the explosion.

'The club's been hit!' exclaimed Coburg.

Sure enough, thick smoke was belching out of the entrance to the Café de Paris. Immediately, Coburg began running towards the club.

'Watch out!' warned Rosa.

'There may be people in there who need our help,' said Coburg, and kept running.

As he got close, some people spilt out of the club onto the pavement, coughing and choking and falling to the ground. Rosa ran to one and started checking for injuries.

'I'm alright,' said the man in between coughs. 'At least, I think I am. But it's carnage in the club. Bodies everywhere.'

Coburg made for the entrance and tried to find the stairs, but the smoke was so thick it was impenetrable. He took his handkerchief from his pocket and tied it behind his head so it covered his nose and his mouth, but his attempts to get down the stairs were hampered by the thick, acrid, black smoke, which completely blinded him.

He stumbled back out into the street.

'It's no good,' he told Rosa in between bouts of coughing. 'The smoke's so thick in there you can't see anything.'

'But people could be alive in there!' burst out Rosa.

'The emergency services will have breathing apparatus and torches,' said Coburg.

'But when will they be here?' she begged, nearly beside herself with agonised frustration.

Just then men appeared in fire brigade uniforms, hauling a hose.

'Stand aside!' shouted one. He pulled on his breathing helmet and made for the smoke-filled entrance, shining his powerful torch.

The men vanished into the thick, dense smoke. Coburg and Rosa attempted to follow them but were stopped by another fireman.

'We have friends in there!' Rosa appealed to him.

'That may be, but it's too dangerous,' the man said.

'I'm a volunteer for St John Ambulance,' protested Rosa. 'I might be able to help.'

'You might also be killed. There's no way of knowing what damage there's been. The roof might be about to collapse. In fact, the whole building above it could fall down.'

'But you're going in,' protested Rosa.

'Only in as far as we can, and we've got breathing apparatus,' said the man. 'Now, move back. There could be another bomb in there, primed to go off. We need the entrance clear.'

Coburg took Rosa's arm and gently pulled her back.

'We can't do anything,' he said. 'We'd only be a hindrance, in the way. If there is anyone alive, they'll find them. We won't be able to.'

'In that case I want to wait here,' she said. 'I want to find out who's survived, and who hasn't. I need to know what's happened to them.'

'We can't,' said Coburg.

'These are my friends,' Rosa appealed. 'People I've played with for years. People I care for.'

'It's too dangerous out in the street,' said Coburg. 'The bombing's still going on.'

11

'But I want to *know*!' she stressed.

'And I'll find out,' Coburg promised her. 'But nothing's going to be known for hours. They won't even be able to *see* in there. I promise you, I'll come back when it's daylight. I'll find out what's happened.'

'What do we do till then?' she asked, looking desperately at the smoke that still billowed out of the club entrance.

'We go home,' said Coburg sadly.

She hesitated, then nodded, took his hand and walked with him along Coventry Street towards Piccadilly.

CHAPTER TWO

Sunday 9th March

Coburg and Rosa sat down to their breakfast porridge, Rosa watching the clock. She was due at the St John Ambulance station at Paddington at 7.30 a.m.

'You don't have to go in this morning,' said Coburg. 'After what happened last night, I'm sure the others will understand.'

'No, I'm going in,' said Rosa. 'Last night made me even more certain I have to go in. There will be people all over London who'll be needing ambulances after last night's attack.'

They had the wireless on in the background tuned in to the BBC Home Service, listening in case there was any news on what had happened to the Café de Paris the previous night, but the only mention of the night's bombing was that Buckingham Palace had been hit during the attack.

'Nothing at all about the Café de Paris,' sighed Rosa.

'They don't like to put out bad news,' said Coburg. 'They think it lowers public morale.'

'Buckingham Palace being struck is hardly good news,' said Rosa.

'Yes, but they think it shows that the royal family are sharing in the war damage,' said Coburg. 'After I've dropped you off at Paddington, I'll try and find out what happened to Ken and

Martin and the others. If it's good news, I'll phone Mr Warren at the ambulance station and leave a message.'

'And if it's bad news?'

Coburg thought it over, then said, 'I'll let you know either way.' He finished his porridge and looked at the clock. 'Time to go.'

Coburg drove Rosa to the ambulance station in the police car he'd been allocated after he'd been barred from using his much-loved Bentley for official purposes because, as he was told, 'it doesn't look good for a detective to be driving around in an expensive car like that when the general public are restricted in their petrol usage'. Especially, it had been added, when the detective concerned is the Honourable Edgar Saxe-Coburg.

'There's a certain feeling of animosity towards the aristocracy by a large section of the public, especially with the rationing, which seems to affect the poor but not the wealthy.'

'I'm not wealthy,' Coburg had pointed out. 'And I don't consider myself as an aristocrat.'

'Others do. Your older brother is the Earl of Dawlish with a country estate. You went to Eton. That makes you one of them.'

And so Coburg had garaged the Bentley.

After dropping Rosa off, Coburg drove to Leicester Square. He parked the police car and walked along Coventry Street to the Café de Paris. Or, rather, where the café had been, for now tape had been fixed across the entrance and a sign said *Danger. No entry.*

'Awful, isn't it, Mr Coburg,' said a voice behind him.

Coburg turned and saw Jeff Watts, a waiter at the café. His face and clothes were still stained with smears of black smoke.

'I was lucky, the fire brigade found me. I was in the kitchen when the bomb went off. They dragged me out.' He shook his head, misery etched in his face alongside the stains. 'I haven't been home. I wanted to stay here. It was almost like I kept hoping they'd turn up.' He let out a groan. 'Ken's dead. So's Martin. Most of the band. Most of the customers who were nearest the bandstand. They reckon forty were killed and eighty injured, so I was one of the precious few who survived.' He gave a sigh. 'You and your wife were lucky. If you'd stayed another ten minutes you'd have been killed as well. That table where you were was flattened.'

'We came back,' said Coburg. 'Rosa and I. We tried to get in to see if we could do anything, but the fire brigade stopped us.'

'You wouldn't have been able to do anything,' said Watts. 'The fire brigade were only able to do what they did because they had breathing apparatus and torches. As it was, they were still taking bodies and the wounded out at four this morning. They reckon the bomb that did it came down the ventilation shaft that runs through the cinema and came out in the club. That's when it blew up.' His face puckered up and Coburg could see he was about to start crying. 'Bastards!'

'Where did they take the injured?' asked Coburg.

'Some to UCH, some to Charing Cross, some to the Middlesex. The trouble was there were so many people wounded last night, all over this part of London, the hospitals couldn't cope.'

Coburg looked around him, taking in the ruined buildings, the pavements burst open, the smell of burning and of death.

'I'd better go and tell Rosa the bad news about Ken and Martin and the others,' he said.

Watts nodded. 'Give her my regards, Mr Coburg. You've got a good one there.'

Coburg nodded and walked to his car, his nostrils filled with the smell of destruction.

He then did a tour of the inner London hospitals, using his warrant card as a Scotland Yard detective chief inspector, to get a list of those who'd been admitted as a result of the bombing of the Café de Paris, as well as those who'd been killed and put into the hospital's mortuary. Along with Ken Snakehips Johnson and Martin Paulson, there were plenty of names he recognised among the dead. Many he didn't, but those he felt had been the customers who'd been caught in the blast. The musicians in Johnson's band were another matter, and Coburg knew how deeply Rosa would feel when she heard these names.

He looked at his watch and saw that it was half past one. Rosa was due to finish her shift at two. He pulled up outside a telephone box and dialled the St John Ambulance depot. The phone was answered by Chesney Warren.

'Mr Warren, it's Edgar Coburg. Is Rosa there, please?'

'She's just pulled in to the yard.'

'Would you let her know I'm in the area and I'll come and pick her up.'

'No problem.' There was a pause, then Warren asked, 'Rosa told us about last night. Are you alright?'

'We're getting there,' said Coburg. 'I'll see you shortly.'

When Coburg pulled into the yard, Rosa was waiting for him outside the office.

'What's the news?' she asked urgently as she got into the car.

'It's not good,' said Coburg. 'Do you want to leave it until we get home?'

'Tell me now,' she said.

'Martin and Ken are dead, along with half the band.'

She slumped in the passenger seat, her hair falling down to cover her face.

'Who?' she asked.

Coburg took out the list he'd made from his visits to the hospitals and gave her the names of those who'd died. 'Some of them are alive, but are still in hospital being treated.' He then read that list of names to her.

'So they made it,' she said.

'So far,' said Coburg. 'What do you want to do now? Go home, or go somewhere else? Maybe go for a drink?'

She nodded. 'Yes, let's go for a drink. We'll raise a glass to toast Ken and the rest of those wonderful players we'll never see again.' She wiped her eyes. 'God, I'm getting maudlin,' she apologised.

'It's allowed,' said Coburg.

He put the car into gear and drove off.

CHAPTER THREE

Monday 10th March

Coburg pulled up outside the small terraced house in Somers Town where his sergeant, Ted Lampson, lived with his young son, Terry. Immediately, Lampson appeared. Coburg vacated the driver's position and moved to the passenger seat, and Lampson slid behind the steering wheel. It was their regular arrangement: Lampson loved driving but couldn't afford a car of his own, so Coburg kept the police car at his block of flats in Piccadilly, and every morning drove it to Lampson's house, and Lampson took over driving duties during the working day. Coburg had suggested once that Lampson could keep the car overnight, but Lampson had pointed out that Somers Town was an inappropriate place to leave any vehicle out at night, especially a police car. It was one of the poorest parts of London, adjacent to Euston station, and with a number of petty criminals living there. A car parked on the street overnight was very likely to be stolen, or – in the case of a police car – badly damaged. The fact that the driver was a police detective sergeant meant very little; the only cars that were safe on the streets of Somers Town were those owned by known and very dangerous criminals.

'Terry alright?' asked Coburg as Lampson drove off, heading for Scotland Yard.

'Fine,' said Lampson. Lampson was a widower and during the working week he took his eleven-year-old son to his parents' flat just round the corner, where his parents gave their grandson breakfast and then took him to school. 'The team played against a church team yesterday. St Adulphus. Won 2–1.'

Lampson and his fiancée, Eve Bradley, a teacher at Terry's school, organised a Somers Town football team that played matches against other teams in the area, mainly from other schools, boys' clubs and church teams.

'How are plans for the wedding going?' asked Coburg.

'Awful,' groaned Lampson.

Coburg looked at him in surprise. 'Eve's not having second thoughts?'

'It's not Eve, it's her mother,' groaned Lampson.

'What's the problem with her?'

'Loads, but the main thing is she doesn't think I'm good enough for her daughter. She'd always hoped that Eve would get hitched to this bloke Vic Tennant.'

'Who's he?'

'He's got his own business, a builder's with a yard at the back of Euston station. Rolling in money, according to Eve's old woman.'

'Did Eve used to go out with him before you and her got together?'

'No, but he was always hanging around, bringing presents. Eve kept giving them back to him and told him to stop, but he started giving them to her mum, Paula, and she lapped it up. Kept on at Eve that she ought to settle down with him, and even now she's giving Eve the tearful earful about how good this Vic would be for her. What she means, of course, is how good

19

he'd be for Paula.' Her gave a sigh, then asked, 'How was your weekend?'

'Tough. We got caught up in the bombing at Café de Paris. Rosa did a set there, and we'd just left when the bomb hit it. It was lucky for us that Rosa was on early shift at the ambulance station on the Sunday morning, so we'd left early.'

'Yes, I heard about it on the wireless,' said Lampson. 'They said it took a direct hit. Lots of casualties. You were lucky.'

'Snakehips Johnson was killed, along with some of his band and customers. We'd been talking to Snakehips and the café's owner, Martin Paulson, just a minute or so before we left.'

'I'd have thought it would have been safe, being underground. Like being in a bomb shelter.'

'That's what we thought, but it seems the bomb came down a ventilation shaft into the club, where it blew up. Forty killed and eighty injured.'

Suddenly the car radio crackled into life. 'Base to Echo Seven. Come in, Echo Seven.'

Coburg reached for the handset and spoke into the microphone. 'Echo Seven receiving. Over.'

'Echo Seven. Reports of a dead man at the entrance to Lord's Underground station. Police constable in attendance.'

'Received and understood, Base. On our way. Echo Seven over and out.' He hung up the microphone. 'Right, Ted, Lord's station it is.'

'Sure they got it right?' asked Lampson. 'Lord's was shut down a year ago. They might mean St John's Wood. That's the one that serves Lord's Cricket Ground now.'

'A constable's in attendance. I'm sure he knows which station he's at,' said Coburg.

'Another disused Underground station,' sighed Lampson. 'We're getting a lot of these lately.'

'It's the Blitz,' said Coburg. 'They need somewhere for people to go to be safe from the bombing.'

They pulled up outside the closed-up Lord's Underground station, where a uniformed constable was standing by the closed doors and another man was bending over a body lying on the pavement.

'Looks like Dr Welbourne is here ahead of us,' said Coburg.

Dr Welbourne looked up as the two detectives neared him.

'What have we got, Doctor?' asked Coburg.

'We have a dead man,' said Welbourne. 'As you'll see, he's black, which is a bit of a rarity.'

Coburg and Lampson looked at the dead man. He was, indeed, black.

'Any idea who he is?' asked Coburg.

'No identification on him,' replied Welbourne. 'No wallet or anything else.'

'So, possibly a mugging?'

'That would be speculation,' said Welbourne. He pointed to the pavement on which the dead man lay. 'One thing I'm sure, he wasn't killed here. The lack of blood around him shows that. What I can tell you is he was beaten to death by some savage blows about the head.' He indicated the dead man's head where the skin had been lacerated beneath his hair, bloody gashes evident. 'I may be wrong, but it wouldn't surprise me to find the weapon was a cricket bat.'

'A cricket bat?' repeated Coburg, surprised.

Welbourne pointed to some splinters of wood he'd taken from

the wounds to the man's head. 'If I'm not mistaken, these splinters are willow that's been treated.' He added, 'My father works for a firm that makes cricket bats. But I may be wrong. I'll be able to confirm it or not once I've looked at them under a microscope.'

'If you're right, it's very appropriate him being found at Lord's,' said Coburg. 'So, there could be a cricketing connection?'

'Possibly,' said Welbourne. 'Although it may be a deliberate red herring to try and confuse any investigation. After all, a man beaten to death with a cricket bat – if that's what it was – and his body dumped outside Lord's Underground station seems a bit obvious. The other thing is he's been badly beaten. Some of his fingers are broken. Again, I'll be able to let you have more details once I've examined him properly.'

Coburg looked at the constable, who was standing watching, taking in the conversation between the doctor and the detectives.

'Were you the one who found the body, Constable?' asked Coburg.

'Constable Riddick, sir,' said the constable, snapping to attention and saluting. 'From St John's Wood station. And no, sir. I was first on the scene, but the man who discovered the body was a bloke on his way to work, and he came and found me. This is my regular beat, you see, sir, around this area. I asked him to stand by the body while I called it in to my station, then I stayed here to wait for you and the doctor to arrive.'

'Have you got the name of the man who found the body?'

Riddick checked his notebook. 'His name's Henry Duggan. He lives near Lord's Tube station. He works at a local butcher's, Dorset's.' He passed Coburg a leaf torn from his notebook on which he'd written the man's name and address, and that of Dorset's the butcher's. 'Here are his details, sir.'

'Did he say at what time he found the body?'

'It was just after eight o'clock.'

'Thank you, Constable. That's very efficient.' Coburg looked at Welbourne. 'Have you nearly finished here, Doctor?'

'I've done just about as much as I can out in the street,' said Welbourne. 'I'm just waiting for an ambulance to arrive to take the body to UCH. Once I've got him on a table I'll be able to tell you more about him, approximately when he died, and if it was the blows to the head that killed him, or something else.'

Coburg nodded. 'In that case we'll see you later at UCH.' He turned to PC Riddick, and said, 'I think you can return to your duties now, Constable. But well done for holding the fort until we arrived.'

'Thank you, sir,' said Riddick, and he gave another smart salute, and then marched off.

'A good bloke,' commented Lampson.

As he followed Coburg towards their waiting car, he said, 'You look like you've had a thought, sir. About the dead man, I mean.'

Coburg nodded. 'When I saw he was black my first feeling was that he could have been a musician. There's quite a few musicians from the West Indies in London at the moment with so many British musicians away in the services. People like Snakehips Johnson and his band. But then I got to thinking about the cricket aspect.'

'That a cricket bat may have been the weapon?'

'That, and the fact it happened here, by Lord's Cricket Ground. I wondered if the dead man could be associated with the British Empire XI.'

'The who?' asked Lampson.

Coburg smiled. 'I guess you don't follow cricket.'

'Not really. Football's my game.'

'The British Empire XI is a team made up of cricketers from Britain and far-flung parts of the Empire, including the West Indies. They're here to play against different English cricket teams. Just like the football season's been abandoned because of the war, it's the same with cricket. It's a chance to see top-class cricketers in action.'

'But without knowing who this dead bloke is, there's not much chance of finding out if he's part of this lot,' pointed out Lampson. 'He could be just anybody.'

'If I'm right about this, I think I know someone who might be able to help.'

'Who?'

'My brother, Magnus. He's a cricket devotee, and also a member of the Marylebone Cricket Club, which owns Lord's.'

'So he might know this bloke?'

'He might. Let's head back to the Yard and I'll give him a ring and arrange for him to meet us at University College Hospital.'

As Lampson drove them to the Yard, Coburg filled his sergeant in on why he thought Magnus might be able to help them. 'He knows everyone in the cricket world. He was also a superb cricket all-rounder. Although Magnus only played as an amateur, he could have been a professional. He appeared regularly for Eton in the Eton v Harrow match, and was usually either top scorer or took the most wickets. He may not know our victim at all, but there's a chance, and – if he does – this will be quicker than going through the usual channels.'

'Is he in London?' asked Lampson. 'I thought he was at the family stately home in the country. Dawlish Hall.'

'Not while this series of cricket matches are happening. He

24

and Malcolm have got their own seats at Lord's.'

'Malcolm likes cricket as well?' asked Lampson.

'Not as much as Magnus, but he's got an encyclopaedic knowledge of who played for who and when, and their scores.' He grinned. 'It irritates Magnus no end.'

It had been a busy morning for Rosa and her co-driver, Doris Gibbs. Their first call had been to a woman with a suspected heart attack. No sooner had they delivered her to the nearest hospital, than they got a radio message instructing them to go to a fallen building. There, they found an elderly man who'd been trapped in the cellar of his house when it had collapsed following the bombing on Saturday night. He'd been found on Monday morning by a team of rescuers who'd responded to reports of knocking from beneath the rubble. They'd cleared the rubble, exposing a wooden floor, and found a trapdoor. They'd forced the trapdoor open, and a torch shone into the darkness beneath illuminated a man in his sixties called Percy, who told them, 'I think my leg's broke.'

Rosa and Doris arrived and fixed a temporary splint around the man's broken leg, then – with the help of members of the fire brigade who'd turned up – managed to get the stretcher holding the injured man up the rickety wooden steps and out through the trapdoor, and into their ambulance.

'It's lucky they put that radio in our vehicle,' said Doris. 'Even though it means we don't get a break between calls.' Gradually the St John Ambulance were able to put two-way radios in more and more of their vehicles, speeding up the time they could attend to an urgent call.

'How are you doing?' asked Doris.

'Better than I was yesterday,' said Rosa. 'Being busy helps keep me from thinking about it too much.'

She was referring to the bombing of the Café de Paris, an event that still haunted her.

'And Edgar?' asked Doris.

'He throws himself into his work even more than I do,' said Rosa. 'Which is a good thing for him. Mind, he wasn't as close to Ken and the others as I was. I'd played with them for years; they were a really good bunch, as well as being fantastic musicians.'

She slowed down as they neared a junction where a double-decker bus was lying on its side.

'We'd better go back and take the long way round,' she said.

'I'll go and tell Percy what's happened and see if he's alright,' said Doris.

Doris moved to the back of the ambulance where their patient lay, holding on to handles to keep her balance due to the ambulance rocking slightly as Rosa reversed it and then did a three-point turn. Doris arrived beside the elderly man.

'There's a bus been blown over,' she explained. 'We've got to take a different route to the hospital. Are you managing?'

Percy nodded. 'What you gave me has helped with the pain,' he said. 'Thanks.'

'It's what we do,' said Doris. 'Hopefully our way will be clear this other way, so we'll soon have you in hospital.'

'Six months,' groaned Percy unhappily.

'What?' asked Doris.

'Six months,' repeated Percy. 'That's how long this bombing's been going on. Every night, and sometimes during the day. How much longer is it going to go on for?'

'Lord alone knows,' sighed Doris.

At the Yard, Coburg telephoned Magnus's London flat. As usual, the call was answered by Magnus's valet, driver and general factotum, Malcolm. The two men had been in the trenches together during the First War, Magnus in command of a unit and Malcolm his batman. Magnus credited Malcolm with saving his life under fire on at least three occasions.

'Once I was all tangled up on barbed wire, and Malcolm cut me free while Jerry kept up heavy fire on our position with their damned machine guns. Malcolm was hit twice. If it hadn't been for him, I'd have been dead.' Then he'd added, 'Mind, I don't talk about it to him. Don't want him to get a swelled head.'

'The Earl of Dawlish's residence,' Malcolm announced in his most official manner.

'Malcolm, it's Edgar. Is Magnus there?'

'He's in the bath at the moment, Mr Edgar. Is it urgent?'

'Not urgent enough to get him out of the bath for. But when he's finished, could you bring him to University College Hospital.'

'Certainly. I believe he's nearly finished. He's stopped that infernal singing of his. Can I tell him what it's about?'

'There's a dead body I'd like him to look at. Along with you, of course. The doctor who examined him believes he was beaten to death with a cricket bat.'

'A cricket bat!' exclaimed Malcolm, his voice filled with outrage. 'Is nothing sacred?'

'We're not sure. The thing is, we don't know who he is and we hope you two might know him.'

'We'll be with you shortly, Mr Edgar. It's the mortuary at UCH, I presume?'

'It is. We'll see you there, Malcolm.'

CHAPTER FOUR

Coburg and Lampson found Dr Welbourne at work on another cadaver's organs when they arrived at University College Hospital's mortuary.

'I haven't had a chance to get round to your man yet,' said Welbourne, pointing to where the dead man lay on a table covered by a sheet. 'I needed to get these bits and pieces examined to determine the cause of death of another victim.'

'That's fine,' said Coburg. 'In fact, it's a stroke of luck because I've invited my brother, Magnus, to come here and take a look at him. We feel he might know who he is. If there is a cricketing connection, that is. He's bringing his old friend, Malcolm, with him. And it'll be easier for them to see if they recognise the dead man before you start slicing him open.'

'The Earl of Dawlish.' Welbourne nodded. 'I saw him play once. He was using a bat my father had worked on. Superb batsman.'

'Yes, well, he and his old army chum seem to know everyone in the cricket world.'

There was a tap at the door, then it opened and a white-jacketed porter peered in.

'Excuse me, sir,' he said. 'There are two gentlemen to see you.'

'Please show them in, John,' said Welbourne.

Magnus and Malcolm entered, and Coburg introduced them both to Welbourne.

'Killed with a cricket bat, I understand,' said Magnus.

'That's what it appears, although I'll know more once I've opened him up and examined him,' said Welbourne.

He walked to the figure lying on the table and pulled back the sheet to show the man's head.

'Good God, it's Desmond Bartlett!' exclaimed Magnus, obviously shocked.

'You know him?' asked Coburg.

'Of course we know him!'

'He's Jamaican,' added Malcolm. 'One of their best bowlers. In fact, we saw him on Saturday.'

'Where?' asked Coburg.

'At Lord's, at the practice nets, along with some of his team-mates. We wanted to see how they shaped up.' He looked ruefully down at Bartlett's dead body. 'What a tragedy!'

'So he was part of the touring British Empire XI?' said Coburg.

'That's not quite correct,' said Malcolm. 'The British Empire XI have yet to start the 1941 season. So far Bartlett's been playing for the West Indies XI.'

'Didn't you see the one-day game they played against Pelham Warner's XI at Lord's?' asked Magnus.

'No, we were rather busy at that time.'

'Learie Constantine was magnificent for the Windies. A complete all-rounder. Bowls as well as he bats. And Len Hutton was superb for Pelham Warner's side.'

'There was one oddity,' interjected Malcolm. 'The Compton

brothers both played in the match, but for opposing sides. Denis Compton was top scorer with seventy-three, and his brother Leslie was made an honorary West Indian for the day.'

'We need to talk to the other players who were at that practice,' said Coburg.

'Your best bet is to talk to Ray Smith and C. B. Clarke,' said Malcolm.

'Ray Smith?' Coburg frowned. 'He's the Essex all-rounder, isn't he?'

'He is,' said Malcolm. 'He's also the captain of the Empire XI. C. B. Clarke is the vice-captain.'

'I don't know him,' said Coburg.

Both Magnus and Malcolm looked at Coburg in disbelief.

'You don't know who C. B. Clarke is?' said Malcolm, shocked by Coburg's ignorance.

'Unlike you two, I have a full-time job that keeps me very busy,' responded Coburg. 'I'm aware of cricket when it happens, but I wouldn't describe myself as an avid follower.'

'Obviously not, if you don't know who C. B. Clarke is,' said Magnus, his tone heavy with disapproval. 'Carlos Bertram Clarke. And, for the record, his team-mates call him Bertie. He's from Barbados.'

'When the West Indies played the Metropolitan Police at Imber Court, he took all ten wickets for just twenty-nine runs,' added Malcolm. 'He was there at the nets on Saturday, as was Ray Smith. If you want to know who else was, ask Ray and Bertie.'

'You seem to know a lot about the team,' commented Coburg. 'What about Desmond Bartlett?'

'I remember he came over with the West Indies team

in 1939,' said Malcolm. 'When they realised that war was imminent, some of the team returned to the West Indies, and some elected to stay here and join up in the forces. Bartlett was one of those who stayed. He joined the RAF as ground crew.'

'Do you know where he was based?'

'No, but I'm sure we can find out.' He looked at Coburg and asked, 'Where was he found?'

'Outside Lord's Tube station.'

'Curiouser and curiouser,' murmured Magnus.

After Magnus and Malcolm had left, Coburg asked Welbourne if he had any idea when the murder took place.

'I won't know until I've checked his stomach contents, worked out mealtimes, that sort of thing. But, from the degree of rigor mortis, I'm guessing between six o'clock and eight o'clock last night.'

Coburg thanked Welbourne, then he and Lampson made their way up from the basement to the street and their car. As they left the hospital, Lampson grumbled, 'Bloody Arsenal.'

'What have Arsenal got to do with it?' asked Coburg, puzzled.

'The Compton brothers, Denis and Leslie. It's not enough they play for Arsenal in the football league, now it turns out they're both top-level cricketers. It ain't right.'

CHAPTER FIVE

Coburg and Lampson returned to Scotland Yard, where they telephoned Lord's, and after being passed from person to person they were eventually given the addresses and telephone numbers for Ray Smith and Bertie Clarke.

'It seems that they are the main organisers for the Empire XI,' said Coburg.

'Hopefully they'll be able to tell us all we need,' said Lampson.

Coburg tried both numbers, but there was no answer to either.

'We'll try them again later,' he said. 'In the meantime, let's go and have a word with Henry Duggan.'

Henry Duggan was a short, burly man working in the small room at the back of Dorset's butcher shop, sawing up the carcases of lambs and pigs, and then chopping and slicing the pieces into smaller cuts to be displayed in the shop. He seemed grateful to step out into the small yard at the back of the shop to talk to Coburg and Lampson.

'It's hot work,' he said, mopping the sweat from his brow with a large red handkerchief.

'Your boss can still get hold of meat,' noted Coburg.

'He's got a pal who's got a smallholding in Essex,' said Duggan. 'He lets us have the occasional pig or lamb, but it's not like before rationing came in. Then, there were five of us butchers here working on the carcases. Now, there's just me and a bloke called Jerry who comes in a couple of days a week.' He looked at the warrant cards that the two detectives held up for him. 'I'm guessing this is about that bloke I found at Lord's station.'

'It is,' said Coburg. 'Can you tell us what happened?'

'Sure. I was walking to work, same as I always do, and I saw this bloke lying on the ground by the entrance to Lord's Underground. At first I thought he might be a drunk sleeping it off; you get them sometimes. Then I saw he was black, which was a bit unusual. But then I thought to myself, *Lord's*, and I remembered that they were putting on this series of cricket matches, English Counties against the West Indians. So I wondered if he might be one of them. There's been a few of them in the area, going to Lord's to practise. I'm not a great cricket fan, football's more my game, but I like to see top-class sports still taking place. Anyway, I went to him and gave him a gentle prod to wake him up, but he didn't respond.'

'Was he on his back or on his front?'

'On his back, so I was able to check if he was breathing without turning him over. And he wasn't. So I checked for a pulse, and there wasn't one of them either. So I knew he was dead. I knew there was a local copper in the area, because I used to see him sometimes when I was on my way to work. Just to nod to, not to talk to. But I knew where he might be found. So I went to look for him. And, sure enough, he was there.'

'Where?'

'Not far up Prince Albert Road. He looked like he was on his way to the zoo. So I told him about the dead bloke and he come along with me. Then he said he'd need to get Scotland Yard to call it in, so he asked me if I'd mind standing by the bloke while he made the call. And that's all there was to it. I waited, and when he came back, I went to work.'

'Did you notice if there was any blood on the ground by the body?'

Duggan shook his head. 'No. I didn't want to start pulling him around because I didn't want to mess things up; I know the police like things left as they are till they've gone over them. But I had a quick look to see if there was any blood, or any indication of what might have happened, but there was none. Do you know yet how he died?'

'He was struck on the back of the head,' said Coburg.

'Poor bloke.'

'What time was it when you found him?'

'Quarter to eight. It only took me five minutes or so to find the copper. Lucky he was right in the area.'

'Thank you, Mr Duggan. You've been very helpful. Oh, and you were right about him being a cricketer.'

Duggan gave a smug smile. 'It was him being at Lord's made me think of it. I'd make a good detective.'

'So, Bartlett was definitely killed somewhere else and then his body dumped,' said Coburg as he and Lampson walked back to their car.

'Why at Lord's Tube station entrance?' asked Lampson. 'Someone trying to send some sort of message? Something to do with cricket?'

'Possibly,' said Coburg.

'In which case, why didn't they dump him at Lord's Cricket Ground itself?

'Too many people there. The Tube station is closed down.'

'It's still odd,' said Lampson.

'I think it might help to find out a bit more about Lord's station,' said Coburg. 'If anyone's got the keys to it, if anyone ever goes in to check it, that sort of thing.'

'Difficult to find out if it's always closed,' observed Lampson. 'No one to ask.'

'Yes there is,' said Coburg. 'The Railway Executive Committee offices at Down Street. Jeremy Purslake.'

'Purslake?' mused Lampson. 'That's the bloke we met over the dead Russian woman.'

'That's right,' said Coburg. 'If there's anyone who seems to know everything about the railway systems in this country, it's Mr Purslake.'

They drove back to Scotland Yard. Once more, Coburg tried the telephone number for Bertie Clarke, but again got no reply. Next, Coburg got the telephone operator to try the Railway Executive Committee, and when he was connected, asked to be put through to Jeremy Purslake.

There was a series of clicks on the line, then the operator said, 'I have Mr Purslake for you, Chief Inspector.'

'Thank you,' said Coburg. 'And thank you for taking my call, Mr Purslake, I know how busy you are.'

'Never too busy to talk to you, Chief Inspector,' said Purslake. 'How may I help you?'

'I'm afraid we have another dead body at a disused Underground station.'

'Oh dear,' said Purslake. 'On the platform, like last time?'

'No. This one was left outside Lord's station. A man.'

'Murdered?'

'Apparently beaten to death.'

'How awful!'

'I'm hoping you can help us.'

'Certainly, but I'm not sure how.'

'If you can let me know about the station. I know that it closed in 1939, once war was declared.'

'Yes. In fact it's got a bit of a convoluted history, which is why I'm able to tell you about it without needing to go into the archives. The station opened under the name of St John's Wood Road in 1868. It was unable to cope with the large passenger numbers who used it to attend cricket matches at nearby Lord's Cricket Ground. As a result, the station was demolished and reconstructed on a larger scale in 1925, opening under the name of St John's Wood. In June 1939 it was renamed again, this time as Lord's. In November 1939 a new Bakerloo line station named St John's Wood was opened to relieve continuing increasing congestion at Lord's station. With the advent of the Second World War, it was decided to close Lord's station, initially for the duration of the war. However, the decision was made to shut the station permanently after the last train on 19th November 1939.'

'I see,' said Coburg. 'Is it operating as an air raid shelter, like many other Tube stations?'

'No,' said Purslake. 'That would require station staff to be on duty, and air raid precautions in that area are already being well taken care of. Members of the public have night-time access to St John's Wood station, which is less than half a mile away from the old Lord's station. Also, Marylebone Borough

Council have constructed an air raid shelter in the crypt of St John's Wood chapel.'

'So at the moment, Lord's station is shut up completely?'

There was a moment's hesitation, then Purslake said, 'To all intents and purposes. The staff at St John's Wood have keys to the doors in case there's an emergency. The same goes for another set of keys left at St John's Wood police station.'

'And have these emergency keys been used much?'

'If they have, no one's felt the need to advise us here at Down Street. My recommendation would to be make enquiries direct to the staff at St John's Wood.'

Coburg looked thoughtful as he replaced the receiver.

'Has he given you something to think about, guv?' asked Lampson.

'Not on purpose,' said Coburg. 'According to him, Lord's station is officially closed and not in use, not even as an air raid shelter.' He got up from his chair and said, 'Purslake also told me that St John's Wood Tube station have got keys to Lord's. I think it might be worth our going to St John's Wood and picking up the keys and having a nosy around, but first I think we need to check out Lord's Cricket Ground itself. If Bartlett's death is connected to cricket in some way, there might be some answers there.'

'I've never been to Lord's,' said Lampson.

'I haven't been for some years,' said Coburg. 'In fact, I think the last time I was there it was to watch my late brother Charles play in an Eton and Harrow match.'

'Charles? Not Magnus?'

'No, Charles was younger than Magnus so he played more recently.'

'You never played?'

'Not at that level. Anyway, I certainly haven't been since it's been taken over for the war effort.'

'Who by? The army?' asked Lampson. 'I know they're stationing troops on some football pitches.'

'No,' said Coburg. 'The cricket pitch and the seating have been left alone so matches can still be played. But there are barrage balloons operated from there, and also part of the grounds has been given over to an RAF Aircrew Receiving Centre, where the new recruits come.'

'With all that going on, will we be allowed in?'

Coburg smiled. 'We will be if we have a member of the MCC with us.' He picked up the phone. 'I'll see if Magnus and Malcolm are free. In which case, we'll do Lord's before we go to the stations at St John's Wood.'

CHAPTER SIX

Magnus and Malcolm were waiting for them at the entrance to the cricket ground.

'You're in luck,' said Magnus. 'Ray Smith and Bertie Clarke are here, in the clubhouse. We've told them about poor Desmond Bartlett. They're both absolutely shocked.'

'We told them you were on your way,' added Malcolm. 'They're looking forward to talking to you, answering any questions you have.'

As they walked towards the clubhouse, Coburg and Lampson looked up at the huge barrage balloons, the defence against low-flying enemy aircraft, floating in the sky above Lord's, anchored to the ground by thick metal cables.

'I see the place is well-protected,' Coburg commented.

'It needs to be,' said Magnus. 'You may remember that last October those swine in the Luftwaffe dropped an oil bomb onto the outfield at the Nursery End. It's hoped that these barrage balloons will put a stop to that sort of thing. The last thing we want are bombs falling when a match is being played. They're controlled by 903 Balloon Barrage Squadron located in the Nursery Ground.'

'Where's the Aircrew Receiving Centre?' asked Coburg.

'At the other end, past the pavilion. Most of the new recruits are billeted in the blocks of flats overlooking Lord's.'

'Luxury accommodation,' commented Coburg.

'Some are, some not so,' said Magnus. 'But I agree, they're better that the usual billets for recruits. Do you want me to see if I can arrange for you to talk to the people at the ARC after you've talked to Ray and Bertie?'

'Would Desmond Bartlett have had anything to do with them?'

'Well, he was in the RAF, but ground crew not aircrew, so I think it unlikely. If I find out he was involved with the ARC in any way, I'll make arrangements for you to talk to the people in charge.'

'Thanks,' said Coburg.

Coburg recognised the tall young man sitting in the bar of the clubhouse as Ray Smith, the captain and all-rounder for Essex. He'd seen him play at a match Magnus had taken him to before the war.

'You've got to see this man play, Edgar. He has the makings of a superb test cricketer.' The man with him, black with tight curly hair, was obviously the renowned Bertie Clarke. Both cricketers stood up as Coburg and Lampson approached with Magnus and Malcolm. Magnus did the introductions, then said, 'Malcolm and I will leave you chaps alone to talk, otherwise Malcolm will fill up the time with cricket anecdotes.'

'I will not!' protested Malcolm indignantly.

'Yes you would, and these chaps have a murder to solve.' Magnus nodded to the four men and he and Malcolm left, Malcolm still complaining volubly.

'Thank you for seeing us,' said Coburg.

'Anything we can do,' said Smith. 'This is appalling.

40

Desmond Bartlett was a vital part of the team.'

'We understand you were here with him on the weekend at nets practice,' said Coburg.

Smith and Clarke both shook their heads. 'On Saturday,' said Clarke, 'but he wasn't here on Sunday.'

'We assumed he'd had to go back to Kenley,' said Smith.

'Kenley?'

'RAF Kenley. That's where he was based. He was ground crew, you know.'

'Yes,' said Coburg. 'Did he travel up from Kenley on Saturday?'

'No,' said Clarke. 'He'd travelled up the day before, Friday.'

'Do you know where he stayed on Friday night?'

'He said he stayed with a friend.'

'Do you know the name of the friend?'

Both men shook their heads. 'No,' said Smith. 'Although it wasn't with one of the team. We'd have known.'

'And do you know if he stayed with this friend on Saturday night?'

'I don't know,' said Clarke. 'I think we assumed so, but when he didn't appear on Sunday we thought there might have been a change in his plans. He might have gone back to Kenley after Saturday's nets practice.'

'His commanding officer will know,' said Smith.

'Do you know his name?'

Smith took out a small notebook and flicked through it. 'I keep a list of contacts for all our chaps in here, in case we need to talk to them. At the moment, with the war on, we never know who might suddenly be not available, and we need to get someone else in.' He beamed as he found what he was

41

looking for. 'Desmond Bartlett, RAF Kenley. The name of his commanding officer was Group Captain Warmsley.' He read out the telephone number for Warmsley at Kenley, and Coburg wrote it down.

'Has he been informed of Bartlett's murder?'

'I believe so, by now,' said Smith. 'Magnus said he'd told Pelham Warner, and he said he'd inform the group captain.' He shook his head, still shocked. 'I can't get over it. Who'd do a thing like that? He was one of the nicest chaps you could ever meet.'

'Did Bartlett have any family over here?'

Smith looked at Clarke, who said, 'Not as far as I know. He never mentioned a wife, or a fiancée, or anything like that. As far as I know all his family are back in Jamaica.'

'We'd like to talk to the other players who were here with him on Saturday,' said Coburg. 'Could you let us have a note of their names and where we can get hold of them?'

'Of course,' said Smith. He took a sheet of Lord's letterheaded paper from a wooden tray on the table beside them. 'While you talk to Bertie, I'll write them down for you. But I'll still be listening in case you need anything from me.'

'Thank you,' said Coburg.

As Smith began to write the names down, Coburg turned to the Barbadian.

'Would you mind filling me in on the Empire XI,' he said. 'Who's in it, what's your playing schedule, that sort of thing. I'm sure my brother Magnus knows all about it, but I'm rather out of the cricketing loop.'

'Of course,' said Clarke. 'You know Pelham Warner?'

'By reputation, but not personally. My brother Magnus is a good friend of his. '

42

'Yes,' said Clarke. 'Well, it all began soon after the war started, when everyone realised that first-class cricket was going to be one of the casualties. With many of the players joining up for active service, and restrictions on matches being played, it looked as if we could forget top-class cricket as long as the war lasted.' He sighed. 'It's been two years now, and there's still no sign of a conclusion. But, hopefully, we shall prevail.'

'We will,' put in Smith, still writing. 'That criminal Hitler mustn't be allowed to win. It would be the end of the world as we know it.' He looked at them, annoyed, as he told them, 'I tried to join up. The army turned me down because I've got flat feet. The navy also, because I can't swim. I've signed up as a special constable and fire watcher, and then this idea came up as a way of raising money for the war effort.' He turned back to writing his list, saying, 'You tell them, Bertie.'

'It was Desmond Donnelly, a cricketer and a recruit at the RAF, who suggested to Plum – sorry, Pelham, that is – the idea of a put-together team touring around the country playing cricket matches against top-class sides, raising money for the Red Cross. A series of one-day matches would draw the crowds, raise morale and ensure that cricket as a first-class game didn't vanish.

'There was a problem, of course, with so many players away overseas in action, so it was proposed it be a British Empire XI, with top-class players drawn from Britain and the dominion and colonies, whoever was available. There's me, of course, from Barbados. I'm available because I'm exempted from serving.'

'He's a doctor,' put in Smith. 'At Guy's Hospital. And a good one.'

'We have quite a few players from England,' said Clarke. 'Along with those from Australia, New Zealand, India and South Africa. And, of course, the West Indies.'

'Ernest Eytle from British Guiana is a particularly fine player,' added Smith. 'As are K. C. James and W. E. Merritt from New Zealand. Especially James, the wicketkeeper.' He pushed the list of names across the table to Coburg, who folded it and put it in his pocket.

'Thank you,' said Coburg.

'As for our list of matches, we tour around. Our next match is against the Combined Services XI here at Lord's, but we played Epsom Cricket Club at Epsom, the RAF here at Lord's, there's a match against an army XI at Gloucester, and then Northamptonshire,' said Smith. 'We travel as a team, either by train or coach.'

'Where to now, guv?' asked Lampson as they left the cricket ground. 'Lord's Tube station? St John's Wood nick?'

'Not at the moment,' said Coburg. He tapped the pocket where he'd put the list of names Ray Smith had given him. 'We need to find out where Bartlett stayed when he was in London. I'll drop you off at the Yard and you ring round all these people who were at the practice on Saturday and ask if any of them know. Meanwhile, I'll head for RAF Kenley and talk to this Group Captain Warmsley.'

'Where's RAF Kenley?' asked Lampson.

'It's one of the three main airfields protecting London from the Luftwaffe, along with Biggin Hill and Croydon. It's at Coulsdon, just south of Purley. I shouldn't be long.' He took out his notebook and copied down the telephone number

Smith had given him for RAF Kenley. 'Here you are,' he said, handing the torn-out page to Lampson. 'If anything comes up you think it's worth letting me know about urgently, call me there. Otherwise, I'll see you when I get back.'

Coburg drove to RAF Kenley and asked to see Group Captain Warmsley.

'I don't understand this at all,' said Warmsley when Coburg explained the reason for his visit. 'Bartlett had no enemies at all. Hugely popular.'

'What was his role in ground crew?'

'He was a sergeant armourer, and one of the very best. There's a lot of publicity in the press about our pilots, and very deserved, but too often the ground crew tend to get overlooked, and without them there'd be no working planes in the sky.'

'I suppose a sergeant armourer makes sure the guns work.'

'To be honest, Chief Inspector, that's a bit simplistic and underrates what an armourer actually does. For example, the armourer harmonises an aircraft's guns to ensure that all bullets fired from a plane's eight machine guns converge at a point several hundred yards ahead of the aircraft. It's highly skilled and requires the use of plumb lines to make sure the guns are properly harmonised. A harmonisation diagram is lined up on the plumblines exactly fifty yards from the front.'

'Yes,' interrupted Coburg politely. 'I'm sure this is very interesting, but . . .'

'I think you need to understand how and why being an armourer is more than making sure the guns have ammunition,' said Warmsley, his tone sharp. 'It gives you an idea of the man.'

I must keep this man on my side if I'm going to get the information and assistance I need, Coburg warned himself. Aloud, he said, 'Of course. I apologise. Please, continue.'

'The harmonisation diagram is a metal frame with a centre upright with arms on which are eight discs – one for each machine gun. These discs are coloured red, blue, yellow and green – four for each wing. The guns are cocked and a bore-sighting instrument inserted into the breech, which allows the armourer a clear view down the barrel. The gun is then adjusted until the appropriate disc is centred in the barrel. It is an immensely skilled operation. If not done accurately, and checked minutely on every occasion the plane is about to go up, the pilot is at risk. Aerial combat is very dangerous.'

'Yes, sir,' said Coburg. 'I understand the importance of the work that Desmond Bartlett was doing. Do you think it may have been connected with his death? The reason someone wanted to murder him?'

Warmsley considered that thoughtfully, then said, 'He will be a great loss to the war effort and our chances of defeating the Luftwaffe, but I cannot see why he should be singled out.'

'Can you think of any reason why anyone should want to kill him? Did he have any enemies?'

'Absolutely not,' said Warmsley firmly. 'He was immensely popular. And everyone here was proud to have a cricketer of such an international reputation working alongside them.' He paused, then said, 'I was told there was a possibility that he was killed with a cricket bat.'

'Yes,' said Coburg. 'That's the theory of the doctor who examined his body, and this doctor has experience of the type of willow used in cricket bats. Do you think there might be a cricket motive for his death?'

'For the life of me I can't think how there could be,' said Warmsley.

'Do you know where he was staying in London?'

'No. I assumed he would be staying with some cricket pals of his. As I said, he was very popular.'

'He gave no clue as to who those pals might be?'

'No. None.'

'When did he leave?'

'Friday lunchtime. He caught the bus to the train station. He travelled light, he had his cricket bag with his equipment and a change of clothes.'

'And he didn't call you to let you know he might be later back than he'd intended?'

'No. We expected him back on Sunday evening. He said he'd come straight here after Sunday's nets practice. When he didn't arrive on Sunday, I left reporting his absence for a bit, in case he'd got caught up with something. He wasn't due on duty until Monday afternoon. And then, on Monday afternoon, I got a phone call from Sir Pelham Warner informing me that he was dead, suspected murdered.'

After leaving the RAF base, Coburg made his way to Kenley railway station, where he asked at the ticket office if a Black man had bought a ticket to London on Friday.

'A black man?' queried the man in the ticket office. 'Do you mean the cricketer Desmond Bartlett?'

'You know him?'

The man smiled. 'Everyone around here knows Desmond Bartlett. He's famous. A test cricketer. A local hero.'

'Did he get a train to London on Friday?'

'He did. He caught the early afternoon train.'

'Which London station was he travelling to?'

'Victoria.'

'Did he say when he was coming back?'

'No, but he bought a return, so he was definitely intending to come back.'

Coburg got back to Scotland Yard as Lampson was replacing the receiver after his phone call to the last person on the list.

'No luck, guv,' he said ruefully. 'I told each one why I was telephoning, gave them the news about Desmond Bartlett's death, assumed to be murder, and asked if they knew where Desmond Bartlett had been staying during the weekend. The answer was the same each time. No.'

'Well, he must have been staying somewhere,' said Coburg.

'He might have been keeping it a secret,' suggested Lampson.

'A woman?' asked Coburg.

'It's a thought,' said Lampson. 'How did you get on at Kenley?'

'I found out in great detail what an armourer does as part of an RAF ground crew serving Spitfires.'

'Any help?'

'None whatsoever.'

'So, what do we do next?' asked Lampson.

'For now, we call it a day and go home. Tomorrow morning, we go to St John's Wood and check out the Tube station and the police station, see if anyone's picked up the spare keys to Lord's Tube station recently.'

'Dr Welbourne said he wasn't killed there.'

'No, but maybe he was killed inside the station and his body dumped outside.'

'Sounds a bit like clutching at straws, guv,' said Lampson doubtfully.

'Yes, it is,' admitted Coburg ruefully. 'But so far we've got nothing else to go on.'

Eve Bradley came down the stairs from her bedroom and stopped before the mirror in the hallway to check her appearance. Her mother, wearing an apron, appeared from the kitchen and looked at her disapprovingly.

'Where are you off to?' she demanded.

'To Ted's,' said Eve.

'What for?'

'He's making a meal for us.'

'But Vic's bought a steak. A real steak!'

'Well, you can have it.'

'He brought it for you.'

'Well, I don't want it. I told you this morning I was eating at Ted's this evening.'

'Yes, but that was before Vic brought the steak round.'

'Like I said, you have it.'

'But what will I say to Vic when he asks if you liked it?'

'Tell him what I've told him: stop bringing things round for me.'

'He only does it because he cares. He knows how tight things are with rationing.'

'Things are tight for everyone.'

'Not for Vic. He knows people. Important people. Like this butcher he got the steak from. What sort of people does Ted Lampson know? Lowlifes.'

'He knows us. Are you saying we're lowlifes?'

'You know I'm not. I'm just pointing out the difference between them. Vic has got his own business. He's got his own house. He's got money. People work for him. What's Ted Lampson got? A grotty little house in a not very good street. And he's never going to have anything better, not on a copper's wages.'

'He's not just a copper, he's a detective sergeant at Scotland Yard, working with a chief inspector who's one of the most respected policemen there. And his brother's an earl, so when you talk about social standing I think that puts Vic Tennant in his place.'

'You're ungrateful, that's what you are. Vic would do anything for you. Money no object. A lovely house. Instead of which you're throwing yourself away on a lowlife who'll never amount to anything.'

'That's where you're wrong. Ted has got a career ahead of him, once he sits the exams. And he'll pass them. He's intelligent.'

'Then why hasn't he made more of himself? If he'd gone into business he could have made money.'

'What sort of business?' demanded Eve. 'The only ones who've made big money are the ones in shady businesses. Like, where does Vic get his money? Just from building?'

'Don't you dare say that,' said Mrs Bradley angrily. 'Vic's straight.'

'So where did he get that steak from?' asked Eve pointedly. 'Something under the counter, I bet.'

'That doesn't matter,' said Mrs Bradley. 'He's no criminal.'

'No, but some of the people he does business with are. What about that load of lead he was talking about laying his hands on?'

'I'm not having this discussion any more,' said Mrs Bradley primly.

'Good,' said Eve, and she took her coat from the peg and began to put it on.

'You realise if you marry Ted Lampson you'll be lumbering yourself with that tearaway son of his.'

'Terry is not a tearaway.'

'No? What about him getting into fights? Is that the kind of kid you want to share your life with?'

'There were one or two incidents when he was provoked,' defended Eve. 'But that's in the past now.'

'Oh yes?' sneered Mrs Bradley. 'You wait and see. Like son, like father.'

'Ted isn't like that at all,' said Eve. 'Now, if you'll excuse me, I've got somewhere to go.' She opened the street door. 'I'll be back later.'

'When?' demanded Mrs Bradley, scowling, acting pointedly. 'Tomorrow morning?'

Eve glared at her, then left, pulling the door shut hard.

At their flat in Piccadilly, Coburg and Rosa exchanged stories about their respective days, Rosa telling Coburg about the different people she and Doris had transported that day, mostly as the results of accidents.

'People falling down bomb craters. People being hit by flying roof tiles loosened during an air raid. It's a dangerous world out there.'

'It certainly is,' said Coburg. 'We had a strange one today. A dead man outside Lord's Tube station.'

'What's strange about that? Dead men are turning up everywhere.'

'But this man was a Jamaican cricketer, as well as a member of the RAF. It looks like he was beaten to death with a cricket bat. Someone hit him over the head with it.'

'A cricket bat?'

'Yes.'

Rosa frowned. 'Now that is weird.'

CHAPTER SEVEN

Tuesday 11th March

When Rosa and Doris arrived at Paddington ambulance station the following morning, it was to find Chesney Warren waiting for them, holding a slip of paper.

'This has just come in,' he told them. 'A young man's been injured at a block of flats at St John's Wood. It looks as if he fell down the stairs. He's unconscious. He's in the RAF. No one's made any attempt to move him.'

Rosa took the slip of paper from him. 'Air Cadet Richard Rhodes-Armfield, Viceroy Court, St John's Wood.'

'It's right next to Lord's Cricket Ground,' said Warren. 'The accident was reported by another cadet, Ben Wright. He's on site waiting for you.'

'Edgar was at Lord's yesterday on a case,' Rosa told Doris as they made their way towards Lord's. 'A dead man found by the old Tube station.'

'Killed by the bombing?'

'No, Edgar says he was murdered. Bashed over the head. A Jamaican.'

'Jamaican?' repeated Doris. 'That's unusual. We don't get many Jamaicans round here.'

'I think there'll be a few more,' said Rosa. 'Edgar says he's a cricketer here to play a series of top-class cricket matches.'

'I don't understand cricket,' sighed Doris. 'All these positions: silly mid-on, long leg. And then they're in when they're out and they're out when they're in. Odd, that's what it is.'

They arrived at Lord's and made for the small block of flats next to the cricket ground. A young man in RAF uniform was keeping alert watch by the main entrance to the block of flats, and gestured for them to enter.

'Air Cadet Ben Wright,' he introduced himself. He pointed to the still body of a young man, also in RAF uniform, lying at the foot of the concrete stairs. 'That's Richard. He and I are billeted together in a flat on the second floor. He left the flat about an hour or so ago, said he was going to the shops. When he didn't come back straight away, I assumed he'd met somebody and got talking. Anyway, I left the flat to report for duty, and when I came down the stairs I found him there, just like that. I guess he must have fallen or something.'

'Has he moved at all since you found him?' asked Doris. 'Made any noises? Grunts? Anything?'

'No. I checked for a pulse and to see if he was breathing, and he was breathing, even though it was shallow. I decided against trying to move him in case I did some damage.'

'Quite right,' said Doris. She knelt down beside the young man and felt for a pulse, then looked at Rosa, a concerned expression on her face. She took a small mirror from her pocket and held it to his mouth, then looked at Ben Wright. 'You said he was breathing and you felt a pulse?'

'Yes,' said Wright. 'We've all had basic first aid training.'

Doris rose to her feet and looked down at Rhodes-Armfield, an unhappy look on her face.

'Can you double-check me on this, Rosa?' she asked.

'What's wrong?' asked Wright, worried.

Rosa knelt down beside the fallen air cadet and, like Doris, felt for a pulse in both his wrist and his neck, then checked his breathing. She looked up at Doris and the young cadet and said, 'I'm afraid he's dead.'

'He can't be!' exclaimed Wright in horror.

'I'm afraid he is,' said Rosa.

She began to examine his head and neck. When her hand came away from the back of his head, they saw there was blood on it.

'This is a case for the police,' she said.

'But it's an accident, surely,' said Wright.

'Even if it is, the police need to be called before the body's moved,' Doris told him. 'Where's the nearest telephone?'

'There's a phone box just outside.'

'I'll do it,' said Rosa quickly and she gave Doris a look that told her there was a reason for her action, but she couldn't tell her why at this moment.

Once inside the phone box, she dialled 999 and asked for the police. When the operator answered, she identified herself as a St John Ambulance driver and gave the details of the dead man.

'I'm also the wife of Detective Chief Inspector Coburg and I feel he needs to be informed of this, because it might be connected with another murder he's working on in this same area,' she said. 'DCI Coburg's call sign is Echo Seven.'

'Thank you, Mrs Coburg,' said the operator. 'I'll get that message to him.'

* * *

At St John's Wood Tube station, Coburg and Lampson were told that no one had asked for the keys they held to the closed Lord's station.

'We only keep them in case of emergencies, Chief Inspector,' the station master, Josiah Riggs, told them. 'About a year ago we were asked for them by the railway committee because they were doing an inspection of the site. Afterwards, with nothing to report except that everything inside the station was in order, the keys were returned to us, and they haven't left here since.'

'I'd like to borrow them, if I may,' said Coburg.

'You want to look inside the station?'

'I do.'

The station master hesitated, then said, 'We'll have to make an appointment so someone can go with you.'

'Thank you, but there's no need for that,' said Coburg. He held out his hand. 'We know where the station is.'

'But we're responsible for the site.'

'Actually, I'm informed that the Railway Executive Committee at Down Street are responsible for all station sites. I also understand that St John's Wood police station have a set of keys.'

'Well, that's true, but . . .'

Coburg once again produced his warrant card and held it out to the man. 'Also, this gives me the authority to enter public premises without being accompanied,' he said.

Reluctantly, the man nodded. 'Very well. But you'll have to sign for them.'

'That's no problem,' said Coburg, putting his warrant card back in his pocket.

'If you wait here,' said the man, and he disappeared into the bowels of the station.

'A bit reluctant,' observed Lampson.

'Yes,' said Coburg. 'I wonder why?'

'Because he's one of these petty bureaucrats who like to annoy people. Jobsworths, I call them, because they always say, "It's more than my jobs worth to do that."'

'Unless he's got something to hide,' said Coburg thoughtfully.

The station master returned and handed him a set of keys bearing a tag that read *Lord's Station*. He opened a ledger and passed it to Coburg to fill in and sign for the keys. Coburg did so, taking the opportunity to check for any previous signatories. There were none.

'So, we're the first to take these keys since it shut,' Coburg said as he and Lampson walked to their car.

'Those particular keys,' pointed out Lampson. 'They've got a set at St John's Wood nick, and at Down Street.'

The ticket office just inside the entrance to Lord's station had a layer of dust over everything.

'Someone's been here recently,' said Coburg, pointing to marks in the dust on the floor where footsteps had scuffed it.

They followed the marks, walking carefully to avoid stepping on the footprints in the dust. They led to a circular metal staircase where the dust had not had a chance to accumulate due to the open pattern of the metal steps. They followed the stairs down to the first subterranean floor. On the tiled surface, again there was a layer of dust that had been recently disturbed. A metal chair had been left, and around it were scattered some cigarette stubs. Coburg got down on his knees and examined the floor.

'Blood,' he said, pointing to some brown spots. He got up. 'This is where Bartlett was killed.'

'With someone having a few ciggies while they did it,' observed Lampson. 'Which suggests they took their time over it. Why?'

'Because they wanted to get some answers from him.'

'About what?'

'I've no idea,' admitted Coburg.

He made for the circular staircase and began to climb up, Lampson following him.

'I'm going to radio for a forensic team to turn up urgently and go through this place with a fine-tooth comb,' he said. 'Ted, I want you to stay here until they arrive. Meanwhile, I'm going to call on St John's Wood police station and have a look at their register and see if anyone borrowed their keys recently. I'll come back and pick you up.'

Leaving Lampson to wait for the forensic team, Coburg drove to St John's Wood police station, where he found PC Riddick at the reception desk talking to the station sergeant.

'Good morning, Constable Riddick,' said Coburg.

'Good morning, Chief Inspector,' said Riddick. He turned to the desk sergeant and introduced them.

'Sergeant Webster, this is DCI Coburg,' he said. 'He was the one who attended the dead body at Lord's Tube station.'

'Eric.' Sergeant Webster smiled, shaking hands with Coburg. 'Have you got any more on the deceased?'

'We have,' Coburg told him. 'We now know that his name was Desmond Bartlett and he was a member of the West Indies cricket team who are currently playing a series of matches against English county teams.'

'A cricketer, eh,' said Webster.

'He was also in the RAF as ground crew. We do know he joined up when war was declared in 1939.'

'Very patriotic,' said Riddick.

'We're also sure he wasn't killed outside the Tube station, but somewhere else, then his body dumped there.'

'Yeah, that struck me as well, after what the doctor said about him having been hit with a cricket bat,' said Riddick. 'I said that to you, didn't I, Sarge, because there'd been no traces of blood at the scene.'

'You did,' said Webster.

'I've come to update you on the situation,' said Coburg, 'and also to see if you'd picked up any more information about it. If anyone else saw the body before Henry Duggan reported it?'

Webster and Riddick both shook their heads.

'No,' said Webster. 'Nothing. But, to be honest, people are more worried about the bombing raids.'

'That's understandable,' said Coburg. 'You hold a set of keys to the station here, I understand.'

'We do,' said Webster.

'Can I have a look at the register?'

Webster shrugged. 'Be my guest,' he said. 'The fact is that no one's borrowed them. Not from us, anyway.'

He handed Coburg the ledger, and Coburg checked the pages. Sure enough, there was no indication of anyone borrowing the keys.

'Can I have a look at the actual keys?' asked Coburg.

Sergeant Webster looked at him, puzzled. 'Why?' he asked.

'I just want to check something.'

Webster turned to PC Riddick. 'Constable, would you go to

the box where the keys are kept and bring back the spare keys to Lord's station.'

'Certainly, Sarge,' said Riddick.

Webster turned back to Coburg and asked, 'What's to check?'

'I just want to have a look at them,' said Coburg.

It was about five minutes before PC Riddick reappeared. There was a worried look on his face.

'They're not there, Sarge,' he said.

Sergeant Webster looked at him, uncomprehending. 'What are you talking about? Of course they're there. We know no one's taken them out.'

'They're not there, Sarge,' repeated Riddick. 'They're not on the hook where they're supposed to be.'

'They must have fallen off,' said Webster. 'Go and have a proper look.'

'I have, Sarge. I looked right through the box, then the desks there. They're not there.'

'Well, where are they?' demanded Webster.

'I don't know, Sarge,' said Riddick. 'I know where they're not.'

Webster looked at Coburg. 'I don't understand it,' he said. 'Someone must have taken them and not put them back.'

'Nor entered them in the register,' said Coburg. He looked enquiringly at the sergeant. 'Any ideas?'

Webster shook his head, stunned and perplexed. 'None.'

'Perhaps you can start an investigation among your staff to see who knows what happened to them,' said Coburg. 'And let me know. If I'm not at Scotland Yard when you call, leave a message.'

* * *

Coburg drove back to Lord's station and found Lampson waiting just inside the entrance.

'No sign of the forensic team?' he asked.

'Not yet,' said Lampson. 'How did you get on at St John's Wood nick?'

'I checked their keys register. Same as at the Tube station, officially no one's borrowed their keys to this station since it closed. But, in reality, their set of keys have gone missing.'

'Missing?'

'Yes. I've asked them to institute a search for them at the station.'

'So someone took them without signing the register,' said Lampson.

'Yes, the same rather obvious thought struck me.'

'What did they say when you told them Bartlett had been killed here?'

'I didn't tell them,' said Coburg.

'Oh? Why not?'

'There's something iffy about that nick,' said Coburg. 'I'm reserving judgement on how much we reveal to them.'

'Think they might be suspects?'

'Not as such, but I get this feeling they're hiding something. At least Sergeant Webster and PC Riddick are. The keys going missing just adds to that.'

'They'll soon find out a forensic team have been here at Lord's station,' pointed out Lampson. 'This is their patch, after all.'

'We'll cross that bridge when we come to it,' said Coburg.

There was a knocking at the door of the station. Coburg opened the door to find a team of four men standing outside, with an old friend of his, Inspector Harry Durward, at the front.

'Forensic team as ordered, Chief Inspector.' Durward smiled. 'What do you want examined?'

Coburg gestured at the ticket office.

'There's been action here,' he said. 'Signs of footwear. Let us know all you can, shoe sizes, whatever. Downstairs you'll find a metal chair. There are some cigarette stubs beside it. A man was tied to that chair and beaten to death with a cricket bat. In fact, I'd like you to go over the whole station, checking all levels.'

'What are we looking for?' asked Durward.

'The spot where the victim was murdered for evidence who did it, and everywhere else for clues as to who else might have been in here recently.' Coburg handed him the spare set of keys. 'These are from St John's Wood Tube station. The station master there is a Josiah Riggs.'

'You want me to take them back to him after we've finished?'

'No, I want you to take them back to the Yard and leave them at main reception for me. I shall telephone Mr Riggs and let him know what's happened when I get back to the Yard. I'm only letting you know in case he turns up here looking for the keys.'

'You think he's likely to?'

'He's quite likely to. He is, in Ted here's phrase, a jobsworth. Poking his nose everywhere.'

Durward grinned. 'Forewarned is forearmed. I'll let you know what we find.'

As Coburg and Lampson arrived back at their car, the radio was calling: 'Base to Echo Seven. Come in, Echo Seven.'

Coburg opened the car and picked up the microphone. 'Echo Seven,' he said.

'Echo Seven, report of a suspicious death at a block of flats near Lord's Cricket Ground. Young man found with head injuries. The informant was Mrs Coburg.'

She then gave Coburg the address of the block of flats.

'Echo Seven to Base, received and understood. On our way there now,' said Coburg. He turned to Lampson. 'Looks like we've got another one.'

Rosa returned to the entrance area of the block of flats and found Ben Wright talking to a small group of cadets who'd obviously just come down the stairs on their way to report for duty, explaining what had happened. Doris stayed beside the dead body of the young cadet to prevent any of the other cadets from interfering with it.

'Do I need to stay?' asked Wright. 'Like the others, I'm due to be at my station, and there'll be hell to pay if I'm late.'

'You can go,' said Doris. 'But first write down your name and address so we can talk to you.'

Ben Wright wrote down his details and handed them to Doris, then he and the other cadets left.

'Sorry I cut in on making the phone call to the police,' Rosa apologised to Doris, 'but last night Edgar told me about a murder he's investigating. A man killed at Lord's Tube station with blows to the head. And here we are at a block of flats next to Lord's with what may be the same thing: a man dead with blows to his head. I didn't want to say anything in front of the young cadet, but I wanted to make sure that Edgar was the one who come to look into this.'

'You think he was killed by the same person who did the other one?'

'I've no idea,' admitted Rosa. 'But that's for Edgar to look into if he thinks there's anything.'

'If you stay here with the body, I'll get Mr Warren on the radio and explain what's happening,' said Doris.

A few moments later she was on the radio to Chesney Warren at their base.

'That air cadet near Lord's,' she told him. 'He's dead, and in suspicious circumstances. We've called for the police and they're on their way, so I think we'd better stay here in case we're wanted.'

'Understood,' said Warren. 'Let me know when you're finished there.'

'Will do,' said Doris. 'Over and out.'

She replaced the microphone and got out of the ambulance in time to see a police car pull up nearby. The door opened and Edgar Coburg got out, as did a tall man, who Doris assumed to be Coburg's sergeant. She called out and waved at them, and pointed towards the door of the block of flats.

'In there!' she called.

Coburg and Lampson made for the door to the flats, pushed it open and found Rosa kneeling beside the body of a young man in air force uniform.

'This him?' asked Coburg.

Rosa nodded. 'He's dead.'

The door opened and Doris joined them. The door was just closing when another man appeared carrying a black medical bag.

'Dr Welbourne,' he introduced himself to the two women. 'We haven't met before, although I know DCI Coburg and Sergeant Lampson well. And I've seen you before, Mrs Coburg, when you were still Rosa Weeks.'

'I still am Rosa Weeks when I'm performing,' said Rosa. 'It's like Jekyll and Hyde: one person, two personalities.'

Welbourne walked to the body of the air cadet and knelt beside him. 'My wife and I saw you at the Hippodrome about a year ago, before all this madness started. Fantastic. I'm glad you're still performing. At a dreadful time like this we need people like you to raise our spirits.'

He examined the body of the young man, checking the flexibility of his arms and legs. He also examined the wound on the back of his head.

'He hasn't been dead long,' he commented.

'What do you make of the wound on his head, Doctor?' asked Coburg.

'Well, it's not from a cricket bat, like the previous one.' Welbourne stood up. 'There's not much more I can do here.' He looked enquiringly at Rosa and Doris. 'Are you able to take his body to UCH? It'll save calling another ambulance out.'

'That's no problem,' said Rosa.

'Thank you,' said Welbourne. 'I'll get back there and alert them that you'll be arriving.'

With that, he left and made for his car.

'I'll go and bring a stretcher,' said Doris, and she headed towards the ambulance.

'She's very good,' complimented Coburg.

'She is,' agreed Rosa. 'I'm lucky to be teamed with her.'

'And thanks for calling this in to me,' said Coburg.

'It was after you'd told me about the other one. The one by Lord's Tube station. I expect it's just a coincidence,' said Rosa, 'but, just in case, I thought it worth contacting the police.'

'And I'm glad you did,' said Coburg reassuringly.

CHAPTER EIGHT

As Coburg and Lampson drove back to Scotland Yard, they discussed the latest turn of events.

'So both the dead men were in the RAF, one in aircrew, the other ground crew.'

'You think they were targeted because they were in the RAF?'

'It's less tenuous than the idea that cricket is the link, just because one was a cricketer and the other lived in a billet overlooking Lord's Cricket Ground,' said Coburg.

'The trouble with the idea of them both being in the RAF as the link is: Rhodes-Armfield was obviously in the RAF because he was wearing a uniform. But Bartlett was in civvies,' pointed out Lampson.

'Yes,' said Coburg thoughtfully. 'The RAF connection only works if the killer knew that Bartlett was in the RAF.'

'So it's someone who knew him rather than just a random attacker,' said Lampson.

'I suggest we split our resources,' said Coburg. 'If you go to Lord's and talk to Rhodes-Armfield's former comrades about the young cadet, I'll go back to Kenley and talk to the other men in Bartlett's ground crew. See if we can find any common thing that links the two, apart from cricket and the

RAF. I'll need the car to get to and from Kenley, so see if you can persuade the motor pool to let you have another. Use my name as authority.'

'I will, but whether they've got anything of any quality is debateable,' said Lampson doubtfully. 'If it comes to it, I can always walk.'

To Lampson's delight, when he called at the motor pool he found an old friend of his, Jonty Miller, in charge.

'You're in luck, Ted,' Miller told him cheerfully. 'A vehicle that was damaged in a bombing raid has just been returned to us, completely repaired.'

'Nothing bad I should know about?' asked Lampson warily. 'Chassis alright? Brakes?'

'Everything's as good as new. In fact, it's in better nick than before it got hit.'

It was with pleasure that Lampson drove the car to Lord's Cricket Ground, reflecting as he did that the car handled better than the one he and Coburg drove around in.

I wonder if we could do a swap? he thought as he made his way to Lord's.

When he arrived at Lord's he introduced himself to the man in charge of the Aircrew Receiving Centre, Group Captain Weymouth, and the purpose of his visit.

'A terrible thing to happen, Sergeant,' said Weymouth. He frowned, puzzled. 'You're saying that it wasn't an accident, that Rhodes-Armfield was murdered?'

'That's right, sir. The medical examiner has confirmed it. With your permission I need to talk to those people here who associated with Cadet Rhodes-Armfield in order to find out

67

what motive could have been behind the attack on him.'

'I think you'll find it was some outsider who came in to try to burgle the place, and Rhodes-Armfield saw him and tackled him about it. I think it highly unlikely that any of our chaps were responsible for this appalling crime.'

'That's very likely, sir, but my boss, DCI Saxe-Coburg, has ordered me to find out as much as I can about the establishment here.'

'Saxe-Coburg?' asked Weymouth. 'Any relation to Magnus Saxe-Coburg, the Earl of Dawlish?'

'His younger brother, sir.'

'Does he play cricket as well?'

'Not to my knowledge, sir. Not to the level of the Earl, at any rate.'

'Pity.'

'DCI Coburg wanted to be here today but he's had to go to RAF Kenley to follow up another line of enquiry.'

'Kenley? What's happening there?'

'I'm afraid I can't say, sir. Security.'

'I understand,' said Weymouth. 'Very well, Sergeant, how can I help you?'

'If you could fill me in on what happens with the cadets, it will help me get a picture of their regular routine.'

'Of course. New recruits are here for three weeks. Aircrew have to be nineteen years old before they can take part in operations. During their time here they receive basic instruction, go through rigorous medical checks, and also a series of tests to identify each cadet for a potential role in an aircrew. After that they're posted to initial training wings around the country.'

'What do they do during the day, sir?'

'The day starts at 7 a.m., when we march them down to Regent's Park Zoo, where they have breakfast. The zoo has been allocated as our canteen. After breakfast, it depends on what their particular course is. The men are assembled into flights, each flight under the command of a corporal.'

'And which particular group was Rhodes-Armfield in?'

'He was training to be a wireless operator.'

'And the name of the corporal who was in charge of his section?'

'That would be Corporal Judkins. A good man.'

'Where would I find Corporal Judkins?'

Weymouth consulted a chart on the wall. 'He's in the wireless shop. He'll have different small groups throughout the day.'

'Thank you, sir.'

CHAPTER NINE

Lampson found Corporal Judkins in the wireless shop and introduced himself, showing the corporal his warrant card.

'Detective Sergeant Lampson,' he said. 'We're looking into the death of Cadet Richard Rhodes-Armfield.'

Judkins frowned. 'Why?' he asked. 'It was an accident. He fell down the stairs and banged his head.'

'That's what was thought at first, but a proper examination has revealed that he was struck on the back of the head, and it was that blow which killed him.'

'Yeah, like I said, when he fell down the stairs.'

'Apparently not. According to the medical examiner, the blow to his head wasn't from contact with the stairs.'

'The bannisters, then.'

'No, they've been examined. He was hit on the back of the head. We're assuming that's what made him fall down the stairs. So, it's murder.'

Judkins shook his head. 'No, I can't believe that. Not here.'

'That may be, Corporal, but that's what it's being called. So, what can you tell me about Cadet Rhodes-Armfield? What sort of person was he? And might anyone have a reason to attack him?'

'No, not at all,' said Judkins. 'As to the sort of person he was, he'd only been here about a fortnight, like the rest of them, so there's really not much time to get to know them individually. He did what he had to do. He didn't particularly stand out.'

'Good at what he was training for? Wireless operator, wasn't it?'

Judkins nodded. 'Passable. Nothing outstanding, but nothing negative against him. He was good enough. Most of them develop and improve when they're actually with a flight as part of a crew.'

At Kenley, Coburg talked to the other members of the ground crew about Bartlett. All of them were shocked to hear of his death, and even more shocked to hear he had been murdered. All of them praised him to Coburg, describing him as 'Really nice. Decent. Trustworthy. Do anything for anyone, which made him a great member of our ground crew.'

None of them could think of any reason why anyone would have wanted to kill him. Also, none of them knew who he would have been staying with while he was in London for his couple of days' nets practice. 'One of his cricket pals,' one suggested.

At Lord's, Lampson was quizzing Ben Wright. The young cadet repeated the story he'd told Rosa and Doris: that he and Richard Rhodes-Armfield had been billeted together in a flat on the second floor. That Richard had left the flat saying he was going to the shops.

'When, after an hour, he didn't come back, I assumed he'd met somebody and got talking. Anyway, I left the flat to report for duty, and when I came down the stairs I found him lying there on the stairs, out cold. That's when I phoned for an ambulance. He was alive when I found him. That's why I was so shocked when the ambulance women said he was dead.'

'How long have you been here?'

'Two weeks. One week more to go and then we move on.'

'Richard arrived at the same time as you?'

'Yes, we were in the same attachment.'

'Did you know him before?'

'No. They just allocated us to the same billet. That's how it works here. Someone points a finger at you and says: 'You and you, Flat 3. You and you, Flat 4.'

'How did you get on with Richard?'

Wright hesitated, before saying, with touch of awkwardness, 'To be honest, we didn't see much of one another. We were in different groups for most things. We saw each other at breakfast because we're all marched to the mess at the zoo en masse.' He grimaced. 'The food's bloody awful, but at least it's something to eat.'

'So who did he hang around with?'

Again, Wright hesitated momentarily, then said, 'I think the other chaps tended to avoid him.'

'Why?'

'He was always on the cadge. We'd only been here two days when he asked if I could lend him some money.'

'How much?'

'Fifteen pounds.'

'Did you?'

Wright shook his head. 'I don't have that kind of spare money. Once he realised I wasn't a touch he sort of lost interest in me. Lucky for me, as it turned out, because some of the other chaps complained to me about him. They wanted me to have a word with him.'

'What about?'

'The chaps who did lend him money in the first week said he never paid them back, even though they asked him. They thought, as he and I shared a billet, I might have some influence with him.'

'I'd have thought that once word went around that he didn't pay back, people would have stopped lending him anything.'

'Yes, that's been the case lately. As the clock ticks on us being moved on, he'd got edgier about getting his hands on some money. I made sure any spare cash I've got is safely tucked away. I wouldn't trust him not to steal it if he could find it. The strange thing is I get the impression he comes from a wealthy family. That's why some of the other chaps thought it was safe to lend him money; they were sure they'd get it back.'

'What gave you the idea he came from a wealthy family?'

'The double-barrelled name to start with. Then his accent. Public school. And he was always talking about his rich father, but mainly he talked about him with resentment. He used to go on something alarming about his father being the tightest person in the world, how he'd let him starve rather than give him a single penny.'

'Did you ever meet his parents?'

'No. Families aren't encouraged to come here during basic training.'

'Why did he need money if he came from a well-off family?'

Wright hesitated, then said reluctantly, 'I think he used to gamble.'

'Cards?'

'No, racing. He was always studying form.'

'Not a lot of form to study,' said Lampson. 'All professional sport like football and everything else has been cancelled. Most of the racecourses have been shut because of the war.'

'Not all of them. I remember from the notes that Richard made. Ripon, Hurst Park and Newmarket still have some racing. Not as often as before, but there are still some. And some of the greyhound tracks keep open.'

'But how does he place bets?' asked Lampson. 'I can't imagine him going to any of those courses, and off-course betting's illegal.'

Wright looked uncomfortable. 'I don't know. I don't bet, so I don't get involved in it.'

Lampson watched the unhappy young cadet and thought: *Oh yes, you know, you just don't want to say.* A thought struck him. Nearly every branch of the services had someone who ran a book. Was that the same here, at this RAF centre? If so, as it was usually one of the non-commissioned officers, he could understand why Wright was reluctant to talk about it. Make an enemy of an NCO and your daily life would be an absolute nightmare. It would be something to look into, but later. Right now he needed to settle the unhappy cadet down, pick his brains about Rhodes-Armfield.

'Tell me about the people he did hang around with here.'

'Like I said, most of the other chaps avoided him over the money business.'

CHAPTER TEN

When Coburg arrived back at Scotland Yard, he found a message waiting for him, asking him to contact Dr Welbourne at University College Hospital.

'Dr Welbourne,' said Coburg. 'Have you got something for me?'

'I have,' said Welbourne. 'First of all, the cricketer, Desmond Bartlett. That was definitely treated willow in the wound at the back of his head, so a cricket bat.'

'Interesting,' commented Coburg.

'The other thing is, once I'd taken his clothes off there were definite signs of ill-treatment. His upper body had been burnt with what looks like cigarette ends. Three of the fingers of his left hand had been broken, and it looks as if they were broken deliberately.'

'Cigarette ends?' echoed Coburg. *So that's why those cigarette ends were by the chair*, he realised. 'So he'd been tortured?'

'That's the conclusion I've come to. Tortured, and then beaten to death with a cricket bat. In my opinion two people were involved in his torture and death. There were marks indicating his arms had been tied to the arms of a chair. To do that and then stub out a cigarette repeatedly on his bare skin and break his fingers, when the victim was a struggling and fit young man, would need two people.

'Turning to the young air cadet found on the stairs. When I examined the wound on the back of his head under a microscope, it indicated the weapon used had a sharpish metal edge.'

'A blade?'

'No, it was heavy but slightly flattened,' said Welbourne. 'I also found traces of grit and boot polish.'

'Boot polish?'

'Which leads me to think he was kicked in the back of the head with a heavy boot that had metal protectors at the front of the sole under the toecap.'

'A service boot?'

'Exactly. I could be wrong, but I think he must have been kicked while he was lying on the stairs, unconscious.'

Coburg hung up, puzzled. Why would anyone kick a fallen air cadet in the head?

He was just pondering this question when the door of the office opened and Lampson entered.

'You're back, sir.' The sergeant beamed. 'How did you get on at Kenley this time?'

Coburg gave a rueful sigh. 'Everyone I spoke to said what a decent bloke Bartlett was, and no one could think of a reason why anyone would want to kill him. No one seemed to know anything about his personal life, whether he had a girlfriend. No one knew who he stayed with when he was in London. What about you? How did you get on?'

Lampson's smile became broader. 'I got us a great car from the motor pool,' he announced proudly. 'Better than the one we've got now. I was wondering if we could do a swap?'

Coburg looked at him uncertainly. 'That may not be easy. You know what this place is like for red tape. We've already got our call sign for the radio in our present car.'

'Surely they could switch that to this other car?'

'They *could*,' said Coburg. 'But it doesn't mean they will.'

'At least come and take a look at it, guv. I haven't taken it back to the motor pool yet; I thought you might want to look over it. Give it a drive, see what you think.'

Coburg nodded. 'Alright, I'll do that, but I'm not making any promises. For a start, someone else might have first claim on it.'

'My pal Jonty didn't say anything about that, and I'm sure he would have.'

Coburg looked interested. 'Is Jonty Miller back at the motor pool?'

'He is,' said Lampson.

'He's an old pal of yours, isn't he?'

Lampson nodded. 'He is.'

'Alright,' said Coburg. 'Where's this wonder car at the moment?'

'In the yard.' Lampson looked thoughtful. 'In fact, there was another thing I discovered at Lord's today.'

'Oh?'

'It was when I was talking to the cadet who was billeted with Rhodes-Armfield. The one who found him.'

'Cadet Wright.'

'That's him. Anyway, he told me the dead kid came from a well-off family, but he was always broke because he gambled, and lost. He'd borrowed money from some of the other cadets, but never paid them back. I've got a hunch he might have owed money to a bookie.'

'If he came from a wealthy family he might have had access to a private bookie, and they usually give a lot of leeway to private clients,' said Coburg.

'But I get the impression that wasn't the case here. He didn't get on with his father, and his father refused to bail him out.'

'So, if he was betting it must have been with an illegal bookie.'

'Yes, that was my thought. And some of these illegal bookies can be quite hard when enforcing payment of debts.'

'You think that's why he was killed?'

'I don't think it was necessarily deliberate. Someone roughed him up and it went wrong and he took a tumble down the stairs.'

'Maybe not,' said Coburg. He told his sergeant what he'd learnt from Dr Welbourne.

'So Bartlett was tortured before he died,' said Lampson.

'That's what it looks like.'

'Do you reckon his fingers being broken relate to him being a cricketer?'

'Yes, quite likely,' agreed Coburg.

'And Rhodes-Armfield was kicked to death? By someone wearing RAF boots?' said Lampson thoughtfully.

'It's got to be: only RAF personnel are at Lord's, no army or navy,' said Coburg. 'We need to find out who his bookie was.'

'He could have had more than one,' said Lampson thoughtfully. 'I had an uncle who used to gamble a lot, and when he owed one bookie too much and the bookie wouldn't take any more bets until he'd paid what he owed, he'd go to another.'

'What happened to him?'

'He did a runner. We think he went to Newcastle, or

somewhere up north. He never let any of the family know where in case someone came after him. Bookies have got long memories.'

'So we definitely need to find his bookie.'

'I had a thought on that. In nearly every organisation, there's usually one person who runs a book on the side.'

'That's true,' agreed Coburg. 'There was one in our unit when I was in the army. A corporal. And he tended to back up his debt-collecting with a couple of heavies from the same unit.'

'So my guess is there's a corporal or something operating here at the recruitment centre. The dead cadet's section leader was a Corporal Harry Judkins. He could be a candidate.'

'Did you talk to him?'

'I did.'

'How did he come across?'

'Shifty.' Lampson shrugged. 'Mind, being questioned by a Scotland Yard detective sergeant, most people are shifty.'

'There was no hint who this bookie might be from his flatmate, young Wright?' asked Coburg.

'No. He said he doesn't bet himself, so he doesn't know. But I bet he knows.'

'I'll have a word with him, see if I can squeeze anything out of him,' said Coburg.

'I had another idea,' said Lampson. 'I thought it might be worth having a word with the dead boy's family, see if they know who he might have been involved with. Apparently, Richard was always moaning about his dad being well-off but tight-fisted and refusing to help him out.'

Again, Coburg nodded. 'Yes. Do you want to take that on? You seem to have a lot worked out already on this case.'

'Actually, I thought it might work better if you had a word with them. They're well-off and they've got a double-barrelled name and I get the idea Richard went to a public school. I thought we might get more out of them if they talked to someone related to the royal family, rather than a working-class oik like me from Somers Town.'

'I'm *not* related to the royal family.'

'Yes, but I bet they jump to that conclusion when they hear your moniker.' He grinned. 'Detective Chief Inspector Saxe-Coburg. The Honourable.'

'On the other hand, they may be completely indifferent. And, don't forget, they'll be grieving the death of their son.'

'I'm not forgetting. I'm just thinking that if there's something dodgy about their son and his money dealings, they might be reluctant to talk about it. But once you open your mouth and they hear that Eton accent . . .'

'I will not play the performing toff,' said Coburg.

'Not even if it gives us a lead into who murdered their son?'

'As I said, I doubt if my accent will make any difference.' Then he gave a grudging sigh and added, 'But it might. You're right, Ted. I'm afraid sometimes I get resentful about the impression people have of me because of my name.'

'Think of it as a bonus,' said Lampson. 'It opens doors that are closed to most of the rest of us.'

'Where do these Rhodes-Armfields live?'

'Some big house in Berkshire. I've got the address. My thought was that if we went there, and you drove, you'd get the feel of the car and see how you feel about it.'

'I'm being manipulated,' accused Coburg.

'But in a good cause,' defended Lampson. 'If you think this

car is any good it'd be a shame to let it go to some herberts who'd just mess it up.'

'You really think this car is better than our usual one?'

'I do. Jonty won't be expecting it back before tomorrow morning, so a run out to Berkshire will fill in the time nicely.'

Coburg got up. 'Right, let's go and see these Rhodes-Armfields. And at the same time see if this car is as good as you say it is. But before we do, I want to get hold of a photo of Desmond Bartlett. It's possible Ray Smith and Bertie Clarke will have one. If not, I'll ask Magnus to get one from Pelham Warner. If that fails, we'll have to make do with one from the mortuary, but I'd prefer one where he looks alive. Can you arrange that?'

Lampson nodded. 'What's the plan for the photo?'

'I want to get it in the daily papers under the headline "Have you seen this man?" Bartlett must have stayed somewhere on Friday night, perhaps Saturday as well. Someone *must* have seen him. I'll start getting hold of newspaper editors who owe us a favour while you sort out copies of the photo.'

'Right, guv. Leave it to me,' said Lampson. 'Can I take the car?'

Coburg nodded, then reached for the phone and his contact list of newspaper editors.

CHAPTER ELEVEN

Coburg and Lampson drove down the long drive towards the luxurious mansion on the outskirts of Binfield in Berkshire, the home of the Rhodes-Armfields.

'Young Wright wasn't wrong when he said the family had money,' commented Lampson. 'I assume they've been told their son's dead?'

'The commanding officer at Lord's told them,' said Coburg. 'Though how much detail he went into, I don't know. These service types tend to keep things close to their chest.'

'Did you fix up with your newspaper pals about the photo?'

'It'll be in most of them in the morning,' said Coburg. 'The ones you sent it to.'

'I did all the ones on that list you gave me,' said Lampson. 'A messenger took them.'

As Coburg parked the car, Lampson asked, 'Well? What's the verdict?'

'Not bad,' said Coburg.

'Better than that!' enthused Lampson.

'I'll give you that it handles better, and the gear change is smoother.'

'So can we keep it?'

'I'll have a word with Superintendent Allison,' said Coburg.

They walked to the front door, which was set in a faux Roman portico, and rang the bell. After a slight delay, a girl of about fifteen wearing a maid's uniform opened the door.

'Yes?' she asked.

Coburg and Lampson produced their warrant cards and showed them to her.

'Detective Chief Inspector Saxe-Coburg and DS Lampson from Scotland Yard to see Mr and Mrs Rhodes-Armfield, if they're available.'

'Did you say Scotland Yard?' asked the girl.

'I did,' confirmed Coburg.

'Would you wait here a moment?' asked the girl.

With that, she shut the door. Coburg and Lampson waited, and a short while later the door opened again and a short podgy man in his fifties looked suspiciously out at them.

'Scotland Yard?' he asked, his tone pugnacious.

'Yes, sir,' said Coburg. 'Are you Mr Rhodes-Armfield?'

'I am. What do you want?'

'We'd like to talk to you about your son, Richard.'

'He's dead,' said Rhodes-Armfield flatly.

'Yes, sir. That's why we're here. May we come in?'

Rhodes-Armfield stepped to one side to let them enter, then shut the front door.

'This way,' he said.

He led them along a corridor adorned with portraits of people from previous centuries, causing Coburg to wonder what their connection was to the family. Mr Rhodes-Armfield's accent was distinctly working-class Birmingham, and the faces in the portraits looked to be aristocratic, certainly in their ornate dress.

He led them into a sitting room, where the furniture and décor again showed off wealth. A slim, well-dressed woman in her fifties rose from the settee she was sitting on and nodded to them.

'My wife, Fiona,' Rhodes-Armfield introduced her.

'Annie said your name was Saxe-Coburg,' she said. 'Any relation to the Saxe-Coburgs of Dawlish?'

'The Earl is my elder brother,' said Coburg.

This seemed to impress her, although it did not impress her husband, who simply scowled. Coburg noticed that her accent was very cut-glass, much higher up the social scale than her husband's. *So that's where the portraits come from*, he thought.

'Our apologies for intruding at this time,' said Coburg gently. 'Please accept our sympathies for your loss.'

She nodded.

'They're here to talk about Richard,' said Rhodes-Armfield, adding, 'You're a bit posh for a copper. Saxe-hyphen-Coburg? Brother of an earl?'

'We can't be blamed for our antecedents,' said Coburg smoothly. 'You, yourself, sir, also have a double-barrelled name.'

'Yes, but mine's only that way because my wife came from that kind of stock. Gentry. So, when we married, I agreed that we'd take on both names. It was what her parents wanted. I'm an Armfield, she's a Rhodes. I'm from good working-class stock. I worked my way up from nothing to get what I've got.'

'You've done very well for yourself,' complimented Coburg.

'And not just for me, Inspector. For my family. My wife's family may have had posh manners, but no money till I turned up.'

84

'Alfred!' protested his wife. 'That's no way to talk in front of strangers.'

'Take me as you find me, that's what I've always said,' snapped Rhodes-Armfield. 'I speak my mind regardless of who I'm talking to. It was my money that saved your family, and it was my money that sent that useless son of ours to public school.' He sneered. 'It would make a gentleman of him, so I was told. Ha! A gentleman who falls down the stairs. Drunk, I suppose.'

'The doctor found no evidence that he'd been drinking, sir,' said Coburg.

'Then it must have been a fight. If so, what was the fight about? Money, I suppose. All his troubles were usually about money. That posh school he was at threatened to expel him for stealing. It was only a healthy payment from me that stopped that happening.'

'Richard had difficulty adjusting to life there,' put in Fiona.

'Why? Because he couldn't flash wads of cash around like some of those types?' He turned to Coburg and Lampson and said, 'I kept him on a tight rein as far as money was concerned. I wanted him to learn value of money, that it doesn't come easy. I fought for every penny I earned.'

'We understand that he asked you for money while he was at the Aircrew Receiving Centre.'

'Not just then! He was always asking me for money. It shows how stupid he was. I told him time and time again not to ask me for money, but he kept doing it.'

'Alfred, this is our son you're talking about!' burst out Fiona accusingly. 'He's just died! Don't you have any heart for him?'

'He took my heart from me years ago with all those sneaky things he did. Stealing from us!'

'He didn't steal! He asked me if he could borrow money from me and I lent it to him.'

'More fool you! Did he pay you back?'

'He tried, but there were always problems.'

'Problems of his own making.' He turned to the two policemen. 'When I found out what was going on, I turned off that tap. I blocked my wife from handing over any more money to him.'

'Leaving him to flounder!' accused his wife.

'If he was going to survive in this world he had to learn to make his own way.'

'But he didn't survive! He died. And it's your fault!'

With that, she put her hand to her face to hide the tears that suddenly began to appear and rushed out of the room. Rhodes-Armfield looked after her.

'I'm sorry for that, Inspector,' he said. 'My wife's distressed.'

'That's understandable, sir, in view of what's happened. Losing a child is always a tragedy, regardless of what may have gone before.'

Rhodes-Armfield looked at Coburg, his expression challengingly defensive.

'You don't like me, do you, Inspector? You think I'm hard.'

'I don't know you well enough to like or dislike you, sir. I sympathise with the loss of your son. I'm sure you and your wife wish things could have been different. But I'm here to investigate his death.'

'What's there to investigate? He fell down the stairs. That's what his commanding officer told me when he rang to inform me. Like I said, I expect it was a fight with someone he owed money to.'

'Since then, sir, new information has come to light that puts a different aspect on the situation. There is every indication that he was struck on the back of the head, and it was that blow that killed him.'

Rhodes-Armfield stared at Coburg, weighing this up. 'You're saying someone murdered him?'

'That seems to be the most likely explanation.'

'Well, who?'

'That's what we're here trying to establish, sir. We've talked to his fellow cadets at the ARC and there is a suggestion that he may have got into financial difficulties over gambling debts. Can you throw any light on his gambling activities?'

'No!' thundered Rhodes-Armfield firmly. 'I don't gamble and I warned him against it. I guessed it must be something like that when he kept begging me for money.' He gave an unhappy sigh. 'So it cost him his life.'

'That's one possibility, but we're also looking into others. Did he used to gamble before he went to the ARC, sir?'

'I don't know. I didn't think so, but it's possible.'

'Did he ever give any indication of who he was gambling with at the ARC?'

'His bookie, you mean? No. But then, he'd never have told me. He knew how I felt about gambling, and he knew if I found out about it he'd be even less likely to get any money from me.'

'So you have no knowledge of who he might have been involved with financially at the ARC? No one he mentioned as asking him for money?'

'No,' said Rhodes-Armfield. Then he frowned. 'But there was one funny thing. About a week ago I had a phone call from his unit officer at the ARC asking if Richard had been in touch with me regarding a mess bill that was due. He said that Richard had told him that he'd been in touch with me regarding it and that I'd said I would settle it, and he needed to know when the money would be forthcoming in order to make the accounts right before Richard was transferred to other units, along with the rest of the squad. I told him that this was the first I'd heard of it, and I had no intention of settling any mess bills, or any other bills my son may have incurred. I told him it was a matter between my son and the RAF.'

'What was the name of the officer?' asked Coburg.

Rhodes-Armfield's face creased into a thoughtful frown as he tried to remember. 'It was a Corporal something. Atkins, or something like that. Atkinson, perhaps? Or maybe it was Judkins.' He shook his head. 'I know it was something like that, but I didn't take it in. I was so angry at the cheek of it, at Richard using this officer to try and get money from me. Outrageous!'

'Corporal Atkins, Atkinson or Judkins,' said Coburg as they walked to their car.

'Corporal Judkins,' said Lampson firmly. 'The one I told you about. The shifty one.'

Corporal Harry Judkins did indeed look shifty as he sat in the commanding officer's office across a tacble from Coburg and Lampson. This return visit by Lampson had unsettled him, especially as the sergeant was now accompanied by a detective chief inspector with a posh accent and a double-barrelled name.

Coburg got down to the matter in hand straight away.

'Corporal Judkins, we've received information that you've been running a book here at the ARC,' he said.

'Running a book? What d'you mean, running a book?' blustered Judkins, attempting a weak and what he hoped was innocent-looking smile.

'Engaging in gambling, taking bets on sporting events.'

Judkins shook his head. 'No,' he said.

'So you won't mind if we examine your bank accounts.'

Judkins scowled. 'Yes, I do mind. Those are private.'

Coburg shrugged. 'Please yourself. We can always get a court order.'

'What do you mean, a court order?' demanded Judkins, bristling.

'Ask your commanding officer; I'm sure he'll explain it to you,' said Coburg. '*If* you want to involve your commanding officer, that is. I wasn't going to involve him, but that's your prerogative.'

Judkins glowered and glared suspiciously at Coburg. 'What's all this about?' he demanded.

'That's up to you,' said Coburg. 'Off-course bookmaking is illegal, but there's so much of it that goes on, especially with the war, that many in the police are happy to turn a blind eye to it. Only in this case, one of your clients, a Richard Rhodes-Armfield has recently tragically died.'

'He wasn't a client, as you call it,' said Judkins. 'He was a cadet here at the ARC. And he fell down a flight of stairs.'

'He was *assisted* in falling down those stairs, according to the medical examiner,' said Coburg. 'A blow to the back of his head. A kick from a service boot, according to our medical expert. What we have to decide is whether it was deliberate, and therefore murder, or an accident. A bit of strongarming over an unpaid debt that got out of hand. No death intended, just an unfortunate accident.'

Judkins fell silent, but they could see from the way his eyes moved warily backwards and forwards, from Coburg to Lampson, then back to Coburg again, that he was weighing up his response.

'What happened to him was nothing to do with me,' he said finally.

'But you were running a book,' said Coburg. 'If you deny it, we can get proof. But that would involve lots of other people having to give evidence in court.'

'Court?' echoed Judkins, horrified.

'Which would take up a lot of people's time when everyone is concentrating on getting this war won. As you are, training up these cadets.'

'I am,' said Judkins. 'It's an important job.'

'Which you wouldn't be able to do if you were in jail for illegal bookmaking. And, I guess, you'd also be discharged from the services. Are you married?'

'Yes,' said Judkins, warily.

'Kids?'

'Two. But what's that got to do with it?'

'I'm guessing your family depend on your wages to get by. Be a pity for you to lose not only your career in the RAF but your income as well.'

'Look, what do you want from me?' demanded Judkins angrily.

'Information about Richard Rhodes-Armfield. How much

did he owe you, and how did he come to tumble down the stairs?'

Judkins fell silent once more, then mumbled awkwardly, 'He owed me fifteen quid.' Then defiantly, he added, 'But I had nothing to do with him taking a fall down the stairs or kicking him. I'm not that kind of bloke. I never laid a hand on anyone.'

'But someone you know might have,' said Coburg. 'Someone who responded to your request for help in getting the money that was owed to you.'

'Look, you don't understand,' appealed Judkins. 'These boys are away from home, some of them for the first time. They need some entertainment to take their minds off worrying about the war and what they're going to be caught up in, but there's nowhere they can go round here. Not really. They're restricted to base and the pub is the only outlet. So having a bit of a flutter gives them a bit of amusement. That's all it is, a bit of fun. As you said, everyone does it.'

'Who did you send to lean on young Rhodes-Armfield?'

'No one!'

'In that case I can only assume you did it yourself. Knocked him down then kicked him in the head.'

'No!' shouted Judkins, leaping to his feet.

'Sit down!' snapped Coburg. 'Or I'll call an escort and have you taken to the guardhouse, with force if necessary.'

Judkins sat down, a look of desperate appeal on his face.

'It wasn't me,' he said.

'Who was it?' asked Coburg.

CHAPTER TWELVE

Wednesday 12th March

Seventeen-year-old Max Baxter unwrapped the oilcloth from the object he'd found in a battered suitcase, which had been lying untouched on the top of a cupboard in one of the barns in the yard at the rear of his mother's pawnshop. The suitcase had been gathering dust there since his father, Marcus Baxter, died six months before. His father had been out at night on a burglary with his pal Dingo Lewis. A bomb had hit the house they were robbing while the occupants were in an air raid shelter. Both Marcus Baxter and Dingo Lewis had been killed. It had been a valuable lesson for Max: don't go robbing at night when the Luftwaffe are bombing London. Do your business during the day.

Baxter's Secondhand Goods was officially a pawnshop where people could come and cash in their valuables for a short while, until they had the money to redeem them and get them back. Unofficially, it was a place where Max's mother, Ma Baxter, bought stolen goods and sold them on. She was always careful in the goods she took in, nothing too distinctive that might be recognised by the former owner. Much of the stuff she took in were items stolen en masse from warehouses.

Max showed the precious object he'd found to his two

younger brothers, sixteen-year-old Monty and fifteen-year-old Micky.

'What do you think of that?' he asked proudly.

Monty and Micky looked at the revolver in awe. Micky reached out to touch it, but Max pushed his hand away.

'Careful,' said Max. 'It's loaded. The bullets are still in it.'

'Will it fire?' asked Monty.

'Bound to,' said Max. 'It's still in good nick. Oiled and everything, and Dad wrapped it in this oilskin to keep it good.'

'What are we gonna do with it?' asked Monty.

Monty was the most nervous of the three boys. Like his two brothers, he was often in trouble, but it was usually because he'd been tagging along with them on some escapade. Monty never started anything himself; he left that to Max and Micky.

'We're gonna use it,' said Max.

'How?' asked Micky.

'Remember last week when we were in Pearce's Greengrocer's and he caught me taking an apple?'

The other two boys nodded.

'One lousy apple!' spat Micky.

'Exactly,' said Max. 'And he threatened to call the police on us. Well, we're going to have our own back on that scab. We're going to go to his shop and show him this gun and tell him to open the till.'

Micky looked excited, Monty doubtful.

'Say he calls the police?' asked Monty. 'That's not just nicking an apple, that's robbery with a gun. You go to prison for that.'

'That's not going to happen,' said Max confidently. 'One

look at this beauty and old Pearce will crumble. He'll have that till open faster than anything.'

'Say he doesn't?' persisted Monty.

'Are you gonna shoot him?' asked Micky.

'Don't be silly!' said Max scornfully. 'I'm not that much of an idiot. No, if he don't do what I say I'm gonna shoot some of his fruit and veg, jut to let him know I mean business.'

'Yeah!' Micky grinned. 'That'll do it.'

'But say the gun don't go off?' said Monty. 'It's been in that suitcase for a long time.'

'Like I say, Dad oiled it and it's been kept wrapped in oilcloth,' said Max.

'But you've never fired it,' pointed out Monty, still not convinced.

'Yes I have,' said Max. 'When Dad was alive he let me have a go with it.'

'I don't remember that,' said Micky.

'You weren't here. You and Monty had gone out with Mum to do something, so Dad said we'd use the opportunity for me to see how it worked. Remember those bales of straw in the yard in case we got a horse?'

'I remember Dad saying we were going to get a horse,' said Micky.

'And we would have done if he hadn't got killed,' said Max. 'Anyway, I fired two bullets into them. Then, after, he showed me how to load it.'

Micky's grin grew broader. 'This is gonna be great!' he said delightedly. 'I can't wait to see old Pearce's face when you start shooting up his shop.'

* * *

Prudence Baxter was sorting through some overcoats that her two minions, Degsy and Bill, had taken in from a customer.

'This is all a load of old tat,' she said disparagingly.

'The bloke who brought it in said it was all top-class stuff. He knocked over some clothing place up the West End.'

Ma Baxter shook her head. 'Well, he can take them back again. I'm not paying good money for this tat. Let him try some other mug.' She looked at the two men. 'Who was it?'

'Eric Dawes,' said Degsy. 'You've done business with him before.'

'Yes, but with better stuff than this.'

'Hello, it looks like the boys are off walkabout,' said Bill, looking through the back window, which looked out on the yard.

Ma Baxter looked and saw her three sons walking across the yard to the open gates, which led out onto Frampton Street. As always, Max was in the lead with Micky close beside him, and Monty bringing up the rear.

'Want me to go out and ask 'em where they're going?' asked Bill.

Ma Baxter shook her head. 'No, they'll just lie. This way, if they get in trouble we can honestly say we didn't know anything about it.'

Coburg had initially wanted to pick up Lance Corporal Huxton the previous day, but by the time they'd finished with Sergeant Judkins, the rest of the training staff had left for the day.

'We could always pick him up at his home,' Lampson had suggested.

Coburg had shaken his head. 'It'll keep till first thing

tomorrow,' he'd said. 'We've had a long enough day. You need to get home to Terry, and I need to get home to Rosa.'

'What if Judkins warns him?' Lampson had asked.

'I doubt it,' Coburg had said. 'I may be wrong but I don't think Corporal Judkins would fancy telling Huxton to his face that he grassed him up to us.'

And so they'd left it until the morning, where they found the lance corporal in one of the workshops soon after the staff arrived at the reception centre.

'Lance Corporal Huxton, we need you to accompany us to Scotland Yard,' Coburg told him.

'Why?' demanded Huxton.

'For the moment that has to remain under wraps,' said Coburg. 'You'll be fully informed when we get to the Yard.'

Huxton shook his head. 'I can't leave the base. I'm on duty here.'

'We've got the permission of your commanding officer to take you,' said Coburg. 'Now we can do this in a civilised manner, or we can take you in handcuffs. It's up to you.'

'What do you mean, handcuffs?' said Huxton, outraged. 'What am I supposed to have done?'

'As I said, you'll be informed of any charges against you when we get to Scotland Yard.'

'What charges?' insisted Huxton.

Coburg gestured towards the police car waiting outside the building. 'In the car, please.'

Huxton scowled, but walked to the car and clambered into the rear seats, next to Lampson. Now, Huxton sat in one of the interview rooms in the basement of Scotland Yard, facing Coburg and Lampson across a wooden table.

'You've been brought in because we've been informed by Corporal Judkins that you roughed up Air Cadet Rhodes-Armfield in order to get him to pay Corporal Judkins the £15 he owed him. During this roughing up, Cadet Rhodes-Armfield tumbled down the stairs, and subsequently died. According to the medical examiner, cause of death was a blow to the back of his head.'

Huxton looked at them, obviously discomforted that Judkins had dropped him in it, telling them what had happened about him being asked to lean on the young cadet.

'I never did anything untoward,' he said defensively. 'I just had a word with him, was all.'

'A bit more than that, by all accounts,' said Coburg, 'seeing as Rhodes-Armfield fell down the stairs.'

'Him dying was nothing to do with me,' said Huxton firmly. 'After he took a tumble, which was a complete accident, I went down to see how he was. He was unconscious, but breathing. And there was no damage to the back of his head. No blood at all. So, if it was the wound on the back of his head that killed him, that was nothing to do with me.'

'No blood at all?'

Huxton shook his head firmly. 'I lifted his head a bit to listen to him, make sure he was breathing. If there'd been any blood it would have been on my hand. There was none.'

'But the ambulance people reported blood on the back of his head, and on the stairs where he was found when they examined him. And they examined him as soon as they arrived.'

'Something must have happened to him between me leaving him and them arriving,' said Huxton.

Coburg looked at him in obvious disbelief. 'You really expect us to believe that?'

'Yes, because it's the truth.'

'What, for example?'

Huxton shrugged. 'Maybe he woke up, tried to get up, then fell and banged his head on the stair.'

Coburg shook his head. 'Can you really see a jury believing that?' he asked.

'I don't care,' said Huxton doggedly. 'I didn't kill him and that's all I know. If someone else came along later and did it, it wasn't me.'

'We've got medical evidence that he was killed by a kick to the back of his head by someone wearing a pair of service boots. Take your boots off.'

'Why?'

'I want our science people to examine them.'

'I tell you I never hurt him!' burst out Huxton. 'I didn't do nothing but have a word with him.'

Gerry Pearce weighed the apples, put them in a brown paper bag and passed them to Tom Brakes.

'There you are,' he said. 'Two shillings.'

Tom handed over a florin, then asked, 'No chance of any bananas, I suppose?'

Pearce looked at him, incredulous. 'Bananas?' he repeated. 'There's been no bananas since the war started, you know that.'

'There were some at first,' Tom countered.

'Yeah, but that was before the U-boats started attacking the merchant ships. No bananas. No oranges. Nothing but what we can grow here.'

'I bet the royal family and the rich toffs get hold of bananas,' said Tom jealously. 'The rich can get everything.'

'I bet they can't get bananas,' said Pearce. 'Even the top restaurants and hotels are having to come up with alternatives. Mashed turnips with sugar.'

'Yuck,' said Tom.

'Don't knock it until you've tried it,' said Pearce. 'I've got some turnips, if you like.'

'Have you got any sugar?'

Pearce shook his head. 'No chance,' he said. Suddenly something caught his eye in the street outside and he said in warning voice, 'Look out. It's them Baxter brothers. If they come in and start nicking my stuff I'll turf 'em out.'

'If you get handy with 'em, you'll have their old woman to deal with, and you know what a terror Ma Baxter can be,' warned Tom.

The door of the shop opened and Max walked, Monty and Micky following him. Usually they swaggered whenever they walked around the town, but today Pearce noticed they seemed a bit edgy. Nervous.

'What can I do for you?' asked Pearce warily.

Max pulled the revolver from inside his jacket and pointed it at the greengrocer. 'You can open the till,' he said.

Pearce and Tom stared at him, and at the gun.

'Have you gone mad?' asked Pearce. 'What are you doing with that thing?'

'What's it look like?' said Max aggressively. 'Open that till.'

Pearce glared at Max, his face distorting into an angry scowl.

'Bugger off,' he snapped. 'You're barred from my shop. If you come in here again, I'm calling the police on you.'

'Do it, Max,' urged Micky. 'What you said. Show him we mean business.'

Max swung round, pointing the gun at the fruit and vegetables on display. There was the deafening sound of the gun going off, and a yell of pain from Micky, who stumbled forward and fell against the food displays.

'You shot me!' howled Micky, and then he slid down to the floor.

Max looked at his fallen brother, then at the smoking gun, in horror. Pearce and Tom stared at the fallen Micky, shocked.

'It jumped!' burst out Max. 'It jumped in my hand!'

Micky struggled to his feet and leant against the food display trays, moaning.

'What are we going to do?' asked Monty, fearful.

'You bring Micky,' said Max urgently. 'We'll get help for him.'

With that, Max ran out of the shop, while Monty put his arm around his younger brother and helped him stagger out into the street.

CHAPTER THIRTEEN

'What's the address again?' asked Rosa.

'43 Rossmore Road,' said Doris. 'It's not far. Old lady fell down the stairs.' She grimaced. 'It'll be the second one falling down stairs this week we've had.'

'Let's hope this one doesn't die on us, like the cadet.'

'If you ask me there was something odd with that one,' said Doris thoughtfully.

Suddenly a teenage boy stepped into the road in front of their ambulance and aimed a pistol at them.

'What the hell?!' shouted Rosa, slamming on the brakes.

'Pull over or I shoot!' barked the youth.

'What the hell is wrong with you?' demanded Rosa.

'Bloody cheek!' said Doris, outraged. 'Run him over.'

'I mean it,' threatened the youth. 'My brother's hurt. He needs help.'

Rosa and Doris looked towards the side of the road and saw two boys, one holding the other up and helping him towards the ambulance. The boy who was hurt was barely able to walk, his face creased in pain, with blood soaking through his shirt and trousers.

'Open the back door,' the youth said. His attention turned to Doris. 'You, get in the back with him and treat him.'

'We'd better do as he says,' advised Rosa. 'He looks badly hurt, and we can't trust this lunatic not to pull the trigger on us.'

With a scowl, Doris got out and went to the back of the ambulance. The youth with the gun got into the passenger seat Doris had vacated, the gun pointing at Rosa.

Rosa heard the sound of the rear door being opened, and someone clambering aboard. There were more noises, then a banging from the rear of the ambulance as a signal.

'Right, get going,' the youth ordered Rosa.

'The nearest hospital is Paddington General,' said Rosa, putting the vehicle into gear.

'No! No hospitals!' snapped the youth. 'Go to Frampton Street. Do you know where it is?'

'Yes.'

'There's a pair of tall double gates about halfway down, painted green. They're open. Drive in and you'll be in a yard.'

'What is it?' asked Rosa.

'I told you, it's a yard,' said the youth.

'He needs a hospital,' said Rosa. 'He's bleeding badly.'

'Shut up and just do what I say,' snapped the youth.

Rosa followed the road until she came to Frampton Street. She found the open green double gates and drove the ambulance in. It seemed to be a yard at the rear of a shop.

The youth got out of the cab and shouted 'Ma! Ma!' He then ran to the double gates and pulled them shut, sliding a pair of bolts in place to secure them.

Rosa looked through the windscreen towards the rear of the shop and saw a plump woman in her forties emerge and run towards the youth with the gun.

'What's going on?' she demanded, bewildered.

'Micky got shot,' said the youth. 'He's in the back of the ambulance.'

The woman let out a shout of 'Degsy! Bill!'

Two burly men appeared from the rear of the shop at a run. Rosa heard the rear door of the ambulance open and shutting, then the two men carried the injured youth into the building. The middle-aged woman followed them. The youth with the gun appeared beside the cab, the gun pointing at Rosa.

'Turn the engine off,' he ordered.

Rosa switched the engine off. Suddenly the youth became aware for the first time of the radio set in the cab.

'Is that a radio?' he demanded, agitated.

'It connects us to our base,' began Rosa, but she was cut short by the explosion of the gun being fired and a bullet smashing into the radio. Rosa looked at the shattered radio in horror.

'What did you do that for?' she demanded angrily.

'Shut up!' barked the youth.

The woman came hurrying out of the shop and charged up to the youth.

'What was that about?' she demanded, her tone as angry as Rosa's had been.

'They got a radio in the cab. I had to stop her sending messages.'

The youth who'd been supporting the wounded boy now appeared from the back of the ambulance. Doris was with him. The clothes of both of them were stained with blood.

Rosa looked enquiringly at Doris. 'How is he?' she asked.

'Just about hanging in,' said Doris. 'He needs a doctor. And not just any doctor, he needs to go to hospital. He's got a bullet in him. He'll need an operation otherwise he'll die.'

'No!' shouted the youth with the gun, and he pointed it at Doris.

The middle-aged woman grabbed hold of the youth by the collar and demanded, 'What happened?' When he didn't immediately reply, she turned to the other youth, and Rosa became aware of the resemblance between the two boys. Brothers, obviously. 'Monty, what happened?'

'Micky got shot,' said Monty.

'Who by?' demanded the woman.

Monty shot an awkward look at his elder brother, who burst out defensively: 'It was an accident!'

The woman let fly with a slap that hit the youth so hard around the head that he stumbled, then fell. The youth tried to scramble up, but the woman kicked him and he screeched in pain and doubled over.

'No, Ma!' he pleaded.

The woman rounded on the younger brother, who flinched and stepped back from her, obviously fearful.

'It was Max's idea to hijack an ambulance,' said Monty. 'He said if we took him to hospital the police would be called. They always are when someone's been shot.'

'That's right,' said Max, getting up from the ground, clutching his painful ribs. 'You always told us, keep the police out of it.'

One of the men who'd carried the boy reappeared from the shop and ran to the woman.

'Degsy's got Micky's clothes off, but he's in a bad way,' he said. 'He needs proper medical help.'

The woman turned to Doris and Rosa.

'You two,' she barked. She pointed at the rear entrance to the building. 'Get in there and save him.'

'We're not doctors,' protested Doris. 'We're just an ambulance crew.'

'You'll know more than we do,' said the woman tersely. 'Now, get in there. If he dies, you die.'

With that, she hurried them towards the rear of the building.

CHAPTER FOURTEEN

With Huxton locked up in the custody suite, Coburg and Lampson took his boots to the reception desk and arranged for a messenger to take them to Dr Welbourne at the mortuary at University College Hospital. Coburg wrote a note to accompany the boots, explaining that they had been taken from a suspect in the case of the dead air cadet. The two detectives then made their way upstairs to their office. As they opened the door, the phone began to ring.

'DCI Coburg's phone,' said Lampson, snatching up the receiver.

'Is the Chief Inspector there?' asked a man's voice. 'Please tell him it's Chesney Warren from Paddington St John Ambulance.'

Lampson held out the phone towards Coburg. 'Chesney Warren from Paddington St John Ambulance,' he said.

Coburg took the receiver. 'DCI Coburg,' he said. 'How can I help you, Mr Warren?'

'I'm afraid Rosa and Doris seem to have disappeared,' said Warren, obviously worried.

'Disappeared?' repeated Coburg, puzzled.

'I sent them on a call to pick up a woman and take her to Paddington General about half an hour ago. They said they weren't far from the woman's address, and they'd radio me when they'd delivered her. I expected them to be in touch quite quickly, but I haven't heard anything from them. Five minutes ago I had a phone call from the woman's daughter to say the ambulance hadn't arrived. I tried calling them on their radio, but there's been no response. It may be that their radio has packed up, but if that had been the case and there was a problem I'm sure they would have phoned in. Both Rosa and Doris are scrupulous like that.'

'Where was the pick-up?' asked Coburg.

'43 Rossmore Road. A Mrs Edna Phipps. I've sent another ambulance, which is on its way, but I'm concerned about Rosa and Doris.'

'Do you know where they were when you gave them the address?'

'No, just that they said they weren't far away. They'd just delivered a patient to Paddington General, so they could have been on their way from there.'

'Right. My sergeant and I will go and check the route from Paddington General to Rossmore Road, so if anything's happened, I'll let you know.'

Coburg replaced the receiver and got to his feet, a concerned look on his face.

'Rosa and her pal Doris have disappeared,' he told Lampson. 'Last known sighting Paddington General and on their way to Rossmore Road.'

'They're not far from each other,' said Lampson, getting up.

'No, so we'll start at Paddington General in Harrow Road, and make our way to Rossmore Road, see if anything's happened that explains it. You drive, I'll look out.'

* * *

Rosa and Doris stood in the back room behind the shop, Rosa watching as Doris cut away the shirt and trousers from the unconscious Micky. His torso was a mess. The bullet had gone into him from the back, tearing through the soft tissue before coming out the front at his side, leaving a gaping exit wound. Blood was pumping.

'We need to clean him up,' said Doris. 'We need some warm water.'

'Max!' shouted Ma Baxter. When there was no response from her son, she shouted: 'Degsy! Bill!'

The two men appeared.

'Where's Max?' she demanded.

'He was upset,' said Bill. 'I think he's gone into one of the storerooms.'

'Right, we need some warm water,' said Ma Baxter.

Bill and Degsy looked at one another; both looked baffled.

'What in?' asked Bill.

'Oh, for God's sake!' shouted Ma Baxter in exasperation. 'I'll do it myself.' She turned to Doris and Rosa and said menacingly, 'Remember what I said. He dies, you die.'

With that, she left. Degsy and Bill hesitated, then followed her. Rosa shot a look at Doris. 'Think we ought to do a run for it?'

'Where to?'

'The ambulance.'

'The doors to the yard are bolted. And she'll be back in a second.'

'You know she's going to kill us anyway' said Rosa grimly. 'Even if we save him. We've seen too much. We know that the oldest boy shot the youngest. We know where they live.'

'We just have to keep letting her think we're working on him,' said Doris. 'So long as he's alive, there's hope.'

'Can you keep him alive?' asked Rosa.

Doris shook her head. 'He's lost too much blood and he's still losing it. There's nowhere we can put a tourniquet on him; we need clamps. Which we don't have. All I can do is see if I can slow down the bleeding. But, with what we've got to work with, I can't see that happening.'

Inside the disused Lord's Tube station, two men packed the electrical apparatus away in its wooden case, then one carried it carefully down the winding stairs to the platforms far below while his companion followed. In the short corridor at the bottom of the stairs that linked the two platforms, the southbound and the northbound, was a door with a faded sign saying *Private*. Inside was a roomy cupboard containing brooms and buckets and other cleaning materials, left there when the station closed in 1939.

The man carrying the wooden box waited while his companion moved the brooms and buckets aside to reveal a hole that had been made in the wall. The man put the wooden box in the hole, then placed a piece of board across the hole to conceal the box before putting the brooms and buckets in front of the board.

'I still think it's dangerous leaving it here,' said the second man. 'Say someone comes and starts moving things round. They'll find it.'

'They won't,' said the other man confidently. 'For one

thing, no one comes down here. And, after what happened, we can't leave it anywhere else.'

'I suppose not,' said his companion, but he didn't sound convinced.

'Nothing so far,' said Lampson. He was driving along Broadley Street, following the route it was thought the ambulance would have taken. 'Maybe they went another way.'

'Possibly,' said Coburg. Then suddenly he was alert. He'd seen a police car parked outside a greengrocer's shop and a uniformed policeman standing outside the shop. He could see through the shop window another police officer inside, talking to some men.

'Over there,' said Coburg. 'That greengrocer's, where the police car is. Something's happened.'

Lampson headed towards the greengrocer's and pulled up behind the parked police car. Coburg got out, took out his warrant card and showed it to the officer outside the shop.

'What's happening, Constable?'

'Attempted robbery, sir. Shots fired.'

Coburg hurried into the shop and introduced himself. 'DCI Coburg, Scotland Yard. I understand there was a robbery. Anyone injured?'

The two civilians tuned towards him, as the officer told him, 'One of the robbers was shot, sir.'

'It was the Baxter brothers!' burst out one of the men impatiently. When Coburg looked at him enquiringly, he added, 'This is my shop.' He gestured toward a sign on the wall that said *G. Pearce. Greengrocer.*

'You know the thieves?' asked Coburg.

'Everyone around here knows them!' said Pearce angrily.

'Trouble since the day they was born. Max, Monty and Micky Baxter. Max is the eldest, seventeen, then there's Monty, who's sixteen, and Micky the youngest is fifteen.'

'What happened?' asked Coburg. 'Was an ambulance involved?'

'An ambulance?' repeated Pearce, puzzled.

'I bet there was!' said another man. 'It looked to me like Max shot Micky. I bet they went for an ambulance to get him help.'

'Tell me exactly what happened,' said Coburg to the man.

'I was here in Gerry's shop looking at what he had. Not that there was much.'

'Things are difficult to get hold of,' protested Pearce. 'You know that, Tom.'

Coburg silenced the greengrocer with a gesture of his hand, but kept his eyes on the witness, Tom.

'The Baxter brothers came in. Usually they're cocky, showing off, but today they looked edgy. Suddenly Max pulls out a gun. "We want what's in the till," he said.' Tom shook his head. 'We were shocked. I knew they were evil little toe-rags, always thieving, but they'd never done anything like this before.'

'What did you do?' asked Coburg.

'Nothing,' said Tom. 'It wasn't my shop, and I never argue with anyone holding a gun.'

Coburg turned to Pearce, who scowled and said, 'There was no way I was going to let them take my money. That's hard-earned, that is. And I didn't believe that little scrote would actually use the gun. I didn't think it was even loaded.'

'But it was,' said Coburg.

'It was,' said Pearce. 'I told Max to get out. That made him angry. He went all white and the next second I heard this bang.

111

I don't think he was aiming at anyone. I think he just wanted to shoot some fruit to let me know the gun was loaded. Anyway, suddenly Micky gave a wail and fell back against the stands. "I'm shot," he says. Well, that was it. The older boys panicked. They held Micky up and helped him out of the shop. I ran into the back where the phone is and called the coppers.'

Coburg looked at the constable, who gave him an apologetic look. 'I'm afraid it took us a bit of a while to get here. We were on another call.'

Pearce gave the constable a derisory sneer. 'Taking a break, I reckon. It was ages before you turned up. Lucky it wasn't someone being murdered.'

'It could have been,' put in Tom. 'Especially with Max Baxter having that gun.'

'Where can I find these Baxters?' asked Coburg.

'They live with their mum in Orchardson Street, over a pawnshop,' said Tom. 'There's a yard at the back of the shop. That's where they park their van. The yard opens out on Frampton Street.'

'Right,' said Coburg. 'Tom, you come with us and show us where their yard is.' He then turned to the waiting police officers. 'I want you to check every street corner between here and Orchardson Street and ask if anyone saw an ambulance.'

'Yes, sir. Where shall we get hold of you?'

'At Frampton Street.'

'Why am I going with you?' asked Tom, puzzled, as Coburg led him towards their car, where Lampson was waiting.

'Because you know where the Baxters' yard is, and I want to look at it.'

Tom got in, as did Coburg, and a short while later Lampson

pulled up beside the double green gates in Frampton Street. Coburg got out and made for the gates. He grabbed hold of the top and pulled himself up, then dropped down and returned to the car.

'Thank you, Tom,' he said. 'We're most grateful. You can go.'

'Where?' asked Tom.

'Wherever you want,' said Coburg.

Tom looked puzzled, but then he got out of the car and walked off, heading back towards Pearce's Greengrocer's to fill in Gerry Pearce on the mystery of this trip.

'The ambulance is there, in the yard,' Coburg told Lampson. 'I hope that means that Rosa and Doris are in the building. I'm going to stay here in case someone appears. I want you to get to the nearest nick and alert them to the situation. I want armed officers to come here to mount a guard front and back. Plus, vehicles to block off the roads. When they're here, we go in. But we've got to handle it carefully. If there's guns in use, we can't risk Rosa and Doris. Tell the officers they're to keep well back, out of sight, and we only go in when I give the word.'

'Right, guv,' said Lampson. 'Marylebone nick is nearest, and I know the sergeant there.'

Paul Huxton sat on the hard bench in the custody cell in a mood of absolute misery. Why him? he thought. Why not Judkins? All he'd done had been what Judkins told him, but he was the one in the police cell.

Murder, they said. It was all wrong; he hadn't murdered anyone. He hadn't even really touched that cadet, just pushed him around a bit to reinforce the demand that he cough up the fifteen quid he owed. And then the stupid bastard had tumbled down the stairs. He must have banged his head against something as he fell, because he was definitely alive when Huxton had gone down the stairs to examine him. Unconscious, but still very much alive. Breathing.

All this nonsense about him being kicked in the back of the head.

Huxton looked down at his stockinged feet, with the big toe of his left foot poking through a hole in his sock. He'd been meaning to darn that. It was unfair the police picking on him and taking his boots away from him like they did.

The question was, if the cadet had been kicked in the back of the head, who by? Had Judkins turned up and seen the boy lying there, maybe coming round and starting to move, and had given him a kick? Why else would anyone want to kick the boy in the head like that? They must have known it could be a killer kick.

Degsy and Bill sat in one of the barns, surrounded by piles of clothes. By rights they should have been sorting through the piles, separating the clothes into good condition, in need of some minor repairs, and the third lot for selling to a rag-and-bone merchant, but, after what had happened, they'd decided the safest place to be was out of the way.

'If Micky dies, she'll go absolutely crackers,' said Degsy.

'Shh,' said Bill, alarmed. 'Don't let her hear you say that.'

'She can't hear me,' said Degsy, but he lowered his voice almost to a whisper. 'She's in that room with Micky and them two women.'

Bill and Degsy had worked for the Baxters for many years. And soon after they began working for the family, both men realised that the power in the family lay with Ma. Marcus had been tough, but nowhere near as tough as his wife. Ma Baxter had been – and still was – ruthless in her business dealings, and protecting her boys. Especially Micky, the baby. Max she tolerated, Monty she mostly ignored, but Micky was special to her.

'Where are Max and Monty?' asked Bill.

'Somewhere around,' said Degsy. 'I think Monty went upstairs to his room. As for Max, he was in one of the barns, keeping away from his ma.'

'D'you think Micky'll make it?' whispered Bill, worried.

'Don't know,' admitted Degsy unhappily. 'I saw a bloke shot like that before.' He shook his head. 'He didn't.'

In the back room, Ma Baxter stood and watched as Doris probed into the wound in her youngest son's torso, pressing her fingers against the wound in a futile attempt to staunch the flow of blood.

'Can't you stop the bleeding?' Ma Baxter demanded.

'Not without the proper equipment,' said Doris. 'We need clamps.'

'We've got clamps here,' said Ma.

'But not the right sort,' said Doris. 'We need medical clamps.' She looked at Ma Baxter in appeal. 'There might still be a chance if we take him to hospital.'

'No hospital,' said Ma firmly. 'You fix him. That's what they pay you to do.'

'No, we're volunteers. We pick up injured and ill people and take them to hospital, so they can be treated.'

Ma Baxter shook her head grimly. 'Save him,' she said. 'Save him.'

CHAPTER FIFTEEN

Coburg saw the police car approaching down Frampton Road. It pulled up just short of the large green gates and the doors opened and Sergeant Lampson got out, accompanied by two uniformed officers, one a sergeant. In the distance, Coburg saw another police car park across the end of the street, blocking it off.

'Another car's going to be doing the same at the other end of Frampton Street,' said Lampson. 'The same's happening on Orchardson Street, a car blocking each end of the road so nothing comes through. We've got three officers authorised to use firearms, all sergeants, and all veterans of the First War, so they're experienced.' He indicated the sergeant standing beside him. 'This is Sergeant Wilson, one of them.'

'Good to have you with us, Sergeant,' said Coburg. 'You've been told what the situation is?'

'I have, sir,' said Wilson. 'We're well aware of Ma Baxter and her lot, though I never thought the boys would do anything like this. They say that Max shot Micky.'

'That's what the greengrocer told us,' said Coburg. 'An accident, by all accounts. I guess the boy hadn't fired a gun before and didn't allow for the kick it gives.'

'Are you armed, sir?' asked Wilson.

'I'm afraid not,' said Coburg. 'Both Sergeant Lampson and

I are authorised, but we never expected to be in this situation, so our firearms are under lock and key at Scotland Yard.' He turned to the constable enquiringly. 'I appreciate you joining us, Constable . . . ?'

'Appleton, sir,' said the constable, saluting.

'Constable Appleton. I'm going to try and get this sorted without bloodshed. Sergeant Lampson and I will approach the pawnshop from the Orchardson Street entrance. Sergeant Wilson, I'd like you and Constable Appleton to be a few houses along from the pawnshop. It's going to depend on who answers the door. If it's Max and he's got his gun, there could be trouble. I'm hoping whoever opens the door will be Mrs Baxter, or someone who isn't armed. In which case we'll call you in and you can help us overpower them if they resist.'

'Right, sir.' Wilson nodded. He gestured towards the police car that had dropped them by the gates. 'That's Sergeant Harpson at the wheel of the car. He knows the area and the family. I'm going to suggest, sir, he stays by the back gates, in case anyone comes out that way.'

'Is he armed?' asked Coburg.

'No, sir.'

Coburg looked doubtful. 'I'm not sure about that.'

'Sergeant Harpson is a very experienced officer, sir.'

'He may be, but experience is no match for someone pointing a gun at you if you're unarmed. Where are the other two armed officers?'

'One at each end of Orchardson Street.'

'Right. We'll go round to Orchardson Street to get to the pawnshop, and we'll send the one there to join Sergeant Harpson in the car.'

'If you think that's best, sir,' said Wilson.

'I do,' said Coburg. He looked at Lampson. 'Ready, Sergeant?'

'All ready, sir,' replied Lampson.

Coburg, Lampson, Sergeant Wilson and Constable Appleton walked to the end of Frampton Street, where a small group of police officers were gathered. Sergeant Wilson called one of the sergeants over.

'This is Sergeant Chester, sir,' he told Coburg.

'DCI Coburg,' Coburg introduced himself. 'I want you to join Sergeant Harpson in his car by the rear gates to the property. There's a chance that if anyone comes out of there they may have a gun. But only use your weapon if you feel you have no other choice.'

'I understand, sir,' said Chester.

'You're a veteran of the last war?' asked Coburg.

'I am, sir.'

'Same here,' said Coburg. He held out his hand. 'Good luck to us all, Sergeant.'

'Thank you, sir,' said Chester. He shook Coburg's hand, then saluted him.

Coburg, Lampson, Wilson and Appleton continued round the corner into Orchardson Street. Just short of the pawnshop, Coburg said, 'Right, you two wait here. I'll blow a whistle if we need you.'

The two uniformed officers made for the doorway to a small house and took up their waiting positions, Sergeant Wilson drawing his revolver and holding it ready to use.

Coburg and Lampson made for the door of the pawnbroker's shop. It was locked. Coburg knocked at the door. When there was no answer he knocked again, harder, and then even harder when there was still no response.

'Alright, keep your hair on!' came a man's voice from inside. 'I'm coming!'

The door opened a crack and a man peered out at them. 'We're closed.'

Coburg and Lampson showed him their warrant cards.

'Not any more you're not,' said Coburg. 'Police.'

The man looked at them warily. 'What d'you want?'

'For starters, you can open this door.'

The man shook his head. 'Can't do that. Got my orders.'

'To remind you, we're the police. Now open this door.'

'Can't do that. What do you want, anyway?'

'We're here to talk to Mrs Baxter.'

'Why?'

'We'll tell her that when we see her.'

The man shrugged. 'She ain't here. You'll have to call back later.'

Coburg gave the man a steely glare. 'You're obviously not getting the message. Either you open this door or I kick it open.'

'You can't do that!' blustered the man.

'Want to bet?' snapped Coburg.

The man shook his head. 'This is illegal.'

'No, what *is* illegal is someone stealing an ambulance. Which theft has been reported to us. And said ambulance is currently in your yard.'

The man looked startled at this. 'No it ain't,' he protested.

'Ted,' said Coburg.

Lampson gave the door a hard kick with the toe of his heavy boot and it thudded against the man, knocking him backwards.

Coburg and Lampson strode into the shop.

'It's the law!' shouted the man desperately.

A middle-aged woman appeared from the back of the shop.

'Who are you?' she demanded angrily. 'You've got no right to barge in like that!'

'And you've got no right to have a stolen ambulance in your yard,' snapped Coburg. 'Where are the crew?'

'What crew?'

Coburg sighed. 'Alright, you want to do this the hard way.' He took out his police whistle and blew two long blasts on it. There was a moment's pause, and then Sergeant Wilson and Constable Appleton came running to the scene.

'Arrest this man and this woman,' ordered Coburg. 'Handcuff them and put them in a car.'

'No!' yelled the woman. But the uniformed officers grabbed hold of Ma Baxter and the man and hustled them out to where the cars were waiting. Coburg gestured to Sergeant Wilson, who had his revolver at the ready.

'Right, we're going in. Only use that if our lives are in danger.'

As they made their way through the shop towards the door at the rear, the door opened and Rosa and Doris appeared. The uniforms of both were spattered and smeared with blood.

'We heard the shouting,' said Rosa, hurrying to her husband and throwing her arms around him. 'Thank God you're here.'

Coburg looked at her blood-spattered uniform.

'Are you alright?' he asked.

Rosa gestured at her uniform. 'This isn't from us. It's a boy who got shot.' She gestured towards the rooms at the back. 'I'll show you.'

'Be careful,' warned Doris. 'The other two boys are around

somewhere, and one of them's got a gun.'

Coburg held his hand out to Sergeant Wilson. 'I'll take your gun,' he said. 'If there's any shooting to be done, it'll be by me.'

Sergeant Wilson handed over the revolver. Coburg turned to Lampson. 'You stay here, with Doris. If you hear any shooting, come through.'

Lampson nodded.

'How many of them are there?' asked Coburg as he followed Rosa towards the door at the back of the shop.

'The two other boys and a bloke who works for Ma Baxter,' said Rosa.

'Where are they?'

'I don't know,' said Rosa.

Coburg took hold of her arm and stopped her.

'You stay here, with Ted and Doris,' he said.

'You don't know where the shot boy is,' said Rosa.

'Tell me.'

'It's the first door on your left. He's on a table.' As Coburg took hold of the door handle, she added warningly, 'He's dying. He may even be dead by now. But watch out for the older boy, the one with the gun. He's dangerous.'

Coburg nodded and pulled the door open. As he did there was the deafening sound of a gun being fired and a bullet smashed into the doorframe beside Coburg. Coburg saw a youth waving a gun, bringing it to bear on him, and ducked back from the doorway as the boy fired again. This time the bullet slammed into the side wall of the rear passage, spraying plaster.

Coburg waited, counted to three, then looked around the door and down the passage. There was no one there. The youth had gone, but where? Coburg saw a flight of stairs leaping to an

121

upper floor. He also saw a door swinging loose at the far end of passageway and realised it led to the rear yard.

Two choices: out into the rear yard or up the stairs? The youth with the gun was in one of those two, ready to shoot. But which one?

Coburg stood, his ears alert for any sound, and heard a shuffling from upstairs. But who was it? There were a man and two boys on the loose. At least one of the boys was armed. Was the other also armed? And what about the man who'd been with Rosa and Doris and the shot boy? Was it him upstairs? Was he armed?

Coburg moved quietly towards the stairs and slowly, carefully, began to mount them, intent on not making any noise to alert whoever was upstairs. He kept the revolver ready, finger on the trigger. As he neared the top of the stairs, he heard the shuffling noise again. Someone was in one of the rooms, waiting for him.

Coburg stopped, listening, trying to work out which room the barely audible noise was coming from. There were four doors on the upper landing, all of them shut. Coburg crept along the landing, listening to each door as he passed it. It was as he pressed his ear to the door of the fourth room he heard the tell-tale shuffling from within. He tried the door handle, but the door was locked. Coburg stepped back, raised his boot, and crashed into the room, sending the splintered door flying off its hinges. Immediately a teenage boy rushed at him, then out of the room and down the stairs.

'He's coming downstairs!' shouted Coburg to the police officers below. There was a commotion from downstairs as police officers ran into the rear passage. Coburg ran out onto the landing and watched as the runaway youth climbed over the bannisters and dropped into the passage, then made for the open door into the rear yard. Two big, burly officers leapt on him and brought him to the floor.

'Max!' called the boy in desperation.

Coburg turned and ran back into the room he'd just come out of. He ran to the window and looked out. The youth with the gun was unbolting the pair of large gates.

Sergeant Wilf Harpson was behind the wheel of one of the police cars making up the police blockade in Frampton Road, close to the gates to the rear yard behind the pawnshop. Sergeant Chester sat beside him, holding a revolver in his hand.

'Something's happening,' said Chester. 'Listen to that shouting.'

Suddenly the large green gates swung open and a youth ran out, a revolver in his hand. Harpson started up his engine and aimed the car to cut off the youth's escape route. As he did so he saw the youth raise the gun and point it at his windscreen. There was an explosion, then a bullet skidded off the roof of his car. Immediately, by instinct of self-preservation, Harpson slammed his foot on the accelerator and the car shot forward. Harpson saw the youth's mouth open in panic, then the front of the car hit him at force and he disappeared beneath the bonnet.

Harpson pulled the car to a halt and he and Chester got out, warily watching in case the youth was going to use the gun again. But as Harpson rounded the front of his car he saw there was little chance of that. The youth was mostly under the car, just his head was visible, and to Harpson he had that dead look he'd seen so often: the eyes and mouth open but not focused.

CHAPTER SIXTEEN

Coburg stood with Rosa, Doris and Lampson in the yard beside the ambulance. Ma Baxter and the man with her, who went by the name of Degsy, had been taken to Marylebone police station, where they were being held awaiting charges for kidnapping. The dead bodies of Max and Micky Baxter had been taken to the mortuary at Scotland Yard. Under the watchful eye of Sergeant Wilson, a team of police officers had been left behind to search the yard and the buildings for stolen goods. The rest of the team had been stood down and returned to their stations, with Sergeants Harpson and Chester about to return to their base to write up their statements on how the death of Max Baxter had occurred.

'We'll seal the building and the barns once the search is over,' Sergeant Wilson informed Coburg. 'Because I'm sure we'll have to come back.'

'And Rosa and I had better get this ambulance back to the Paddington depot,' said Doris.

'I don't think you driving is a good idea after what you've been through,' said Coburg.

'We can't leave it here,' said Doris. 'Someone will nick it.'

'And I'm alright to drive,' added Rosa. 'I'm a little shaky, I admit, but I can do it. And Doris will be with me.'

Coburg thought this over, then said, 'Alright, but let us

follow you, just in case you feel you need help. Then after, we'll run you both home. That alright with you, Ted?'

Lampson looked doubtful. 'We've got to take care of charging Mrs Baxter, the other bloke we arrested, and the kid,' he pointed out. 'It's kidnapping and threats of death. I can do it, if you like. I'll grab a lift to Marylebone nick and do the paperwork on them while you run Rosa and Mrs Gibbs home.'

Coburg nodded. 'Thanks, Ted. I owe you one.'

'We both owe you for saving us,' said Doris. 'They were going to kill us, you know. There was no way we could save the boy, and she told us if he died, so would we. And I believe she meant it.'

'Sergeant Harpson will run you to Marylebone,' offered Sergeant Wilson.

Lampson thanked him, then gestured for Coburg to leave the group so they could talk privately.

'After what Rosa's been through today, you ought to stay and look after her,' he said quietly. 'I can do the paperwork on Ma Baxter and the bloke, and the two dead boys, then report to the superintendent at the Yard on what happened.'

Coburg looked towards Rosa and Doris. Despite their outwardly stoic appearances, he could tell both women were badly shaken by their experience.

'Are you sure?' he asked, concerned.

'Absolutely,' said Lampson.

'Thanks, Ted,' said Coburg. 'I'll see you tomorrow morning. Same time as usual.'

Lampson nodded, then set off to find the two sergeants and their car to arrange a lift to Marylebone.

* * *

At Marylebone police station, Lampson sought out the station sergeant.

'My guvnor, DCI Coburg, has told me to do the official charging of Mrs Baxter, the kid, and the man she was arrested with,' he told him.

'Derek Harvey, known as Degsy.' The sergeant nodded. 'We've got them in custody. We're not sure what to do about the kid, Monty, because he comes under juvenile. I'm guessing he'll be sent to borstal to await trial.' He took three forms from a drawer. 'I've drawn up the charge sheets for each of them. All they need is your signature.'

'Thanks,' said Lampson. 'I'll talk to the adults both first, in case there's anything I need to add to their charge sheets.'

'Who do you want first?'

'Mrs Baxter,' said Lampson.

'She's going to be the worst,' warned the sergeant.

'Has she been told two of her sons are dead?'

'No.'

'Then I'd appreciate having a couple of officers in the room with me when I tell her. She looks like the kind of woman who could go berserk.'

'She is,' said the sergeant. 'I'll get a couple of blokes to bring her to the interview room, and tell them to stay.'

'Thanks,' said Lampson.

He walked down the corridor to the interview room. It was a spartan, windowless room, the only furniture a bare wooden table with two chairs, one on either side. Lampson settled himself down on one of the chairs, took out his notebook and a pencil, which he placed in front of him, then waited. After five minutes the door opened and two uniformed constables entered, ushering Prudence Baxter in. Lampson noticed that she was handcuffed. A precaution in case she went on the attack when she heard the bad news, he supposed.

The officers pushed Mrs Baxter down onto the empty chair, then stepped back from her, but not too far, Lampson noticed.

'Mrs Baxter, I'm Detective Sergeant Lampson from Scotland Yard.'

'You're the one who came knocking at my door with that other one. The posh one.'

'DCI Coburg,' said Lampson. 'He's otherwise engaged so I'm doing this official interview.'

Baxter flourished her handcuffed wrists. 'Do I need to have these on?' she demanded.

'Not if you behave,' said Lampson. He looked at her steadily. 'I regret to tell you, Mrs Baxter, your son Micky is dead.'

She fell silent, but Lampson could see the anger and hatred in her eyes.

'Your lot killed him,' she said, her voice low and unemotional, but there was no mistaking the bitterness in it.

'With respect, Mrs Baxter, your son Micky was shot by your son Max. If you'd let the ambulance crew take him to hospital he might have been saved.'

'Those women would have saved him if your lot hadn't turned up. They were trained.'

'They didn't have the necessary equipment, nor the medical skills, to perform the sort of operation he needed. Micky died because your son Max shot him, and because you refused to let him be taken to a hospital where he could have been treated by trained medical staff. Your refusal was why he died.'

She looked at him and her hatred and anger filled her face. He fists clenched together, and Lampson was glad of the handcuffs and the presence of the two police officers.

'I also have to tell you that your son Max is dead.'

At this, she sat bolt upright, and for a moment Lampson thought she was going to launch herself at him. Slowly she brought herself under control. Through clenched teeth she asked, 'How? Who killed him? One of your lot?'

'Max ran out through the gates of your yard into Frampton Street. He took a shot at a police officer sitting in a car who was watching the gates. The officer was forced to take evasive action using the car.'

'He ran him over?'

'Not deliberately. He was trying to stop him shooting at him again, or at anyone else. Unfortunately, the car collided with your son.'

'He killed him,' she hissed, and her eyes were like a snake's now, a venomous and angry snake.

'He didn't have a lot of choice,' said Lampson. 'Your son was armed and shooting at people. He shot at my boss and just missed him.'

'Pity,' she said bitterly. She fell silent, taking this in, then she said, 'So, thanks to your lot, two of my sons are dead.' Again, she fell silent, then she asked, 'What about Monty?'

'He's in custody. He'll be charged with robbery, aiding and abetting in a kidnap, and obstructing the police in the course of their duty. Most likely, because of his age, he'll be remanded to borstal.'

She glared coldly at him. 'I'm going to have you for this. You and your boss. For the deaths of my sons. You killed them.

You've no idea how much pain I'm going to put you through.'

'Threats, Mrs Baxter? That'll go on the charge sheet, in addition to the kidnapping and keeping the ambulance crew hostage.'

'They're not threats,' she said icily. 'They're promises.'

'You're talking yourself into a longer prison sentence,' said Lampson.

'I don't care. One day I'm gonna be out and then you and your boss are gonna pay for what you've done to me and my boys.'

Lampson made a note in his notebook then asked, 'Where did Max get the gun from, Mrs Baxter?'

She sat defiantly upright and did her best to fold her arms, even with the handcuffs in the way.

'I'm saying nothing more,' she said.

Lampson nodded.

'Take her back to the custody cell,' he told the two officers.

CHAPTER SEVENTEEN

Coburg, in his police car, followed the ambulance into the yard at Paddington's St John Ambulance station. He parked up and joined Rosa and Doris as they walked towards the office, just as Chesney Warren came out. Warren looked at the two women's blood-saturated uniforms in horror.

'My God!' he exclaimed.

'It's alright, it's not ours,' said Doris. 'It's from a boy we were forced to take on board.'

'At gunpoint,' added Rosa. She pointed to the ambulance. 'He also shot the radio, so that'll need replacing.'

'What happened?' asked Warren.

Between them, Rosa and Doris filled him in on their adventure.

'Luckily, as a result of your phone call, we were able to find them,' Coburg told Warren.

'And the boy?' asked Warren.

'He's dead,' said Coburg. 'As was the boy who shot him, his brother.'

'My God!' said Warren.

'With your permission, Mr Warren, I'll run Doris and Rosa home,' said Coburg. 'They've had a shocking day.'

'Of course,' said Warren.

'No,' said Rosa. 'We're alright, and we're needed.'

'If we went home we'd only brood about it,' added Doris. 'Better to be working.'

'I know you feel that way at the moment,' said Warren. 'But you need to recover from your ordeal.' When he saw that they were about to argue with him, he pointed at the ambulance and said, 'And your ambulance is going to need checking over, if he shot the radio out.'

'Mr Warren's right,' said Coburg. 'You're going to need another ambulance. At least until this one's been repaired and checked out.'

Doris and Rosa looked at one another, then Doris said, 'Alright. But we'll be in tomorrow, and we'll take another ambulance while this one's being sorted out.'

When Rosa saw that Warren was about to protest, she said firmly, 'We need to be working. If we're at home, all we'll do is relive it.'

Warren looked at the firm expressions on both women's faces, then nodded. 'Very well. I'll arrange another vehicle for you for the morning.'

'Thank you,' said Doris.

Rosa looked at Coburg. 'You can take us home now, Edgar,' she said.

Lampson sat in the same interview room where he'd talked to Prudence Baxter. This time the person facing him across the table seemed far less of a potential threat to him, or to anyone else for that matter. Degsy Harvey was an ineffectual-looking man in his fifties, wearing old clothes that had been badly mended. His long thin hair hung down either side of his thin face. He looked to Lampson like one of life's losers, the type who gets kicked around and can't muster the courage to fight back.

'Derek Harvey,' said Lampson. 'You are charged with kidnapping two members of St John Ambulance and making threats of death against them. You are also charged with aiding and abetting a gunman who was shooting at people.'

'He's just a kid.'

'Was,' said Lampson.

Degsy frowned. 'Was?' he repeated.

'Max is dead.'

Degsy stared at him, shocked. 'Does his mum know?'

Lampson nodded. 'I told her.'

'And Micky? The one who was shot?'

'He's dead, too.'

Degsy sagged on his chair. 'She'll go mad,' he said.

'She could have stopped it,' said Lampson. 'If she'd let the ambulance crew take him to hospital. You, too. You could have saved him if you'd let them take him to where he could get proper treatment.'

'She wouldn't let me,' said Degsy.

'Who's the other man who was with you at the yard?'

'What other man?' asked Degsy.

'Oh come on,' scoffed Lampson. 'There were two of you. We caught you but the other one scarpered.'

Degsy shook his head. 'No idea what you're talking about,' he said.

Lampson looked at him levelly. 'You are being charged with offences that could end up with you being in prison for a very long time. If you've got any sense you could get the length of time you spend in jail reduced by being helpful. So let's start with this one: who's the other man who was with you at the yard?'

Again, Degsy shook his head. 'There wasn't anyone else. Now, do I get a solicitor?'

Lampson signed the charge sheets for Prudence Baxter, Degsy Harvey and Monty Baxter and handed them to the station sergeant.

'Keep them in custody overnight,' he said. 'My guvnor will be in tomorrow morning and he'll be in touch. My gut feelings is he'll sort out a solicitor for them if they don't have one of their own, and after that he'll say to put them in jail on remand, but I don't want to second-guess him in case he decides different. After all, it was his wife who was kidnapped and threatened with death.'

The paperwork done, Lampson grabbed a lift with a car that was being sent to Scotland Yard. When he got back to the office, he found a message for DCI Coburg from Dr Welbourne asking him to contact him, with a telephone number at University College Hospital.

'Dr Welbourne,' said Lampson. 'It's DS Lampson, DCI Coburg's sergeant. I'm afraid Coburg's away for the rest of the afternoon.'

'That's no problem, Sergeant,' said Welbourne. 'I'm just getting back to him about that pair of boots he sent me. There's no trace of blood on them. They weren't the ones used to kick the young RAF cadet to death.'

'He might have cleaned them?' suggested Lampson.

'He might, but there's usually some vestige left. That's not the case here. Sorry.'

Lampson hung up, then made for Superintendent Allison's office.

'Sorry to trouble you, sir,' he said, 'but DCI Coburg wanted me to inform you about an event that happened today that we were involved with.'

'What sort of event?' asked Allison.

'A robbery followed by a kidnapping and siege, which resulted in the deaths of two teenage boys.'

The superintendent looked at Lampson, shocked.

'Deaths?' he repeated.

Lampson related the events of the afternoon to him in detail, closing with: 'So DCI Coburg has taken his wife and the other St John Ambulance crew member home to recover.'

'Coburg's wife was actually taken hostage?'

'Yes, sir. At gunpoint. He should be at home now if you'd like to talk to him, sir. But he'll be in tomorrow morning. He said he'll see you then.'

'That'll be fine, Sergeant,' said Allison. 'Fortunately, it ended well.'

'Except for the deaths of the two boys, sir.'

'Of course. I was referring to the safety of the two poor women and the police officers involved. It could have been a complete tragedy on their parts. You and DCI Coburg are to be congratulated on managing a very difficult situation.'

'Thank you, sir, but it was primarily at the direction of the chief inspector, along with vital assistance from Marylebone station.'

Lampson then returned to the office and telephoned the chief inspector at his flat to update him.

'Ma Baxter, Monty Baxter and Degsy Harvey have all been remanded in custody through Marylebone,' Lampson told him. 'I signed the paperwork, but Marylebone would be grateful for a call from you tomorrow with instructions about legal representation and all that sort of stuff.'

'No problem,' said Coburg. 'I'll deal with that as soon as we get in tomorrow. Thanks, Ted.'

'One other thing: Dr Welbourne has made his report on Huxton's boots. He says there are no traces of blood on them.'

'He could have cleaned them.'

'That's what I said, but Dr Welbourne says they weren't the ones that killed that RAF cadet.'

'So, another dead end,' said Coburg ruefully.

'What do you want me to do about Huxton?'

'Keep him in custody overnight,' said Coburg. 'He's involved in the cadet's death, even if he didn't do it himself. I'll sort that out tomorrow.'

'You're going to be busy tomorrow,' said Lampson. 'I also filled in Superintendent Allison on what happened at Marylebone today. I told him you'd see him tomorrow in case he's got any questions.'

'Alright, Ted. Thanks for everything. I'll see you in the morning at the usual time.'

'How's the missus holding up?'

'Very well,' said Coburg, 'considering what she's been through.'

'She's a warrior, that one,' said Lampson.

'She is,' agreed Coburg.

* * *

'What was that about me?' asked Rosa as Coburg replaced the receiver.

'You're a warrior, according to Ted Lampson,' Coburg told her. 'I was just agreeing with him.'

The telephone rang and Coburg picked it up.

'Coburg,' he said.

'You're supposed to say your number,' reprimanded Magnus. 'Otherwise people might think they haven't got through to the right person.'

'How many people do you telephone called Coburg?' asked Coburg, slightly piqued.

'I'm just making a point,' said Magnus. 'We wondered if it was convenient for Malcolm and I to call round? We think we've got some information about the murder of Desmond Bartlett.'

'Oh?'

'Which I'd rather not talk about on the telephone. People listen in.'

'By all means. When do you want to call?'

'Now, if that's convenient.'

'We look forward to seeing you. We'll put the kettle on.'

He hung up, and Rosa asked, 'Magnus?'

'It seems he and Malcolm have some information about Desmond Bartlett.'

'The cricketer who was murdered?'

'Yes, but he doesn't want to talk about it over the phone.'

'It sounds like he might have the name of a suspect.'

'Yes, it does. I just have to hope it's something, because we're going around in the dark at the moment.'

'You've got the man who killed that air cadet.'

'Who we *think* killed him.'

'You're not sure?'

'In all probability he did, and his defence story is so ludicrous it's laughable. But I actually get the impression he might be telling the truth. Although, with some people, they're convinced it's the truth, even though all the evidence is against it.' He looked at Rosa, concerned. 'You're sure you're alright about this, Magnus and Malcolm coming after the dreadful experience you've had today?'

'Yes,' she said. 'But I'd rather not tell them about it. Let's just hear what they have to say.'

Coburg nodded. 'If that's what you'd prefer.'

'It is,' she said.

CHAPTER EIGHTEEN

Magnus and Malcolm settled themselves down on the settee, sipping at the cups of tea they'd been served.

'We've been doing some asking around,' said Magnus, 'and one of the stewards at Lord's mentioned that Desmond and some of the other players in the Empire XI have come under a bit of pressure of late from an illegal bookie who's operating in the area.'

'This wouldn't be a certain lance corporal in the RAF, would it?'

'What? Good God, no. Absolutely not.' Magnus sounded shocked at the suggestion. 'I'll let Malcolm tell you because he was the one who got the story from the steward.'

'The steward's name is John Evans,' said Malcolm. 'According to him, threats have been made to some cricket players by thugs who work for an illegal bookmaker called Jimmy Webster. In particular, these thugs have been pressuring those playing for the Empire XI, offering them bribes to get bowled or caught out, or miss catches.'

'Why?' asked Coburg. 'I would have thought that cricket was one sport where this sort of thing didn't happen. We all know that fixing is rife in horse-racing and boxing, and there have been some dubious results in football matches, even in snooker and billiards, where the bookies have cleaned up as a result.'

'Yes, but these are different times,' said Magnus. 'Most of the big sporting events have been cancelled since the war started. In football there's been a ban on long-distance travel to save fuel for the war effort, and also many professional footballers have left their clubs to enlist in the armed services.

'All tennis tournaments have been suspended, even Wimbledon. The World Snooker Championship suspended. All professional boxing tournaments have been replaced with inter-services boxing competitions, like the navy versus the army. All major athletic events have been cancelled. There are no professional golf tournaments, and even horse-racing has been taken off the calendar with the big races, like the Grand National and the Cheltenham Gold Cup, both cancelled.

'Evans told me that all of this has drastically affected the gambling industry,' said Malcolm. 'Especially the illegal off-course bookies. As you said, these bookies have been known to fix matches and races, but the current climate makes things much harder for them to do this. It's become harder to fix boxing because, with no professional boxing, the inter-services tournaments are about military pride, with one service against another, rather than money. Horse-racing is erratic, with meetings being cancelled. It seems the series of one-day matches being played by the British Empire XI offers the crooked bookies such as Webster a real opportunity to "fix" matches.'

'You still haven't said how Desmond Bartlett figures in all this,' said Coburg.

'According to Evans, Bartlett was one of the players who

Webster's people leant on to try to fix a match: miss a catch, bowl a foul ball, that sort of thing. Evans got on well with Bartlett, they often used to chat, and when Evans noticed that Bartlett seemed worried, he asked him what was going on, and Bartlett told him about the threats he'd had if he didn't comply. There was talk of breaking his fingers, which, for a cricketer, would have been a career-finisher.

'Evans advised Bartlett to go to the police. Bartlett told Evans he'd done just that, reported these threats to the station sergeant at St John's Wood. But the station sergeant dismissed his complaint.'

'Was this station sergeant called Eric Webster?'

'Yes,' said Magnus. 'According to Evans, he's the brother of the illegal bookie, Jimmy Webster.'

'My God,' exclaimed Rosa. 'It's blatant corruption!'

'Do you know this Sergeant Webster?' asked Malcolm.

Coburg nodded. 'I met him when I went to St John's Wood to see if they had any more information about Bartlett's murder.'

'You see why we had to come and see you and tell you face to face, rather than over the phone,' said Malcolm.

'Have any other players been threatened by this Jimmy Webster's thugs?' asked Coburg.

'I don't know. Evans didn't tell me about any others, and we were concentrating on Bartlett.'

'Is this steward, Evans, prepared to give evidence in court against the Webster brothers?' asked Coburg.

'I don't know,' said Malcolm unhappily. 'He only told me about this because he felt guilty about what happened to Bartlett. He wondered if he'd said anything before, Bartlett might still be alive. But I could tell he's frightened for his own safety.'

'I need to talk to Evans,' said Coburg.

'The problem with that is, once it's known that Evans has been talking to the police, the same might happen to him as happened to Bartlett. Is there a way round it? A way you can dig about, but without Evans being named.'

'I'll do my best,' said Coburg. 'The last thing I want is anything bad to happen to Mr Evans.'

Malcolm nodded. 'In that case, if you can come to Lord's tomorrow morning, I'll introduce you to him.'

'Thank you,' said Coburg. 'Would eleven o'clock be alright? I've got a few things to attend to first at Scotland Yard.'

'Eleven will be fine,' said Malcolm. 'I'll see you at Lord's.'

'One other thing,' said Magnus. 'You asked me about Bartlett's private life, to see if there were any skeletons in his cupboard. As far as Malcolm and I could find out, Bartlett led a completely blameless life. He didn't drink, didn't womanise, just played cricket and was very popular with his comrades.'

After Magnus and Malcolm had left, Coburg and Rosa settle down with a sandwich and a bottle of wine.

'We could always go out for a meal, if you'd prefer,' suggested Coburg.

'No thanks,' said Rosa. 'After what we've been through today, I need to feel safe and secure here in our own home.'

'Until the air raids start,' said Coburg ruefully.

'If they do, we've got the air raid shelter in the basement,' said Rosa.

'I fancy it's more *when*, rather than *if*,' sighed Coburg.

* * *

Lampson looked at his watch. Half past five. It was good that today he'd been able to get away from Scotland Yard at a reasonable time. It meant he'd be able to spend more time with Terry. Too often lately he hadn't been able to get to his parents' flat to collect his son until half past six. Then it would be a case of hurrying home to give him his tea – although usually Mrs Lampson had given Terry something to eat when he came home from school – and then settle down to look at the newspapers together, and sometimes listen to the wireless if there was a comedy programme on. Since he and Eve had got engaged, Eve often came round to spend the evening. For Lampson, this was great, because she had a special affinity with Terry. They'd talk about things that had happened at school, with the pair of them laughing at something particularly ridiculous that had struck them that day. This had come as a great relief to Lampson, who'd worried how Terry would react to his father marrying his schoolteacher, especially as she had a reputation as a tartar in the classroom, a real dragon. But once Terry had realised that Eve wasn't a dragon at all, but a lovely human being with a similar sense of humour to his own, everything had been fine. No, better than fine.

He turned a corner into the street where his parents' block of flats was situated, and found his way barred by three tough-looking men. He heard a noise behind him and turned to see a fourth had appeared behind his back.

'Ted Lampson, I presume,' said one of the men, a scornful look on his face.

'Who wants to know?' demanded Lampson, tensed for trouble.

'Someone who's got an interest in you,' said the man.

'What sort of interest? And who is he?' And Lampson looked around for any person who might be lurking nearby, watching.

'Oh, he's not here. Not in person. More in spirit,' said the man. 'He sent us to give you a message.'

'It needs four of you to give me a message?' said Lampson sarcastically.

'He thought it might need that many to drive it home,' said the man.

'Alright then,' said Lampson. 'What's the message?'

He heard a rustle behind him, then the man at his back had grabbed the collar of his coat and pulled it down, trapping his arms. At the same time, two of the men in front of him had stepped forward and taken hold of his arms. Instinctively, Lampson kicked out as the two other men moved towards him, catching one in the knee. The man let out a cry of pain and sank to the ground.

'Naughty, naughty,' said the man who'd done all the talking. 'Hold him, fellas.'

One of the men took hold of Lampson's hair and pulled his head up, and the man who'd done all the talking smashed his fist into Lampson's face. He then proceeded to pile punches into Lampson's chest and brought his leg up to knee Lampson in the groin, but Lampson saw it coming and managed to get his thigh in the way.

Another punch struck him full in the face, then another, and blood spurted from his nose and a cut above his eyebrow.

'The message is,' grated the man, 'no wedding for you to Eve Bradley.' With that, the man delivered another full-blooded punch to Lampson's stomach, doubling him over in pain. 'Vic Tennant says so.'

The man nodded to the other three, who released Lampson and let him fall to the pavement. As Lampson lay on the ground, the man kicked him savagely in the ribs. 'Just so you don't forget the message.'

With that, the four men walked away, leaving Lampson lying on the pavement.

Bert Lampson was playing draughts with his grandson when he heard the knocking at the door.

'I wonder who that is?' he said.

'It'll be Ted,' said his wife.

'No, Ted's got his own key,' said Bert.

'I'll go,' said Terry, and he started to move towards the door, but his grandfather stopped him.

'No,' said Bert. 'It could be strangers, and I'm always wary of opening the door to people we don't know.'

Bert headed for the street door and opened it, and as he opened it, his son fell into the house and lay on the floor. Bert looked down in horror at his son's blood-streaked face.

'Ted!' he called. 'What's happened?'

'Dad!' shouted Terry in alarm, as he came into the hallway.

Alerted by the sound of upset, Mrs Lampson came hurrying to the door.

'Oh my God!' she cried out as she saw the state of her son.

Bert Lampson lifted his son up, but he couldn't manage to get him far enough off the ground to be able to carry him.

'Take his feet,' he told his wife. Then, to Terry: 'Hold him under his right arm; I'll take the other. We'll drag him into the living room.'

Once they'd got Ted fully into the hallway, Mr Lampson

pushed the street door shut. They managed to haul his heavy body along the passageway and into the sitting room, where they manoeuvred him onto the sofa and laid him out.

Mrs Lampson hurried to the kitchen to collect her first aid box, in which she kept a variety of liniments and ointments, along with rolls of bandages of different sizes.

'What happened?' demanded Bert Lampson.

'I had an accident,' muttered Ted through blood-soaked lips.

'Oh, come on!' snorted his father in blatant disbelief. 'Who did it?'

'He'll talk later,' said Mrs Lampson. 'Let me get to work and patch him up. Terry, go and get a damp flannel from the kitchen. Make sure you use warm water from the kettle. Not hot, warm.'

'Right, Nan,' said Terry, and he scuttled off to the kitchen.

Bert Lampson looked at his badly beaten son, a look of thunderous anger on his face.

'Someone's gonna pay for this,' he said vengefully.

The wail of air raid sirens echoed eerily through the streets around and along Piccadilly. Coburg and Rosa picked up the bags left by their flat door into which they'd put provisions to get them through their time in the shelter in the basement of their block of flats.

'At least we don't have to hurry through the open streets like the majority of people,' said Rosa as they descended the stairs.

'We're also lucky where we are,' added Coburg. 'I can't help but think about the people living in the docklands area in the East End, which seems to be the Luftwaffe's favoured target.'

'And anyone living near a major railway terminal,' said Rosa. 'Like Ted and his family in Somers Town, right next door to Euston, St Pancras and King's Cross. I think, if that was us, I'd suggest moving somewhere safer.'

'People in those places can't afford to,' said Coburg.

As they reached the ground floor, the door of one of the flats opened and John and Isobel Whitcombe appeared, also carrying bags laden with supplies.

'Here we go again,' said John Whitcombe. Proudly, he held up one of the bags. 'I've got something here to keep us entertained. A friend sent me this new board game from America. It came out over there just a couple of years ago and there's talk of them producing it in Europe, but for the moment we've got one of the first in this country. It's called Criss-Crosswords, and it's amazing. You're going to love this!'

Ted Lampson and his parents and Terry made their way towards the air raid shelter deep beneath the Maples furniture repository. Every step was painful for Lampson.

'You three go on,' he urged his parents. 'I'll catch up with you.'

'Not likely,' said his mother firmly. 'We stay together.'

She'd treated the cuts and bruises on his face with a purple antiseptic lotion, and strapped his ribs with rolls of thick bandage.

'Put your arm round my shoulder,' his mother ordered. To her husband, she said, 'Bert, you keep hold of Terry. Terry, hold on to your grandad's hand.'

'I'm too heavy,' protested Lampson.

'You're not too heavy for me,' said Mrs Lampson. 'I'm your mother.'

Lampson groaned but put one arm across his mother's shoulders, doing his best to keep from putting pressure on her. His father appeared on his other side and slipped his son's other arm over his shoulder, while keeping a firm hold on Terry with his other hand.

'There's no need,' protested Lampson.

'Walk, don't talk,' said his father curtly.

They were able to increase their speed enough to get to the entrance to the shelter. Just as they did there was a series of explosions behind them. Terry turned to look back.

'It looks like Euston station's been hit,' he informed the others.

'Walk, don't talk,' repeated Bert Lampson, and he jerked Terry's hand to urge him into the shelter.

Inside, one of the first people they saw was Eve, standing watching the entrance anxiously. She hurried towards them, then stopped, a look of horror on her face as she saw the livid purple paint on Lampson's.

'What's happened to you?' she asked.

'I had a bit of an accident,' said Lampson.

'Cuts and bruises,' explained Mrs Lampson. 'I put some stuff on 'em.' She looked around, then asked, 'Is your mum here?'

'No. She's gone to Vic Tennant's house. He's got a shelter there now. He had his blokes put one in.'

'You didn't go?' asked Lampson.

Eve shook her head. 'No. I knew you wouldn't want to go there, and my place is where you are.' She looked at his injured face and asked, 'What happened?'

'Like I said, I had an accident.'

'No, he didn't,' said Bert Lampson. 'Someone did it to him, but he won't tell us who.'

'But he'll tell you,' said Mrs Lampson. 'At least, he ought to. You'll be husband and wife in ten days, and married people shouldn't have secrets from one another.' She then looked accusingly at her husband and said pointedly, 'At least, they're not supposed to.'

'When did I ever hide things from you?' demanded Bert Lampson indignantly.

'Plenty of times,' retorted Mrs Lampson. She took hold of Terry and said, 'Come on, Terry. Let's find a spot. And you, Bert. Leave this pair to talk.'

Eve and Lampson watched Lampson's parents guide Terry through the crowd in the basement.

'Your mum's wonderful,' said Eve.

'Yes, she is,' agreed Lampson.

Eve ushered Lampson to a spot where there was an upturned wooden box.

'This'll do,' she said, sitting down.

Lampson sat down beside her.

'Right,' she said. 'Talk. Who did it?'

'I ran into some of the blokes who work for your precious Vic Tennant,' said Lampson bitterly.

'He's not my precious,' said Eve sharply.

'Alright, your mum's,' Lampson corrected himself. 'But he wants to be yours. Anyway, these blokes said they had a message from Tennant. Don't marry Eve Bradley, they said. And, to reinforce it, three of them held me while the fourth went to work on me.'

Eve looked at him, shocked.

'Are you sure?'

'They quoted his name at me to make sure I knew who the message was from,' said Lampson.

'You've got to report it to the police,' said Eve angrily. 'Have them put in jail. All of them. Including Vic Tennant.'

'It won't happen,' said Lampson. 'The blokes who did it will deny it, so it'll be my word against four of them. Tennant wasn't even there.'

'But you can't let them get away with this!'

'I don't intend to,' said Lampson harshly.

'No, Ted,' said Eve. 'If you take the law into your own hands, you'll be the one who goes to jail.'

'I'm not going to do anything stupid,' Lampson assured her. 'Trust me, I'm a copper. I know the law.'

'So what are you going to do?'

He looked thoughtful. 'I'm thinking about it,' he said.

'So am I,' said Eve. 'And tomorrow I'm moving out of my mum's house. I'm having nothing to do with Vic Tennant ever again. I've already told my mum to tell him I don't want him coming round; well, now I'm telling her I never want to see him again, and this will make sure of that.'

'Where will you go?' asked Lampson.

'I've got a cousin, Betty, who's got a flat in Camden Town. I've always got on with her. She'll let me stay there. After all, it's only for just over a week. Saturday the 22nd we get married, and then I'll be in your house with you.'

'You could always move in before,' suggested Lampson.

She shook her head. 'People will talk.'

'Let them.'

'No. It won't be right for Terry, and we don't want our

married life to start off on the wrong foot. He's important to you, and so he's important to me.'

Lampson nodded. 'Alright, but your mum ain't gonna like it.'

'That's her problem,' said Eve.

CHAPTER NINETEEN

Thursday 13th March

With the all-clear sounding, and daylight filtering in through the landing windows, Coburg and Rosa mounted the stairs to the top landing and their flat.

'If I never see another game of Criss-Crosswords, I'll be very happy,' moaned Coburg.

'I enjoyed it,' said Rosa. 'I thought it was fun.'

'It'll never catch on,' prophesied Coburg. 'Not over here, anyway.'

He put the key in their door and they walked in to a scene of devastation. The windows of their flat had been blown in by a bomb blast and glass was scattered across the floor and the furniture of their living room.

'Bastards!' said Coburg angrily. 'Well, that's blown my day. By the time I've cleared all this up and got hold of a glazier, I can forget about work. I'd better phone Malcolm and let him know our meeting this morning is off.'

'No,' said Rosa firmly. 'You need to see this steward. You've got a murder to solve and the longer you leave it, there's less chance of you catching whoever did it. Plus, you've got the charging of the people who were involved in kidnapping me and Doris yesterday, which you said you needed to do this morning. And then there's the airman you suspected of killing the air cadet to deal with.'

'But the mess here and getting the windows fixed . . .' protested Coburg.

'The managing agents will arrange that,' said Rosa. 'That's what we pay them for.'

'I suppose so,' said Coburg grudgingly.

'You go to work and I'll phone them as soon as their office opens.'

'What about your work?'

'You heard Mr Warren yesterday; there's no guarantee he'll have another ambulance for us, and ours has got to be repaired. I'll phone him and let him know what's happened, and I'll be in late. Now clear some of this broken glass off the table so I can fix breakfast, and then you can get off to Somers Town and pick Ted up and get to work.'

When Coburg pulled up outside Lampson's house to pick up his sergeant, he was shocked to see the bruises and cuts on his sergeant's face.

'My God, what happened to you?'

'Someone sent a small party of blokes to tell me to cancel the wedding.'

'This bloke you told me about, Vic?'

'Yeah.'

'You reported it?'

'No. Vic wasn't with them. I don't know who these blokes were. Vic'll just deny it. He'll have an alibi for when it happened.'

'So what are you going to do?'

'Deal with it,' said Lampson tersely. 'I'm not going to have this toe-rag mess things up for me and Eve.'

'You'd better be careful,' Coburg cautioned him. 'You go looking for revenge, you could end up in jail.'

'I'll sort it out,' said Lampson. 'It was a bad air raid last night.'

'Tell me about it,' grumbled Coburg. 'Our windows were blown in. Luckily we were in the shelter last night instead of in our flat, or we'd have been shredded by the broken glass.'

'You got anyone to replace the glass?'

'Rosa's dealing with it. She's getting onto the managing agents. I picked up something interesting yesterday from Malcolm and Magnus about Desmond Bartlett.'

'Oh?'

'He was being leant on by a street bookie to throw cricket matches.' Coburg told Lampson what he'd heard from Malcolm about the threats. 'It included threatening to break Bartlett's fingers. Considering that's what happened to Bartlett, this sounds very likely. The problem is the bookie, Jimmy Webster, turns out to be the brother of Sergeant Eric Webster at St John's station, and when Bartlett tried to report the threats to him, Sergeant Webster sent Bartlett off with a flea in his ear.'

'And possibly told his brother about Bartlett reporting it.'

'Exactly.'

'What are we going to do about it?'

'We'll have to tread carefully because it involves a senior police officer, so I'm going to talk to Superintendent Allison. Then I've arranged with Malcolm to talk to this steward, John Evans, at Lord's at eleven, after we've got all the other stuff sorted out: Huxton, the Baxter woman, and her last remaining son.'

153

'D'you want me to come to Lord's with you?' asked Lampson.

Coburg shook his head. 'I get the impression from Malcolm that this steward is pretty scared, so I think it'll be better to see him one-to-one, rather than scare him off by us arriving mob-handed.'

They arrived at Scotland Yard and, on the way into the building, Coburg stopped at a newsvendor's stand to buy a paper.

'That piece about Bartlett is in,' he said, showing Lampson the page with the photo of Bartlett, alongside a headline: *Have you seen this man recently?* 'Hopefully it'll prod someone into getting in touch. We really need to find out who Bartlett was staying with over the weekend.'

When they got to their office, Coburg checked for any messages, then made for Superintendent Allison's office, taking the newspaper with him.

'I hear you had a difficult day yesterday,' said the superintendent, gesturing for Coburg to take a seat. 'Not just you, but your wife as well.'

'Yes, sir.'

'How is she now?'

'She's recovered. Thank you for asking. On that score, I've arranged for the three people we arrested, Mrs Baxter, her accomplice Derek Harvey, and her teenage son Monty, to be remanded in prison until they come to trial.'

'They'll need legal representation.'

'Yes, sir. I think that might be likely in the case of Mrs Baxter. According to Marylebone station she's a long-standing criminal. People like that usually have a tame solicitor on call.

If not, I'll arrange for a duty solicitor to attend them.'

He then showed the superintendent the newspaper with the piece about Desmond Bartlett.

'This has appeared, so I'm hoping it might produce some information for us,' said Coburg.

'Yes, Chief Inspector, I saw it,' said Allison, gesturing to the copy of *The Times* on his desk. 'Any further information on that case?'

'Yes, sir, there is. I received information from a very reliable source that indicates the dead man, Bartlett, was being threatened by an illegal bookmaker trying to get him to throw the series of cricket matches the Empire XI is playing. I'm seeing the source of this information at Lord's this morning.'

'Very good,' said Allison.

'The problem is, sir, that this bookie, Jimmy Webster, is the brother of the station sergeant at St John's Wood, Eric Webster; and when Bartlett reported to threats to Sergeant Webster they were dismissed.'

The superintendent looked at Coburg, concerned. 'You realise the implication of this?'

'I do, sir.'

'If it turns out that one of our own station sergeants was complicit in this murder . . .'

'Exactly, sir. It needs to be handled with discretion.'

'Discretion, but with justice at the forefront of our minds. If we have a rotten apple, we have to deal with it. But without publicity. At this difficult time we can't afford to have doubts about the honesty of the police being aired publicly.'

'I understand, sir.'

'What do you intend if you get confirmation of this alleged

collusion between this bookie and his brother?'

'Take them both into custody and keep them here at Scotland Yard, with strict orders to the custody staff that nothing about this must be leaked, especially to the press.'

Allison nodded. 'Very good,' he said. 'What about the air force cadet, the one at Lord's? I believe you have someone in custody.'

'We do, sir, but Dr Welbourne has now cast doubt on whether he was responsible. There's no doubt he threatened him, but I'm not sure if he was the one who kicked him to death.'

Allison fell silent, weighing this up, then said, 'If you aren't able to charge him, you'll have to release him.'

'I know, sir. I'm going to have a last interview with him and see if he changes his story. If not, we'll release him, but under investigation, with orders to remain within the jurisdiction.'

'Right,' said Coburg as he and Lampson walked down the stairs to the custody suites, Coburg carrying Huxton's boots. 'There's just time to have a word with Huxton before I head for Lord's.'

'What about Marylebone?' asked Lampson.

Coburg shook his head. 'I'll have to do them later. Can you phone them and tell them I've been delayed?'

'No problem,' said Lampson. 'Are you planning to release Huxton?'

'We'll see how it goes,' said Coburg. 'But the fact is we haven't got any hard evidence to hold him.'

'I still think he's the most likely,' said Lampson. 'Let's face it, there wasn't much time between the cadet taking a tumble down the stairs, and Ben Wright finding him, not if Wright is telling the truth about when he found him. And I can't think why he'd lie about it.'

The two detectives were admitted to the custody suite and the cell where Huxton was sitting on the bench. Coburg handed the airman his boots, and Huxton immediately put them on and began to lace them up.

'Is that it, then?' asked Huxton. 'Does this mean I can go?'

'That depends,' said Coburg, sitting down on the bench next to Huxton, while Lampson remained by the door. 'Let's say, for argument's sake, you're telling the truth about Rhodes-Armfield. That you didn't kick him in the head.'

'I am!' said Huxton desperately. 'I didn't! He was alive when I left him.'

'So, who did? Bearing in mind there wasn't very much time between you pushing him down the stairs and his billet-mate finding him.'

Huxton scowled. 'If you ask me, you ought to take a look at his billet-mate. That Ben Wright.'

'Why?'

'Well, there was something between them.'

Coburg looked at him inquisitively. 'When you say "something between them" . . . ?'

'No, nothing like that,' said Huxton quickly. 'At least, as far as I know. There was bad feeling between them.'

'What sort of bad feeling?' asked Coburg.

Huxton shrugged. 'I don't know. All I know is that that Sergeant Pringle, who's in charge of accommodation, was approached by Rhodes-Armfield to request a transfer to another billet. I was in the office with Pringle when Rhodes-Armfield asked.'

'Why did he want a transfer?'

'He wasn't specific. Said something about he wasn't getting on with his billet-mate. Said there was bad feeling between them, which was affecting his training.'

Lampson leant close to Coburg and whispered, 'The money. Rhodes-Armfield always on the cadge.'

Coburg nodded, then asked Huxton, 'What did Sergeant Pringle say?'

'He told Rhodes-Armfield there was nothing to be done, that's how billets were allocated and he'd just have to get on with it. Then – and this is the odd thing – Rhodes-Armfield said the reason was because Wright wasn't an appropriate billet-sharer for him, and he had proof.'

'What sort of proof?'

'Rhodes-Armfield never said. Sergeant Pringle said he wasn't interested. Said he only had just over a week left to share, and to get on with it.'

'Did Corporal Judkins know about this?'

Huxton looked uncomfortable. 'He might have.'

'Because you told him?'

'That was one of the reasons he paid me. To keep an eye on the youngsters, find out any weak spots.'

As Coburg and Lampson made for the turnkey's reception desk to fill out the release form, Coburg said, 'I don't think the problem was about Rhodes-Armfield badgering Wright for money, otherwise it would have been Wright asking to change billets, not the other way round. No, there's something else.'

'Corporal Judkins knows,' said Lampson as they signed the

release form and handed it to the waiting turnkey. 'The shifty one.'

'I'll pay him another visit after I've finished with Malcolm and the steward,' said Coburg. 'After all, I'll be at Lord's already.'

The turnkey unlocked the cell and escorted Huxton out of the custody suite.

'You're free to go,' Coburg told him.

'How do I get back?' asked Huxton. 'I've got no money on me.'

'I'll give you a lift,' said Coburg.

Huxton looked doubtful. 'It won't look good, me stepping out of a police car in front of everyone.'

'It's that, or you can always walk,' said Coburg. He turned to Lampson. 'I should be back in a couple of hours,' he said. 'If you need me, leave a message at Lord's clubhouse.'

Lampson returned to their office, while Coburg escorted Huxton up the stairs and out to the car park.

'I didn't do it,' said Huxton again, as they got into the car.

CHAPTER TWENTY

As the car neared Lord's, Huxton asked plaintively, 'Can you stop before we get there and let me out? Then I can just walk in.'

Coburg pulled up a short distance from the cricket ground.

'Remember what I said: don't leave the district,' he warned Huxton.

Huxton got out and walked towards the entrance to the cricket ground. Coburg drove into the cricket ground and parked by the clubhouse, where he found both Magnus and Malcolm waiting.

'I decided to come along as well because John Evans knows me,' said Magnus.

'He knows me as well,' said Malcolm, obviously piqued. 'You just wanted to be nosy.'

'I'm here as a member of the MCC,' said Magnus primly. 'If Evans has any concerns about what he's being asked by Edgar, I can reassure him he's doing his duty to the MCC by answering them honestly.'

The three men entered the clubhouse and Magnus led them to a table where a man in a steward's jacket sat. John Evans was a small, thin man in his fifties, with hair so sparse and thin his pink scalp was clearly visible through it. He looked decidedly uncomfortable at the fact he was about to be questioned by a Scotland Yard detective chief inspector.

'This is my brother DCI Edgar Coburg, Evans,' began Magnus. 'He's in charge of the investigation into the murder of poor Desmond Bartlett. I want you to tell him what you told Malcolm and myself about Bartlett being threatened.'

'Yes, Your Grace,' said Evans. He looked at Coburg and said defensively, 'Perhaps if I'd said something sooner he might still be alive, but when he told me that the police weren't interested, I didn't know who else to suggest he approach about it.'

'I understand.' Coburg nodded sympathetically. 'I know Magnus and Malcolm will have already heard what you have to say, but I'd appreciate it if you could start from the very beginning so I've got all the facts.'

'It was about two weeks ago,' said Evans. 'I noticed that Mr Bartlett seemed unhappy and preoccupied. Which wasn't like him, because he was always cheerful. He was a great joker, always making the others in the team laugh, and the staff here. There was no side to him, he treated everyone the same, whether they were a top-class cricketer or the groundsman, or the people who did the laundry. And he was approachable, not like some. So I didn't think he'd be offended when I asked him if everything was alright, and if there was anything I could do for him.'

'"I'm afraid not, John," he said. And that was a lovely side of him, he always called the staff here by their Christian names, not their surnames, like most people did.'

'Surnames has always been the usual protocol here,'

explained Magnus defensively. Coburg gestured for him to stay quiet.

'Did he say what was troubling him?' asked Coburg.

'He said he'd been approached by a couple of men – thugs, he described them as – who said it would be worth his while if the Empire XI were to lose their next match. Mr Bartlett said he told them that was in the lap of the gods and depended on the wicket. He then started to walk off, but they stopped him. "It also depends if a member of your side drops a few catches, or gets bowled out," one of them said.

'"That depends on the players," Bartlett told them, and the man who did all the talking said, "Exactly. It would be distressing if someone who had the opportunity to earn a few bob by dropping a catch, or getting bowled out, didn't do it when he'd been asked. It could be injurious to his health." The man then looked at Mr Bartlett's hands and said, "For example, it would be a pity if those fingers of yours, that work such magic, got broken. A top-class cricketer needs his fingers. But our boss needs your side to lose their next match."'

'When is the next match?' asked Coburg.

'This coming weekend, against the Combined Services XI,' said Magnus. 'It's here at Lord's, before the team begins to tour.'

'Did they tell Mr Bartlett who was behind this threat?' asked Coburg.

'Yes. They said their boss, Jimmy Webster, was a very influential man who could be very generous if he was happy, or very angry if he was displeased. Mr Bartlett was angry about this, and upset, and even more so because he'd gone to the local police station to report the threats against him, and even named Jimmy Webster as being behind them, but the sergeant at the police station dismissed the threat. He told Mr Bartlett that he knew Mr Webster and he was a respectable local businessman. He then threatened to charge Mr Bartlett with wasting police time.' Evans gave a heavy sigh and shook his head. 'As I say, Mr Bartlett was really upset. He didn't know what to do.' He looked at Magnus. 'I suggested he talk to you, Your Grace. He said he'd think about it, but first he wanted to talk to some other members of the team, see if anyone else had been threatened.'

'And had they?' asked Coburg.

Evans nodded. 'Last week he told me he'd spoken to some of the other team members and discovered that two of them had also been approached.'

'You didn't tell me that when we spoke,' said Malcolm, offended.

'I wasn't sure how much to say, sir,' said Evans.

'Who were the other two?' asked Coburg.

'Tate Babcock—'

'He's Australian,' cut in Malcolm.

'And Bob Appleyard.'

'From South Africa,' cut in Magnus quickly, before Malcolm could speak again.

'But they didn't end up like Desmond Bartlett,' observed Coburg. 'I wonder why not?' He looked at Evans. 'Do you know this Jimmy Webster?'

'Not personally,' said Evans. 'I don't gamble, but I know that some of the staff do.'

'Who, for example?' asked Coburg.

Evans looked uncomfortable. 'I'd rather not say,' he said. 'I don't want to get anyone in trouble.'

'It's a bit late for Desmond Bartlett,' said Coburg gently. 'But it might stop anyone else getting hurt. I need to talk to this Jimmy Webster, which means knowing where I can find him, and what he looks like.'

Evans hesitated, then reluctantly nodded. 'I think Melvyn, the assistant barman, bets with him now and then.'

Magnus got to his feet. 'He's in the stock room at the moment. I'll get him.'

'Thank you,' said Coburg.

As Magnus left, Coburg asked Malcolm, 'Can you arrange for me to see the other two men, Tate Babcock and Bob Appleyard?'

'I'll let Magnus fix that up,' said Malcolm. 'Otherwise he'll accuse me of interfering.'

Lampson caught the bus to Somers Town. His beating by Vic Tennant's thugs, with the threat of more to come if he didn't call off the wedding to Eve, made him angrier than he'd been in a long while. Despite what Coburg had said, he knew there was only one way to put a stop to this.

When he arrived in Somers Town, he walked to the local boxing club where he knew he'd find his cousin, Peter Webb. Bert was a stoker on a blast furnace who worked the late shift and kept his days for training in the ring. Bert was a useful middleweight who'd gained a great reputation when he boxed for St Pancras Boys when he was younger, winning every bout he fought in, and now was working towards a professional boxing career. Lampson found Webb practising on the punchbags.

'Hello, Ted,' Webb greeted him. Then, when he caught sight of the marks on Lampson's face, he let out a whistle. 'What you been up to?'

'I had a bit of a disagreement with some blokes whose boss objects to my getting married to Eve.'

'On what grounds?'

'He wants her for himself.'

'And what does Eve say to that?'

'She's made it clear she's not interested in him.'

'What's his name? This boss?'

'Vic Tennant. He's got a building firm back of Euston station.'

Webb nodded. 'I know it. And he did this?'

Lampson shook his head. 'No, he couldn't punch his way out of a paper bag. He got three of his blokes to have a go at me. Two held me while the third gave me what's for.'

'Bastards. So, what's the plan? A bit of retribution?'

'I hope it doesn't come to that,' said Lampson. 'I'd hate you to get nicked for belting someone, especially with your career in the offing. No, I thought if we made a mob-handed visit to Tennant's yard it might make these blokes of his think twice before they try anything again. It should also make Tennant wonder about the wisdom of doing it again.'

'No punch-up?' said Webb, disappointed.

'Well, that depends on them. If they start anything, whatever we do will be self-defence.'

'True,' said Webb. He looked around the gym. 'In case there's a bunch of 'em when we get to the yard, it'd be a good idea to take a few blokes with us, just to show we mean business.'

'Okay,' said Lampson. 'But let 'em know we're not there to

start trouble, but if they do, we can finish it.'

Webb grinned. 'Sounds good to me, Ted. Let me sort out some likely lads.'

Coburg sat in the members' lounge opposite a very unhappy Melvyn Peake. Magnus and Malcolm were there, too. Personally, Coburg would have preferred to conduct his interview with Peake away from their stern looks, but he had to admit that without their assistance he'd never have got this far, so he resolved to put up with them being there and hoped they wouldn't intervene too much. The main thing he had to do was calm Peake down; he was obviously upset at being quizzed by a Scotland Yard detective chief inspector, and especially in front of a member of the MCC.

'Now, you're not in trouble, Melvyn,' Coburg did his best to reassure the barman. 'It's just that I need to get hold of Jimmy Webster, and I understand you occasionally lay a bet with him.'

'No,' said Melvyn quickly. 'That's illegal, that is.'

Coburg leant forward and looked the man in the eyes, firmly but sympathetically.

'I stress again, you're not in trouble. But you will be if you don't co-operate. All I need you to do is sit in the car with me and direct me to where Jimmy has his pitch. You don't need to get out of the car, just point him out to me. Then you can go. That's all there is to it.'

'Will I be getting him in trouble?' asked Peake, worried.

'Not if he hasn't done anything wrong,' said Coburg.

Peake fell silent, torn by indecision.

'Or you can come with me to Scotland Yard and we can

discuss your job here and what effect it may have on it if you are arrested.'

Peake looked at him, shocked. 'Arrested?' he echoed, horrified. 'You said I wasn't in trouble.'

'And you're not, providing you do this one small service for me. It's up to you.'

'Do I have to come with you?' asked Peake anxiously. 'He'll see me.'

'No, he won't,' Coburg reassured him. 'You'll be in the back seat of the car crouching down. It would help if you tell me where I'm aiming for.'

'The corner of Hamilton Street and Marlborough Place,' said Peake. 'There's a phone box there.'

Yes, thought Coburg, street bookies usually chose their pitch where there was a phone box handy so they could check in with the latest odds, and what was happening at the different venues.

Coburg went to the office and used the telephone to call Scotland Yard. He was informed that Sergeant Lampson wasn't available. Instead, he asked to be put through to the duty sergeant.

'Sergeant, this is DCI Coburg. I need four uniformed officers and a car to come to Lord's Cricket Ground. I shall be in the members' bar.'

'Yes, sir. I'll send them over immediately.'

Fifteen minutes later, three burly uniformed policemen marched into the bar.

'I asked for four,' said Coburg.

'PC Nixon's outside in the car,' he was told.

'Excellent,' said Coburg. 'We have allegations of a street

bookie operating in the area. We'll need two cars. One of you go and join PC Nixon, the other two come with me to my car.' He looked at Melvyn Peake, who looked even more unhappy at the arrival of the uniformed policemen. 'This is the part where you come in, Melvyn,' he said.

They left the members' bar and got into the cars, and within a short time they were approaching the corner where Hamilton Street met Marlborough Place. A man in a camel-hair coat was standing inside the telephone box talking on the phone. Two men stood outside the box, obviously keeping lookout.

'That's him,' said Peake. 'In the camel-hair coat.'

'The other two are his touts, I presume?'

'They work for him.'

'Right, Melvyn, your job here is done. We'll go a bit further on and then you can slip out of the car and head off.'

'You won't use my name?' asked Peake anxiously.

'I have no idea who you are,' said Coburg. He coasted a few more yards, then pulled the car to a halt. Peake slipped out and vanished up a side street.

'Right,' said Coburg. 'Now we pick them up. The bookie comes in the car with me, his two henchmen in the other car.'

'Yes, sir,' said one of the officers. 'Where are we taking them? The local station?'

'No. Scotland Yard. And don't give them time to talk to one another.'

As Coburg drove towards the junction, one of the officers commented, 'You'd think that, seeing two coppers' cars approaching, they'd have been off on their toes instead of just waiting there.'

'Yes,' mused Coburg. 'Interesting, isn't it. It's almost as if the sight of a couple of police cars doesn't worry them.'

The two police cars pulled up beside the phone box. When Coburg got out, the two men on lookout suddenly looked alarmed.

'Arrest them,' ordered Coburg. 'The charge is aiding and abetting an illegal bookmaker.'

As the two lookouts were hustled to the second car, Coburg strode to the door of the phone box and pulled it open. Jimmy Webster looked at him, affronted.

'What's your game?' Webster demanded.

'James Webster, my name is DCI Coburg. I am arresting you on a charge of illegal bookmaking.'

Webster looked at him in disbelief.

'Nark it!' he said. He gestured with the telephone receiver at Coburg. 'I'm on the phone to my wife.'

'Well, tell her you just got nicked,' said Coburg.

He took the phone from Webster and hung it up, then pointed to the waiting car.

'Will you come quietly or do I need cuffs?' he asked.

Webster scowled. 'You're making a big mistake,' he spat.

Coburg took the bookie by the arm and led him to the car.

At the offices of the Railway Executive Committee in the former Down Street Underground station, Jeremy Purslake stared in bewilderment at the photograph of Desmond Bartlett in *The Times*. He reread the text next to it in disbelief. Then he picked the paper up and made for the office where his assistant, Peter Etheridge, was going through some papers.

'Peter, I don't know if you've seen the papers today?' he asked.

Etheridge was a small thin-faced man in his late twenties, dark-haired and clean-shaven and with traces of a Caribbean accent when he spoke, the result of having been born and raised in Jamaica.

'No. I must admit I tend to avoid them,' he said. 'They're always so full of doom and gloom. Is there anything I should know about?'

Purslake produced his copy of *The Times* and showed him the photograph of Desmond Bartlett.

'I remember you said you had a friend coming to stay with you last weekend, a cricketer called Desmond Bartlett.'

Etheridge took the newspaper and as he read the text, his face registered shock and horror.

'"This is a photograph of Desmond Bartlett. He was the victim of a murderous attack, his body being found outside Lord's Tube station on the morning of Monday 10th March. The police are eager to find out where he was staying from Friday 8th to Monday 10th. Anyone with any knowledge of his movements over that weekend, please contact DCI Coburg at Scotland Yard." Dead?' said Etheridge, stunned. 'Desmond's dead?'

'He did stay with you, didn't he?' asked Purslake.

'Er. Y-yes,' stammered Etheridge. 'On the Friday and Saturday night.' He looked shocked. 'They say his body was found outside Lord's Tube station on Monday morning.' He looked at Purslake. 'This is appalling. He left my place on Sunday morning to go to Lord's and told me he'd be going on afterward to the RAF base at Kenley, where was serving, after the practice.'

'We ought to let DCI Coburg know,' said Purslake. 'He's

in charge of the investigation into Bartlett's murder. He telephoned me and told me a man had been murdered and his body found outside Lord's Tube station, but he didn't mention the name of the man. Can I call him? I'm sure he'd want to talk to you.'

'Of course. Absolutely,' said Etheridge. He looked at the newspaper, shocked and stunned. 'I can't believe it!'

CHAPTER TWENTY-ONE

The four blokes who'd attacked Lampson were lounging about in Tennant's builder's yard, along with five more men, when the detective sergeant walked in.

'Well, well, look who's here.' The one who'd done most of the pounding when they'd attacked Lampson smirked. 'Come for a second helping?'

'More of a return bout,' said Lampson. 'With the scores evened up.' He let out a shrill whistle, and Peter Webb and six other men appeared from round a corner where they'd been waiting.

The effect on the men in the yard was one of instant consternation.

'It's Peter Webb and his mates from the boxing club,' whispered one to the others. The others nodded nervously; they were well aware of Peter Webb's reputation, and that of the other members of the boxing club.

The tubby figure of Vic Tennant appeared from the office, obviously worried at this arrival of a bunch of tough-looking men in his yard.

'What's going on?' he demanded.

'Just the man I've come to see,' said Lampson grimly. He pointed to the bruises on his face. 'I've come to pay you back for these. You and the blokes who did it.'

'We was only following orders!' bleated the leader of the thugs urgently. He pointed at Tennant. 'It's him you want, not us!'

Lampson began to stride towards the men, Peter Webb and the boxers following him. Suddenly the men ran for it, rushing out of the gate and into the street, leaving Vic Tennant standing alone and panicking in the yard. As Lampson headed towards him, Tennant ran towards his office, but in his panic he tripped and fell sprawling on the ground.

Lampson glared down at him. 'Get up,' he snapped.

'No! You'll kill me!' moaned Tennant.

Suddenly the fear became too much for him, and he wet himself, urine soaking his trousers.

Lampson shook his head.

'A fine specimen of a man you are,' he sneered. 'I wouldn't lower myself by hitting you, though you deserve it. Just take this as a warning. If you try anything like that again, you will suffer. Not your men, but you. In the meantime, stay away from Eve. Got it?'

The petrified Tennant nodded.

'I said, got it?' demanded Lampson, his voice harder this time.

'Got it,' said Tennant, his voice quavering.

Lampson nodded, then turned on his heel. 'Rights, lads,' he said to the others. 'All over.'

As the boxers followed Lampson out of the yard, one of them could be heard complaining to Webb, 'I thought we was gonna have a scrap.'

'Only if they started it,' Webb told him.

* * *

At Scotland Yard, Coburg handed Jimmy Webster and his two lookout men to the custody officer to be locked up. 'No one's to talk to them except me, when I return.'

With that, Coburg returned to the reception hall where the four officers were waiting for him.

'Right, we now do the next part, which you aren't going to like, but it has to be done.'

'Which part is that, sir?' asked one of the men.

'We're going to St John's Wood police station to arrest the station sergeant, Eric Webster, and maybe someone else.'

The men looked at him, shocked. 'Arrest one of our own?'

'That illegal bookie we've just arrested and locked up is the brother of Sergeant Webster, and there are allegations of collusion and corruption between them in a serious case,' Coburg told them. 'I can't go into details, but it's part of something big.'

'Two cars again, sir?' asked one of the officers.

'Two cars.' Coburg nodded. 'We're not sure who else we'll have to bring in.'

In two cars, they drove in convoy to St John's Wood police station. The first person Coburg encountered as he walked into the station was Constable Riddick.

'Hello again, Chief Inspector.' Riddick beamed. 'What can we do for you?'

'You can accompany two of these officers to one of the cars we've got outside,' said Coburg. 'You're under arrest.'

'Under arrest?' echoed Riddick, shocked. 'What for?'

'Everything will be explained when we get to Scotland Yard,' said Coburg.

He nodded to two of the officers, who took Riddick by the

arms and escorted him out of the station.

'What's going on?' demanded an angry voice. Coburg looked up to see Sergeant Eric Webster looking at him. 'Where are you taking Constable Riddick?'

'To Scotland Yard,' said Coburg. 'Along with you. Eric Webster, I am arresting you on suspicion of corruption and collusion to commit a crime. You don't have to say anything, but anything you do say—'

'Yes, I know the rest,' snapped Webster. 'This is ridiculous.'

Coburg nodded to the two constables, who took charge of Eric Webster and led him out to the waiting cars. A constable who had been in the station at the reception desk looked on, bewildered.

'What's happening?' he said. 'What do we do without the station sergeant?'

'Get someone else to take charge of the desk,' said Coburg.

Once at Scotland Yard, Coburg had Webster and Riddick taken to the custody suite and locked up. He then dismissed the uniformed officers and made his way up to his office. As he walked in, he found Lampson on the phone.

'One moment, Your Grace,' said Lampson. 'He's just walked in.'

He held out the receiver and Coburg took it.

'Yes, Magnus?'

'I've made contact with Babcock and Appleyard. They're staying in separate hotels. I'll give you the phone numbers of their hotels and you can make arrangements to see them. I've told them what it's about, and they both say they'll be pleased to help.'

Coburg thanked his brother, then replaced the receiver.

'Where did you get to earlier?' he asked Lampson.

'I had some business to attend to,' replied Lampson.

'So did I,' said Coburg. 'I've arrested both Webster brothers, plus Jimmy Webster's lookout men, and PC Riddick. Unfortunately, you weren't around, or else you could have taken part.'

'I'm sorry,' apologised Lampson. 'I didn't know.'

Before he could go on to explain, the phone rang.

'DCI Coburg's phone,' he said. Then he held out the receiver to Coburg. 'It's Mr Purslake from Down Street. He needs to talk to you urgently.'

Coburg took the phone. 'Yes, Mr Purslake?'

'Chief Inspector, I've only just learnt from the newspaper the identity of the dead man found at Lord's station. They say he's Desmond Bartlett, the cricketer. Is that right?'

'It is, yes.'

'The story I read said that the police are trying to track his movements from Friday 8th March until the time his body was found early on the morning of the 10th.'

'That's also right.'

'Well, I think we can help you. Mr Bartlett was staying with one of my work colleagues, Peter Etheridge, during that weekend.'

Coburg's heart gave a leap. At last, a lead!

'Is Mr Etheridge with you at the office at this moment?' he asked.

'Yes, that's why I'm telephoning you. When I saw the story in the paper, I remembered he'd told me that me that Mr Bartlett would be staying with him. They're old friends from

Jamaica. Mr Etheridge came to Britain about four years ago and I believe he and Mr Bartlett had kept up a correspondence. I understand Mr Bartlett had been to stay with him a couple of times since he came to England.'

'Is Mr Etheridge a cricketer?'

'No, but he doesn't live far from Lord's Cricket Ground, which is why Mr Bartlett asked if he could stay with him over the weekend while he was there doing some nets practice.'

'Could you ask Mr Etheridge to remain there, please, Mr Purslake. Tell him I'm on my way now to talk to him.'

Coburg hung up and told Lampson the reason for Purslake's call. 'We now know where Bartlett was during the weekend he came to London. He was staying with an old friend of his from Jamaica. It seems that this old friend, a Peter Etheridge, works for the Railway Executive Committee at Down Street, so that's where I'm going.'

Lampson frowned. 'I don't recall anyone black being there when we were at Down Street before, investigating that Russian woman's murder. You sure he's from Jamaica?'

'Maybe he was out when we were there.'

'What about the Webster brothers and Riddick?'

'I'd like you to deal with that while I'm out. Get in touch with their families and inform them that we have them in protective custody as part of an investigation into a case. Assure them that they're safe and well, and ask them if they have a solicitor, as we'll need to get in touch with their representative. They're bound to ask what all this is about, but tell them at this stage you're not allowed to say.'

'And if they get stroppy? I don't think that'll be the case with the bookie's missus, she must be used to him getting nicked, and the same goes for his two lookouts, but the bookie's brother and PC Riddick are a different kettle of fish.'

'If anyone's difficult, tell them DCI Coburg will be in touch with them later. If you need me urgently, I'll be at Down Street.'

As he drove to the former Tube station, now the offices of the Railway Executive Committee, Coburg reflected on Purslake's call. The mystery they'd been unable to solve had been finding out where Bartlett had stayed in London, and who with, immediately before he was killed. At last, there was a breakthrough. Coburg hoped that this Peter Etheridge might be able to fill in the timeline of Bartlett's movements. According to Dr Welbourne, Bartlett had been killed at some time during the Sunday evening.

On his arrival at Down Street, Coburg was taken by Jeremy Purslake to Peter Etheridge's office. Purslake made the introductions, then discreetly left. Etheridge gestured for the detective to take a seat, then said apologetically, 'I'm afraid I'm still quite shaken with this news about Desmond.'

'I can understand, sir,' said Coburg. 'And please accept my sympathies for the loss of your friend. You were friends, I assume?'

'From our teens,' said Etheridge.

'You're from Jamaica, sir?'

Etheridge nodded. 'Yes.' He gave a rueful smile. 'I'm guessing you expected someone black, did you, Chief Inspector? Not all Jamaicans are black. Plenty of us are white. But if we were born on the island, we're all Jamaican.'

'I believe Desmond Bartlett stayed with you on the weekend when he met his tragic end.'

'Just the Friday and Saturday. He arrived on Friday late afternoon and stayed the night, then went to nets practice at Lord's on Saturday, then again on Sunday. He told me he would be heading back to Kenley after nets practice, so he took his bag with his cricket equipment with him and his overnight bag when he left on Sunday morning.'

'May I ask how you knew Mr Bartlett?'

'We both come from Kingston in Jamaica. As teenagers we both went to the same places to listen to the same music.'

'Music?'

'Specifically, jazz. Not only did we enjoy listening to it, we discovered we also liked playing it. Desmond on trumpet and me on drums. It may surprise you, Chief Inspector, but Jamaican music isn't all calypsos, or mento.'

'Mento?'

'The Jamaican version of calypso. Calypso itself comes from Trinidad and Tobago. But for Desmond and myself, the real music was jazz. Jamaica has some great jazz musicians. Do you know Jiver Hutchinson, the trumpeter? Or Leslie Thompson? Another trumpet player and also a wonderful trombonist?'

'That name's familiar. Wasn't he with Snakehips Johnson's band?'

Etheridge smiled. 'You know your jazz, Chief Inspector. But then, you're married to Rosa Weeks. I saw a photo of you two in the papers.' His face looked serious as he said, 'I think I read somewhere you were both caught up in the dreadful bombing at the Café de Paris.'

'Yes,' said Coburg quietly. 'We were talking to Ken that evening before we left.'

'A wonderful musician,' said Etheridge. 'But an ambitious and dubious operator.'

'Dubious?' queried Coburg.

'He joined Leslie Thompson's band, the Emperors of Jazz. In fact it was Leslie Thompson's band that Snakehips took over as the result of some dodgy legal wrangling. Snakehips pushed Thompson out, and they became the West Indian Dance Orchestra. Jiver Hutchinson had been one of Thompson's sidemen, but he carried on with Snakehips and the band.'

'I'm surprised. Ken always struck me as a straight type of guy.'

Etheridge laughed. 'An interesting phrase to use about an openly gay man.'

'I meant in his business dealings. His band stayed with him.'

Etheridge shrugged. 'Yes, well, it's all in the past now. I'm sorry Ken's gone. I liked his music. But ask your wife about Leslie Thompson and Jiver. She must have run into them at some time during her career; she seems to have played with nearly everyone of note.'

'I will,' said Coburg. 'Getting back to Desmond Bartlett, you said he arrived on Friday.'

'He did,' said Etheridge. 'We had this regular routine whenever he arrived. We'd dig out some of our favourite records and then we'd play along to them, Desmond on trumpet and me keeping rhythm on an old suitcase.'

'Did he have his own trumpet?'

'He did, but he left it with me. He preferred to keep that side of him apart from his cricketing world. The sad fact is that many sportsmen seem to be musically tone deaf. There are exceptions, of course. I know some cricketers who are also adept pianists.' He looked inquisitively at Coburg and asked, 'It said in the paper that Desmond had been attacked. In what way? A knife?'

'Not as far as we know,' said Coburg. 'All we know is that he was killed by a blow to the back of his head from a cricket bat.'

'A cricket bat?'

Coburg nodded. 'But before his death he was tortured.'

Etheridge looked at the detective, obviously even more shocked than he had been on discovering that Bartlett had been killed.

'Tortured?' he repeated in bewilderment.

Again, Coburg nodded. 'Three of his fingers had been broken, and there were burns on his upper body, made by a lighted cigarette.'

Etheridge's mouth dropped open, then suddenly he got up and rushed out of the room. Coburg heard a noise from the next room, which sounded like a metal wastebin being knocked over, and then the sound of retching, followed by violent vomiting.

He sat, waiting for Etheridge to return. First, there was the sound of footsteps, then another door being opened and a clonk as the metal wastebin was put down, then the sound of a toilet being flushed, and running water.

Shortly after, Etheridge returned and resumed his seat. He was deathly pale and his eyes red-rimmed.

'I apologise for that,' he said. 'That information caught me off guard. It was completely – and horribly – unexpected.' He gulped, then gave a huge breath out, then in, obviously still recovering his composure. 'I'm sorry,' he said. 'This is the worst possible news. I . . . I think I need to go home. I'll have to explain to Mr Purslake.'

'I can do that for you, if you'd like,' offered Coburg. 'You've had a bad shock.'

Etheridge hesitated, then he said, 'I'd be grateful if you could, if you wouldn't mind. This has hit me rather hard. Please tell him I'll be in again tomorrow.' He stood up, then said, 'He'll give you my address, if you need to talk to me again. It's in Abbey Road, not far from Lord's, which is why Desmond chose to stay at my place.'

He made for the door. At the door he stopped and turned to face Coburg. 'I'm terribly sorry about this. It's so . . . horribly unexpected.'

With that, he left.

CHAPTER TWENTY-TWO

Coburg arrived back at the office to find Lampson beaming. The sergeant pointed at the phone and told him, 'All contacted. No problems with either of the Webster brothers' wives, which suggests to me that Sergeant Webster's missus knows something about what may be some dodgy activities on his part.'

'Collusion with his brother, the bookie?'

'That was my thought.' Lampson nodded. 'The only one I had trouble with was Mrs Riddick. She got in a right strop. Demanded she be allowed to come in and see her husband. She's not at all happy.'

'I'll give her a ring,' said Coburg. 'Have you got her number?'

'She's not on the phone,' said Lampson. 'I had to leave a message with the laundry where she works. She phoned me back from a phone box.' He gave a rueful look at Coburg. 'She's a sharp one. She even reversed the charges.'

'Okay, I'll try her at the laundry.'

Lampson handed him a piece of paper with the telephone number of the laundry on it. 'How did you get on at Down Street?'

'For starters, Peter Etheridge is a white Jamaican. He and Desmond Bartlett knew one another when they were teenagers. They had a mutual interest in jazz.'

Coburg filled his sergeant in on the conversation he'd had with Etheridge, then said, 'The interesting thing was his reaction when I described how Bartlett had died. Being tortured, the broken fingers, the cigarette burns. He ran out of the room and vomited.'

'Vomited?'

'He was so overcome with the shock of it. Perhaps I was too graphic in my description. In fact he was so shaken by it he had to go home to recover.'

'Sounds a bit extreme as reactions go,' said Lampson thoughtfully. 'Were they close, Etheridge and Bartlett?'

'Long-standing friends. Bartlett often stayed with Etheridge.'

Lampson looked enquiringly at his boss. 'What d'you reckon, guv? Lovers?'

'Men often stay with a friend without there being anything like that between them,' said Coburg.

'Yeah, but from how you describe it his reaction was a bit more than just an old pal getting done in.'

'It was unexpected,' pointed out Coburg.

'Yeah, but I could only imagine that sort of reaction from someone who was . . . well, romantically involved,' said Lampson, obviously uncomfortable. 'Anyway, if he reacted like that it indicates he didn't have anything to do with Bartlett's murder.'

'Unless he's a very good actor,' said Coburg. He picked up the phone and dialled the number for the laundry that Lampson had given him.

'Good afternoon,' he said. 'Is Mrs Riddick there? This is Detective Chief Inspector Coburg from Scotland Yard calling for her.'

'I'm sorry, she's gone home,' said the woman at the other end.

'Oh dear. Not to worry, Will she be in tomorrow?'

'She's usually here,' said the woman.

'Would you ask her to call me. The telephone number is Whitehall 1212. Thank you.' He hung up. 'Right, that's us for the day, I think.'

'What about the other two cricketers we need to talk to?'

'I'll phone them when I get home and make arrangements to see them both tomorrow, before we talk to the Webster brothers. The more information we've got on the threats being made to the Empire XI cricketers, the better.'

The telephone rang.

'DCI Coburg,' he said.

'Sorry to trouble you, sir, it's Sergeant Wattis at the reception desk.'

'Yes, Sergeant?'

'We've got a problem, sir. There's a lady here demanding to see you, a Mrs Riddick. She's very angry. She's demanding to see her husband.'

In the background, Coburg could hear a woman's angry voice shouting.

'You'd better get someone to bring her up to my office,' said Coburg. 'We don't want a scene like this in public.'

'Shall I send a WPC up with her, just in case things turn nasty?'

'You think that's likely?'

There was another outburst of shouted abuse directed at the unfortunate sergeant, who said regretfully, 'I'm afraid I do, sir.'

'In that case, get a WPC to bring her up to my office and

ask her to stay. She can escort her out afterwards.'

'Right, sir.'

'This doesn't sound good,' commented Lampson. 'Do you want me to stay?'

'No. You get off. No sense in both of us suffering an ear-bashing.'

Vera Riddick stormed into Coburg's office, a WPC close behind her, and stood pugnaciously glaring at the detective chief inspector, who looked up from the papers he'd deliberately arranged on his desk.

'Mrs Riddick.' Coburg nodded. 'I'll be with you in one moment.'

He made an elaborate signature on one of the sheets of paper.

'Yes, Mrs Riddick,' he said. 'I understand you want to see me.' He gestured to the empty chair on the other side of his desk. 'Do take a seat.'

'You're the bloke who's had my husband locked up?' she demanded angrily, remaining standing.

'Your husband is in protective custody,' said Coburg calmly. Again, he gestured at the empty chair. 'Please, do take a seat.'

'What's that mean?' she demanded. 'This protective whatever it is.'

'Protective custody. It means we are keeping him safe and ensuring he doesn't come to any harm.'

'Harm from who?'

'It's possible there may be people out there who believe your husband has evidence that can be used against them.'

'What evidence? Against who?'

'Will you please sit down,' said Coburg, his tone firmer this time. He waited until she'd reluctantly settled herself in the chair, before saying, 'That's what we're trying to ascertain. I cannot tell you the details, Mrs Riddick, because it's a matter of national security, but we have had information that suggests your husband is privy to details of a criminal conspiracy, although he may not be aware of the full implications. Until we've established the facts, it was decided to give your husband full protection, and the only way to ensure that is by what we call "protective custody".'

'Locking him up!'

'He's safe twenty-four hours a day, guarded night and day. There is no way he can be protected if he was out on the street.'

'He's in prison!' she shouted. 'Jailed, like a common criminal!'

'He's not in prison, he's in the custody suite here at Scotland Yard. We have an investigation currently going on that we hope will get to the truth of the matter very swiftly. That's what I was out doing when you telephoned earlier.'

She fell silent, but looked at Coburg suspiciously.

'What sort of copper are you?' she asked.

'As I've already said, I'm a detective chief inspector.'

'Yeah, but the way you talk isn't like any copper I've ever met. That posh accent. And the sergeant at the desk said your name was Saxe-hyphen-Coburg. What is that? Special Branch?'

Coburg fell silent for a moment, then said, 'I'm afraid there's a great deal I'm not allowed to reveal at this moment because of national security. But I can assure you that things are moving on this case.'

'When will Arnold be out?'

'I have some important meetings connected with the case tomorrow and the day after. It is my hope we can reach a conclusion. Providing I'm assured of your husband's safety, he will then be returned to you.'

She fell silent, studying Coburg carefully.

'Who's after him?' she asked. 'Is it the Germans?'

'As I said, I'm afraid national security precludes me from revealing anything further. But rest assured, we're doing our best to reach a speedy resolution.'

Once he'd got rid of Vera Riddick, Coburg drove to Marylebone police station. He felt bad about not going to the station before, especially as Sergeant Wilson and the team at Marylebone had been so vital during the rescue of Rosa and Doris.

'My apologies for not getting here before, Sergeant,' he said when he walked in and found Sergeant Wilson at the desk.

'I understand, sir. Sergeant Lampson telephoned to say you were held up on another case.'

'Two cases, I'm afraid,' sighed Coburg ruefully. 'I meant to call before to thank you and your team for your excellent work the other day, and to finalise any paperwork that's needed.'

'Sergeant Lampson signed off the remand documents, so they're done. We sent Mrs Baxter to Holloway and Harvey to Pentonville. Mrs Baxter gave us details of her solicitor and we've been in touch with him.'

'Who is it? Anyone I know?'

'Jason Fermoyle.'

I don't know him,' said Coburg.

'He tends to be the mouthpiece for most of the local villains in this patch.'

'What's he like?'

'A pain in the neck. But he's sharp, which is why he earns a good living off them.'

'What about the boy? Monty Baxter?'

'We'd intended to send him off to borstal on remand pending trial, but Fermoyle turned up and started quoting chunks of the Children and Young Persons Act 1933 at us, stating that he had the authority from the boy's mother to act in loco parentis for him and as he was confident of obtaining Mrs Baxter's release shortly he would be bringing a restraining order against us to prevent us transferring Monty anywhere while he was in discussions with the magistrates over Mrs Baxter's legal situation.' He sighed. 'Like I said, Fermoyle's sharp. He knows what he's doing, and the last thing we need is to find ourselves on the defensive against some smart-alec solicitor.'

'Where is Monty at this moment?'

'He's still here. The restraining order is in force for forty-eight hours, so my guess is Fermoyle will be very busy trying to get Mrs Baxter's release early tomorrow.'

'Do you think he'll achieve it?'

'It depends on which magistrate he draws. My guess is Fermoyle will play the grieving mother card. If the magistrate is soft-hearted there's a good chance he'll succeed. If, on the other hand, they're the hang 'em and flog 'em type, he may not.'

When Coburg got home, he made phone calls to the hotel where the two cricketers were staying. At the first, he was informed that Mr Appleyard was out and they didn't know when he'd return.

'In that case I'd like to leave a message for him. My name is Detective Chief Inspector Coburg from Scotland Yard and I'd appreciate it if Mr Appleyard could contact me.' He then gave him the number at Scotland Yard, and at his flat.

He had more success with Babcock.

'Yes, Chief Inspector,' said the Australian. 'Your brother said you'd be getting in touch with me. This is about what happened to Desmond?'

'It is,' said Coburg. 'But rather than talk about it over the phone, I'd prefer for us to meet face to face, if that's alright.'

'Fine by me. When?'

'Is tomorrow morning suitable?'

'Where? Here?'

'I'd prefer to talk at Scotland Yard.'

'So, this is official?'

'It is.'

'In that case I'll be there. What time? Nine o'clock okay?'

'Nine o'clock will be perfect. I look forward to seeing you.'

'Me, too, Chief Inspector. If I can do anything to help you nail the bastard who killed Desmond, I will.'

Coburg hung up and then set about preparing a meal for himself and Rosa. He had intended to take her out for dinner, but decided to stay at the flat in case Appleyard telephoned.

Rosa arrived home just as Coburg was finishing the meal.

'Mmm, that smells good. What is it?'

'Spaghetti with a tomato sauce, seasoned with bay leaves and pepper,' said Coburg.

'My, you're becoming a culinary gourmet,' said Rosa. 'What's the occasion?'

'I remembered you were on a later shift today, so I wanted to surprise you.'

'Consider me surprised,' said Rosa. 'I'll just change out of this uniform, then we can eat.'

When they were seated, eating, Coburg said, 'I met an interesting man today. Peter Etheridge. Desmond Bartlett stayed with him at his flat on the weekend he was killed.'

'Really? How did you find him out? Through the cricketing grapevine?'

'No, it was as a result of that piece we put in the papers that said, "Have you seen this man?"'

'So, is he another cricketer?'

'No, he works for the Executive Railway Committee at Down Street. He's also a jazz fan, as was Bartlett. They knew one another in Jamaica. They used to play jazz together. It seems that Bartlett played jazz trumpet.'

'Really? I don't think I've heard his name on the circuit.'

'Etheridge mentioned another couple of names he thought you might know. Leslie Thompson and Jiver Hutchinson.'

'Yes!' exclaimed Rosa. 'I played with both of them!'

'I thought you might have. Etheridge mentioned something about a dispute between Thompson and Ken Johnson.'

'Ah,' said Rosa warily.

'You know about that?'

'I've heard some things, but I don't know how much is true. I didn't ask because I didn't want to get involved if people were taking sides. I liked Leslie and Ken both, very much.'

'According to Etheridge, Ken joined Leslie Thompson's band, the Emperors of Jazz, then eased him out of it and took it over.'

'I don't think it was that simple,' said Rosa. 'There was more going on.'

'What more?' asked Coburg.

Rosa hesitated, then said, 'Whenever there's a band or any group of musicians, sometimes there start to be differences. Someone doesn't think they're getting the right solo they deserve. Sometimes it's about differences of musical style. Someone wants to play freestyle, someone else wants to play cool jazz. Sooner or later, there's a split, with some of the band going with one of the guys who wants one style, and the others going with the one who wants a different way.' She shrugged. 'It happens. In the case of Ken and Leslie, Ken had the residency at the Café de Paris. Very popular. Leslie was more diverse.'

'Diverse?'

'He began playing with Spike Hughes. Then, a couple of years later, he toured Europe with Louis Armstrong.'

'Armstrong?' said Coburg, impressed. 'He must have been good.'

'He was,' said Rosa. 'Still is. After he left Armstrong's band, he formed his own outfit.'

'The Emperors of Jazz.' Coburg nodded. 'Etheridge told me.'

'This Etheridge knows his jazz,' said Rosa.

'He knows Jamaican jazz,' said Coburg.

'After the split with Ken, Leslie went on to play trumpet with Benny Carter, and then double bass with Edmundo Ros,' Rosa told him.

'He certainly found good company,' commented Coburg.

'As I said, he's a good player. One of the best.'

Rosa finished her spaghetti and gave Coburg a wicked smile.

'I was just thinking,' she said, 'about dessert.'

'I haven't prepared anything,' said Coburg apologetically.

Her smile widened.

'I was thinking of a different kind of dessert,' she chuckled. 'With the air raids, it's difficult to snuggle up in an air raid shelter like we like to. So . . .'

Coburg returned her smile, got up and took her hand as she stood up.

'Now that is a lovely idea,' he said.

At that moment the telephone rang. Coburg sighed.

'Leave it,' said Rosa. 'I expect it'll just be Magnus again.'

'It could be a call I'm expecting about the Bartlett case,' said Coburg. He picked up the phone and said, 'Coburg.'

A man's voice with a strong South African accent said, 'Bob Appleyard. I got a message to call you. I'm guessing this is about what happened to Desmond Bartlett. At least, that's the impression I got from Magnus Coburg, your brother. Although his full name is Saxe-hyphen-Coburg and someone told me he's an earl.'

'He is. And yes, that's right about our family name.'

'So, when do you want to meet?'

'Are you available tomorrow?'

'I'm busy in the morning, but how does lunchtime sound? Say just before noon?'

'Just before noon will be fine. Do you know where Scotland Yard is?'

Appleyard chuckled. 'Everyone knows where Scotland Yard is.'

'In that case I'll see you there tomorrow just before noon.'

He hung up the phone and grinned at Rosa.

'All business over,' he said.

'Time for dessert?' she asked.

He pulled her to him and kissed her. 'Perfect,' he said.

CHAPTER TWENTY-THREE

Friday 14th March

Peter Etheridge looked apologetically at Jeremy Purslake.

'I'm so sorry for the way I acted yesterday, Mr Purslake,' he said. 'Leaving so abruptly like that, without asking your permission, was unforgivable. Completely unprofessional.'

'That's alright, Peter. I do understand. To hear the dreadful details of what had happened to your friend would have shaken anyone. Are you sure you're alright to return to work?'

'Absolutely,' Etheridge assured him. 'The work we do here is absolutely vital to the war effort. The absence of just one person can have a derogatory effect on the efficiency of the train system. I promise you, it won't happen again.'

As Etheridge returned to his own office, he felt laden down with guilt. Guilt for the way he'd abandoned his post the day before, after DCI Coburg had told him the graphic details of how Desmond had been tortured to death, and guilt because he knew he was to a large part responsible. If he'd acted differently, Desmond might even be alive. But Etheridge hadn't foreseen what would happen. He'd trusted someone, believed what they told him, and as a result Desmond had died the most painful death imaginable. The thought of Desmond's broken fingers, the cruel burns on his flesh, and that final death blow once more made the vomit rise in his throat, but he fought to keep it down.

He had to do something. Desmond's brutal death demanded justice, but Etheridge knew he couldn't go to the police, not without putting himself in mortal danger. He knew who'd killed Desmond, and why. The issue now was what to do about it. Nothing he could do would bring Desmond back, but he needed to make sure that Desmond's death received justice. It would not come from the law, so he would have to take steps to make sure it came from him. The person who killed Desmond would have to die, and just as painfully as Desmond had.

Tate Babcock was a tall, tough-looking Aussie who was too large for the wooden chair on which he sat in Coburg's office. He looked at Coburg and Lampson, a grim expression on his face.

'Just to double-check, your brother Magnus said this was connected to what happened to Desmond. Is it?'

'It's possible. We know he was threatened by some men working for an illegal bookmaker who wanted him to perform badly in the matches.'

'If it was them, I'm sorry I didn't hit them harder.'

'You hit them?'

Babcock nodded. 'Two guys, thought they were tough. They stopped me when I was coming from the pavilion after nets practice. At first I thought they were just after my autograph – we get a lot of that. But then they started playing the heavy, telling me it would be good for my health if I managed to drop a few catches, let myself be bowled out. I knew what this was about; I've known it happen with boxers being paid to take a dive. Only these two weren't offering me money.'

'So you hit them?'

'Just to let them know I wasn't the kind of guy who they could lean on and get away with it.'

'You didn't think of reporting it to the police?'

Babcock shook his head. 'Desmond told me how he'd had the same sort of threats, and what had happened when he reported it to the police. They sent him off with a flea in his ear. So I knew that was a waste of time. Anyway, I've been used to sorting things out for myself. So I gave them a look and said, "Are you threatening me?" And one of them smirked and said, "That depends on you." And then he pulled this bike chain from his pocket and sort of flicked it around. So I let him have one right in the mouth. He went cross-eyed and fell over, out cold. That's when I turned to the other one and let him have a boot in the groin.' He gave a harsh grin. 'I'm guessing you call it grievous bodily harm. When the second guy stopped screaming and crying, I held him up against a wall and warned him what would happen to his pal and him if they tried this again, with me or with anyone else.'

'Was this before or after Desmond Bartlett was found dead?'

'Oh, before. But it was after Desmond had been threatened.' He looked thoughtful and added, 'I told Desmond about it, and when I described the men I'd encountered, he said they sounded like the same guys who'd threatened him.'

'You didn't think to report what had happened after you knew that Bartlett had been found dead?'

'Who to? The police? After what had happened when Desmond reported it? Waste of time. Plus, there was a good chance I'd find myself arrested for assault.' He shook his head. 'Let's face it, Chief Inspector, who are the police going to believe? I'm a foreigner, an Australian; these blokes were local.'

'I'm a police officer, and I believe you,' said Coburg.

'You may, but after what happened when Desmond tried to lay a complaint, I wasn't taking any chances.'

'Did you talk about this to Bob Appleyard?'

'Bob?'

'Yes. We understand he was also pressurised by these men.'

Babcock shook his head. 'Not the same ones. Bob told me about it. The guys who approached him didn't threaten him; they offered him money to mess things up.'

'And what did Appleyard do?'

Babcock studied Coburg. 'You met Bob yet?'

'No,' said Coburg. 'I'm planning to.'

Babcock smiled. 'Bob is a big guy. I mean, *big*. With *big* hands. He grabbed 'em both by the throat with his huge hands and gave a little squeeze while he told them what he felt about people who tried to fix cricket matches. Bob is passionate about cricket. For him, it's the purest game there is. It's more than a game, it's a religion for him. And, to make sure they didn't kick him or anything while he was giving them this talk, he stood on their feet. And Bob has got big feet. *Big* heavy feet.'

'Again, he didn't report it?'

'Like I said, Bob had heard what the reaction of the police had been to Desmond when he went to the station. So, like me, he made sure these guys got the message.'

'Did they say who they were working for?'

Babcock shook his head. 'No.'

'You didn't ask?'

'No. Me and Bob just sent our own message. We were sure that message would get passed back to whoever had sent them.'

'We have a couple of men in custody who we suspect may have been involved. Would you mind taking a look at them and seeing if you recognise them?'

'Not at all,' said Babcock, getting to his feet. 'Are you coming to see us in action tomorrow?'

At his words, Coburg suddenly remembered what Magnus had told him about the Empire XI's schedule: their next match at Lord's was to be on 15th March.

'Against the Combined Services XI.' Coburg nodded. 'I'm afraid not, much as I'd like to. This search for Desmond Bartlett's murderer is keeping me occupied six, sometimes seven, days a week. This weekend Sergeant Lampson and I only have Sunday off, but even that's starting to look precarious.'

Coburg and Lampson led the way out of the office and down to the basement and the custody suite.

'This gentleman is here to take a look at some of the prisoners,' Coburg told the turnkey.

'Which ones?'

'Jimmy Webster, Joseph Jackson and Walter Millen.'

The turnkey nodded. 'I'll bring them out and get them to stand outside their cells.'

'Thank you,' said Coburg.

The turnkey took his keys and unlocked three of the cells, called the prisoners out and lined them up. Webster and his two lookouts regarded Coburg and Lampson with contempt, and gave puzzled looks at the big Australian.

Babcock shook his head. 'Sorry, Inspector. Never seen these guys before.'

'Thank you,' said Coburg. He gestured to the turnkey to put the three back in their cells.

'When are you gonna let us go?' demanded Webster.

Coburg ignored him and escorted the Australian back upstairs.

'Sorry it wasn't them,' said Babcock.

'So am I,' said Coburg. 'But thank you for coming.'

'What next?' asked Lampson after Babcock had gone. 'Question the bookie and his brother?'

'Later,' said Coburg. 'After Bob Appleyard has been. In the meantime, I'm going back to Lord's to talk to Corporal Judkins. I need you to hang on here in case Appleyard tuns up early. If he does, do the same thing as we did with Babcock: show him the prisoners and see if he recognises them.' He paused, then added pointedly, 'And no slipping off.'

'It won't happen again, guv,' Lampson promised.

Prudence Baxter was accompanied by her solicitor, Jas Fermoyle, as she walked out of Holloway prison, where she'd been on remand.

'You took your time to turn up,' she complained.

'It wasn't easy to get bail arranged for you,' defended Fermoyle. 'Kidnapping two St John Ambulance people. Making death threats. It was only because I laid it on thick about you losing two of your sons that softened the magistrate at the hearing.'

'What about Monty?' she demanded. 'Where is he? Why haven't you got him out?'

'That's next,' said Fermoyle. 'I got a restraining order stopping the law from moving him from Marylebone nick to a borstal until your case had been heard. Now you're out, we can get Monty out into your care.' He patted his jacket and its bulky inner pocket. 'I made sure I got a court order to that effect.'

Coburg found Judkins in charge of a group of trainees in a workshop and gestured to the corporal to come outside so they could talk.

'We've let your man, Huxton, go,' he told him.

'I know, I saw him. He never done it.'

'He's still in the frame. We're just letting him go for the moment. But you're also still in the frame, Corporal Judkins.'

'Why? I've told you all I know. I wasn't even there when Rhodes-Armfield died!'

'Huxton told you about Rhodes-Armfield going to see Sergeant Pringle and asking for a change of billet because there was bad feeling between him and Cadet Wright.'

Cautiously, Judkins nodded. 'What of it?' he asked warily.

'As a bookie it's in your interests to know what's going on with people who bet with you, especially when they owe you money, like Rhodes-Armfield did. So what did you find out?'

'What about?' asked Judkins, even more warily.

Coburg gave a sigh of impatience. 'Look, Judkins, we've got you bang to rights on the illegal bookmaking. We can have you chucked out of the air force and put in jail. Give me what I want to know or go to jail. It's your choice. What was Rhodes-Armfield's beef against Wright, and what was this proof he said he had?'

Judkins hesitated, then said reluctantly, 'It was nothing to do with the money he owed me. So it's nothing to do with anything between him and me and Huxton.'

'What was it to do with?'

'Rhodes-Armfield said that Wright was homosexual. He had this proof, which was a love letter he found from Wright's boyfriend back home.'

'How did he find it?'

'I didn't ask him. Knowing Rhodes-Armfield, I guess he searched Wright's belongings when he was out at some time, looking for money to nick. He was a right scumbag, was Rhodes-Armfield, for all his double-barrelled name and his posh school accent.'

'Where's Cadet Wright at the moment?'

'He's with his group in the next shop. Corporal Merton's in charge there.'

'Right, you come with me there and authorise Cadet Wright to come out and talk to me.'

A short while later, Coburg was standing in the corridor with Ben Wright, who looked puzzled why he'd been asked to come out from the group.

'I need your boots,' said Coburg, pointing at the boots on Wright's feet.

'Why?'

'We're checking everyone's boots, one at a time. We're starting with you.'

'When will I get them back?'

'Hopefully, tomorrow. After the laboratory's examined them.'

'Why mine?'

'It's a process of elimination. You're the one who found him, so you're first.'

Wright shook his head. 'No. I need my boots. These are the only pair I've got. If I'm caught without them I'll be on a charge.'

'No you won't, because I'll arrange an "excused boots" chit for you,' said Coburg.

'What am I supposed to wear?' demanded Wright.

'Ordinary shoes until you get them back,' said Coburg. 'Let's go to your billet and you can change.'

'I can change and bring them to you later, after I've finished this session,' said Wright. 'It's an important one.'

'Now,' said Coburg firmly.

After getting his boots from the reluctant Wright, Coburg drove to University College Hospital and left the boots for Dr Welbourne, with a note of explanation. He then made for Scotland Yard.

Bob Appleyard had arrived earlier than scheduled, because when Coburg walked into his office he found a large man sitting with Lampson. He was, as Babcock had said, big. Very big. Well over six feet tall and all of it solid muscle, with enormous hands. Appleby stood up as Coburg entered and Lampson made the introductions, and the two men shook hands.

'Thank you for coming in, Mr Appleyard,' said Coburg.

'If it means you can lay hands on the bastards who killed Desmond Bartlett, it'll be my pleasure,' said Appleyard grimly.

Coburg took Appleyard down to the custody suite. The turnkey opened the cell doors, and as the three prisoners came out, Appleyard blurted out, 'That's them!'

Jackson and Millen looked at the big South African, alarmed, and backed away.

'Don't let him near us!' shouted Jackson in panic as Appleyard moved towards them.

Coburg laid a restraining hand on Appleyard's arm. 'You're sure these are the men who approached you about throwing a cricket match?'

Appleyard snarled, 'Am I! You bet! Let me have a few moments with them.'

'No!' wailed Millen, and he darted back into his cell.

Coburg pointed at Jimmy Webster, who looked shaken. 'What about him?' he asked.

Appleyard shook his head. 'No, he wasn't there, just those other two. But if he's the one pulling the strings and was behind it, I'd like a private word with him.'

Webster shrank back and called out plaintively, 'He's not allowed! I demand protection!'

Once the three men had been put back in their cells and the big South African had departed, after being promised that he'd be kept informed of progress on what had happened to Desmond Bartlett, Coburg told Lampson, 'We'll talk to Jackson and Millen first. Let's get as much as evidence against Jimmy Webster as we can before we quiz him. He's a slippery character.'

Jackson and Millen were escorted to an interview room, where Coburg and Lampson faced them across the bare wooden table.

'Jimmy Webster asked you to have a word with the big South African. And you did, and he sorted you both out. We know that because he told us what happened, he identified you, and the way you acted when you saw him confirms it.

However, the Australian said you weren't the ones who tried to pressure him, but it was still someone working for your boss, Jimmy Webster. So who was it?'

They both shook their heads. 'We don't know anything about that.'

Coburg gave a weary sigh. 'This is getting boring,' he said. 'We've got you bang to rights on pressuring the South African cricketer in order to try and make him throw matches. Two other cricketers from the Empire XI suffered the same: the Australian you saw earlier, and a Jamaican. The Jamaican was beaten to death. In my book, the finger points to you. Not for the Australian, but for the Jamaican. So it's murder, and you'll hang.'

'We don't know anything about any Jamaican!' burst out Millen. 'Honest!'

'Then tell us who were the ones who Jimmy Webster set on the Australian. You must know because he beat them up, so word will have got back to you. They're the ones we're looking for. If you don't say, then you two will be the ones swinging from a rope.'

Jackson and Millen exchanged awkward looks, then Millen said, 'Tug Jenkins and Wally Dibbs.'

'And why did Webster choose you two to pressure the South African?'

Looking completely defeated, Jackson said, 'Because, after what happened to Tug and Wally, they told Jimmy they weren't going to do any more. They were both hurt bad.'

'Instead, you got hurt,' pointed out Coburg.

'It wasn't supposed to happen,' said Millen. 'Jimmy told us, after what that Aussie bastard had done to Tug and Wally, not to do any threats involving violence. He told us to try bribery. Which is what we did.'

'We never expected that big bear of a South African to react the way he did,' said Jackson with a groan. 'We was polite. We wasn't violent or threatening.'

'Where do we find Tug Jenkins and Wally Dibbs?' asked Coburg.

'Tugs lives in Paddington and Wally in Warwick Avenue.'

Coburg pushed a sheet of paper across the table to them, along with a pencil. 'Write down their addresses.'

Once they had done so, Coburg passed the paper to Lampson. 'Bring 'em in,' he said.

Fortunately for Lampson, both Tug Jenkins and Wally Dibbs preferred to spend the morning in bed, so they were at home when Lampson and a couple of constables turned up. Coburg telephoned Babcock to tell him they had another pair of men in custody who they'd be grateful if he would come in and take a look at. When Jenkins and Dibbs were brought out from their custody cells and saw the Australian, they flinched, just as Jackson and Millen had done when confronted with the South African, Appleyard.

'That's them,' said Babcock grimly.

'We've never seen this bloke before!' protested Jenkins.

Babcock stepped towards purposely towards them, rolling up his sleeves.

'Maybe I'd better remind you how our last encounter went,' grated Babcock.

'No!' yelled Dibbs in panic. 'He's not allowed to touch us!'

As Babcock moved nearer to the pair and there was no sign

of the two detectives or the uniformed officers making a move to intercept him, Jenkins shouted desperately, 'Alright! Yes, it was us!'

'Thank you, Mr Babcock,' said Coburg, moving to head the Australian off. 'My sergeant will take a statement from you confirming your identification of these two men as the ones who assaulted you.'

'It was him who assaulted *us*!' protested Dibbs.

After Jenkins and Dibbs had been returned to their cells, Coburg asked Babcock, 'You told me before that the description Desmond Bartlett gave of the two men who intimidated him sounded like the men who had tried the same with you, these two. Having seen them again, does that still stand?'

'From the way Desmond described them, it does,' said Babcock. 'That tattoo one of them had on the back of his hand, for example. And the other one's broken nose. They sound like the same guys to me.'

CHAPTER TWENTY-FOUR

Once Babcock had departed, Coburg had Jenkins and Dibbs brought to the interview room to be quizzed by himself and Lampson.

'We know you threatened the Australian. We also know that it was you two who tried the same with the Jamaican and that you threatened to break his fingers.'

'We didn't *say* that to him,' said Dibbs defensively. Then he added, awkwardly, 'Although we may have hinted it.'

'The Jamaican was later found dead, beaten to death, with his fingers broken and cigarette burns on his body. Would you like to tell us about that?'

'It wasn't us!' said Jenkins and Dibbs in frantic unison.

'We never touched him!' insisted Dibbs.

'So it's just a coincidence that the man whose fingers you threatened to break had his fingers broken shortly after?'

'Absolutely!' said Jenkins.

Coburg gave a chuckle. 'Even you have to admit how unlikely that sounds,' he said.

'It's true!' insisted Dibbs. 'We never actually touched him.'

'What did you do?'

'Just talked to him.'

'Threatened him.'

'Not as such.'

'What did Jimmy Webster tell you to do to him?' asked Coburg.

'Just . . . lean on him,' said Jenkins.

'Rough him up? A few punches?'

'No.'

'So if you did, it was on your own volitions, not because he told you to?'

'We didn't!' insisted Dibbs. 'Ask that Australian. We didn't do anything to him, just gave him a warning. A bit of gentle advice.'

'Gentle?' said Coburg incredulously.

'There was no violence until he started it,' said Jenkins. 'He's an animal. It was the same with the black bloke.'

'So you got violent with Desmond Bartlett?'

'No! I meant we did the same thing to him, just talked to him.'

Coburg looked at them firmly. 'You're both being held in custody on suspicion of the murder of Desmond Bartlett. If you'll give us the details of your solicitor, we'll have him informed. If you don't have a solicitor, one will be provided.'

'We didn't murder anybody!' said Dibbs desperately.

Coburg turned to the two uniformed officers accompanying. 'Take them back to their cells,' he said.

When Jenkins and Dibbs had gone, Coburg said to Lampson, 'What do you think?'

'They're guilty,' said Lampson. 'If it's not them, it's

Webster's other pair of thugs, Jackson and Millen.'

'Then I think it's time for us to see what Mr Webster himself has to say,' said Coburg.

Prudence Baxter put on the kettle to make a cup of tea. Her son Monty, released from custody, sat and watched her apprehensively. She was fuming with anger, and when she was in this mood people around her were likely to get a beating from her.

She turned from the stove and said to Monty, 'I want the people who killed your brothers, dead.'

Monty looked at his mother, worried.

'Max killed Micky,' he said. 'He shot him. I was there.'

Prudence Baxter grabbed him by the arms and pushed her face towards his, glaring fiercely into his eyes.

'It was an accident,' she said harshly. 'Those two ambulance women could have saved him if that copper hadn't turned up and interrupted things. DCI Coburg, he was the one in charge, so he's responsible for Micky dying like he did. Then there was the copper who deliberately ran Max down and killed him. His name's Sergeant Wilf Harpson and he works out of Marylebone nick. Those are the two.' She looked at him intently. 'It's your duty to avenge your brothers.'

'How?' asked Monty.

'Shoot them,' she said flatly.

'I can't,' said Monty.

Suddenly Mrs Baxter lashed out, slapping Monty hard around the face. 'You can and you will.'

'I've never fired a gun,' Monty appealed. 'I don't know how to use one.'

'It's simple. You aim it and pull the trigger. The closer you are, the better. Get right up close to them and push it in their back. That way, you can't miss. I'll get Bill to teach you and practise with you.'

Coburg and Lampson faced Jimmy Webster across the bare wooden table in the interview room.

'We have received information that you act as an illegal off-course bookmaker,' Coburg said.

Webster shrugged. 'It's not a crime.' Then he gave a shrug of apology. 'Alright, technically it is, but it's not a real crime. Not like robbery or murder or anything.'

'But it can be associated with both those.'

'Maybe, but not involving me. I'm straight, I am.'

'Do you deny putting pressure on a man called Desmond Bartlett, a cricketer from Jamaica who played with the West India cricket team, to throw matches? Drop catches. Get bowled out. That sort of thing.'

'Of course I deny it! Why on earth would I?'

'Because I'm reliably informed that the Empire XI are the odds-on favourites to win the next few matches, so if they lose you'll make a lot of money. And your two thugs, Jenkins and Dibbs, have confirmed that you sent them to lean on Desmond Bartlett.'

'Rubbish!' said Webster.

'Then how do you explain the fact that someone beat him up very badly before he died? Someone burnt his body with the lighted end of a cigarette. They broke his fingers, and then beat him over the head with a cricket bat. Torture and threats of violence.

'The charge you're facing, Mr Webster, is murder. Three cricketers with the Empire XI were targeted by your blokes to try and make them throw some cricket matches: an Australian called Tate Babcock, a South African called Bob Appleyard and a Jamaican called Desmond Bartlett. Tate and Appleyard have identified the men who tried it on with them, who have admitted they were doing it on your instructions. We have their written confessions. The Jamaican was less fortunate; he was beaten to death after first being tortured. All on your orders, Webster, so it's a charge of murder.'

'No!' burst out Webster. 'It was nothing to do with me!'

Leaving Lampson to return Webster to his cell and then go to the office to check if there were any messages, Coburg made his way to Superintendent Allison's office to make his report.

'It looks as if two men, Tug Jenkins and Wally Dibbs, may be the ones who tortured and killed Desmond Bartlett, acting on the orders of an illegal bookmaker called Jimmy Webster. All three deny it, but then, of course, they would. There are another two heavies who do enforcement work for Webster who are called Jackson and Millen. They're also possible culprits for Bartlett's murder. I'd like to have those five remanded in custody on suspicion of conspiracy to commit murder while we continue with our investigations.'

'Very well,' said Allison. 'What about this police officer you mentioned, the bookie's brother?'

'Sergeant Eric Webster,' said Coburg. 'If Webster and his thugs are guilty, then there's a case that can be made against Sergeant Webster for collusion. There's still a question mark over the keys to Lord's Tube station going missing from St John's Wood police station.'

'Very well,' said Allison. 'Good work so far, but be very careful. Until we have concrete evidence that incriminates them, it's still supposition, and a good defence barrister could find holes in the prosecution case. What we really need are confessions.'

'Yes, sir. Sergeant Lampson and I are about to interview the two key suspects from St John's Wood police station, Sergeant Eric Webster and PC Arnold Riddick.'

'You'll have to be even more careful with them; they're in the force and they know the ropes. If you're wrong, it could create a scandal that might well affect police morale.'

'Yes, sir. We've decided to do the interviews on a one-to-one basis: I'll take Sergeant Webster and Sergeant Lampson will take Riddick.'

'Why do you think this PC Riddick might be involved?'

'It's just a feeling, sir. Plus, he seems to be a confidant of Sergeant Webster. And, if Sergeant Webster is corruptly involved with his brother, he'd need a fellow conspirator in the station to protect his back.'

'Two rotten apples, eh.'

'If we can prove it. And, if we can, there may even be more.'

CHAPTER TWENTY-FIVE

Coburg had decided to question Eric Webster on his own. He hoped there was more chance of the sergeant opening up if there were just the two of them in the room, with no other police present. He also hoped that Eric Webster might even make a slip because he was off his guard as a result of it just being one-to-one. However, the steely glint of wariness in Webster's eyes suggested that any chance of the sergeant making a give-away slip in his responses was remote.

'Let's start by talking about your brother, Jimmy's, activities,' said Coburg.

'What do you mean, his activities?'

'His illegal gambling business, for starters.'

'That's nothing to do with me, Chief Inspector.'

'It ought to be. You're a sergeant with the Metropolitan Police and your brother's running an illegal gambling business.'

Webster shook his head. 'Come off it, Chief Inspector. You know the way it is, with the war on. It's generally accepted about giving a nod to gambling while the war's on. The posh people do it, and it's the only release ordinary people have got. It's having the odd flutter that keep everyone going.'

'I'm not just talking about the illegal gambling,' said Coburg. 'The bigger issue is your brother's thugs beating up the players to pressurise them to throw a match. Players like Desmond Bartlett, who was beaten to death with a cricket bat.'

Webster stared at Coburg.

'The murder?!' he exclaimed, astonished. 'You're thinking Jimmy had anything to do with that?' He shook his head. 'You're totally wrong. Absolutely not.'

'We have a witness who informed us that Desmond Bartlett was threatened by two men who work for your brother in order to pressurise him to throw the match. Bartlett came to you to report it, and you dismissed it.'

'Because I knew it was a load of crap! It was a lie!' snapped Webster. 'He was lucky I didn't do him for defamation of character.'

'And yet someone killed him. Beat him to death after he was tortured. His fingers broken and cigarettes stubbed out on his bare flesh.'

'Jimmy had nothing to do with that!'

In the other interview room, Sergeant Lampson encountered the same stubborn defiance in Constable Riddick right from the start, although Riddick's style was to play amenable, eager to please.

'Constable Riddick, this interview is part of an investigation into the death of Desmond Bartlett, whose body was found at the former Lord's Underground station,' said Lampson.

Riddick nodded. 'Yeah. I can see that, as it was me who reported the body.'

'After it had been brought to your attention by the witness, Henry Duggan.'

Again, Riddick nodded. 'That's him. The butcher.'

'How well do you know Jimmy Webster?'

Riddick looked at Lampson, bewildered. 'Who?'

'Jimmy Webster. The brother of Sergeant Webster at your station.'

'I don't know him at all.' Then he changed tack. 'That is to say, I don't know him as such. I saw him once about six months or so ago when he popped into the station to see Sergeant Webster. But we were never introduced. Did you say his name's Jimmy?'

'So we understand.'

'Yeah, well, like I say, I know him to see, but I just saw him that once, and then only for a minute while he was in the station.'

'What did he talk to his brother about?'

'I don't know. He popped into the sergeant's office and I guess they talked, and then he went.'

'And Sergeant Webster didn't tell you what they talked about?'

'No. There was no reason for him to. I assumed it was family business, and so nothing to do with me.'

'And how long was Jimmy Webster in the office with Sergeant Webster?'

'Not long. Two or three minutes. And then he left.'

'How did you know he was Sergeant Webster's brother?'

'Because when he came in he asked if Sergeant Webster was around. When I said he was, and in his office, he said, "Could you tell him his brother's here and would like a word." I knocked on the door of the sergeant's office and told him, and he told me to send him in. Which I did.'

'And Sergeant Webster never told you what his brother's visit was about?'

'No. Why all these questions? What's going on?'

'Do you know what Jimmy Webster does for a living?'

'No idea. The sergeant's never talked about his brother.'

'He's a bookie.'

Riddick frowned. 'A bookie? What, a real one? Does the racecourses?'

'No, he's off-course.'

'With an office?'

'No, he's an illegal bookie.'

Riddick looked at Lampson, then laughed. 'No! You're making this up!'

Lampson shook his head.

'Well, that's a shock,' said Riddick.

'You had no idea?'

'No,' said Riddick. Then he asked, curious, 'So what's this have to do with the dead bloke?'

'An allegation has been made that Jimmy Webster pressurised some sportsmen to throw games. In this particular case, he's accused of threatening the dead man, Desmond Bartlett, with violence if he didn't throw some of the cricket matches he was due to play in.'

Riddick shook his head. 'No, I can't believe that. Not the sergeant's brother.'

'It's an allegation that's got to be investigated. We've also had an allegation that Desmond Bartlett came to St John's Wood police station to report these threats to Sergeant Webster, unaware that Jimmy Webster and the sergeant were related. The sergeant refused to investigate the allegations and sent Mr Bartlett away. Were you at the station when Mr Bartlett arrive to make this complaint?'

'No, I'd never seen the dead bloke before. I'd have recognised him if I had.'

When they returned to the office to swap notes, Coburg and Lampson both expressed their feelings of frustration at their interviews.

'Nothing doing,' groaned Lampson. 'Riddick's like a clam, but an oily, greasy clam. I thought he might be prepared to sell out Sergeant Webster to save himself, but no luck. He just plays ignorant.'

'Same with Webster,' sighed Coburg.

'Think we'll have to let them go?' asked Lampson. 'Without a confession to the actual murder, we only have two of the thugs for making threats.'

'I know,' admitted Coburg unhappily. 'Have we got fingerprints of all of them?'

'All of them,' confirmed Lampson.

'Good,' said Coburg. 'I'm hoping that Harry Durward may turn up something at the Tube station. Fingerprints on the chair, for example. Maybe even the cigarette stubs?'

Lampson shook his head. 'Unlikely, guv. The fag ends, I mean.'

There was a knock at the door, which opened and Harry Durward entered. He carried two large bulging sacks.

'Forensics report,' he said. He grinned and put the two sacks on Coburg's desk. 'Plus something a little extra special.'

'We were just talking about you,' said Coburg. 'Wondering if you'd found anything.'

'We did as you asked and searched the whole premises, and we found these in a store cupboard right at the bottom of the stairs,' said Durward. 'Take a look, but put some gloves on first, and handle everything with care otherwise you might smudge any prints.'

Coburg took some gloves from his desk drawer and pulled them on. Durward put on a pair of gloves himself, then opened one of the large sacks and took out a wooden box. Coburg studied the box.

'It looks like a radio,' he said.

'It is, one that receives and transmits,' said Durward.

Coburg examined the lettering on the box. 'German,' he said.

'Exactly,' said Durward. 'Whatever went on at Lord's Tube station, we have a nest of spies involved. Once we realised what it was, we took care to handle it wearing gloves. If we're lucky, there'll be fingerprints on it. Find out who the prints belong to and you'll have the people who killed your cricketer.'

'Put it back in the sack, if you would, Harry,' said Coburg. 'I'll run it down to MI5 and let them examine it.'

'There was this in the store cupboard as well,' said Durward. He opened the other sack and took out a long leather bag.

'A cricket bag!' exclaimed Coburg.

'Exactly,' said Durward. 'I thought you'd be interested.'

'Have you opened it?'

'Of course,' said Durward.

Coburg opened the bag and let out an appreciative whistle when he saw the contents.

'This is gold dust,' he said, complimenting Durward.

'This looks like Bartlett's cricket things.' He pointed at the cricket bat. 'Including the murder weapon, if I'm not mistaken.'

'Yes. I had the same thought when I saw the bloodstains.'

'I'll let MI5 check it all for prints, then I'll pass it on to Dr Welbourne,' said Coburg. 'He'll be able to confirm if the blood on the bat belonged to Bartlett.' He turned to Durward and said, 'Well done, Harry, to you and your team. If this means we nail our murderers, it'll be thanks to you.'

The phone ringing interrupted them. Lampson picked it up.

'DCI Coburg's phone,' he said. He held the receiver out to Coburg. 'It's Dr Welbourne.'

'You're busy,' said Durward. 'Let me know how MI5 get on with the box, and you get on with the cricket gear.'

'Will do,' said Coburg. 'And thanks again, Harry.' Into the receiver he said, 'Coburg.'

'Dr Welbourne. Those boots you sent me are the ones. The metal plate at the front matches the wound, and there are traces of Rhodes-Armfield's blood on one of them.'

'Thank you, Doctor. That's the second piece of good news I've had in the last couple of minutes.'

'Oh?'

'Our forensics team examined Lord's Tube station and it looks like they've found Bartlett's cricket bag, including the cricket bat that killed him. I need MI5 to take a look at everything first, then I'll get the cricket bat to you.'

Coburg was smiling when he turned to Lampson. 'It looks like our luck's turned. I'm going to take this stuff to Inspector

Hibbert, along with the fingerprints we took from the Webster brothers and the rest, so Hibbert can check them against any on the box. While I'm doing that, I'd like you to get another car from the motor pool, go to Lord's and bring in Ben Wright. You'd better take a couple of uniforms with you in case he proves awkward.'

CHAPTER TWENTY-SIX

The car that Jonty was able to provide for Lampson this time was slightly battered, but Lampson reflected that it was only for picking up a suspect, not for impressing anyone. Group Captain Weymouth seemed a troubled man when Lampson entered his office with two uniformed officers in tow, and the reason for his concerned look became apparent as soon as Lampson told him they were there to pick up Cadet Ben Wright.

'I'm afraid Cadet Wright has vanished,' said Weymouth. 'He's now officially AWOL, absent without leave.'

'That's unfortunate, sir,' said Lampson. 'Do you have his personal details? His home address, names of his parents, that sort of thing?'

Coburg was never sure whether Inspector Hibbert would be at MI5's temporary HQ at Wormwood Scrubs prison or out hunting spies. But, even if he wasn't, it was important to deliver the items Inspector Durward had found at Lord's Tube station quickly so they could be examined. This business of a German radio added a new and unexpected dimension to the murder of Desmond Bartlett, the real possibility that it was connected to an illicit German spy ring operating in Britain.

But what could the connection be between a German spy ring and a Jamaican cricketer?

Luckily for Coburg, today Hibbert was at Wormwood Scrubs. He looked with a puzzled expression at the contents of the two sacks.

'A German transmitter and a bag of cricket gear?' he said.

'They were both found at the same place,' Coburg told him. 'Hidden in a store cupboard in the abandoned Lord's Tube station. The same place where a West Indian cricketer called Desmond Bartlett was tortured and killed.'

'Yes, I saw about it in the papers,' said Hibbert thoughtfully. 'You think he found out about the radio and that's why he was killed?'

'We don't know,' said Coburg. 'He wasn't working for you, was he?'

'Bartlett? No, absolutely not.' Hibbert looked at the radio transmitter. 'How many of your blokes have handled this?' he asked.

'Two, and both with gloves on,' said Coburg.

Hibbert nodded. 'Leave it with me,' he said. 'I'll get my men on it. What are you looking for?'

'Identifying any fingerprints on the articles.'

'If there are any on the radio, we might have them in our records. But I'm not sure if we'll be able to help you with the cricket gear.'

'If the same people were involved, the chances are whoever handled the radio also handled the cricket stuff.'

'Yes, that makes sense,' said Hibbert. 'I suppose you want the information yesterday?'

'Today would be good,' said Coburg. He held out the sheets

223

of paper containing the fingerprints they'd taken from the prisoners in custody. 'These are from the people we're currently holding in custody on suspicion of the murder, if they're any help.'

Hibbert took the sheets and looked at the clock. 'It's gone five,' he said. 'Most of my team have gone home. Tomorrow?'

'If you can,' said Coburg. 'You're looking for spies. I'm looking for murderers.'

'Who might be one and the same,' said Hibbert. 'I'll see what we can do.'

When Coburg and Lampson met up at Scotland Yard, Lampson told him about Wright having gone AWOL.

'I've got the address of his parents in Essex. If what Judkins said about Wright having a boyfriend at home is correct, I think it'll be worth making a trip out there tomorrow. If I can borrow the car.'

'Agreed,' said Coburg. 'You head for Essex. I'll stay here at the Yard and see if Inspector Hibbert turns up with any information. How's everything going for the wedding? Eve getting nervous?'

'Not so you'd notice.'

'What about her mother pushing the merits of this other bloke?'

'She tried, but Eve told her where to go. In fact, Eve's moved in with a cousin of hers for the run-up to the wedding. You're still on for it are, you?'

'Unless you've got a male relative you'd like to do it. An uncle or a cousin?'

Lampson shook his head. 'I want this wedding to have some class, for Eve's sake. Trust me, my uncles and cousins may have some qualities, but class ain't one of them.'

'In that case, I've been working on my best man speech. I've been told the tradition is to make jokes about the bridegroom.'

'I think you're also supposed to say what a good bloke he is,' said Lampson doubtfully.

'I will,' Coburg assured him.

'And be careful about anything too clever. I know what you Eton blokes can be like. Classical references will go right over the head of my relatives. And mine, as well.'

'Noted.' Coburg nodded. 'So, no Horace and Cicero.'

'Who are they? Some upper-class comedy double act?'

'Horace was a Roman historian, poet and philosopher, famous for erudite quotations: "*Brevis esse laboro, obscurus fio*. I strive to be brief, and I become obscure". Cicero was a politician from around the same time. "*Mens cuiusque is est quisque*. The spirit is the true self". All clever stuff.'

'Too clever,' commented Lampson. 'Any witty sayings, Tommy Trinder will be alright. But not Max Miller.'

'Understood,' said Coburg. 'Oh, and I think we'll release Riddick.'

'Why?'

'If he is involved in any way, I think he'll be more help to us outside than in. I get the impression he's a bit of a ducker and diver. I'll see if we can get someone to keep an eye on him.'

That evening, Mr and Mrs Lampson called for Terry and took him to stay the night at their flat, 'To give Ted and Eve some privacy, for once'.

'They'll have plenty of privacy after they're married,' complained Mr Lampson.

'I thought you liked having Terry to stay over?' said Mrs Lampson.

'Well, I do,' said her husband. 'But Vic Oliver's on the wireless tonight, and Terry isn't keen on him. He'll start whistling.'

'If there's another air raid, we'll all be down the shelter,' Mrs Lampson pointed out.

So Terry went off with his grandparents, and that evening, Eve called to spend time with Lampson.

'One more week to go,' Lampson said to Eve when she'd arrived and been enveloped in his arms. 'Mr and Mrs Lampson.'

'It'll take me some getting used to,' said Eve.

He hugged her close and whispered, 'As Terry's out for the night, what do you say to going upstairs for a bit of a cuddle?'

'Is that supposed to be a romantic advance?' she asked with a smile. 'It's not exactly Douglas Fairbanks.'

'I can still carry you up those stairs like he would,' said Lampson, lifting her up.

'No thank you,' she said, forcing him to put her down. 'It would be just our luck for you to trip and drop me a week before our wedding.' She took his hand. 'Yes to the cuddle, but I'll walk up.'

Afterwards, when Lampson brought them cups of tea in bed, she asked, 'Are we still on for the football on Sunday?'

'St Ethelred's Boys Choir,' said Lampson. 'Should be a tough game. Those choirboys can be right hard cases. I wouldn't miss it for the world.'

'You may not want to, but you never know what's going to happen in your job.'

'No, I've definitely got Sunday off. I know one thing: I've got to go out to Essex tomorrow and see if I can bring someone in.'

'What's he done?'

'If the evidence is right: murder.'

'Sounds dangerous.'

'Don't worry, the boss has told me to take a uniformed officer with me, just in case he resists.'

'Say he's armed?'

'He's not. He's just a scared teenager.'

'Like the one you were talking to me about who threatened to shoot your boss's wife?'

'Well, yes, I suppose you could compare them,' admitted Lampson awkwardly. 'But this one's very different. He's a cadet with the RAF.'

'Who are trained to use weapons.'

'Not this one,' insisted Lampson. 'Look, Eve, there's no danger here, I promise.'

'There'd better not be,' said Eve. 'We're supposed to be getting married a week tomorrow, and I want you there all in one piece.'

'I will be. I promise.'

'Your boss still on for being best man?'

'He is.'

'And, since my mum's being difficult, I was thinking of asking his wife if she'd be my maid of honour. Do you think she'd agree?'

'What about Betty? Your cousin?'

'I did sound her out, but she's very shy. Really shy. She's got a thing about everyone looking at her.'

'Tell her on the day everyone will be looking at the bride.'

'I tried that, but it didn't work. She got terrified at the thought.'

'Alright, I'll ask the guvnor to ask Rosa.'

'That's not the way things are done, Ted. It's for me to ask her in person.' She thought it over, then said, 'But maybe you could come with me when I talk to her about it. You've been to their flat before, so you know where it is. And it might make things easier.'

'No problem, I'll find out if they're going to be in tomorrow evening. Am I allowed to do that?'

She kissed him. 'You are,' she said.

CHAPTER TWENTY-SEVEN

Saturday 15th March

Next morning, after Coburg had picked Lampson up and taken them both to Scotland Yard, Lampson took the car to the motor pool, where, with Coburg's official backing and Jonty Miller's technical expertise, the new car radio call sign was officially changed to their call sign of Echo Seven. That done, Lampson collected Jim Kent, the uniformed constable who was to accompany him to Essex, from the reception area.

'Where are we headed for, Sergeant?' asked Kent as they set off in the car.

'A little village out Braintree way in Essex. An RAF cadet's gone AWOL and I've got a suspicion he'll be hiding out at a pal's of his.'

'What made him go AWOL?' asked Kent.

'We're pretty sure he kicked another cadet to death, and when he knew we'd taken his boots in for forensics to check them, he decided to do a runner. At least, that's the way me and my guvnor see it. Of course, it could be just a wild goose chase.'

'What's your guvnor like to work for?' asked Kent. 'DCI Saxe-Coburg, ain't it?'

'It is,' said Lampson. 'And he's the best.'

'Upper-class, though,' said Kent uncertainly. 'Part of the royal family. That's a bit odd for a Scotland Yard copper.'

'He's nothing like that at all,' said Lampson. 'No airs and graces. Just an all-round decent bloke.'

When they arrived at the address they had for Ben Wright, Lampson told Kent to stay with the car while he made the visit.

'I can't see him trying anything with his parents there. And I'd rather not leave the vehicle unattended. Even police cars have been known to get nicked.'

Mrs Wright was the only one in the house. At least, that's what she told Lampson after he'd showed her his warrant card and explained the reason for his visit: wanting to talk to her son, Ben.

'My husband's out at work,' she told him. 'He works at the railway station.' She frowned, puzzled. 'Why have you come here to talk to Ben? He's at that RAF place at Lord's, the cricket ground.'

'Well, he should be, but it seems he's gone AWOL. Absent without leave. We wondered if he'd been in touch with you?'

'No. What d'you mean, he's gone absent without leave?'

'We needed to talk to him about an incident that happened, but for some reason he left before we could talk to him.'

'What incident?'

'Another cadet was injured and the evidence suggests that Ben may have been responsible.'

'Is that what this other cadet said?'

Lampson hesitated, then said awkwardly, 'I'm afraid the other cadet hasn't said anything. He died.'

Mrs Wright looked at him, shocked. 'Not Ben! Ben wouldn't do anything to harm anyone!'

'At the moment everything is just circumstantial, which is why we need to talk to Ben to get his side of the story.'

'Well, he hasn't been here.'

'We understand that Ben has got a good friend who lives around here. Someone he saw quite a lot?'

'You must mean Colin Dent,' said Mrs Wright. 'Him and Ben are best mates. Always hung round together before Ben signed up for the RAF. They used to talk about both going in at the same time, but Colin failed the medical.'

'Do you have an address for Colin? It might be useful if we talk to him. He might have heard from Ben.'

'Colin lives with his parents at the other end of the village. You can't miss it. Colin's dad, George, is a blacksmith. He's got a forge with a sign outside: George Dent, blacksmith.'

Inspector Hibbert arrived in Coburg's office.

'We managed to get some prints off that radio,' he said. He pulled a chair to Coburg's desk and sat down. 'Three people. Two we don't know, but the third we've got his prints in our "people to watch" file. A man called George Grimshaw.'

'Who's George Grimshaw and how does he fit in with this?'

'Someone reported him because he was heard expressing unpatriotic views in a pub one night. He was saying the war was out of control, that Churchill didn't know what he was doing. He said it was Churchill's fault that all the people had died during the Blitz. He said we should have got the deal that Chamberlain had made with Hitler in Munich. He said that Hitler never wanted to go to war with Britain. The end result was someone took a swing at him and it degenerated into a punch-up. The police were called.'

'Was Grimshaw charged?'

Hibbert shook his head. 'The thing was, it was the other bloke who started the actual fisticuffs, so it was decided to drop any charges against both of them. We didn't want the publicity that goes with someone mouthing off anti-patriotic views; it can encourage others. We took the fingerprints of both men and kept Grimshaw's on file. We also kept an eye on him for a while, but after that he seemed to watch what he said. His prints on the radio appear to indicate he's moved on from just having anti-Churchill opinion to actively working with the Germans.'

'As a spy.'

'Not necessarily. We know that he was working at an electrical shop at the time he got into the fight in the pub, so it's my guess that he put his skills to work doing the radio bit, passing information on to the Germans.'

'So he's a technician rather than a spy?'

'That's my feeling. The questions is, who's passing him information that he radios to Germany?'

'Pull him in and ask him.'

'Unfortunately, he's vanished. I sent a couple of blokes to the address we had for him during the time of the pub fight, but the street's gone, bombed out.'

'Maybe he was killed?'

'No, that street was bombed four months ago. These fingerprints are much more recent than that. At the moment we're trying to find out where he's gone to.'

'What about the shop where he was working?'

'We tried there. The bloke who owns it, Ben Daly, sacked Grimshaw after he heard about the punch-up in the pub.

He told us, "I don't employ traitors," and got rid of him. My guess is Grimshaw managed to get another job with another electrical place. The trouble is, we don't know where.'

'Any ideas on the other two sets of fingerprints?'

'None.'

'What about the cricket gear?'

'Grimshaw's are on the cricket bag and the cricket bat. So are three others, as yet unidentified. I'm assuming one lot belongs to the dead man, Bartlett.' He looked at Coburg, curious. 'You look like you've had a thought.'

'I've had a couple,' said Coburg. 'If we're talking about some German spy ring being at the heart of this, maybe they tortured Bartlett to find out something about the RAF. After all, he held a senior position as a technician at Kenley.'

'Yes, it's a possibility,' said Hibbert. 'But it's an odd sort of thing to do, snatch him off the street.'

'Unless they knew he had specific information that they needed,' said Coburg. He remembered what Group Captain Warmsley had told him about Bartlett's work, about the harmonisation diagram, and how important it was to the accuracy of the RAF fighter pilots. Could it be they were after technical details about the equipment in order to use it in some way to the advantage of the Luftwaffe?

'You said you had a couple of thoughts,' Hibbert reminded him.

'The second is just a bit of a hunch.'

'What sort of hunch?'

'I'm going to get the fingerprints off someone and bring them to you for you to check against all this stuff.'

'Whose fingerprints?'

'A friend of the cricketer who was killed, Desmond Bartlett. Bartlett was staying with him on the weekend he was killed.'

'We're looking for German agents. Do you think this character might be one?'

'He doesn't strike me as such. At the moment I'm clutching at straws.'

'But sometime a straw turns up good,' said Hibbert. 'Anyway, you've got nothing to lose. Except scaring this bloke off. He might do a runner.'

'If he does, we'll know my hunch was right.'

'Which won't be much good if he's vanished.'

'I'll make sure he doesn't,' said Coburg.

When Magnus and Malcolm arrived at Lord's to watch the Combined Services XI against the British Empire XI, they were surprised to see Sir Pelham Warner and the Empire XI's captain, Ray Smith, waiting just inside the entrance.

'Magnus!' exclaimed Warner. 'We were hoping you'd come.'

'We wouldn't have missed it,' said Magnus. Then he caught their worried expressions and asked, 'What's the matter? Has something happened?'

'John Winkler has dislocated his shoulder. So we're a man down,' said Warner.

'I'm afraid this has happened to us before,' said Smith. 'One match, one of the team fell ill and we had to ask the umpire to play for us, and we had a scorer step up to take the place of the umpire.'

'The problem is compounded because the players we considered for back-up aren't in London at the moment.'

'So what can we do to help?' asked Magnus. 'You want us

to see who we can rope in as replacement?'

'No,' said Smith. 'We'd like you to play, Magnus, if you agree.'

'Me?' said Magnus stunned.

Malcolm looked at him. 'You can't,' he said firmly. 'You're too old. You can't run like you used to. You're liable to fall over and break a leg.'

'You're not too old,' said Smith firmly. 'We talked about it, Pelham, Bertie and myself, and we all agreed you are the perfect substitute. You may not be as young as you were, but you were a top-class player, and there's no reason why you still can't be these days.'

'And we need you,' said Warner.

'I'm not sure,' said Magnus doubtfully.

'At last, some common sense,' said Malcolm tersely.

'You can come in at the tail-end of the innings,' said Smith. 'And we'll put you on the boundary when it comes to fielding. What do you say?'

'We need you, Magnus,' urged Warner. 'We have to have a team of eleven, and at the moment we've only got ten.'

Lampson pulled up outside George Dent's blacksmith's forge. Once again, he told Kent to stay with the car while he went in and talked to the Dents. This time, George Dent was at work in the forge, while Mrs Dent was out.

Lampson showed his warrant card and asked if Colin Dent was around.

'Why?' asked Dent suspiciously.

'We're just hoping he might be able to help us get hold of his friend Ben Wright.'

'He's in London,' said Dent. 'At the RAF camp they've set up at Lord's Cricket Ground.'

'He seems to have vanished,' said Lampson. 'We're hoping Colin may have heard from him.'

'If he has, Colin hasn't said anything about it.'

'Can I have a word with Colin?'

Dent shrugged. 'If you must,' he said.

Lampson followed him as he walked out of the forge and towards the small cottage. 'Colin!' he called. 'Colin!'

A young man appeared from the cottage.

'Colin, this chap wants to have a word with you about Ben,' said Dent.

Colin Dent gave Lampson a look of puzzlement.

'What about him?' he asked.

'It seems that Ben has gone absent without leave from the RAF base at Lord's. We're trying to find him.'

'Why?'

Lampson's police experience kicked in, almost a sixth sense. He could see that Colin Dent was suddenly very nervous and on edge.

'We just need his help with something,' said Lampson. 'Have you seen him lately?'

'No.' The answer was too quick, abrupt, defensive.

'Have you heard from him? A letter? Phone calls?'

'We're not on the phone,' said Colin. 'And no, I haven't heard from him.'

'What's going on?' demanded Dent. He, too, had caught the tension emanating from his son and was worried by it.

Lampson nodded. 'I understand. In that case we'd like you to come with us.'

'Where to?' demanded Colin, and now he was definitely on edge.

'Yes, where to?' echoed his father. 'Where are you planning to take him?'

'To Scotland Yard,' said Lampson, putting on his friendly face. 'Orders from Detective Chief Inspector Coburg. You can telephone him, if you like. He'll confirm it. The phone number is Whitehall 1212.'

'We're not on the phone,' said Dent defensively.

'I saw a phone box in the village,' said Lampson. 'We passed it on the way here.'

Dent scowled. 'I don't like this,' he said. 'I'm sure you need my permission to take him.'

Lampson gave a friendly sigh and shook his head. 'I'm afraid that doesn't apply in a case where national security is involved.'

'National security?' said Dent, bewildered. 'What's Ben got to do with national security? Or Colin, for that matter?'

'It's an RAF matter,' said Lampson. 'I can't go into details at this stage.' He turned to Colin, who was getting even more agitated. 'If you'd get into the car, please, Colin.'

'No,' blurted out Colin. 'You can't make me.'

'I'm afraid I can,' said Lampson. 'However, I think we'd all prefer it if we can do this without having to use force.'

'What's this for?' demanded Dent, anguish in his voice. 'Colin hasn't done anything.'

'In that case we'll be able to return him to you, once DCI Coburg's had a word with him.' He again looked at Colin, and gestured towards the car.

Colin flinched and backed away from him. 'No,' he said again.

Lampson sighed and took a pair of handcuffs from his pocket. 'I'd prefer it if I didn't have to use these,' he said. 'But that's down to you.'

'Not handcuffs!' implored Dent. 'People will see him and think he's done something bad.'

'It's up to him, Mr Dent,' said Lampson. 'As I say, I don't want to use these, and if he gives me his word he'll come along with no trouble, I won't have to. Once the chief inspector's talked to him, we'll be able to return him to you straight away.'

Colin looked at his father for help. Mr Dent gave an unhappy sigh.

'Go with them, son,' he said. 'We know you haven't done anything. This is just something to do with Ben.' He looked urgently at Lampson. 'You will send him back?'

'I promise,' said Lampson.

Reluctantly, Colin began to walk slowly towards the waiting police car, Lampson beside him. Suddenly, Colin stopped.

'I need to get something,' he said. 'From my room.'

'Sorry,' said Lampson.

PC Kent had seen them approaching and got out, opening the rear door of the car.

'PC Kent will sit with you in the back,' said Lampson.

The unhappy Colin got into the back of the car, Kent joining him and pulling the door shut. Lampson got behind the steering wheel, started the car up and drove off.

Ben Wright looked out of the tiny window in the attic above the blacksmith's forge and watched the police car drive off. Why had they taken Colin? Where to? Was he under arrest?

Wright felt sick. He'd arrived late at night and managed to

get Colin on his own and explained the situation to him.

'I'm in trouble. I need somewhere to hide until I can get away.'

'Why? What's happened?'

'Do you remember that letter you wrote to me about us being together?'

'Yes, of course.'

'Well, the chap I was billeted with found it. He was a complete scumbag. He tried to blackmail me. He said if I didn't pay him he'd send it to my commanding officer, and my parents.' He'd hesitated, then said, 'There were parts of it that could be misinterpreted.'

'What did you do? Pay him?'

'I couldn't – I didn't have the money. Anyway, he got into a fight with someone and fell down the stairs, and died.'

'Died?'

'The police think I killed him. So I need somewhere to hide while I work out what to do.'

Dent had fallen silent, thinking, then he'd said, 'The attic over my dad's forge. He never goes there. It's full of junk. You could hide out there. I'll sneak you in some food while we work out a plan. I've got some money.' Then he'd asked, 'Why do they think you killed him?'

'Because when I found him unconscious, I kicked him, and they say it was that kick that killed him. But it wasn't! It was him falling down the stairs that did it, I'm sure of that.'

'Why did you kick him?'

'To put him out of action for a week, in the medical quarters. That was the time I needed. After that, I'd have been sent to some placing where he couldn't find me. The trouble

239

is the policeman who's in charge, a detective inspector at Scotland Yard called Coburg, and his sergeant, someone called Lampson, are convinced I'm guilty.'

And now it was this same Sergeant Lampson who had taken Colin away, thought Wright bitterly. How did they know about Colin? How did they find his name and address? He'd destroyed the letter. His parents must have told the police about Colin. That was the only way they could have found out about him.

He wondered what they would do to Colin. Pressurise him to make him tell them where Ben was. He shuddered at the thought of Colin in their hands, undergoing interrogation. The police hadn't treated him badly when they'd questioned him, but that was because it had been at Lord's on RAF territory. Colin wouldn't have that safety.

CHAPTER TWENTY-EIGHT

Malcolm sat next to Magnus and looked at him disapprovingly as he strapped on his pads in readiness for going out to the crease.

'This is madness,' snorted Malcolm. 'Sheer vanity.'

'It is not vanity ' it is responding to an urgent appeal by our captain, Ray Smith, and the President of the MCC. Did you know that Plums was born in Trinidad?'

'Of course I did,' said Malcom indignantly. 'I also know that he was educated in Barbados, before he went to Rugby.'

'My point is,' continued Magnus, 'that although he's counted as an English cricketer, playing for England in many test matches, he is ideally qualified to be associated with the Empire XI as a son of the empire himself.'

'At least he's got the good sense not to put himself in danger at his age. Unlike you.'

'I'm years younger than Plum,' protested Magnus. 'He's nearly seventy. And what's all this eyewash about danger?'

'I've seen their fast bowler in action,' said Malcolm. 'Freddy Pearce. The man's a menace. That ball will come flying at you like a cannonball.'

'In my time I've faced some of the best fast bowlers in the world,' said Magnus.

'But you were younger then!'

'Which means I'm experienced. I'll watch Pearce's feet; that's always an indication of the speed he'll be delivering at.'

'If you've got any sense, you'll let yourself be bowled first ball,' said Malcolm.

Magnus looked at him, shocked. 'Macolm! In all the long years we've known one another I've never heard you say anything so unsporting!'

'It's not unsporting; it's about survival. You can't move as fast as you used to.'

Magnus looked around the dressing room. 'I'm glad there was no one else here to hear you say that. If there had been you'd have been disbarred from the MCC.'

'I'm just thinking of you,' insisted Malcolm. 'If you ask me, Plum and Ray Smith acted irresponsibly in asking you to play today. When was the last time you wielded a bat competitively?'

There was the sound of cheering from outside, and loud applause, signifying one of the batting pair at the wicket was out and was making his way back to the pavilion.

Magnus stood up.

'I refuse to have this conversation any more,' he said. He picked up his bat and tucked it under his arm. 'Freddy Pearce awaits me.'

Coburg mounted the stairs to Peter Etheridge's flat in the small block close to Lord's Cricket Ground and rang the doorbell. Etheridge opened the door and looked at Coburg warily.

'Good morning, Mr Etheridge,' said Coburg. 'I'm sorry to disturb you on a weekend, but we've found some items belonging to Desmond Bartlett, and we need to check everyone's fingerprints against those on the items in order to eliminate people we're sure weren't involved in his murder.'

'What items are these?' asked Etheridge.

'His cricket bag. His bat was inside it.'

'The bat he was killed with?'

'Yes.'

'Where was it found?'

'Hidden in a store cupboard at Lord's Tube station.'

'So whoever murdered him must have done it there.'

'That's how it appears.'

Etheridge fell silent, thinking it over, then said, 'My prints will be on Desmond's bat. He used to show me how to hold it to make different shots. And on the bag because I remember I carried it into my flat.'

'In that case I'm sure you'll have no objection to my taking your fingerprints so we can eliminate you from the investigation.'

'Of course,' said Etheridge. 'I assume that once you've eliminated mine and Desmond's fingerprints, whoever's are left on the bat will be those of the person who killed him.'

'Possibly,' said Coburg. 'Although we may not know for sure.'

'I assume you'll be taking the fingerprints of the cricketers he practised with at the weekend. Some of them will have held his bat.'

'Of course,' lied Coburg smoothly. He took the ink pad and paper from his pocket. 'This won't take a minute, I promise you.'

Once Coburg had taken Etheridge's fingerprints, he made his way back down the stairs to the street, where he'd left two detective constables waiting, Fred Armstrong and Derek Burton.

'Right,' he told them, 'it's possible Mr Etheridge might do a runner. If he does, you know what your instructions are.'

'We follow him, one in the lead and the other keeping some distance behind. After a while we switch over,' said Armstrong. 'That way if he spots one of us, he'll think we were on our own, doing it solo, or it was just a coincidence.'

'And before that?' prompted Coburg.

'One of us goes up to his flat, knocks, and asks if a Mr Bedford lives there. If he asks what it's about, we say an insurance claim. Once he's told us no Mr Bedford lives there, we apologise and walk off.'

'That way one of us knows what he looks like and can describe him to the other,' finished Burton.

'Good,' said Coburg. He handed a piece of paper to Armstrong. 'This is my home phone number, in case anything untoward happens. But hopefully, if he does go out, it'll be uneventful. Your job is to make sure where he goes and who he sees.'

'Yes, sir,' said Armstrong. 'You can count on us.'

Coburg left them to it and made for Wormwood Scrubs. Inspector Hibbert had gone, but Coburg left Etheridge's fingerprints with a note for Hibbert to check them when he returned.

Lampson drove to the local police station and left Colin Dent in the car with PC Kent while he went in to talk to the desk sergeant. He introduced himself and told him the reason for his visit.

'Do you know Ben Wright? He lives with his parents in the village.'

'The one who went off to join the RAF?'

'That's him. He seems to have vanished. We think he might be hiding out at George Dent's blacksmith's place. You know it?'

'Everyone knows George's forge.'

'Colin Dent has agreed to come with us to Scotland Yard to answer some questions about Ben. I'd be grateful if you could keep a watch on the forge, and the house. See if Ben Wright is spotted around there.'

'And if he is?'

'Pick him up and let us know at Scotland Yard. Ask for DCI Coburg or DS Lampson, and we'll come and pick him up.'

With that in place, Lampson returned to the car and they headed for Scotland Yard.

Simon Roche entered the small electrical shop. George Grimshaw was behind the counter, wearing a brown overall. He looked quizzically at Roche.

'What can I do for you, sir?' he asked.

Roche looked around, then murmured, 'Is the boss around?'

'No,' said Grimshaw. 'It's Saturday. Sometimes he likes to take a Saturday off.'

'Anyone else around?'

'No, just you and me.'

'So what was all that "What can I do for you, sir?" business?'

'Just being careful in case anyone came in. We can't take chances.' He regarded Roche with curiosity. 'So, what's up?'

'There's been activity at the Tube station, so I went in to check on things. The radio's gone. And the cricket bag.'

Grimshaw thought this news over, then said, 'It must be the police.'

'How? We've got both sets of keys,' said Roche.

'There's a third set, which were left at St John's Wood Tube station. If you remember, we decided to leave them there because we didn't want to arouse suspicion if all three went missing.'

'That was a mistake.'

'It may have been, but we couldn't foresee what would happen,' said Grimshaw. 'The thing is, we can't send any more messages. Not for the moment.'

'So we try and get the radio back?'

Grimshaw shook his head. 'No. Either the police have it, or they'll have passed it to MI5. Either way, MI5 will have put a tracking device inside it. Our best bet is to abandon it and get another.'

'From Jurgen?'

Grimshaw nodded. 'I'm seeing him later. Right now, our main problem is the two weak links that we have to deal with.'

'Etheridge?'

'And the policeman who sold us the keys. We have to silence them both. I suggest you deal with Etheridge. He knows and trusts you. I'll deal with the policeman.'

Ben Wright entered the phone box. He'd been very careful. He'd seen the policeman watching the forge, so he'd slipped out of the back door and then followed a circuitous route across the fields before going back into the village from the other direction.

His fingers trembled as he dialled Whitehall 1212. When the operator answered with 'Scotland Yard', he said, 'Can I speak to Detective Inspector Coburg, please?'

'Who's calling?'

'Tell him it's RAF Cadet Ben Wright.'

'One moment.' There was a pause, then the operator said, 'There's no answer to DCI Coburg's phone. Would you like to leave a message?'

'No thank you. I'll try again later.'

Damn! thought Ben as he left the phone box. What were they doing to Colin?

Simon Roche was also on the telephone, in his case dialling Peter Etheridge's number. When Etheridge answered, Roche said, 'Peter, we need to talk.'

'About what?'

'We can't talk on the phone. Can I come to your place?'

'No,' said Etheridge. 'Not after what happened.'

'That's what I want to explain,' said Roche. 'It wasn't me.'

'Who was it?'

'That's what I want to tell you.'

There was such a long pause that Roche wondered if Etheridge had hung up. 'Peter, are you there?' he asked.

'Yes,' said Etheridge. 'Very well, we'll meet. At the place it happened.'

'Why there?' asked Roche.

'Because it's the right place,' said Etheridge.

'When?'

'Tomorrow morning.'

As Roche hung up, Grimshaw looked at him questioningly. 'Everything alright?'

'No,' said Roche. 'He wants to meet inside Lord's Tube station.'

'Why?'

'That's what worries me.'

'I think we should both be there.'

'He won't talk if you're there as well,' said Roche.

'I'll hide myself,' said Grimshaw. 'I'll only come out if there's trouble.'

CHAPTER TWENTY-NINE

Ben Wright had intended to leave it for an hour or more before trying DCI Coburg again, but his concern for Colin impelled him to dial Scotland Yard's number again. Once more, he gave his name to the switchboard operator and waited nervously as he heard the same series of clicks. This time he heard a man's upper-class accent say, 'DCI Coburg.'

'Chief Inspector, it's Ben Wright. Your sergeant has arrested Colin Dent. That's not fair. He had nothing to do with what happened to Richard. You have to let him go.'

'At the moment he's not here,' said Coburg. 'But then, if Sergeant Lampson has only recently collected him, it will be a while before they're back at Scotland Yard. The best thing for everyone is for you to hand yourself in and tell us what happened. If you'll tell me where you are, I'll get someone to collect you.'

'Colin had nothing to do with this,' repeated Wright firmly. With that, he hung up.

Good work by Ted, thought Coburg as he replaced the receiver. The sergeant had gone to Wright's home village in Essex, identified this friend of his, and was now bringing him in. Wright had sounded rattled. Wright was obviously still in the village and must have seen Lampson drive his friend away.

If we handle this one carefully, he'll deliver himself to us, thought Coburg. He could hear the desperation in the cadet's voice.

Grimshaw had been waiting opposite the entrance to St John's Wood police station for half an hour, and was concerned that unless the person he was waiting for put in an appearance soon, he was in danger of being arrested for loitering with intent. It was with relief that he saw the uniformed figure appear from the station and began to walk ponderously along the street. Grimshaw made his way across the road and intercepted the policeman with a cheery smile.

'Hello, again,' he said.

The uniformed officer returned his smile with his own cheerful, 'Hello yourself.'

'I was wondering if you could help me with a small favour,' said Grimshaw. 'A paying one, obviously.'

'More keys?'

Grimshaw shook his head. 'Not this time, something much simpler. But the money's still the same. Are you interested?'

'I'm always interested where money's concerned.'

'In that case, can we meet somewhere more private than here? Someone's bound to spot us with money changing hands in broad daylight.'

'No problem,' said the uniformed man. 'Where do you suggest?'

'Do you know The Dog and Duck?'

'In Pilbeam Mews?'

'That's the one. Say nine o'clock tonight? On the corner outside it, near the toilets?'

'By the toilets it is.' The uniformed man nodded. 'Nine o'clock.'

Lampson walked into the office, a smug smirk on his face. Coburg looked enquiringly at him, looking to see if anyone was with him. When it became apparent that Lampson was on his own, he asked, 'So, what have you done with him?'

'Done with who?' feigned Lampson.

'Ben's friend Colin,' said Coburg. 'I heard you'd picked him up.'

'I booked him into the custody suite downstairs,' said Lampson. 'I'm guessing you're not going to charge him and that he's bait.'

'He is,' agreed Coburg, 'and our fish is already biting. Wright phoned me to tell me that Colin had nothing to do with what happened to Rhodes-Armfield and we should let him go.'

'What did you say?'

'I told him to hand himself in.'

'Do you think he will?'

Coburg nodded. 'I believe so. The longer Colin's here with us, Wright's imagination will be working overtime worrying what we're doing to his pal. I'm guessing he might come in tomorrow, after he's had a whole night to worry about him.'

'Tomorrow won't be good for me, guv,' Lampson said doubtfully. 'We've got a football match tomorrow against St Ethelred's Boys Choir.'

'Don't worry, I can handle him,' said Coburg.

'You're down to have tomorrow off as well,' Lampson reminded him.

'I'll explain it to Rosa. She'll understand.'

'So long as that's alright,' said Lampson.

'It is,' said Coburg. He became aware that his sergeant was hovering, as if weighing up something he wanted to say, but was unsure how to express it. 'Yes?' he asked.

Lampson sat down.

'Talking of Rosa,' he said, 'I've got a favour to ask. Actually, it's Eve who wants to ask her a favour.'

'What sort of favour?'

'I'm not supposed to tell you, Eve says it's for her to ask, but the thing is she needs a maid of honour for the wedding.'

'I thought her mother was doing that?'

'She was, but Eve and her mum have had a bit of a bust-up.'

'Over this Vic character?'

'Yes. Paula says if Eve goes ahead with marrying me, she won't condone it by being her maid of honour.'

'That's a bit harsh.'

'It is. Eve got upset with Paula going on about Vic all the time and how I wasn't right for her, so Eve quit her mum's house. She's staying with a cousin of hers, Betty, before the wedding.'

'Can't this cousin act as her maid of honour?'

'Betty's not keen. She's very shy. And Eve really wants this to be a special day.' Lampson hesitated, then said awkwardly, 'So, she'd like to ask Rosa if she'd be her maid of honour.'

'Rosa?'

'Yes. Rosa as maid of honour, you as best man. At least you'd know you two would get on. I've known some weddings where the best man and the maid of honour hated each other. Ruined the whole occasion.'

'Well, all I can do is ask her,' said Coburg.

'That's the thing. Eve's a stickler for protocol about doing everything the right way, and she says she's got to be the one to ask Rosa.'

'I see.'

'So I was wondering, would it be alright if Eve and I called in this evening, early-like, and Eve could ask her? Unless you've got arrangements already made for this evening.'

'No,' said Coburg. 'Not as far as I know, anyway. Yes, alright. We'll see you later.'

'You won't tell her why we're calling?' asked Lampson, concerned. 'Only Eve . . .'

'Wants to ask Rosa herself.' Coburg nodded. 'No problem. My lips are sealed.'

They were interrupted by the telephone ringing. Lampson picked it up.

'DCI Coburg's office.' He listened, then said, 'Yes, he's here, Mrs Coburg. I'll put you on to him.' He held out the receiver towards Coburg and whispered, 'Talk of the devil, it's herself.'

'Yes, I got that impression when you called her Mrs Coburg,' said Coburg. He took the phone. 'Is everything alright?'

'Everything's fine,' said Rosa. 'I'm calling because I thought you might like to know that Magnus is playing at Lord's today.'

'What?' said Coburg, bewildered. 'What do you mean? Playing cricket?'

'What else would they be playing at Lord's?' asked Rosa.

'But how?' asked Coburg.

'I don't know the details, it's just that I've just had a phone call from one of your newspaper pals, Bernie Rich.'

'He does the sports column for *The Times*.'

'Exactly. He's at Lord's for this special cricket match today.'

'The Empire XI against the Combined Services XI,' interrupted Coburg.

'Yes, that's what Bernie said. And it's been announced that due to one of the Empire team being injured, His Grace the Earl of Dawlish, Magnus Saxe-Coburg, will be playing in his place.'

'My God!' said Coburg. 'This is unbelievable! Magnus playing at Lord's!'

'Surely he's played there before.'

'Yes, but that was before the war. And I'm talking about the First War. Did Bernie say where he was in the batting order?'

'No.'

Coburg looked at the clock. 'I'm guessing he's at the tail end, if the Empire team went in to bat first. I can't imagine him opening. At least we've got a chance to see him fielding.'

'See him?' asked Rosa.

'Of course. We can't miss this opportunity. It will never come again. Get your coat; I'll pick you up.'

'We won't be able to get in. Bernie said Lord's is packed out.'

'Not for Magnus Saxe-Coburg's brother and his sister-in-law. If they try to stop us going in, I'll produce my warrant card and say I'm on official police business.'

'With your wife?'

'An important material witness,' said Coburg. 'I'll see you shortly.'

He hung up, and Lampson looked at him, impressed.

'Magnus playing at Lord's? That's *the* cricket ground, isn't it?'

'The cricket holy of holies,' confirmed Coburg, getting to his feet and reaching for his coat. He hesitated, then said to his sergeant, 'You aren't a cricket man, are you?'

Lampson rose, grinning happily. 'I'm prepared to be converted,' he said. 'Are you sure it'll be alright me coming along?'

'Let anyone try and stop us,' said Coburg determinedly.

Bill Biggs sat in the poky room in the run-down lodging house that was his home. It wasn't much of a place, one room in a tall crumbling Victorian house that had been divided into eight 'flatlets', as the landlord called them. These so-called flatlets – basically bed-sitting rooms – were crammed into three floors of the old house. There was a toilet on each of the three landings. No bathroom. Ablutions took the form of filling an enamel bowl with water and washing different parts of your body at a time. That was if you wanted an all-over wash. In truth, Bill, like most of the other tenants of the house, made do with a cursory under-arm rinse and a quick douse of his privates, what his mum used to call a whore's wash. And she would have known.

As he sat there, he thought again of what had happened at the yard. He knew what had happened to Max because he'd seen the police car hit him. Bill had ben lurking in the yard after Ma Baxter and Degsy had been taken by the law, dodging from barn to barn, on the lookout for an opportunity to get away. Max opening the gates and running out had been his chance, especially once the copper had run Max down. All attention had been on Max under the car, and Bill had sneaked out and then run off without being spotted. Bill assumed that Micky had died, which meant Monty was the only one of the boys to survive.

Bill wondered how Degsy was. Was he in prison? Was Ma in prison as well? And Monty? Part of him kept expecting the law to come looking for him, but then he told himself that Degsy would never do that. Degsy would never grass him up.

Bill had started working for Marcus and Ma over twenty years before, soon after he'd come out of prison. The charge had been causing criminal damage while drunk; the sentence had been twelve months. It had been a bloke he'd met inside who'd suggested he contact Marcus Baxter when he got out. Bill did, and for the past twenty years he'd become fixture at the pawnbroker's and the yard. Degsy had arrived eight years ago. Luckily, they'd hit it off. They trusted one another and they watched each other's backs, especially against Ma. Ma could be vicious, and dangerous. He wondered what would happen to Ma and Degsy. More importantly, he wondered what was going to happen to him. Without Ma running the business, he was out of work. No income. No way to pay his rent for this crummy little room, let alone buy food and drink. The only thing he could do to survive was sell off things in the yard and the barns. But would he be able to get to them? The law would surely be keeping an eye on the place. The two St John Ambulance women would have told the police there'd been two men at the place. They already had Degsy under lock and key, so they'd be looking out for him. He might have to leave the area. Start somewhere new. Maybe up north? Or the Midlands?

A loud banging on his door pulled him out of his reverie.

Who was that? Had Degsy decided to grass him up and

given the police his address? They would have made him an offer: a lighter sentence if he gave up the bloke who'd been with him.

The banging came again, even louder, and this time a hard woman's voice came with it: Ma Baxter.

'Bill, open this door! I know you're in there!'

Biggs unlocked the door and pulled it open, and Prudence Baxter pushed past him into the room.

'You're out,' said Biggs in surprise.

'Of course I bloody am!'

'What about Degsy? And Monty?'

'Monty's out. Degsy's still in. I'm gonna see what I can do. Where did you get to?'

'I managed to get away.'

'But you know what happened? To Max and Micky?'

Biggs nodded.

'That's why I'm here. I want you to teach Monty to shoot a gun.'

'Why?'

'Because I said so.'

'But why?'

'Because Monty's brothers are dead and he needs to understand that if you're going to get on and be top dog in this business, and he will be, you have to make sure people know you're capable of dealing with revenge personally.'

Biggs looked at her, shocked. 'You want him to shoot someone?'

'Two people. The copper who stopped those ambulance women working on Micky. And the copper who ran Max down.'

Biggs shook his head. 'No, you can't. Monty's not like that.'

'No, he isn't, but he will be.' She fixed him with a steely glare of anger. 'At the moment he isn't tough like Max or Micky. He was the runt of the litter. The weak one. And we know why. Because he's yours!' She sneered at him. 'I should never have shagged you. It only happened because Marcus was in the clink and I hadn't had any for a long time. I never thought I'd get pregnant, but I did, and now the other two are gone, he's all I've got. So I want him to step up. You teach him.'

'No,' said Biggs.

She swung her hand, smacking him on the side of the face. 'Don't you ever say no to me,' she snarled.

CHAPTER THIRTY

As had been forecast, the audience for the cricket match at Lord's was packed, but Coburg had used his brother's name to gain admission, and they found themselves squeezed into seats in a privileged area along with Sir Pelham Warner and Malcolm.

'I'm so glad you made it,' said Warner. He smiled at Rosa. 'It's a pleasure to finally met you, Mrs Coburg. And you, too, Mr Lampson.' He leant towards Rosa and whispered, 'I heard you on the Henry Hall show on the wireless. Absolutely superb.'

There was a round of enthusiastic applause from the crowd to greet the Empire XI walking out ready to take their fielding positions.

'How did Magnus do in the batting?' Coburg whispered to Malcolm.

'Better than expected,' admitted Malcolm. 'He hit a couple of good singles before being bowled. Not bad, especially against a demon like Freddy Pearce.'

They watched Magnus walk towards the boundary and take up a position along the perimeter.

'Deep extra cover,' Malcolm informed Rosa. 'At least he's not in the firing line.'

Rosa looked enquiringly at Coburg, who explained, 'The fielders grouped closest to the batsmen – slips, silly point, silly mid-off, silly mid-on, leg, short leg, and so on – are the ones most likely to find themselves trying to catch a ball travelling at its fastest. Possibly for someone like Magnus, a deep position – long on, long off, deep fine leg or those others – hopefully keeps him out of harm's way.'

'There's no guarantee of that with someone like Magnus,' commented Malcolm dourly.

Coburg recognised the giant figure of Bob Appleyard, the South African, tossing the cricket ball in his hand as he and the rest of the team watched the opening pair for the Combined Services XI walk from the pavilion towards the wicket.

'Eddie Hearne and Freddy Pearce,' Malcolm told Rosa. 'Top class, both of them. Pearce, in particular, is a magnificent slogger. Hits them high and wide.'

'Freddy Pearce,' remembered Rosa. 'He was the one who bowled Magnus.'

'Well remembered,' Malcolm complimented her. 'We'll make a cricket fan of you yet.'

The two batsmen took their places at their respective wickets, with Pearce facing the bowling of Bob Appleyard to open.

Appleyard walked back from the wicket for what seemed like a long distance, turned, and then hammered towards the wicket surprisingly fast for such a large man. He let fly with a scorcher of a delivery, which hurtled towards Pearce. Pearce lifted his bat, stepped back, and then swung. The crack of willow against leather echoed all round the ground, and with the force of the collision the ball soared high up into the sky, and then began to drop, right to where Magnus was standing. Magnus put up both hands and collected the falling ball. For a second he seemed to stumble from the impact, then he nearly recovered his balance, but fell to his knees on the grass. However, he raised his right hand, proudly showing the ball in his hand.

'Out for a duck!' shouted Coburg. He rose to his feet and began applauding. 'He got Pearce out for a duck! What a catch!'

'Sheer showmanship,' sniffed Malcolm disapprovingly. 'All that dropping to his knees nonsense. Completely unnecessary. I'll have something to say to him later.'

'Oh come on, Malcolm,' said Coburg. 'You've got to admit, that was something special. To catch out someone of the calibre of Feddy Pearce. And first ball!'

'It was thanks to Appleyard's delivery,' said Malcolm. Then, grudgingly he added, 'Still, not bad for a man his age.'

The game ended with a narrow victory for the Empire XI.

'You've got to admit it, Malcolm,' said Coburg. 'If Magnus hadn't got that catch, Freddy Pearce would have decimated the bowling.'

'Possibly,' said Malcolm reluctantly. 'Anyhow, I shall now go and congratulate His Grace and toast his performance with good brandy in the members' bar. Will you join us?'

'Thank you, Malcolm, but I have some unfinished business I need to attend to.' Catching Rosa's surprised look, he whispered to her. 'I'll tell you later.'

'Is this business going to take all evening?' she asked.

'No,' said Coburg.

'Then can I suggest we take Magnus and Malcolm out

for a celebratory meal this evening? After all, today has been something special.'

Coburg looked at Malcolm. 'What do you think?' he asked.

'I think that is a lovely idea,' he said. 'Magnus can spend the evening showing off, and I know a lovely restaurant that has a piano, and it would make it really special if you could serenade us, Rosa.'

'I'd be delighted,' said Rosa.

Malcolm turned to Coburg. 'What time will this unfinished business be finished?'

'Er, how does seven o'clock sound?' asked Coburg.

'Seven o'clock it is,' said Malcolm. 'Come to the flat and we'll go from there. It's not far.'

'It's still our treat,' said Rosa.

As Malcolm went in search of Magnus to tell him the news, Coburg, Rosa and Lampson joined the throng flooding out of Lord's and made for the car park, where Coburg had parked their police car.

'Want a lift back to Somers Town?' Coburg asked Lampson as they reached the car.

'No thanks, guv. I'll make my own way back. And, er . . .' Lampson looked meaningfully at Coburg and gave him a conspiratorial wink, before walking off.

'What was all that?' asked Rosa, intrigued.

'All what?' asked Coburg.

'That wink Ted gave you. What are you two up to?'

'A wink?' said Coburg, putting on an air of innocence.

'Oh come on, Edgar, you don't fool me. Was that this unfinished business you were talking about?'

Coburg gave a sigh. It was true, he couldn't fool Rosa. He

unlocked the car and, as they got in, he thought about his promise to Lampson not to tell Rosa about Lampson and Eve calling, and their reason, and decided it was impossible. For one thing, Rosa would be furious with him for not warning her in advance that Lampson and Eve would be calling. And, once he'd told her they'd be calling, she'd want to know why. As far as Coburg was concerned, it was absolutely a no-win situation for him, and if he didn't want to spend the evening being lectured to at great length by Rosa on the fact that his first loyalty was to her and not to his sergeant and his fiancée, he needed to warn her. And, also, to swear her to silence about knowing why they were coming.

'Ted and Eva will be popping in,' he said. 'Possibly soon after we get home, I expect.'

She looked at him, puzzled. 'Why?' she asked.

Coburg gave a sigh. 'I'm not supposed to tell you because Eve wants to ask you herself, but she wants you to be her maid of honour.'

'Me? Why me?' asked Rosa.

'Her mother was supposed to do it, but she's pulled out.'

'Pulled out?'

'Yes.'

'Why? Cold feet?'

'Not just that, I get the impression she's unhappy about the whole wedding. She tried to get Eve to call it off.'

'Why?'

'She doesn't like Ted. She thinks he's low. She wants Eve to marry some other chap, a local builder. Someone with more money than Ted.'

'What an awful woman!'

'I agree. But when Eve asks you, act surprised. I'm not supposed to have said anything about it. I promised Ted.'

'Don't worry. I'll act surprised, and I'll also be gushing in my enthusiasm for doing it.'

'No too gushing,' warned Coburg. 'It might make her suspicious.' As he started the car up, he said ruefully, 'While it's confession time, I need to go into the office tomorrow for a short while.'

'On a Sunday? I thought we could have the day off and go somewhere nice.'

'So did I, but I'm hoping a murderer will come in and make a confession. Ted can't be there to deal with it, he's got a football match, and I'd quite like to wrap this murder up.'

'What makes you so sure this murderer will come in?'

Coburg sketched out the story for her: Ben Wright going AWOL, and his alleged boyfriend being brought in to Scotland Yard as bait to reel him in.

'You really think he'll come in?'

'I do. But I could be wrong.'

'You have my blessing,' she said. 'We'll always have another Sunday. And we will have this evening as a celebration.'

As they walked into their flat, the telephone was ringing. Coburg picked it up.

'Coburg,' he said.

'It's DC Burton,' came the constable's apologetic voice. 'I'm sorry to report, sir, we lost the suspect.'

'What? How?'

'He didn't come out for ages, but when he did we put your orders into practice. I led, then after a while Armstrong took

264

over from me, then I took the lead again. The suspect went into a few shops and browsed.'

'What sort of shops?'

'Record shops and bookshops. And then he went into a hotel. He went to the lounge and ordered a pot of tea and a cake. After he'd finished he went to the desk and paid, and then went to the gents' toilet. After he didn't come out after fifteen minutes, I went to the gents'. He wasn't there, but I discovered there was another entrance to the toilets, which led to a back corridor. He must have gone out that way.'

Damn, thought Coburg. Aloud, he asked, 'What happened next?'

'We went back to his flat. This time Armstrong went up to the flat to try the Mr Bedford trick, but there was no answer.'

'Do you think he spotted you?' asked Coburg.

'I don't know, Maybe was just being cautious.'

No, thought Coburg. *He spotted you.*

Coburg hung up, then asked the operator to get him MI5 at Wormwood Scrubs. As he anticipated, Inspector Hibbert wasn't in that day.

'Could you get a message to him at home, or leave one for when he comes in,' said Coburg. 'Tell him Chief Inspector Coburg called. With reference to the set of fingerprints I left for him earlier today, I had two constables tailing the suspect after I visited him at his flat. Unfortunately, they lost him. I don't know if the suspect has returned to his flat or gone somewhere else.'

He replaced the receiver with a sigh of annoyance.

'Problems?' asked Rosa. 'Has this murderer you're hoping will call in tomorrow done a runner?'

'No, it's another suspect in another case who seems to have vanished.'

'What's this one done?'

'I'm not sure. He could be involved in a murder, or it might be espionage.'

'A spy?'

'Possibly, but at the moment I don't know. I'm clutching at straws.'

There was the sound of their doorbell ringing.

'I'm betting that could be Ted and Eve come to ask their favour,' said Coburg.

'In that case, I'm prepared to be happily surprised,' said Rosa as she made for the door.

She opened it and found Lampson and Eve on the doormat.

'Why, hello!' She smiled. 'Is this an official call, Sergeant?' Then she chuckled. 'I guess not as Eve is with you. Come in, both of you.'

Lampson and Eve returned her smile and entered the flat.

'Edgar, it's Ted and Eve!' called Rosa. 'This way.'

She ushered them into the living room, where Coburg had picked up a newspaper and was sitting pretending to read it. Coburg stood up and gestured for them to sit.

'Well, this is a pleasant surprise,' he said.

'We're sorry if we're interrupting anything,' apologised Eve.

'You're not interrupting anything,' said Rosa.

'We're here because I've got a favour to ask,' said Eve. 'You know we're getting married next Saturday.'

'Indeed,' said Rosa. 'Edgar's been practising his best man speech. The wedding breakfast after is to be at your school, I believe.'

'It is,' said Eve. 'The headmaster has generously said we could have the hall. The thing is, I've got a problem with my maid of honour. Or, rather, the person who was going to be my maid of honour.'

'Oh?' said Rosa, putting on a look of puzzlement.

'Yes. My mother was going to do it, but I'm afraid we've had a bit of a falling-out. It looks like she's not even going to be at the ceremony.'

'Oh dear!' said Rosa. 'Why?'

'I'd rather not go into details,' said Eve. 'It's just something that blew up, as these things sometimes do. Anyway, I know it's short notice, but I wondered if you'd agree to be my maid of honour?'

'Me?' said Rosa, surprised. 'But shouldn't it be one of your family, or a best friend?'

'Because of the issue with my mother, I'd rather not ask a relative, otherwise it's about them taking sides. And for friends, I haven't really got any who I'm close to, except for Ted.'

'And I'm already involved as the bridegroom.' Lampson grinned.

'So, I know it's a bit of a cheek, but I'd be so grateful . . .'

'No, I'm the grateful one!' Rosa beamed. 'I've never been a maid of honour before. This is so flattering to be asked. Of course I'll do it, and with the greatest of pleasure. Do we need a rehearsal, so I know what to do?'

'Yes please,' said Eve delightedly. 'Are you free on Tuesday? If so I can arrange with the vicar for us to meet at St Pancras Church after school finishes and we can go through the procedures.'

'Tuesday will be perfect,' said Rosa. 'I'll arrange for an early shift at the ambulance station. Will the vicar be free at, say, four o'clock?'

'I'll check and let you know,' said Eve. 'But I'm sure it'll be alright. He's being very supportive.'

Rosa turned to Edgar and said, 'This call for a celebration! Open a bottle.' Then she asked Eve and Lampson, 'If that's alright with you?'

'Yes, please,' said Eve. She smiled at Rosa and said, 'I'm so grateful for this. It will make our wedding perfect. You as my maid of honour, the chief inspector as Ted's best man, and Terry's agreed to be a page.'

'Dressed up in a medieval pageboy's outfit?' asked Coburg.

'In a suit,' said Ted. 'Anything else would have been asking too much, especially if his mates saw him.'

Coburg opened a bottle of white wine. 'It should be champagne,' he said as he poured it into four glasses, 'but this'll have to do.'

The four sat and toasted the bride and groom, then discussed the details of the actual wedding: who'd be attending and if the couple had any plans on where to spend their honeymoon.

'We've decided to leave any honeymoon until the war's over,' said Eve. 'Travelling anywhere is dangerous. Even the seaside towns are getting bombed.'

They chatted for a brief while longer, then Coburg apologetically excused himself and Rosa. 'I'm sorry to cut this short, but we're having dinner with my brother this evening to celebrate his appearance at Lord's Cricket Ground today,' he explained. 'And I know, at his age, he'd like to get home before the bombing starts tonight. *If* it starts, that is.'

'Yes, Ted told me about the cricket match,' said Eve. 'Your brother must be very proud.'

'He is, but quietly,' said Coburg. 'He's never been one to boast about his achievements.'

After Lampson and Eve had left, Coburg hugged Rosa to him and kissed her.

'You were magnificent,' he said. 'You should have been an actress.'

'It's what performers do,' she said. 'We put on a show and hope it's convincing.'

'You were absolutely convincing,' Coburg told her. 'Now to join the Laurel and Hardy of the cricketing world.'

By quarter to seven, Coburg and Rosa were seated with Magnus and Malcolm at a small but exquisitely decorated restaurant in Piccadilly.

'We chose this because the food is first-rate, and also because it's not too far from your flat,' said Magnus. 'So, if the Luftwaffe decide to start earlier tonight, you haven't got far to go to get to your shelter.'

'On the other hand, Reginald, the owner, has a large cellar beneath this restaurant, which would afford us a place of safety if the swines attack while we're dining,' said Malcolm. He smiled. 'It also serves as his wine cellar, so we'd be well supplied with some excellent liquid refreshment.'

Talk naturally turned to the match that had been played that day, with Malcolm waxing lyrical about the performance of the Empire XI batting.

'There was one absolutely spectacular performance by this youngster, Trevor Bailey. And I do mean youngster. Just a schoolboy. He plays for Dulwich College. An incredible performer. He's just what . . . eighteen?'

'Seventeen, I believe,' said Magnus.

'Top of Dulwich's batting and bowling averages in 1939 and 1940,' enthused Malcolm. 'He's one to watch for the future, I promise you.' Then he gave a rueful sigh as he added, 'Although I understand he's planning to join the Royal Marines, so what sort of future there is for him is in the lap of the gods.'

'Talking of performances, that was a wonderful catch you made today,' said Rosa to Magnus.

'A touch of luck.' Magnus smiled modestly.

'No, it was a good catch,' said Malcolm firmly. 'I must admit, Magnus, I had my doubts about how you'd do today. But you proved me wrong. However, I do hope you won't let it go to your head and engage yourself in any more matches at that elite level.'

'If I'm asked, I might consider it,' said Magnus.

Coburg saw that Malcolm was about to give a retort, and, determined to avoid any kind of row between the two old friends, he changed the subject.

'Rosa and I are involved in a wedding next weekend as best man and maid of honour,' he announced. 'My sergeant, Ted Lampson, who you met today, is marrying Eve Bradley, a teacher at the Somers Town primary school.'

'The local registry office, I presume,' said Malcolm.

'No, it's at St Pancras New Church, that large Roman-style church in Euston Road on the corner of Woburn Place, just across the road from Euston station.'

'Ah yes,' said Magnus. 'Very grand. Do you know why it's called St Pancras New Church?'

'No,' said Malcolm, 'but I'm sure you're going to tell us.'

'A friend of mine is on the synod and he's an expert on old churches.'

'But St Pancras Church isn't an old church,' pointed out Coburg. 'I believe it was built in the middle of the last century.'

'Yes, but the clue is in the fact that it's called *New* Church. There's an *old* St Pancras Church in a public gardens on Pancras Road, close to St Pancras railway station. It was built, so it's believed, around about AD 314, when the Romans were still in Britain. It's one of the oldest sites of Christian worship in England.'

'Who was St Pancras?' asked Rosa.

'He was a Roman citizen who converted to Christianity,' said Magnus. 'He was beheaded for his faith when he was just fourteen.'

'Fourteen!' exclaimed Rosa, horrified.

'Age has never been a bar to punishment,' observed Magnus. 'Even as recently as the last century, children could be hanged for certain offences.'

'Including theft,' added Coburg.

'Can I suggest we change the subject,' said Malcolm, 'This is supposed to be a celebration, yet here we are talking about hanging children.'

'Good point,' said Magnus.

Malcolm looked across the table at Rosa and said, 'Would you mind making this evening perfect with a song, my dear? I've had a word with Reginald and he'll be absolutely delighted if you'd play his piano.'

'Of course.' Rosa smiled.

Malcolm was just raising his hand to summon the maître d'

over, when they heard the wail of the air raid siren start up in the street outside. Immediately the diners began to gather their things and settle their bills. There was no rush or panic; everyone knew that this signalled the first sightings of the German heavy bombers and their Messerschmitt escorts coming over the Channel towards the English coast. It would take them a while before they reached London.

'Another time,' said Rosa. 'Next time you're at the flat. A small private concert.'

Magnus cocked his head, listening for the sound of approaching aircraft.

'Typical Germans,' he grumbled. 'No ear for music.'

CHAPTER THIRTY-ONE

Sunday 16th March

The morning of one of their football matches invariably meant people calling at Lampson's house to inform him that their son was unable to play that day for illness, injury, or family issues; so when there was a knock at his door as he was going through Terry's football kit to make sure it was all in order, he assumed it would either be yet another apologetic parent, or someone reporting local bomb damage after last night's raid. When he opened his front door he was surprised to see Eve's mum, Paula Bradley, standing there. Before Lampson could open his mouth, she was on the attack.

'I heard what you did to Vic Tennant,' she said angrily.

'I didn't lay a finger on him,' said Lampson, doing his best to contain his temper at her aggressive attitude.

'You knocked him to the ground.'

'I didn't touch him!'

'Then how come he was in a state?'

'Because he didn't expect me to have words with him after he got his men to beat me up.'

'Beat you up?' she said in disbelief.

'Yes. He thought I'd be scared off.'

'You liar! You went to his yard and threatened him.'

'I wanted to let him know I wasn't going to be scared off from marrying Eve, no matter how many men he sent to attack me.'

'You liar! Vic's a gentleman. Unlike you. Well, let me tell you, Mr Lampson, that there's not going to be a wedding. Not to you, anyway. It's off.'

'How are you going to stop it?'

'By not giving my permission.'

'That won't wash. Eve's old enough to go ahead without your permission.'

'She may not think that when I tell her that if she goes ahead with it, I won't be there. And nor will any of our family.'

'Eve's already left your house,' said Lampson.

'And that's your fault as well,' snapped Mrs Bradley. 'Telling her lies about Vic.'

'Vic Tennant got his men to beat me up.'

'Lies! We'll see what Eve says when I tell her I won't be at your so-called wedding.'

'That's your prerogative,' said Lampson. 'If you choose to boycott your own daughter's wedding that's up to you. Now get off my doorstep.'

With that, he shut the door very firmly.

Coburg sat in his office and stared at his phone, willing it to ring. He'd felt sure that Ben Wright would either call at the Yard and hand himself in, or telephone again. It was now ten o'clock and there'd been no word from him.

Maybe I was wrong, he thought ruefully. *In which case, I'll have blown the chance for Rosa and I to have a lovely day together, and we'll just have to turn Colin Dent loose and mount a large police search for Wright in his home village.*

Then the phone rang. Trying not to sound eager, he picked it up.

'DCI Coburg, there's a call for you from St John's Wood police station.'

'Thank you,' said Coburg.

'DCI Coburg,' said a voice. 'Sergeant Ernie Ward, acting duty sergeant at St John's Wood.'

'Yes, Sergeant Ward. What can I do for you?'

'A dead body was found this morning outside the toilets by The Dog and Duck pub in St John's Wood. He was one of our own, a constable called Arnold Riddick, although he was in civilian clothes, not in uniform.'

'How did he die?'

'Stabbed in the heart.'

'Where's the body?'

'Gone to UCH. Dr Welbourne attended. Detective Inspector Nokes was the attending officer from the murder squad. He said he'd be in touch with you when he'd got back to the Yard, but we knew you'd had dealings with Arnold Riddick, so I thought I'd phone to alert you in case Inspector Nokes is delayed. He said he'd be calling on Arnold's widow to talk to her.'

'Thank you for letting me know,' said Coburg.

Damn, thought Coburg as he hung up the receiver. He wondered what had happened to the watch he'd asked to be put on Riddick. Somebody bungling, he guessed. Someone who had decided there was nothing to see so they'd taken a long break. And now Riddick was dead.

Coburg thought that Inspector Nokes would very likely

be delayed in returning to the Yard, once he became involved with Vera Riddick, if his own experience was anything to go by.

The phone rang again. This time it was the reception desk.

'There's a young man here wants to see you, Chief Inspector,' said the reception sergeant. 'He says his name's Cadet Ben Wright.'

'Could you have him escorted to my office,' said Coburg.

He hung up with a feeling of satisfaction. He'd been right.

A few minutes later, there was a knock at his door, and at his call of 'Come in!', it opened and Ben Wright entered, accompanied by a uniformed constable.

'Take a seat, Ben,' said Coburg, gesturing to the chair opposite him. 'You too, Constable.' As the constable took the other remaining chair, Coburg explained to the young cadet, 'He's here as a witness to our talk. Think of him as your protection, so you can be assured that nothing you say in here will be distorted or twisted.'

Coburg pulled a notepad towards him and took out a pencil as Wright sat down.

'I have to do a formal caution,' Coburg told Wright. 'It's for your protection.' He then spoke the words of the official caution about how anything the person said would be taken down and might be used in evidence against him.

'Now,' he said, 'Richard Rhodes-Armfield.'

'He was evil,' said Wright.

'You kicked him,' said Coburg, keeping his tone gentle and sympathetic. 'In the head.'

'I didn't mean to kill him!' burst out Wright. 'I just wanted to . . . shut him up for a bit.'

'Go on,' said Coburg.

'He was always on about needing money. It was all he talked about. Then he found this letter from my friend.'

'Colin Dent?'

Wright nodded. 'He put a filthy slant on it,' he said, his voice filled with disgust and anger. 'He said he was going to show it to our commanding officer unless I gave him the money he needed. Fifteen pounds. I told him I didn't have it. He said in that case he'd also send it to my parents. I didn't know what to do.'

'You thought he'd carry out his threat?'

'I knew he would!'

'So when you found him lying unconscious on the stairs . . . ?'

'I kicked him. I didn't mean for him to die. I just wanted to put him out of action for a week, until the training was ended and we'd moved on and I was far away from him, out of his clutches.'

'What about the letter?'

'I found it in his things later. I destroyed it.' He looked imploringly at Coburg. 'I didn't mean to kill him, you must believe that. And Colin had nothing to do with any of it.'

Coburg nodded. 'Do you have a solicitor of your own?'

'No.'

'In that case I'll arrange one for you. You'll have to be detained, I'm sure you understand that. But hopefully the solicitor might be able to get you bail.'

'What about Colin?'

'He'll be released immediately,' said Coburg.

'Can I see him?'

'I'm afraid not. Not at the moment. But that may change,

if your solicitor is able to sort something out. It will be a duty solicitor, but I'll do my best to get you a very good one.' He stood up. 'Right, let's get down to the custody suite and book you in. And, I assure you, you'll be safe here.'

Once Coburg had booked Ben Wright in and seen him taken away to the cells, he signed the papers to get Colin Dent released. When Dent arrived, he said, concerned, 'I saw Ben being taken to the cells.'

'Yes. He handed himself in. That's why I've just signed your release.'

'What will happen to Ben?'

'I'm arranging a solicitor for him. He'll be given every help to explain what happened.'

'He didn't mean to kill him.'

'I know, he told me,' said Coburg.

'So it wasn't murder.'

No, thought Coburg, *if his solicitor is any good it'll be manslaughter with extenuating circumstances. But he'll still go to prison.*

'Do you have the money to get home?' Coburg asked. 'Or I can arrange a car. After all, we brought you here.'

'No thank you,' said Dent. 'A police car coming to the village will only cause gossip. I'll make my own way home.'

Coburg shook Dent's hand, then watched him walk out of the building. He was just making for the stairs up to his office, when he was hailed by the sergeant at the reception desk.

'Sorry to trouble you, Chief Inspector, but there's a phone call for you. It's the station master at St John's Wood Tube station and he sounds very upset.'

Coburg took the receiver from the sergeant. 'DCI Coburg,' he said.

'Chief Inspector,' said the voice of Josiah Riggs. He sounded very agitated. 'We've just had a man come in to tell us he was passing Lord's Tube station when he heard the sound of screams coming from within. He saw the notice on the door saying that any enquiries about the station should be made to the Railway Executive Committee or us here at St John's Wood station. We cannot gain entry to the station because you have not yet returned the keys to us. I must insist that be done as a matter of urgency.'

'Of course,' said Coburg. 'But first I'll visit the station and investigate these reports of screams. A crime may well have been committed.'

'In that case, I will be there as well,' said Riggs. 'We are in part responsible for the station.'

Coburg hung up the phone and said to the duty sergeant, 'I need a constable, urgently, to accompany me to Lord's Tube station.'

The sergeant gestured to a uniformed officer, who hurried over.

'PC Dibworth, accompany DCI Coburg,' the sergeant told him.

'Thank you,' said Coburg. 'If Inspector Nokes comes looking for me, tell him I'll be back when I've sorted this out.'

As Coburg made for the Tube station, PC Dibworth next to him in the passenger seat, he reflected on how his day had turned out. He'd only come in in the hope that Ben Wright would appear. Although Wright had arrived, so had the reports of PC Arnold Riddick stabbed to death, and now screams heard from the abandoned Tube station.

Josiah Riggs was waiting impatiently outside the entrance to the Tube station when Coburg pulled up. Coburg hurried to the door and unlocked it, stopping Riggs as he was about to enter. 'Be careful,' he said. 'If there were screams, the assailants could be here. If a crime has been committed, we don't want any evidence disturbed.'

Coburg led the way, followed by Dibworth and the station master. The first sight that met their eyes was the body of a man lying just inside the entrance. His face had been demolished with brutal force, blood and brains scattered around the remains of what had once been a human head.

'Oh my God!' burst out Riggs, and then came the sounds of retching, and vomit cascading onto the metal floor. Coburg stepped nimbly back to avoid his shoes being splattered.

'Wait here,' Coburg told the unfortunate station master. 'There might be more.'

Coburg gestured for Constable Dibworth to follow him and he began to descend the circular stairs. He didn't have to go far before they came to a second body who'd been similarly battered and mutilated.

'Stay here,' Coburg ordered the constable.

He began to descend further down the stairs, being careful to keep watch for any movements. A few steps down he came upon a heavy hammer, the head and the handle very bloodstained.

He must have dumped the hammer down the stairs, Coburg reasoned. In which case, the attacker must have fled the scene.

Coburg climbed back up the stairs, gesturing to the

constable to follow him up to ground level.

'I think it's just those two,' he said. He looked at the station master, who was leaning against the wall, his face as white as a sheet. 'Stay here with him,' said Coburg to Dibworth. 'I'm going to call it in and get a forensics team out.'

CHAPTER THIRTY-TWO

The football match had started badly for Somers Town Boys; St Ethelred's Boys Choir's centre forward had scored inside two minutes, but instead of being demoralised and playing negatively, Somers Town Boys responded with attacking vigour, and as the whistle went for half-time they were 3–1 up, with Terry having scored two of their goals.

'I thought their heads would go down and they'd give up,' said Eve, a broad beam on her face, 'but they didn't.'

'You've trained them well,' said Lampson.

'*We've* trained them well,' Eve corrected him. She looked at him with a fond smile on her face. 'I want to kiss you and hug you right here.'

'So do I, but we can't,' said Lampson. 'That would put the boys off.' He looked at the boys of his team, animatedly talking about the key points in the first half that had turned the game in their favour.

'Good game,' said Mr Lampson, as Lampson's parents joined their son and future daughter-in-law. 'Terry's second goal was a cracker.'

'Everything alright for next Saturday?' Mrs Lampson asked Eve.

'Everything is,' said Eve. 'In a week's time there'll be two Mrs Lampsons.'

'Any word from your mum?'

'No,' said Eve. 'But that's her lookout. If she decides to boycott it, that's her problem.'

'Surely she'll at least turn up,' said Mrs Lampson, concerned.

'That's up to her,' said Eve. 'I haven't heard from her, so I hope she'll turn up. But she may not.'

'She's a stupid cow,' snorted Mr Lampson indignantly.

'Now, now, no need for that sort of talk,' admonished his wife. She turned to Eve and asked, 'If she doesn't, what are you going to do for a maid of honour? Betty?'

Eve shook her head. 'I asked her, but she doesn't want to.' She smiled as she said, 'Ted's boss's wife is doing it.'

'The jazz singer?' said Mrs Lampson, impressed. 'Rosa Weeks?'

'That's right. I asked her last night, and she said yes. She's a really lovely woman. So, we'll have her as my maid of honour, and her husband as Ted's best man.'

'A famous jazz singer and a member of the royal family!' said Mrs Lampson, awed. 'This is going to be the most impressive wedding we've ever had in Somers Town!'

Coburg sat in the police car and radioed through to Scotland Yard, reporting the discovery of the two dead bodies.

'I need a doctor and a forensics team as a matter of urgency at the abandoned Lord's Tube station. Can you see if Inspector Durward is available? Over.'

'Message received, Echo Seven. Please stand by and I'll get back to you after I've made contact.'

'Thank you, Base. Echo Seven over and out.'

Coburg hung up the receiver and stepped out of the car,

then went into the station entrance where the ashen-faced Josiah Riggs was leaning against a wall. He looked like he was going to be sick again.

'I've reported it in, Mr Riggs,' said Coburg. 'A doctor and a forensics team should be on their way. I'll wait here for them. I'll need to hang on to the keys to the station for a bit longer, while the investigation continues.'

Riggs nodded in agreement. He looked in no fit state to argue for the keys to be returned to him.

'There's little more you can do here, so I suggest you go home and I'll make contact with you once I've got something to report.'

Riggs looked at him, shock still showing on his face.

'In all my years I've never seen anything as bad as that,' he said. 'There have been fatalities, people throwing themselves under trains, but this . . .' He dried up. 'How do you cope with it?'

'I'm afraid it's part of being a detective with the murder squad,' said Coburg. 'But you never get used to it.'

Riggs stumbled out of the station and made for his car, parked a few yards away.

'Are you alright to drive?' Coburg called out to him, concerned.

'I will be,' said Riggs. And he got into his car and drove slowly away.

Coburg turned to the waiting Constable Dibworth. 'I'll be in the car if you need me, waiting for a call from Base. Your job is to stop anyone else coming in. You never know when some tramp or other might wander in if he sees the door ajar.'

* * *

Rosa was sitting reading the Sunday newspapers when the phone rang. *Edgar*, she thought hopefully, *telling me he's on his way home and we can go out somewhere after all.* Instead, it was a man's voice she didn't recognise.

'Good afternoon, Mrs Coburg. I'm sorry to trouble you on a Sunday, but this is Inspector Hibbert of MI5. Is DCI Coburg there.'

'No, he's at Scotland Yard.'

'Oh? I thought he had today off.'

'So did I,' said Rosa ruefully.

'So I should be able to get hold of him at Scotland Yard?'

'Unless he's out on a case. If he contacts me, I'll tell him you called.'

As she hung up the phone she thought ruefully, *Even less chance of me seeing Edgar today.*

Coburg got the message over the radio to tell him that Dr Welbourne was on his way, as was a forensic team led by Inspector Durward. Relieved, he returned to the station.

'The medic and forensics are on their way,' he told PC Dibworth. 'Once they're here we can leave them with the keys and get back to the Yard.'

Dr Welbourne was the first to arrive. He took a look at the bodies and said, 'You don't need to be a detective to see that whoever killed these two men had a lot of rage in him. I've arranged for an ambulance to pick them up and take them to UCH.'

'Can you hold off on that for the moment?' said Coburg. 'I've got a forensics team coming and I'd like them to take a proper look at everything in situ before the bodies are taken.'

'That's fine by me,' said Welbourne. 'Can I leave it with you to arrange the transfer of the bodies to UCH once forensics are ready? If the ambulance turns up, give them my apologies for calling them out prematurely.'

'Thanks, Doctor. And next time we get something like this, I promise I'll let you know how bad the situation is first.'

As Dr Welbourne left, an ambulance was just pulling up. Welbourne explained to them in a few words that they weren't needed at the moment, and then departed. As the ambulance moved off, the forensic team arrived from Scotland Yard. Coburg greeted Harry Durward with a handshake, and handed him the keys to the station.

'We haven't explored the place; we thought it best to leave it to you and your men rather than trample all over it and mess up any evidence,' said Coburg, indicating the station entrance. 'Inside you'll find one body, with his head obliterated, in the ticket reception area, and another with the same kind of injuries partway down a flight of stairs. Fingerprints of both bodies are going to be essential if we have any chance of identifying them. We'll leave you to do your work. I'm heading back to Scotland Yard, if anything comes up here you feel is urgent.'

'I'm guessing it's all urgent, if we want to catch whoever did it,' said Durward. 'I thought you had this Sunday off.'

'So did I,' said Coburg ruefully.

Coburg summoned PC Dibworth and the pair made their way back to Scotland Yard.

'Thanks for your help today,' Coburg said to the constable.

'I felt like a spare part for most of it, to be honest, sir,' said Dibworth.

'I know the feeling,' said Coburg.

He made his way up the stairs to his office. As he entered his office, his phone was ringing. It was Inspector Hibbert.

'I thought you'd be at home today,' said Hibbert.

'So did I.'

'Yes, I got that impression from your wife.'

'You phoned the flat?'

'I did. I thought you'd want to know about the prints you supplied. We've got a match. This chap Etheridge.'

Coburg nodded. 'On the cricket bat. He told me he'd handled it when Bartlett was staying with him.'

'Not just the cricket bat,' said Hibbert. 'They're also on the radio.'

'You're sure?'

'Absolutely. Etheridge is one of this ring of spies, along with George Grimshaw, and one other unknown.'

'You got my message about him giving my men the slip?'

'I did. I hope you gave them hell.'

Rather than answer, Coburg asked, 'What about the other prints I gave you?'

'None of them match with the radio, the cricket bat, the cricket bag, or anything else. I'm going to see if this Etheridge has returned to his flat. Do you want to come along?'

'I'm afraid I've got to be here in case Inspector Nokes arrives. He's investigating a murder.'

'Connected with your cricketer?'

'It could well be. One of the policemen at St John's Wood was stabbed to death last night. Nokes is supposed to be coming here with his report. The trouble is I keep being called out. I'm not long back from Lord's Tube station, where there's been a double murder.'

'Who got killed?'

'It's hard to say. Both men have had their faces obliterated with a heavy hammer. One of them may even be Peter Etheridge.'

'Where are the bodies? I'll check their fingerprints, or did our murderer smash their hands up?'

'No, their hands looked intact. Harry Durward and his forensics team are there at the moment, going through everything.'

'Will it be alright if I go there? If one of them turns out to be Etheridge, it'll save me looking for him.'

'Be my guest. You know Harry Durward, don't you?'

'I do. Good bloke. I'll let you know how I get on.'

No sooner had Coburg replaced the receiver, than his phone rang gain. This time it was the reception desk.

'Sorry to trouble you, sir, but Inspector Nokes is here with a Mrs Vera Riddick, who wants to see you. Would you prefer to see her here in reception, or . . . ?'

'No, I'll see her here in my office. Please tell Inspector Nokes to bring her up.'

Vera Riddick was understandably in an antagonistic mood, although not as combative as on the previous occasion. Even as Inspector Nokes was opening his mouth to introduce her, Mrs Riddick beat him to it.

'You told me my Arnold was in danger,' she said accusingly. 'Protective whatever it was, you said.'

'Protective custody.'

'To save his life. But it didn't work. Who did it? Who were you trying to protect him from? Who killed him?'

'We don't know, Mrs Riddick.'

'But you must have some idea! You took him into that protective whatever. Who did you think was after him?'

'That's what Inspector Nokes and I are looking into.'

'Was it the Germans? You said it was about national security.'

'Did he have any contact with Germans?' asked Coburg, intrigued that Vera Riddick had raised the matter.

'No, he didn't.'

'Were there any criminals who might have wanted him dead?'

She shook her head. 'Arnold didn't get involved with criminals. He mostly stayed at the station doing paperwork. He did his beat patrols, same as the rest of them.'

'Can you think of anyone who might have wanted to harm him?'

'No. Everyone liked Arnold.' Suddenly she began to cry. 'I don't know what I'm going to do without him.' She became angry and accusative again as she said, 'It's got to do with what you said before, this protective custody business. That's the only thing it can be. You knew about it, so you must know who you were protecting him from.'

'I'm sorry, Mrs Riddick, I wish I could tell you, but at the moment we have no information as to who might have been a danger to your husband.'

'But you must have or you wouldn't have locked him up.'

'There were unspecified threats being talked about aimed at some of the staff at St John's Wood police station. Your husband was just one of those staff we brought into protective custody. When there was no further information forthcoming, it was decided it was a false alarm and they were allowed to go home.'

'And Arnold was killed!' She pointed an accusing finger at

him. 'This is your fault! He's dead because of you! Because you didn't do your job properly!'

'Mrs Riddick—' began Coburg, but she cut him off.

'I'm going to get justice for my Arnold. I'm going to have this investigated. I'm going to complain to the commissioner of police, and I'm going to report it to my member of parliament. You're not going to get away with this!'

'You're entitled to raise it with your MP, Mrs Riddick, and with the commissioner. I will make myself available to them for any questions they might have. All I can say at this moment is I'm very sorry for your loss.'

'You're going to be even sorrier!' she snarled.

With that, she strode to the door and left, slamming the door behind her.

Inspector Nokes looked at Coburg apologetically. 'I'm sorry about that, sir, but she insisted on seeing you. I didn't know what else to do.'

'You did the right thing,' Coburg reassured him. 'All we can do now is find out who killed him, and why.'

CHAPTER THIRTY-THREE

After the tirade from Vera Riddick, and the events of the day, it was with a sense of relief that Coburg made his way home.

'Bad day at the office?' asked Rosa as she saw the unhappy expression on his face.

'Dreadful day,' said Coburg. 'Thanks God it's over.'

'It's not quite over,' said Rosa. 'Inspector Hibbert phoned for you just before you walked in. He asked if you could call him as soon as you get home.' She picked up a sheet of paper and handed it to him. 'I wrote his number down.'

'Thanks,' said Coburg. 'I'll phone him and get it over with.'

'Would a whisky help?' asked Rosa as Coburg picked up the phone and asked the operator for the number.

'It would be manna from heaven,' said Coburg gratefully.

After a series of clicks from the phone, he heard the voice of Hibbert.

'Coburg,' he said. 'You asked me to call you.'

'I've just got back from Lord's Tube station,' said Hibbert. 'I checked the fingerprints of both the dead men, as well as those on the hammer. Neither were Etheridge. George Grimshaw is one of the dead men; his body was the one found lying down the stairs. The other dead body, the one just inside the entrance, is the unidentified man whose prints were also on the radio.

Peter Etheridge's prints are on the handle of the hammer. So it looks like he's killed both of his fellow spies. I'm on my way to his flat with a couple of men to pick him up, in case he came back. I thought I'd let you know.'

'Thanks,' said Coburg.

Coburg hung up and gave Rosa an apologetic look. Then he took the receiver off the hook and laid it down.

'There,' he said. 'If anyone tries to phone us again tonight, they'll be unlucky. Our day off has already been ruined. I only went to the office in the hope that Ben Wright, this RAF cadet, might come in, which he did. But I've also had three more murders, two of them committed by our Jamaican jazz fan, Peter Etheridge.' He shook his head. 'Hardly what I'd call a day off.'

Inspector Hibbert rang the bell of the flat again. Again, there was no answer. Hibbert turned to the two men he'd brought along to accompany him.

'Shardlow,' he said. 'Open it.'

Gerald Shardlow took a bunch of skeleton keys from his pocket. In his other pocket he kept a pack of lockpicks, just in case none of the skeleton keys worked.

'Think he might be lying in wait, guv?' asked Terry Maris, the other man, his hand resting on the pistol in his pocket.

Hibbert shook his head. 'If anything, he'll have topped himself. Taken a handful of sleeping pills, or hung himself.'

'Not many places to hang yourself in these modern flats,' said Shardlow, trying the skeleton keys. 'The ceiling's aren't high enough.' He gave a triumphant smile as one of the keys worked. He pushed open the door.

'Me first,' said Hibbert, entering the flat.

He walked through the flat, finding no sign of anybody, and no sign of any disturbance.

'Check the cupboards,' he told his two men.

Shardlow and Maris checked the cupboards, and bathroom and toilet. There was no one in the flat.

Hibbert led his two men out of the flat and relocked the door. Then the inspector rang the bell of the flat opposite. They had to wait a short while before it was opened by a woman in her seventies who looked out at them suspiciously.

'Yes?' she asked.

Hibbert produced his warrant card and showed it to her. 'Inspector Hibbert from MI5,' he informed her.

'MI5?' she repeated with a frown. 'Hang on. I'll get my husband. He deals with that sort of thing.'

Hibbert exchanged puzzled looks with his two men. *He deals with that sort of thing?* Did that mean that MI5 often called at this flat?

The woman reappeared, accompanied by a man who looked even older than his wife. In his eighties, Hibbert guessed.

'My wife said you were from MI5.'

'Yes, sir,' said Hibbert.

'Let's see your ID.'

Hibbert produced his warrant card and showed it. The man looked at Shardlow and Maris. 'And theirs.'

Hibbert gestured to Maris and Shardlow, who produced their own warrant cards, which they held out to the man. He studied them, then nodded. 'They look in order. What can we do for you?'

'We want to talk to Mr Peter Etheridge,' said Hibbert.

The man nodded towards Etheridge's flat. 'He lives opposite.'

'Yes, I know. He's not in at the moment. We wondered if you might know where he might be?'

'No,' said the man. 'We don't have much to do with him. We say hello if we pass on the stairs. That's about all.'

'Would you mind giving us your name, Mr er . . . ?' asked Hibbert.

'Why?'

'It makes it easier to have a polite conversation.'

'What do we have to have a conversation about?'

'About Mr Etheridge.'

'I've just said, we don't have much to do with him.'

'No, I understand that. The thing is, we do want to talk to him. I wonder if it would be possible for one of my men to stay in your flat to watch his door, in case he comes back.'

'No. I don't want strangers in my flat.'

'But this is a matter of national security.'

'I don't care if it's by order of the King himself. A man's home is his own.'

Hibbert struggled with how to handle this. Usually the very words 'MI5' were like an 'open sesame' in any difficult situation, with people eager to help. This old man was obviously not one of these helpful types.

'Would you have any objection if one of my men sat on the stairs and kept watch on Mr Etheridge's flat?'

The man looked as if he was about to dismiss this idea, too, but fortunately his wife spoke up.

'I don't think we'd have any objection to that, would we, Erasmus? And if he's there for a long time, I could always make him a cup of tea.'

The old man scowled, then shrugged. 'If that's what you want do,' he said. 'I can't stop you.'

With that, he walked back indoors.

'Thank you,' said Hibbert to the woman. 'Mrs . . . ?'

'Nitts.'

Hibbert shot a warning look at his two men to make sure neither laughed at the name.

'Thank you, Mrs Nitts. Your help is very much appreciated.'

'I'll bring you a cup of tea in about an hour,' she said. 'And if you need to use the toilet, just ring the bell. Erasmus isn't as grumpy as he seems.'

'Thank you,' said Hibbert again.

As Mrs Nitts disappeared into her flat and the door closed, Hibbert turned to his two men.

'Right, take turns watching. If he comes back, grab him.'

'We don't know what he looks like, guv,' pointed out Shardlow.

'If anyone goes to that door, grab him,' said Hibbert. 'Any trouble, phone me.'

With that, he left.

Coburg sat half-reading the Sunday newspaper, at the same time listening to Rosa as she sat at the piano and ran through some of her favourite songs. It was to keep her fingers supple, and also to remind herself that – even with the desolation and destruction of the war going on – there were still things of beauty that made the world a better place. They were interrupted by the ringing of their doorbell.

'Who can that be?' grumbled Coburg as he got up and

went to the door. He opened it and found Inspector Hibbert standing there.

'Sorry to call on you,' said Hibbert, 'but we've got an urgent problem. I tried phoning, but the exchange said your phone was out of order.'

'Come in,' said Coburg.

He walked into the living room, Hibbert following. Coburg picked up the telephone receiver and put it in its cradle. 'It must have fallen off,' he said with a sigh.

Hibbert made a little bow towards Rosa. 'My apologies for the interruption, Mrs Coburg. Please don't let me stop you playing. I've always liked listening to you on the wireless.'

'Thank you,' said Rosa. 'But don't let me stop what I guess is important business.'

Hibbett turned to Coburg and said, 'Etheridge has definitely done a runner. I've got two men watching his flat, but neither of them knows what he looks like. I can't get a photo of him from the Railway Executive Committee because it's closed. I've told them to pick up anyone who calls at the flat, but I'd prefer them to get the right man. The two men you put on him, the ones who lost him, know what he looks like. Can you send one of them over to Etheridge's flat? He'll find one of my men sitting on the stairs by the landing.'

Coburg walked to the phone, checked his list for the home number of the two detective constables, then asked the operator to put him through to Armstrong's home. When Armstrong answered the phone, Coburg told him the problem.

'Inspector Hibbert of MI5 wants you to go to Etheridge's flat and tell his man there what Etheridge looks like. Can you do that?'

'No problem, sir,' said Armstrong.

Coburg hung up the phone.

'All done,' he said.

'Thanks,' said Hibbert. He gave a wry smile. 'You can let it fall off the hook again. I promise you I won't be back tonight, even if we catch Etheridge. I'll call you at the office in the morning.'

CHAPTER THIRTY-FOUR

Monday 17th March

Lampson looked to be in a good mood when Coburg picked him up in Somers Town on Monday morning.

'Good day yesterday?' asked Coburg.

'Very good,' said Lampson, sliding into the driving seat. 'We beat the choirboys 4–1. Great stuff. And Eve was in an even better mood because of your missus saying she'd be her maid of honour. That made her day. I'm sorry we interrupted your evening on Saturday. But I hope you had a good Sunday off together.'

'Unfortunately, we didn't.'

Coburg then listed the events of Sunday: the arrival of Ben Wright to make his confession, the discovery of PC Riddick's dead body, and the two men found beaten to death at Lord's Tube station.

'Also, the chap who Desmond Bartlett spent the weekend with before he was murdered, Peter Etheridge, turns out to be part of this ring of spies, and also it appears he was the one who beat the two men to death at Lord's station. He seems to have done a runner. So, all in all, did Rosa and I have a good Sunday? No. I hardly saw her.'

'I'm sorry, guv. You should have come and got me. Or sent someone for me. I'd have come in.'

'Thanks, Ted, but I didn't expect such a blizzard of things to happen all at the same time.'

'So, what's the schedule for today? What do we look at first?'

'I've got Inspector Nokes looking into Arnold Riddick's murder.' He gave a groan. 'And on that subject, I had Mrs Riddick in my office yesterday telling me she's reporting me to the police commissioner and her MP. She blames me for her husband getting murdered.'

'Why?'

'You remember we brought PC Riddick in for questioning. Well, when she came in and demanded to know why he was in a cell, I told her it was protective custody. Now someone's killed him, she's demanding to know who we were protecting him from.'

'Difficult,' said Lampson sympathetically.

'Very,' said Coburg. 'By all accounts, Peter Etheridge is the key to much of what's happened, including the murder of Desmond Bartlett, so the big thing is to find him.'

When Coburg and Lampson reached Scotland Yard, they were surprised to find Inspector Nokes waiting in reception for them.

'I've got some news I needed to share with you, and I wanted to pass it on before you got started on your day,' he said. 'I had a call from Harry Durward. He found a knife at Lord's Tube station yesterday, not far from where Grimshaw's body was. He found it further down the stairs on the next landing. It must have fallen from Grimshaw's pocket or his hand when he was attacked. Grimshaw's prints were on the knife handle. I suggested he take it to Dr Welbourne, which he did. Welbourne says the knife matches the stab wound that killed PC Riddick.'

'Why would Grimshaw kill Arnold Riddick?'

'That's a question for you, Chief Inspector. The issue is how much you want to pursue it.'

'Have you told Mrs Riddick?'

'Not yet. We can tell her that the man who killed her husband is dead, but how much do you want to dig into Riddick's activities? We're talking a serving police officer who may be involved in espionage.'

'Yes, good point,' said Coburg. 'I'll think about it and talk it over with Superintendent Allison.'

'So, I can leave Mrs Riddick with you?'

Coburg nodded. 'Unfortunately, yes.'

Inspector Nokes left them and Coburg and Lampson made for the stairs, but before they got to them, they were hailed by the sergeant at the reception desk.

'There was a phone call for you, Chief Inspector,' he said. 'Inspector Hibbert, MI5. He asked me to tell you that he had men watching Mr Etheridge's flat all night, but he never returned. He's gone.'

Coburg thanked him.

'Well, there's a turn-up for the books,' said Lampson.

'Not really,' said Coburg. 'I expected Etheridge not to return to his flat.'

'I meant Riddick being killed by Grimshaw. Does that mean Riddick was part of the spy ring, or did he stumble onto them and had to be silenced?'

'As both Grimshaw and Riddick are dead, finding Etheridge in case he might have the answer to that is our only hope,' said Coburg.

When they got to the office, Coburg put in a call to Jeremy Purslake at the Railway Executive Committee.

'Good morning, Mr Purslake. It's Chief Inspector Coburg.'

'Yes, Chief Inspector. What can I do for you?'

'Is Peter Etheridge with you?'

'No, and we haven't heard from him, which is most unusual. Peter is usually very conscientious. If he's unable to get in for any reason, he'll always make sure we're contacted, if not by himself, by someone else.'

'Would you mind if I came to see you?'

'When?'

'I was hoping I could call now.'

'It sounds urgent.'

'It is. I'll explain in detail when I get there, rather than over the phone.'

Coburg hung up and told Lampson, 'I'm going to the Railway Executive Committee to talk to Jeremy Purslake about Etheridge. I'd like you to hang on here and hold the fort, in case we get phone calls about all the different things we've got going on.'

'No problem,' said Lampson. 'I'll know where you are if something important turns up.'

Coburg arrived at the former Down Street Tube station and was shown immediately to Jeremy Purslake's office deep below street level.

'Is there a problem about Peter?' Purslake asked anxiously.

'We're concerned there might be,' said Coburg. 'When did you last see him?'

'Here, at the office, on Friday.'

'How did he seem?'

'He seemed like his usual self. He's not a person who

chats; he very much concentrates on his work, which is why he's such a valuable member of staff. When he didn't arrive for work today, I got one of my assistants to telephone his flat to make sure he was alright. As I said, he's usually so very reliable. But there was no answer. I wondered whether I ought to alert someone, in case he's had an accident. He could be lying incapacitated at home.'

'MI5 have already checked. He's not at home.'

'MI5?' echoed Purslake, obviously disturbed.

'There is a possibility he may have been involved in an unfortunate incident.'

'What sort of incident?'

'Unfortunately, a murder. In fact, two murders.'

Purslake stared at him, shocked. 'You're not serious.'

'I'm afraid I'm very serious.'

Purslake gulped, then asked hesitantly, 'Was one of them this cricketer friend of his?'

'Not at the moment, as far as we know. This is about two men who were found beaten to death at Lord's Tube station. It's possible they may have been the people who killed Desmond Barlett.'

'So . . . this could have been revenge for his murder?'

'That's possible, but we won't know until we talk to Mr Etheridge. Do you know of any friends he might have who he sometimes stays with?'

'Not as far as I know,' said Purslake. 'To be honest, I've always found him to be a private person, not much given to personal chatter about himself. In fact the only thing I can recall him saying about himself lately was when he told me about that cricketer staying with him. I believe he was quite proud of having a friend of such international standing, which was why he was so devastated when he found out what had happened to him.'

'Yes, of course. You don't happen to know if there was anywhere he stayed sometimes, any particular hotel, or club? I know many servicemen who sometimes stay at the Army and Navy Club, for example.'

'Etheridge wasn't in the services,' pointed out Purslake.

'No, but there may have been somewhere else he frequented, however occasionally.'

Purslake looked thoughtful, then he said, 'I remember one occasion when he'd come to work straight from one of the jazz clubs he went to. He'd been trapped by a bombing raid and couldn't get home, so he'd decided to stay there until the raid subsided. As it turned out, it didn't finish until daylight, so he came straight here. He was very apologetic because he hadn't had a chance to wash and shave and change his shirt. He was able to wash here, but he didn't have a change of clothes. Ever since then he's kept a spare shirt and a razor in his locker, in case it should happen again.'

'Would you mind checking if they're still in his locker?'

'Not at all. If you'll hold on a moment.'

Purslake left the office and returned a few moments later. 'His things are still in his locker, Chief Inspector. His shirt and razor.'

'Thank you. One last question: do you happen to know the name of the jazz club, or clubs, he used to frequent?'

'I'm afraid not. He never volunteered that sort of information; he was always scrupulous about keeping his social life separate from his work.'

* * *

Coburg returned to his office at the Yard and found Lampson on the phone.

'One moment, Inspector. Chief Inspector Coburg has just returned.' Lampson held out the receiver and whispered, 'Inspector Hibbert.'

'Coburg,' said Coburg.

'I just wanted to make sure you got my message about Etheridge.'

'That he's vanished,' said Coburg. 'Yes. I've just come from the offices of the Railway Executive Committee at Down Street, trying to find out where he might be, if he's lying low.'

'Any luck?'

'All they could suggest was he used to frequent jazz clubs.'

'Not much help,' said Hibbert. 'Who's the main man at the Railway Executive Committee?'

'Jeremy Purslake is the man in charge. He's very helpful.'

'Right. I'll give him a call and see if he's got a photo of Etheridge he can let me have. Once I've got that, I'll put out an alert for him.'

'We'll keep in touch,' said Coburg.

He handed the receiver back to Lampson, who said, 'Jazz clubs?'

'It looks like we're going to have to mount a search of the jazz clubs of London,' said Coburg. He groaned. 'And there are a lot of them.'

'Your missus should be able to help you out,' said Lampson. 'I bet she's appeared in most of them.'

Coburg grinned broadly. 'Brilliant, Sergeant! She's out with the ambulance today, but I'll ask her tonight for the names of some of them, and tomorrow we'll go searching. Right now, I'd better go and talk to the superintendent about Arnold Riddick and Grimshaw.'

Coburg made his way to Superintendent Allison's office, entering at the command of 'Come in' after he'd knocked.

'Yes, Chief Inspector?' enquired Allison.

'You know that a police constable was found stabbed to death yesterday morning,' said Coburg. 'PC Arnold Riddick.'

'Yes. What happened? I thought you'd put a watch on him?'

'I did. I can only think that someone slipped up.'

Allison gave a sigh of annoyance, then said, 'I see that Inspector Nokes is the investigating officer.'

'That's right, sir. It now appears Riddick was killed by a man called Grimshaw, a known traitor who is suspected of being part of a German spy ring. Grimshaw, himself, was killed yesterday by a man called Peter Etheridge, who we're currently searching for. But there is a suspicion that the dead constable, Riddick, was involved in some chicanery with Grimshaw, the German spy.'

'Do you mean that Riddick was working for the Germans?'

'Not necessarily. My gut feeling is that Riddick was working for himself. Remember I said I felt there was something wrong at St John's Wood. Initially I thought it related to Sergeant Webster and his brother, Jimmy, the illegal bookie. I thought there was something rotten there from the fact that Sergeant Webster sent Desmond Bartlett off with a flea in his ear when Bartlett complained about Jimmy Webster's thugs threatening him. I still think Eric Webster is a wrong 'un. I thought that Riddick was part of a conspiracy with the Webster brothers, and he may have been. But I also think Riddick was open to bribes. Remember I told you the keys to Lord's Tube station had disappeared from St John's Wood police station. I now believe that was Riddick. He stole them and sold them to Grimshaw. I think Grimshaw killed Riddick to silence him, or maybe Riddick had tried blackmailing him.

'The problem is, we have to decide what to tell Mrs Riddick. Do we tell her that her husband was engaged in some criminal conspiracy and possible espionage, even though he may not have been aware it involved espionage?'

'It won't look good,' said Allison thoughtfully.

'No, it won't,' agreed Coburg. 'But we have to tell her something. She's talking of complaining to the police commissioner and her MP about the fact that her husband was brought in for protective custody, and he was killed after he was released.'

The superintendent looked questioningly at the chief inspector. 'Something in your voice suggests you have an idea.'

'It's more about putting a different slant on the facts we have. Grimshaw stabbed Riddick to death. Riddick was up to something with Grimshaw, but not in any official capacity. Could we tell Mrs Riddick that we believe her husband had suspicions about a possible nest of German spies operating in the St John's Wood area, and he decided to investigate of his own accord? Before he could go to the authorities with what he'd discovered, the spies found out what he was doing and killed him. The spies then fought amongst themselves and were killed.'

'It's a bit far-fetched,' said Allison after he'd digested the proposal.

'It is, but I'm sure Mrs Riddick would prefer to believe that her husband was a hero and a patriot – even anonymously – rather than a traitor.'

The superintendent weighed this up, then nodded. 'In the circumstances, that might be best.'

CHAPTER THIRTY-FIVE

When Coburg returned to the office, he found Lampson slumped over his desk, holding his stomach and groaning. The sergeant pushed himself upright. That he was in pain was evident from his face, which was deathly pale, sweat running down it.

'What's up?' Coburg asked. 'You look terrible.'

'I don't feel good,' Lampson admitted. 'I think it might be something I ate.'

'Why, what have you eaten?'

'I didn't get breakfast this morning, so I grabbed a bite in the canteen while you were out at Down Street. There was fish pie on the menu, so I had some of that. It tasted a bit funny, but then so much food does these days because you never know what's actually in it.'

'Have you been sick?' asked Coburg.

'No, but I feel like I'm going to be.'

'Maybe you ought to go and see if you can be sick. Put your fingers down your throat.'

'I tried that,' said Lampson. 'No luck. Maybe it's not what I ate.'

Coburg made for the door. 'Stay here. I'm going to talk to the canteen manager, see if anyone else has reported any symptoms.'

Arthur Delton, the canteen manager, looked like a man

under pressure when Coburg called on him.

'What can I do for you, Chief Inspector?' he asked.

'The fish pie you served today,' said Coburg.

Delton let out a groan. 'Not you as well?'

'What do you mean, me as well?'

'I had four people who'd had it come to me and say it had made them ill. You'll make it five.'

'I didn't have the fish pie – Ted Lampson did,' said Coburg. 'So it was off?'

'It shouldn't have been,' said Delton defensively.

'What was in it?' asked Coburg.

'Fish, obviously,' said Delton.

'What sort of fish?'

'Well, that's debateable,' admitted Delton. 'This bloke turned up with it and offered it to me cheap. I'd had stuff from him before that had been alright, so I thought this would be fine. Fish pie is usually a mix of odds and ends, cuttings from a fishmonger's slab. Trust me, I won't be having any more stuff from him.'

Coburg returned to his office.

'Food poisoning,' he told Lampson. 'The fish pie. Arthur Delton confirmed it. Four other people who had it were taken ill.' He looked at his watch. 'I suggest you get off and see if you can see a doctor, or find a chemist open.'

Lampson pushed himself to his feet. 'I will. I'll see if my Mum's got anything for it. She's usually got something in her cupboard. If she hasn't, she makes something up. She's better than a chemist.' He looked at the clock. 'I'll be there for Terry when he leaves school, so I can take him home and then rest

309

up. I'm sure I'll be alright in the morning.'

'If you're not, don't come in.'

'I will be,' said Lampson. He picked up his coat and pulled it on. 'That's the last time I eat fish pie.'

Vic Tennant sat in his car, his eyes fixed on the front door of Lampson's house. He knew Lampson was in there; he'd seen him enter the house, accompanied by his son. Tennant should have taken action then, as soon as he saw the man arrive: start the car, put it into gear and drive fast and hard at him, smashing him against the wall. But the sight of Lampson's son had made him pause. Say he hit the boy instead?

Forget the boy, the target was Lampson. But by the time he'd summoned the nerve to do it, regardless of the boy, Lampson had unlocked his front door and he and his son had gone in.

I'll get him, Tennant vowed. The emotional pain and anger of the humiliation he'd suffered at Lampson's hands in his own yard burnt in him. *I'll never forgive him for that, never!* The trouble was Lampson was big and tough, too tough for Tennant to confront. And he had friends, those thugs of boxers he'd brought with him to Tennant's yard, who'd scared off his own men. So it would be no use getting his men to give Lampson a going-over, like they'd done before. No, it had to be this way. Wait till Lampson appeared from the house and run him over. The heavy rain was a godsend; it would cover the noise of the car engine starting up and the tyres on the road. When Lampson had arrived home, he'd been wearing a distinctive black oilskin waterproof coat and a hat pulled down to protect him from the rain. Providing the rain kept up, Lampson would be wearing the same outfit, cutting off his vision and hearing. Perfect.

The question now was how long it would be before Lampson

came out into the street. As far as Tennant was concerned, he would wait as long as it was necessary. It was starting to get dark, which was even better. If Lampson didn't appear after an hour or so, then Tennant would get him out. He'd throw a pebble at his window. One thing was sure, tonight he would get his revenge. If he was lucky, Lampson would die tonight. Even if he didn't, he'd be so badly injured there'd be no chance of him marrying Eve on Saturday. If at all. And, once Lampson was out of the way, things would be so much easier for Vic Tennant.

Suddenly Tennant became alert as someone else approached the house, and his heart gave a leap as he saw it was Eve. She was wearing a coat that offered little protection against the driving rain, and Tennant wanted to get out and offer her shelter in his car, offer to drive her to her own house; but before he could do that Eve had taken a key from her pocket and was unlocking the front door.

This action of hers filled him with emotional pain; she had a key to that thug's house! For Tennant this meant yet another nail in Lampson's coffin.

Sooner or later, after Eve had gone, Lampson would be sure to come out, even in this weather. And when he did, Tennant would sort him out. If not tonight, then tomorrow night. Or the night after. Tennant could wait. He'd waited this long for Eve, he could continue to wait. So long as what he had to do was done before the day of the wedding.

Prudence Baxter sat in the back room of her shop. Her last surviving son, Monty, and Bill Biggs sat on the settee opposite her, their unhappy faces showing their unwillingness to get involved in her plan. *But they'll do it*, she thought angrily. *If they don't, they know what will happen to them.*

On the table between them lay the pistol.

'This is going to be easy because we'll keep it simple,' she said. 'I've got the information about them, their addresses, where they work, their regular routines. What's going to happen is that you, Monty, will follow them around, Coburg first, and then that Sergeant Harpson, the one who killed Max. You'll wait till each one is on their own. You walk up to them, push the gun in their back and pull the trigger. Then you run. Bill, your job is to make sure that Monty runs the right way. Suss out the area. Alleyways, canal paths, that sort of thing. Monty, you follow Bill. After each one, once you're clear, you come back here. You got that?'

Both Biggs and Monty nodded.

Ma Baxter laid her hand on the pistol. 'You still haven't got this right, Monty. You got it stuck in your pocket. You let the barrel wave about all over the place. You can't be doing that. You pull it out of your pocket quickly and neatly and you push it against his body, all in one go. Then you pull the trigger. Then you run. That's it.'

She turned to Biggs. 'He needs more practice at pulling it out of his pocket and pushing it into the body. Spend tomorrow in the barn with him, practising. I'll come in later and see how he's got on. I want this done, and I want it done soon. Tomorrow, you do Coburg. The day after, Wednesday, you do Harpson.'

That evening at the flat, Coburg sat and read the papers while Rosa played the piano.

'I love listening to you play,' he said. 'You're really something special.'

'It's all about practice,' she said, and she ran through a series of riffs and chords.

'You know that jazz fan I told you about, Peter Etheridge,' said Coburg.

'The one from Jamaica?'

'Yes. Well, we need to get hold of him because I think he holds the key to the whole Desmond Bartlett case.'

'The cricketer who was murdered.'

'Yes. It now looks like Etheridge killed two men. Beat them to death at Lord's Tube station on Sunday morning.'

'Do you know why?'

'I suspect because these two men killed Desmond Bartlett.'

'Revenge?'

'That's my theory. I'll only know for sure once I've talked to him. The problem is, he's vanished.'

'So he could be anywhere.'

'He could be, but my guess is he's taken refuge in a jazz club. One that specialises in Caribbean jazz.'

'Oh yes, I remember now. You said he mentioned players like Leslie Thompson and Jiver Hutchinson.'

'That's right. So I wondered if you knew which jazz clubs might specialise in Caribbean musicians.'

She sat, thinking it over, then said, 'Off the top of my head, there's Blue Note, The Pigeon, Al's Hot Spot and The Rumbaba.'

'Do you know where these places are?'

'I've played the Blue Note and Al's Hot Spot. I've been in the other two, to check out players.'

'Would you come with me to them tomorrow?'

'You think he might be in one of them?'

'He might. They're the kind of places where he feels safe. The thing is, if I turn up as DCI Coburg asking about him, no one's going to help me. It's the way it is in the Soho clubs.'

'But you think they'll talk to me?'

'You're Rosa Weeks, one of their own.'

'So I'm to be your stool pigeon?'

'No. I just want you to get me through the door. I know what Etheridge looks like. If he's in one of them, I'll spot him.'

'And you'll arrest him?'

'At this stage I just want to talk to him. But I hope he'll come with me.'

'Without a fuss?'

'He doesn't strike me as a man who makes a fuss.'

'But he kills people. Beats them to death.'

'And then leaves the hammer he did it with behind. I also suspect he doesn't have a gun, or he'd have used that. He's unarmed.' Coburg looked at her. 'Look, I understand if you don't feel happy about doing this, betraying a fellow jazzer.'

She shook her head. 'No, it's not that. Of course I'll do it. What's the plan?'

'We park up somewhere in Soho near to one of the clubs and pop in. You introduce me to the owner and I'll tell him who I'm looking for, but assure him I just want to talk to him about something. Nothing heavy. If he's not there, we try another, and keep trying and hope that he's in one of them. If we find him, you go back to the car and wait for me there while I talk to him.'

'Or I could stay and listen to the music,' said Rosa.

'Whichever you'd prefer,' said Coburg.

'Okay. We're agreed. But it's not worth going before lunchtime. That's when they open. So I'll do my ambulance shift in the morning, and then you can pick me up at the depot.

I'll also phone around a few pals this evening and see if anyone knows any new clubs that have opened. Jazz clubs are closing down and opening all the time.' She held out her hand. 'Hand me the phone.'

'Thanks,' said Coburg.

Lampson lay on the sofa, his face and body soaked in sweat. He groaned, and Terry looked down at him anxiously.

'Are you going to die, Dad?' he asked.

'No,' said Lampson. He groaned and said ruefully, 'It just feels like it.'

'You shouldn't say things like that, even as a joke,' Eve rebuked him.

'I'm not joking,' Lampson gasped. 'It's food poisoning. I had fish pie at lunchtime, and it turns out that everyone else who had it has gone down with this.'

'I'll go to the chemist and see if he's got anything for it,' said Eve.

Lampson shook his head. 'Mum's making me up something. I told her about it when I picked up Terry and she's got some old family recipe she said she'd make up. I said I'd go back and collect it.' He struggled to push himself up off the sofa, but fell back on it.

'You're not going anywhere,' Eve told him firmly. 'It's chucking it down with rain outside. That'll finish you off.'

'I'll go,' offered Terry.

'No,' said Eve firmly. 'I'll go.'

'You can't go out in this weather,' said Lampson. 'Your coat is no protection.'

'I'll take yours,' said Eve.

'I'll be too big for you,' said Lampson.

'Nonsense,' said Eve. 'I'm almost as tall as you. It'll keep me dry.'

'You'll need Dad's hat as well,' suggested Terry.

'Yes, I will,' agreed Eve. And she went out to the hallway where the hats and coats hung.

'Be careful out there,' called Lampson.

'I will!' she called back.

Terry looked at his dad. 'D'you want me to make you a cup of tea, Dad?' he asked.

The sound of a crash outside the house interrupted Lampson before he could reply. Alarmed, he pushed himself up off the settee and stumbled towards the hallway and the front door. Unhampered by illness, Terry got to the front door before him.

'It's Eve!' he shouted.

Lampson made it to the door and stumbled out into the street and the pouring rain. Eve lay half on the pavement, half in the gutter. Lampson crawled to her and checked her pulse. She was unconscious and blood trickled from her nose.

'Go to the phone box on the corner,' Lampson ordered his son. 'Dial 999. Tell them we need ambulance and police. And it's urgent. I'll stay with her. Be quick!'

Terry needed no further urging; he was already running for the telephone box, his shoes splashing through the puddles and the cascading rain.

At their flat, Rosa hung up the phone. 'That was a pal of mine called Petra Kelly. She says there's a new jazz club opened in Soho where they've had some West Indian musicians. It's called Windies. I suggest we start there as our first port of call tomorrow.'

'Sounds good,' said Coburg. 'We won't be as much in the dark as we would have been without your knowledge and contacts.'

'It doesn't mean we'll find him at any of the clubs,' pointed out Rosa. 'If he's distressed at what's happened, he might have killed himself. He sounds a sensitive sort of person.'

'He is,' said Coburg. The phone rang and he picked it up. 'Coburg,' he said.

'It's Ted, guv,' said Lampson's voice, and immediately Coburg knew from his tone that something was very wrong. 'Eve's been run down by a car. She's in hospital, but they're not sure if she's going to pull through. I'm phoning to let you know I won't be in tomorrow. I need to be at the hospital and see how she is.'

'Which hospital is she in?'

'UCH.'

'Rosa and I will be along immediately,' said Coburg. 'We'll see you there.'

When Coburg and Rosa arrived at University College Hospital, they found Lampson sitting on a hard wooden bench in the reception area. At this time of night, nearly all the other benches were empty, most people opting to make for the security of an air raid shelter. Lampson got to his feet as he saw them arrive.

'How is she?' asked Coburg. On their journey to the hospital he'd dreaded asking this question in case the very worst had happened, but the fact that, although Lampson was obviously distressed, he seemed to be holding himself together suggested she was still alive.

'She's in the operating theatre,' said Lampson. 'One of

her arms is broken, and they're not sure if there's any internal damage. They've advised me to go home and come back tomorrow, but I've told them I'll wait. I want to make sure she's alright.'

The sound of footsteps approaching made them look up, anticipating a doctor come to report on Eve's condition, but it was Lampson's mother.

'I've left your dad looking after Terry,' she said. She nodded to Coburg and Rosa. 'You and I have met before, Chief Inspector, but I've not met your wife.'

Rosa reached out a hand to shake Mrs Lampson's.

'Rosa Coburg,' she said. 'It's a pleasure to meet you, Mrs Lampson, although I wish it could be in better circumstances.'

'How did you get here, Mum?' asked Lampson.

'I walked, of course.'

'We'll run you home after,' said Rosa.

'Once I know that Eve's going to be alright,' said Mrs Lampson. 'What's the news?'

'She's in the operating theatre,' Lampson told her.

'They'll look after her here,' said Mrs Lampson. 'It's a good hospital. Very good staff.'

Coburg got up. 'I'll just go and have a word with the people at reception,' he said.

'Why?' asked Rosa.

'See if there's any news.'

'If there was, they'd have come and told us,' said Rosa.

'Not necessarily,' said Coburg.

'I don't want you upsetting them,' said Rosa firmly.

'I won't be upsetting them,' said Coburg defensively. 'I'm just going to talk to them.' He looked agitated and added, 'I'm not good at just sitting waiting. I need to know what's going on.'

'Then I'll ask,' said Rosa, getting up. 'You sit down.'

'Why is it okay for you and not for me?' demanded Coburg.

'Because you'll upset them if you start pulling rank.'

'Rosa's right,' said Mrs Lampson. 'I know the people here. Good people with a job to do.' She got up. 'I'll go with Rosa and talk to them. You stay here with Ted.'

Coburg gave a sigh of resentment and sat down, while Mrs Lampson and Rosa made for the reception desk.

'I thought I might have some clout,' he said ruefully.

'Not here,' said Lampson. 'Mum's in charge. She always has been. Dad thinks he is, but Mum's the one.'

The two met sat in thoughtful silence for a few moments, then Coburg asked, 'What actually happened? How did she get hurt?'

'Eve went out to get some medicine for me from my mum. Terry and I heard this bang, and when we went out, there she was, on the ground. A car must have come out of nowhere and hit her.' He shook his head. 'It was raining, but he must have seen her.'

'How is the food poisoning now?' asked Coburg.

'Eve being hit like that, I've got over it. Strange.'

'No it isn't,' said Coburg. 'The same happened to me when I was in the trenches during the First War. You're suffering from something and you think you can't go on, and then something big happens and you've forgotten what you're suffering from and you're running.'

Suddenly, Lampson put his hands together, and in a voice filled with agony burst out passionately, 'Oh, dear God, please please please let her live.'

He stood up expectantly as he saw his mother and Rosa approaching.

'No news,' said Mrs Lampson. 'They'll let us know as soon as there's anything to tell us.' She sat down. 'All we can do is wait.'

Two hours later, with still no news of Eve's condition, Lampson suggested to Coburg and Rosa they go home.

'This could take a long time, and you've both got to get to work in a few hours.'

'What about you?' asked Coburg.

'I'll be alright here,' said Lampson.

'And I'll stay here as well,' said his mother.

Coburg nodded. 'Alright,' he said. 'But let us know what happens. And don't try and come in tomorrow.'

He and Rosa got up.

'We'll be thinking of you and Eve,' said Rosa. 'If there's anything we can do, just let us know.'

'The thing to remember is that Eve is a strong person,' said Coburg. 'The longer this goes on, the better it is. It shows she's hanging in there.'

CHAPTER THIRTY-SIX

Tuesday 18th March

Vic Tennant stood in front of the mirror in his hallway, checking his clothes. He wanted to make sure he was dressed properly when he called on Eve and Paula to offer his condolences. He had his story ready: he'd heard there had been an accident and Ted had been injured.

'If there's anything I can do,' he'd offer, making sure his voice had just the right touch of sympathy and sincerity.

He went out to where his car was parked on his driveway, and stopped. There was a dent on the front wing and what looked like blood on the radiator grille. He went back inside and soaked a flannel in cold water, then came out and wiped the blood off. It wouldn't do to arrive at the Bradleys' house with blood on his car.

He drove to the street where Eve and her mother lived, parked, and walked towards their house. A man was standing outside. He appeared to be standing guard over the door. He looked at Tennant as he arrived.

'No one's going in today,' said the man. 'We're taking turns to tell people. There's been a bad accident in the family.'

'Yes, so I heard,' said Tennant. 'That's why I'm calling to offer my condolences. I'm a friend of the family. I know Eve and her mum very well.'

'That may be, but no one's going in today. Eve's mum needs to be left in peace.'

Tennant nodded. 'Alright, but will you let Eve know I called?'

The man frowned. 'I thought you said you'd heard?'

'I did. Someone told me Ted Lampson was knocked down last night.'

The man shook his head. 'Not Ted. It's Eve. She was the one who was run over last night. Really badly hurt. It's possible she might not make it.'

Tennant stared at the man in disbelief. 'Eve?'

The man nodded. 'She went out to get some medicine for her fiancé and some bastard ran her down. Didn't even stop. Just drove off.'

As the realisation of what he'd done hit Tennant, he began to shake uncontrollably. He fell back against the wall of the house, unable to breathe. The man looked at him, puzzled.

'Are you alright?' he asked.

'No.' Tennant was barely able to force the words out. 'I didn't know. I thought it was Lampson.' He backed away from the house, feeling sick. He had to get away, get back to his yard.

'I'll tell Paula you called,' said the man. 'What's your name?'

Tennant shook his head, unable to speak. He turned and stumbled away.

If she dies, it was me who killed her! The words tore through him. He felt himself burning from within. *It was me who killed her!*

Despite his determination to stay awake, Ted Lampson had fallen asleep leaning back against the bench. His mother, sitting beside him, saw the doctor approaching them and jogged him awake. He opened his eyes and saw the doctor, and immediately got to his feet, as did his mother. Lampson looked at the doctor's face, trying to work out from his expression if it was good news or bad, but the doctor gave nothing away until he spoke.

'Well, she's out of surgery,' he said. 'She's got a broken arm and fractures to her skull. We've patched her up. Luckily, she's a strong person. There doesn't seem to be any internal damage, but we're going to keep her in to keep an eye on her.'

'Can I see her?' asked Lampson.

The doctor shook his head. 'At the moment she's still unconscious, and we're going to keep her that way for a while. She's going to need time to recover. So, no visitors today. Perhaps tomorrow, if she's recovered enough, and then only for a few minutes. Are you on the telephone?'

'No,' said Lampson. 'But we don't live far away. Just across Euston Road, in Somers Town. We gave reception our address. Will it be alright if I call in later and see how she's doing?'

'Alright, but leave it till later this afternoon. And you won't be able to see her.'

'I understand,' said Lampson. 'And thank you.'

As he and his mother walked out of the hospital into the early morning sunlight, Lampson was filled with a huge sense of relief. Eve was alive!

'She might not be back on her feet in time for the wedding,' warned his mother.

'That doesn't matter,' said Lampson. 'What's important is she's alright. She'll recover. We can get married any time.'

'Maybe, if she's still in the hospital, the vicar can come here and perform the ceremony,' said Mrs Lampson thoughtfully.

'I'm not sure they'd allow it,' said Lampson.

'You leave that to me,' said his mother determinedly.

When they got to his parents' flat, they found that Mr Lampson had come back after taking Terry to school.

'I'll go back there and ask them to pass on to him that Eve's alright,' he said. 'Terry was worried and will want to know.'

'She's not out of it yet,' said Lampson. 'They've told us no one is to go in and see her today. Maybe tomorrow. So I'll go home and put my head down for a couple of hours.'

'Are you going to be alright?' asked his mother.

'I am, now I know that Eve's alive and she'll recover.'

Lampson headed for his own house, but instead of going to bed, he made himself a cup of strong tea. The thought of what had happened, and who'd done it, nagged at his mind.

Sone bastard had run her down and then just driven off. How had it happened? Yes, it had been raining, but it looked to Lampson like the car had mounted the pavement. An accident, or had it ben deliberate? But who'd want to run Eve down?

But Eve had been wearing his coat and hat. If it had been deliberate, then whoever did it had thought it was Lampson he was aiming at. And there was only one person who'd want to do that to Lampson.

Lampson arrived at Vic Tennant's yard as an ambulance was driving out through the gates. A uniformed constable Lampson knew, Joe Plender, was in the yard watching the ambulance drive away. Plender looked at Lampson awkwardly.

'Morning, Ted,' he said. 'I heard about Eve. Awful.

Shocking. I'm so sorry. If there's anything I can do . . .'

'Do you know if Eve's mum has been told?' Lampson asked. 'I was going to call and see her, but she's not very fond of me.'

'Yes,' said Plender. 'Someone from the station called last night and informed her Eve was in hospital. She got them to take her to UCH, and when she got there she was told that Eve was in surgery. The coppers brought her back home and a WPC stayed with her for a bit. She was in a right state. The neighbours are mounting a guard on the house today to stop people knocking at the door. You know what people are like, calling to offer condolences. It's the last thing she needs at the moment.'

Lampson gestured along the road. 'What was the ambulance for?'

'D'you know Vic Tennant? This is his yard.'

'Yes,' said Lampson.

'He hung himself this morning. Did it here. The ambulance has taken his body away.'

Lampson looked at Plender, stunned. 'Hung himself?'

Plender nodded. 'His secretary came in to work and couldn't find him. Then she went to look in the outbuildings and found him hanging from a beam in one of them. That's why there's no one here. His blokes have all gone home. His secretary had hysterics and she's gone. The offices are all locked up. I'm just off myself.' He looked at Lampson, curious. 'What are you doing here, Ted?'

'There was something I wanted to see Tennant about.'

'Important?'

Lampson shook his head. 'Not now. Are you closing the gates?'

325

Plender shook his head. 'The sarge said to keep 'em open in case anyone comes to deliver anything. I'll come back at the end of the day and shut 'em. After that, it depends on what they decide to do about the business.'

'I suppose that depends on his family,' said Lampson.

'He didn't have any, according to his secretary. Not local, anyhow. He had a brother in Manchester, so I suppose he'll be next of kin. His secretary said she'll get in touch with Tennant's solicitor to sort things out.' He sighed. 'Dreadful. You wonder what makes people top themselves. Business worries, I suppose.'

Lampson watched the constable walk out of the yard and away along the street.

No, not business worries, he thought angrily.

He walked around the yard until he came to Tennant's car, a blue Ford. He saw the deep dent in the wing, and the marks where someone had wiped a damp cloth over the dent and the radiator grille.

The proof, he thought. The real reason Tennant had killed himself. But what should he do with it? He could tell Eve's mother, but she would refute the idea that Tennant had been the one who ran Eve down. Eve would believe it, but did she really need to know it? Not at this stage. She was in no fit state to do anything other than use every ounce of her strength – mental and physical – to recover. He wanted to smash the car, set fire to it, destroy it. But if he did that, the evidence that Tennant had run Eve down would be gone.

He turned and walked out of the yard. *Forget about Tennant. Concentrate on Eve and helping her get well.*

CHAPTER THIRTY-SEVEN

Coburg was sitting in his office at Scotland Yard, looking at the empty desk where Ted Lampson usually sat, wondering how his sergeant and Eve were doing, when the telephone rang. The caller was Inspector Hibbert.

'Just keeping you in the loop,' said Hibbert. 'There's still no sign of Etheridge.'

'I thought that might be the case,' said Coburg. 'I'm going out in search of him today.'

'Where?'

'Jazz clubs,' said Coburg.

'What makes you think he'll be in them?'

'Things he told me, and things other people who know him have said. He hangs around in London's jazz clubs.'

'It doesn't sound much,' commented Hibbert.

'It isn't,' agreed Coburg. 'But it's the only lead I've got. I'm going round the jazz clubs this afternoon.'

'Do you want any help?' asked Hibbert. 'I can let you have some men.'

'No thanks,' said Coburg. 'The kind of places we're going to, they don't offer to help the police.'

'Who are you going with? Your sergeant?'

Coburg wondered whether to tell Hibbert about Lampson,

and Eve's accident, but decided against it. It was Ted's private business.

'I'm going with my wife.'

'Oh, of course. She's a jazzer. Think she might know where he is?'

'No, but she knows most of the clubs.'

Coburg replaced the receiver, as the door opened and Lampson entered. Coburg looked at him in surprise, and with concern.

'What are you doing here?' asked Coburg.

'I'm here to work,' said Lampson.

'You should be at the hospital,' said Coburg.

Lampson shook his head. 'I was. They told me Eve was in a ward and the signs of a recovery were positive. But they won't let me see her today. They said I might be able to see her tomorrow. I sat there in the reception area in case there was any further news, but there wasn't. Just that she was doing okay. In the end I decided I'd be better off doing something here. It won't take my mind off what happened, but it'll go a way towards it.'

'Any word from the local police on the accident?'

'It wasn't an accident,' said Lampson.

Coburg looked at him, warily. 'What do you mean?'

'Eve was wearing my coat and hat when she was run down. The car had to go on the pavement to hit her.'

'You mean someone ran her down deliberately?' said Coburg, incredulous.

'They did, but they thought it was me.'

'But why?'

'For the same reason Vic Tennent got his blokes to beat

me up. He wanted me out of the way so he could marry Eve himself.'

'You don't know that.'

'I do,' said Lampson. 'I went to Tennent's yard to face him about it this morning, and found out he'd hung himself. His car was there in the yard with a damaged wing and radiator where he'd hit her.'

Coburg stared at his sergeant, stunned. 'What are you going to do about it?' he asked.

'Nothing,' said Lampson. 'He's dead. It's over and done.' He looked at Coburg. 'Give me something to do. I need to be busy.'

'Do you feel up to driving?'

'Yes.'

'Right. You can be our driver.'

'*Our?*'

'I'm putting your suggestion into practice. Using Rosa's special knowledge of jazz clubs. We're going to go round the jazz clubs she knows about, especially those that cater for West Indian jazzers. Your job will be to drive us to the ones she directs you to. You park up and wait while we go in. If he's in one of them, she'll come back and join you in the car while I try and talk him into surrendering. If he's not in one, we both come back and you drive us to the next one Rosa directs you to. Are you alright with that?'

'Say he tries something? He might be armed.'

'I don't think so. If he had been he wouldn't have beaten those two chaps to death with a hammer.'

'You can't be sure of that.'

'No, I can't be.'

'It might be safer for you if I come in with you.'

Coburg shook his head. 'I smell like a copper, but with Rosa on my arm, I can get in. They'll clam up as soon as they lay eyes on you.'

Coburg and Lampson picked Rosa up at the St John Ambulance station at Paddington. First, she changed out of her uniform into her civilian clothes.

'No one's going to believe I'm Rosa Weeks if I'm in uniform,' she told them.

They then set off for the first club on their list, Windies. As the name suggested, it was a club for West Indians, but there was no sign of Peter Etheridge there.

'It could be I'm the problem,' said Coburg. So, for the next club, Coburg hovered just inside the entrance door, while Rosa sought out someone she knew. Once again, they'd had no sighting of Peter Etheridge at the club, although they confirmed he was a regular visitor to their sessions. It was the same story at Blue Note, Al's Hot Spot and The Rumbaba. It was at The Pigeon they struck lucky.

As Rosa walked in, the first person she saw was an old friend of hers and fellow musician, Jiver Hutchinson.

'Jiver!'

'Rosa! Hi! What are you doing here?'

'I'm looking for someone.'

Hutchinson grinned. 'If it's me, I'm here.'

Rosa laughed. 'The man I'm looking for is not a player. He's a dedicated fan. Especially of Jamaican jazz.'

'Does he have a name?'

'He does, but I doubt if you'd know it. As far as I can gather he's someone who goes to clubs a lot, but doesn't get involved too much.'

'Try me. You'd be surprised who I talk to.'

'His name's Peter Etheridge. He's from Kingston, but he's been working in Britain for a few years.'

Hutchinson looked suddenly wary. 'White dude?'

'Yes,' said Rosa. 'You know him?'

'I do. We've talked over the years, mainly about Jamaica and jazz.' Then his expression became sad. 'But right now he's in a bad place.'

'What makes you say that?'

'Because he came in here yesterday and hasn't left. The owner hasn't liked to turn him out. Etheridge has always seemed a good guy, never any trouble, not like some people who are enthusiasts.'

'Has he said what the trouble is?'

'No, but it's all there in his face and his whole body. It's like he's in hiding. Not just from people and things, but from himself. Why are you looking for him?'

'Because I heard he was in trouble, and I've got someone with me who wants to help him.'

'How did you hear he was in trouble?'

'It's a long story,' said Rosa. 'Is he here at the moment?'

Hutchinson hesitated, then asked, 'Is it the police?'

'Jiver, I've never lied to you or played false with anyone. You know that. Yes, the person who wants to talk to him – and I stress just talk – is my husband, and he's a policeman.'

'The one the papers talk about. DCI Saxe-Coburg, one of the royal family?'

'He's not part of the royal family, although he is distantly related to them,' said Rosa. 'The thing is, you said yourself Peter's in a bad place. My husband, Edgar, can help him. Not as a police officer, but as a person. At this moment he just wants to talk to him.'

'Not arrest him? Take him into custody?'

'Edgar won't do anything without Peter's agreement. Trust me. You can trust him.'

Hutchinson thought it over. 'Where is this policeman husband of yours?'

Rosa gestured towards Coburg, who was standing just inside the entrance, watching them. Hutchinson thought it over, then signalled for Coburg to join them.

'This is Jiver Hutchinson,' said Rosa when Coburg reached them. 'Jiver, this is my husband, Edgar, DCI Coburg.'

Coburg held out his hand. 'It's an honour to meet you, Jiver,' he said. 'Rosa has told me so much about you.'

Jiver took Coburg's hand and shook it. 'You're looking for Peter the white Jamaican dude.'

'I am,' said Coburg.

'He's fragile,' warned Hutchinson. 'He's in a very bad place.'

'I've told Jiver you only want to talk to him at the moment,' said Rosa.

'And I've never known her tell a lie,' said Jiver pointedly to Coburg.

'I promise, that's all I want to do at the moment.'

'And later?'

'That depends on Peter, but I promise you, I won't harm him or force him. You have my word.'

Hutchinson nodded. 'Okay. He's in the kitchen, getting himself some coffee.'

'It's taking him a long time,' pointed out Rosa gently.

'Everything's taking him a long time at the moment,' said Jiver. 'He'll be sitting there, drinking it. If you come with me, I'll take you in. But let me do the talking at first.'

Coburg nodded. Coburg and Rosa followed the tall Jamaican to the far end of the club and a door marked *Staff only*. Hutchinson knocked, then gently opened the door.

Peter Etheridge was sitting at a table, a cup of half-drunk coffee in front of him. He looked dreadful: unshaven, pale-faced, hollow-eyed. He looked at this interruption uneasily.

'Some people want to talk to you, Peter,' said Hutchinson. 'It ain't trouble. They promise that. Just want to talk.'

Etheridge looked at Coburg and Rosa. 'DCI Coburg,' he said. 'And Rosa Weeks. You tracked me down.'

'We just want to talk,' said Coburg. 'If you'd like to.'

'Yes, I think I would,' said Etheridge. 'I need to talk. Get some things off my chest that have been troubling me.'

'You want me to leave?' asked Jiver.

Etheridge hesitated.

'Perhaps it might be a good idea if Jiver stayed,' said Coburg. 'You'll know you've got at least one good friend here with you for your protection.'

Etheridge nodded. 'Yes. I'd like that, if you wouldn't mind, Jiver.'

'It'll be my pleasure,' said Hutchinson. He took a chair and sat down at the table.

'I'd better go and join a friend of ours who's waiting outside,' said Rosa. 'Otherwise he'll wonder what's happened to us. And you won't want a crowd in here.'

'Another policeman?' asked Etheridge.

'At the moment he's off duty after a private tragedy, so no, not at the moment,' said Coburg. 'This isn't a trap, Peter.'

Etheridge nodded. Rosa, in her turn, nodded to Jiver, Coburg and Etheridge, and made for the exit.

'You want to talk to me about Desmond,' said Etheridge. His voice was dull, unemotional.

'I do,' said Coburg, keeping his voice gentle, understanding. 'And what happened at Lord's Tube station.'

'I killed two men there,' said Etheridge; still his voice expressed no emotion. 'Battered their faces with a hammer.'

'One of them was a man called George Grimshaw,' said Coburg. 'We're not sure who the other man is.'

'His name was Simon Roche,' said Etheridge.

'Why?'

'Because of what they did to Desmond.'

Out in the street, Rosa climbed into the car next to Ted Lampson.

'Well?' asked Lampson.

'He's there,' said Rosa. 'Peter Etheridge.'

'And the guvnor's there with him alone?' said Lampson, concerned.

'They're not alone. A jazz musician friend of mine is with them. And Etheridge poses no threat, I'm sure of that.' She looked at him and said, her voice full of sympathy, 'I'm so sorry about Eve, Ted. If there's anything I can do . . .'

He nodded, held up his hand with two fingers crossed and said, 'Fingers crossed for a full recovery.'

Inside the club, Jiver Hutchinson watched as Coburg and Etheridge talked.

'You were part of a spy ring with George Grimshaw and Simon Roche,' said Coburg.

'I didn't think of it as a spy ring. It was more . . . trying to stop the war,' said Etheridge. 'I met Simon Roche at a jazz club. Like me, I think he found listening to jazz was a way of escaping what was happening. The war. The bombing. One evening we got talking and I mentioned that I wished the war would stop. Not that we should surrender, not at all. I suppose all the bombing and the death had made me think about things. Especially pacifism. I'd already decided that if I was called up, I'd be a conscientious objector. I said this to Simon. I was surprised when he said, "I share your feelings, Peter." Then he added, "But at the moment it's not the right time to express them. Not in public. People would misinterpret them. To even say that there should be peace would be misinterpreted as saying Britain ought to surrender. Neither of us wants that. We're patriots, for God's sake, both of us. But patriots who want peace. Peace with honour."

'He told me he had a cousin in Germany who felt the same. "Walter. He hates Hitler and the whole Nazi regime. So much so that he left Germany and now lives in Switzerland. At least it's a neutral country. It means we're able to exchange letters, although we have to be careful in what we say in case they're intercepted. He thinks there might be a way to bring this dreadful war to an early conclusion."

'"How?" I asked. I suppose I was being gullible, but I was so desperate for the bombing and death to end.

'"These bombing raids the Germans are carrying out," said Simon. "They rain death and destruction down on us, mainly killing the civilian population, the ordinary people, but

335

Churchill and his crowd insist that Britain must fight on. To what end? That more people die?"

"'You're not suggesting we surrender?" I said to him, disturbed.

"'No, no," said Roche, very quickly to reassure me. "Absolutely not. What Walter said to me was he wondered if there might be a way to ease the bombing and destruction of our ordinary citizens, and at the same time put pressure on the government to consider a peaceful solution to what's going on."

'I must admit, I was intrigued. This was the sort of thing I wanted, too, but I had no idea how to achieve it.

"'How?" I asked him.

"'If the Luftwaffe could be persuaded to change their targets from the civilian areas to something that might make the British sue for peace. With honourable terms, of course. Not a surrender."

"'What do you mean?" I asked him. I was still confused.

"'Take, for example, the railway network," he said. "It's vital to the war effort."

"'It is," I agreed. "There's no doubt that without it our war effort would be crippled. That's why the job I do is so important."

"'It is," said Roche. "As it is for Germany. If their railway system were to be disrupted they'd be forced to seek a way of getting an honourable peace, too. And Walter knows what he's talking about. Before he fled over the border to Switzerland, he worked for the German government. He still has contacts there."

"'Surely not if he fled to Switzerland," I pointed out. "That would be counted as treason."

'"Not to the people Walter knows. They know him to be a true patriot, but many of them share his desire for this war to reach a swift end. Not that they can declare it publicly, no more than you or I can say it out loud here. Trust me, Peter, there are more people than you realise both in this country, and in Germany, who want peace, and would do anything to achieve it."'

Etheridge looked unhappily at Coburg. 'On reflection I realise now he was playing me. Hindsight is a wonderful thing. But at the time I fell for it. I really felt it could shorten the war and save lives.'

'You gave him details of train movements, which he sent by radio to this cousin, Walter?'

Etheridge nodded. 'Or someone else. Later on I began to think there was no cousin. Especially when I met Grimshaw. If Simon hadn't kept him under control, I think he would have revealed himself to me to be the Nazi he so obviously was. But I took what Simon told me about him at face value, that he was another pacifist who only wanted peace. He was also an electronics expert.'

'He was in charge of the radio transmitter?'

'Yes.'

'When did Lord's Tube station come into it, for sending transmissions?'

'It didn't. Not until the weekend that Desmond stayed with me. Desmond arrived back from nets practice on Saturday and we spent a pleasant evening together, as we did whenever he came to visit, talking and playing music. On Sunday morning, while I was preparing breakfast for us, Desmond started looking through my records to see if I'd got anything new. While he was doing this, he noticed the transmitter next to my record player. Simon, Grimshaw and I had been using it during the day, while Desmond was at practice.

'I should have got them to take it away, but we decided to leave it as we were going to be using it again on Sunday, once Desmond had gone. Desmond, being a technician with the RAF, recognised what it was. He asked me what I was doing with a German transmitter. I made up some story about it being a new thing to improve the quality of the record player, but he didn't believe me. He kept pressing me about it, and because of this he was still there when Simon and Grimshaw arrived. They realised Desmond had found out about the transmitter. It was Grimshaw who said they needed to talk to him, and they needed to do it in private. Desmond began to protest, but Grimshaw produced a gun to quieten him.

'Simon knew that one of my activities, my hobby, you could call it, was visiting abandoned London Underground stations. I find them wonderful, the haunting atmosphere inside them. I think of them as ghost stations. It's part of my whole fascination with railways. I'm lucky in that I have access at Down Street to the keys to all the former Underground stations. Perhaps it was because Desmond was coming to stay that I selected Lord's for my most recent visit. Simon asked me if I had keys to any nearby Underground stations, and I told him I had the keys to Lord's.

'They left, taking Desmond with them, along with his cricket gear. Simon assured me Desmond would come to no harm; they just wanted to talk to him. They were gone for about an hour, and then Simon returned on his own and told me: "I'm afraid things went wrong."

'"What do you mean?" I asked him.

'"We were talking to him and suddenly he attacked us, trying to get away."

'I remembered the gun that Grimshaw was holding and said: "You shot him?"

'"Of course not!" said Simon. "I told you we wouldn't be doing anything like that, just talking. We struggled, and suddenly he fell and hit his head. He's dead. I'm sorry. I did everything I could to stop something like that happening."

'"What have you done with him?"

'"We left him outside the Tube station. Someone will find him and think it was an accident, or a mugging. The thing is, we have to keep our nerve. We also need to move the radio to a safer place. If the authorities find out he was staying with you, they'll come here. We can't afford for them to spot it."'

He looked at Coburg, appeal in his eyes. 'I know, when I hear myself saying it, how stupid it sounds. So naïve. Anyway, Simon took the radio away, and that was it. Or so I thought. I believed Simon, until you told me how Desmond had been tortured. Cigarette burns. His fingers broken. Then the awful fact he'd been beaten to death with his own cricket bat. I was so angry. Simon had lied to me, and he and Grimshaw had tortured and killed Desmond deliberately. I didn't know what to do. I wanted to shop them, tell the police, but I couldn't do it without betraying my own part in the radio transmissions.

'Then Simon phoned me and said we needed to talk. I'd made up my mind that he and Grimshaw would pay for what they'd done to Desmond. If his death had been an accident, as Simon had said, I could have lived with it, but not the way they'd done it. The sadistic brutality.'

'So you arranged to meet him at Lord's station.'

'Yes. And as soon as Simon opened the door and let me in, I let him have it with the hammer.'

'At this time, Simon Roche was on his own?'

'Yes, but suddenly Grimshaw appeared from up the stairs. He was carrying a knife and he went for me. So I hit him with the hammer.'

'And carried on hitting him?'

Etheridge nodded. 'I had to protect myself from him.'

Lampson sat in the car and talked. He hadn't intended to. It started slowly, with his and Eve's first date, fire-watching on the roof of the furniture repository, and then going to the pictures, and both of them becoming aware that the companionships they had together was more than being just good friends.

'It was like soulmates,' said Lampson. 'We knew what each was thinking, was feeling, without needing to say. Neither of us had ever known anything like that before. And Terry liked her. I thought he'd be upset at having her come and live with us, but no, he was fine with it. Better than fine.'

He told Rosa of their plans for the future. 'She reckons we could get a place of our own. I'd never thought of that. Everyone in our family has always rented, except one of my cousins who married a bloke with money. But Eve had worked out how we could do it. She's clever like that. Much brainier than me. She said we could get a place in the country, a cottage. She'd get a job teaching at a village school and I could join the local police force. She reckoned I'd be an inspector because of my experience at Scotland Yard. She had plans.'

But mostly he talked of how much he loved her, and how

much she loved him. Once more, he used the phrase 'twin souls'. And then he stopped as he saw two figures walking towards the car: Coburg and Peter Etheridge.

'Looks like he's done it,' he said.

Coburg arrived by the car and opened the rear door and held it open while Etheridge climbed in and slid along the rear seat.

'Peter has decided to come in,' said Coburg.

Coburg climbed in beside Etheridge and pulled the door shut. Lampson started the car up and they moved off.

Bill Biggs stood with Prudence Baxter in the barn at the back of the yard, looking at the bales of straw piled up against one wall. In her hand she held a pistol. She gestured with it at the targets that had been propped up against the bales.

'We won't need those,' she said. 'All he needs to know is how to pull the trigger. He'll be doing it up close so he doesn't have to worry about aiming.' She took two large, thick cushions from a sofa and plonked them in front of the bales. 'Just get him to push the end of the barrel of the gun into the cushions and pull the trigger. When he's done it a few times and got used to it, take him to the address we've got for this DCI Coburg. When he opens the door, Monty's to push the pistol into him up close, then pull the trigger. Bang. That's it. If anyone is with him, he's to shoot them as well. Then you take him to this Sergeant Harpson's house and do the same to him. Got it?'

Biggs nodded. Ma Baxter handed him the pistol.

'Let me see you do it,' she said. 'I want to make sure you do it properly. No shaking hands. Then I'll bring Monty in.'

Again, Biggs nodded. He checked the gun was loaded and

that there was a bullet ready to be fired. Then he brought his arm up, pointed the gun against Ma Baxter's head and pulled the trigger. The bullet tore through her skull, ripping her brain apart, before spurting blood out of the other aside of her head.

She hit the ground, her eyes and mouth wide open in shock.

Biggs took a cloth and wiped the gun's handle, then, holding it with the cloth over the barrel, he pushed it into her hand and wrapped her fingers round it.

'Suicide,' he said quietly. 'Losing her two sons like that pushed her over the edge.' He looked down at her dead body. 'You're free of her now, son.'

CHAPTER THIRTY-EIGHT

Wednesday 19th March

Lampson was in the reception area of the hospital early, but his request to visit Eve Bradley was turned down.

'Visiting hours are 11 a.m. until 11.30 a.m., and 4 p.m. until 5 p.m.,' he was informed.

'But she's my fiancée and we're due to be getting married this Saturday,' he told the receptionist. 'I need to see her to find out if she's fit enough to go through with it, or if we have to cancel. If we do, I need to inform that vicar at St Pancras Church.'

The receptionist fixed him with a firm look. 'You can see her at 11 o'clock,' she said. 'Before then the doctors are doing their rounds.'

Resignedly, Lampson made his way to one of the wooden benches and sat down. *The guvnor wouldn't allow this to happen to him*, he thought. *He'd be flashing his warrant card, and because he's got a fancy double-barrelled name and a posh accent they'd let him go up to the ward.* He considered going to fetch his mother in to exert pressure, but he knew she'd side with the receptionist.

'People have got to be allowed to do their jobs,' she'd say. He looked at the clock. Half past nine. An hour and a half to go.

The wait seemed frustratingly endless, and he wondered if he went back to the receptionist and tried pulling rank as a detective sergeant with Scotland Yard it would carry any weight, but one look at the severe expression on the receptionist's face told him such a plan would not only be futile, it might even be counter-productive. The receptionist would possibly have him forcibly escorted from the hospital. He knew that had happened before to people they considered 'difficult'. He was therefore taken aback when, at a quarter to eleven, the receptionist approached him.

'Mr Lampson. I've had a word with the sister on your fiancée's ward and she said the doctors have finished their rounds, so in these special circumstances she will allow you to go up now.'

Lampson stared at her, stunned; it was not the attitude he was expecting. Then he stood up.

'Thank you,' he said. 'I really appreciate this.'

'Ward three,' said the receptionist, and she pointed to the stairs.

Once at the ward, he walked along the row of women in beds, around some of which the curtains had been drawn for privacy, until he came to Eve sitting up in bed. Her left arm was in plaster and a sling, and she had a large bandage wrapped around the top of her head, almost like a turban. There were some magazines in front of her, one of which was open, and she closed it when Lampson arrived.

He kissed her gently, then sat down on the chair beside her bed.

'Magazines,' he said, adding apologetically, 'I should have thought of that and brought something in for you to read.'

'These are from my mum,' said Eve.

'Your mum?' said Lampson in surprise. 'She's been allowed in?'

'No, but she left these for me, with a letter.'

She took a letter from her bedside table and handed it to Lampson. Lampson read it and looked at Eve in surprise.

'She's coming to the wedding?'

'Yes.'

'We don't even know if you'll be in a fit state to do it.'

'Yes I will.'

'You won't be able to walk down the aisle.'

'It's my arm that's broken, not my legs.'

'But you've got a fractured skull. Say you fall over?'

'I won't. I'll have support. Read the rest of the letter. Because Dad's away on active service, she's offered to give me away. So Rosa will be on one side of me, and my mum on the other.'

Lampson looked at her in astonishment. 'That's a bit of a turnaround.'

'She says she came to the hospital and they warned her I might die, so it made her think about what was important. That's why she wants to be at my wedding.'

'Even though you'll be marrying me.'

'Yes. Even with that. My guess is she talked to Betty, and when Betty told her your best man was a member of the royal family . . .'

'He's not really,' said Lampson. 'At least, that's what he keeps telling me.'

'His name's Saxe-Coburg, which was the name of the royal family before they changed it to Windsor, and his brother's the Earl of Dawlish. That's what Betty told her, and she didn't argue. The clincher was when Betty told her Rosa was going to be my maid of honour. My mum's a real fan of Rosa's. She listens to her on the wireless.'

'I always said your mum's a snob.'

'Yes, she is, But she's my mum. And I'm glad she's coming.'

'Then so am I,' said Lampson.

It seemed as if all of Somers Town had turned out for the wedding of Ted Lampson to Eve Bradley and were either in, or outside, St Pancras New Church. Boys from Somers Town football team and their families, staff from the school, along with many of the children and their families, some of Lampson's old pals from the local police stations, and sundry other local people.

Inside the church, Lampson stood beside Coburg at the altar in front of the waiting vicar. In the front pews, Ted's parents sat, looking resplendent in their best outfits, reserved for weddings and funerals.

'It's quite a turnout,' Coburg whispered to Lampson. 'Did you expect this many?'

'No,' admitted Lampson. 'I hope they don't all expect to come to the afters. Mum's only catered for a handful.'

'You're sure Eve's up to this?' asked Coburg.

Lampson nodded. 'If she says she is, she is.'

Someone had obviously given the signal to the organist, because the opening bars of 'The Wedding March' swelled out, filling the church, then the doors opened and Eve appeared, flanked on each side by Rosa and Paula Bradley, with Terry following proudly behind. Lampson and Coburg watched nervously as Eve and her companions made their way sedately and at a gentle pace down the aisle. The strict rationing brought in because of the war meant that the traditional flowing wedding dress was virtually impossible. Most women wore dresses that had been handed down through the family from their grandmothers and even great-grandmothers. For Eve, Mrs Lampson had adapted a lilac-coloured dress she'd inherited from her own mother that she'd been keeping for special occasions, and none was more special than the wedding of her son to the woman he loved. Eve was wearing a headdress and veil that concealed the bandage around the top half of her skull, and a bouquet of flowers nestled in the crook her of damaged arm, partly covering the plaster cast and the sling.

The bridal party arrived beside Lampson and Coburg, and the vicar went through their vows, with Eve and Lampson pledging to be faithful to one another until death did them part. Coburg produced the ring, which Lampson slipped onto Eve's finger, and then Lampson raised Eve's veil and kissed her tenderly.

'Hello, Mrs Lampson,' he whispered.

It was then Lampson's turn to take Eve's good arm and support her carefully along the aisle back to the entrance to the church, although both his mother and Mrs Bradley remained hovering alongside the pair in case they were needed. It was when they reached the door that Paula Bradley sidled over to Lampson's side.

'I admit I was wrong about you,' she whispered. 'I know now you're a good man. But take note of this, Ted Lampson. If you hurt her or make her unhappy in any way, you'll have me to deal with. And even the wrath of God can't match me when I get angry.'

'I'm aware of that,' Lampson whispered back. 'But I promise you, Eve will be safe and happy with me. And you'll always be welcome.'

Coburg, who had accompanied Rosa along the aisle behind the newly married couple, whispered to her, 'It looks like the war between groom and mother-in-law is over. They were just talking.'

'At least one war is over,' said Rosa, then she and Coburg moved to one side and watched as Lampson and Eve stepped out through the church doors and the spectators outside applauded and began to shower them with confetti.

ACKNOWLEDGEMENTS

Much has been written about the heroism of the soldiers, sailors (both Royal Navy and merchant) and aircrews during World War II, and rightly so. But one group who I feel have not been given the praise they are due are those who served at home in defence of these islands. The intense bombing during the Blitz led to firestorms that had to be controlled to prevent vast urban areas from going up in flames, because one of the Luftwaffe's favoured bombing weapons was the incendiary device. To prevent such disasters the firewatchers and volunteer fire crews were vital. It was dangerous work and many lost their lives. My own father had a reserved occupation as a plumber with the local council so he volunteered as a firewatcher and fireman, and most of his nights during the Blitz were spent fighting fires in the Euston/Kings Cross area. In this, he was just one of many thousands who volunteered to put their lives on the line.

After the war there were many films lauding the heroic actions of the RAF (The Battle of Britain, Dambusters, etc), the navy and soldiers (D-Day landings), but to a great extent those who served courageously at home were overlooked. This is just to remind those who read about the war that those in less glamorous roles also served heroically and deserve our gratitude.

JIM ELDRIDGE was born in central London towards the end of World War II, and survived attacks by V2 rockets on the King's Cross area where he lived. In 1971 he sold his first sitcom to the BBC and had his first book commissioned. Since then he has had more than one hundred books published, with sales of over three million copies. He lives in Kent with his wife.

jimeldridge.com